"Erin. It's okay, honey…"

As the reassuring strength of Gabriel's hold surrounded her, reality flooded in a rush. Mortified, Erin twisted against him, desperate to escape. Still, the wall at her back and the large man in front of her had her trapped. Sinewy arms held her tight to his body and the melodious baritone crooned in her ear. Warm breath whispered over suddenly fevered skin, and Erin succumbed, too exhausted to fight herself and the comfort he offered. She lifted her arms to wrap them around his waist.

When he felt her capitulate, Gabriel sighed in baffled triumph. Tenderly, he kissed her temple, then her forehead. As she calmed down, he pressed his lips to the crown of her silky black hair.

"Gabriel."

What she started to say got lost beneath the firm lips that glided over her mouth, careful to taste, but not to take. Erin leaned into the kiss, lulled by its charm. There was no urgency to sink inside, no frantic mating to tie her stomach into knots. But how could she have expected that a first kiss could settle nerves and arouse desires at the same time? Wonderment blossomed and she parted her lips to invite more…

NEVER TELL

Selena Montgomery

St. Martin's Paperbacks

NEVER TELL

Copyright © 2004 by Stacey Y. Abrams.
Cover photo by Herman Estevez.

ISBN: 0-312-99306-4
EAN: 80312-99306-1

Printed in the United States of America

St. Martin's Paperbacks edition / June 2004

St. Martin's Paperbacks are published by St. Martin's Press, 175 Fifth Avenue, New York, NY 10010.

10 9 8 7 6 5 4 3 2 1

NEVER
TELL

PROLOGUE

Strange fits of passion have I known:
And I will dare to tell,
But in the Lover's ear alone,
What once to me befell.

—*William Wordsworth*

MARCH 2002
San Cabes, California

She stumbled into the cabin. He shoved hard, and she cried out as her knees crumpled beneath her. The vicious kick to her side slid her across the Aubusson rug. With a sickening thud, her head rapped against the base of the rocking chair. She fell against the corded timbers of the wall. Shivering on the floor, she lay stunned and tearless.

In the cold dark of the isolated cabin, where she'd thought to hide until Sebastian came for her, her labored breaths echoed and filled the space with fretful sound. The flames from the fireplace had died down. Occasionally, embers spat out angry sparks. Wood cracked and broke against the hearth. A storm raged in the thick of the forest, wind and rain lashing at the old mission stones. Inside, the air seethed with obsession and mania.

"You're mine, Analise!" Nathan stalked her, loomed over her. "Don't ever run from me again!"

The command, and the accompanying strike to her hip from his muddied boot, snapped her head back and opened her swollen eyes. Analise tried to push herself up using the hand beneath her, but the wrist he'd fractured gave way.

It was not the first time she'd felt the brutal ache that seemed to burn her skin, tasted the metallic flavor of blood on her tongue. It was not the first time she'd wanted to whimper for mercy, beg for the pain to cease.

Bending beside her, Nathan could see her drifting away from him. He wouldn't allow it. Lately, she had forgotten who was in charge. That she was his to command. He wanted to kick her again, to smash at her fragile ribs, but he controlled the rage that poured into him. The pleas for mercy gratified him, but they were not enough. She had to understand where she belonged. To whom.

He slapped her then, so hard, his ring dislodged and tumbled to the ground. When she barely reacted, he thought she wasn't sufficiently afraid. Just because he'd never gone this far before, she doubted him. She wouldn't after tonight.

"Look at me, Analise!" he barked as he shoved his hand into his pocket.

She did and her eyes widened when she saw the gun. He held it steady, aimed at her head. "God, Nathan. No. Please."

"I told you not to leave me, Analise. I told you you had nowhere else to go. No one else to turn to." Drawing the cool barrel along her chin, he relished the purity of the fear he could nearly touch. He slid the hard metal along her bruised cheek to rest at her temple. "Your parents are dead. You have no family, no friends. Why would you try to leave me?"

Because of what she'd heard. What she'd seen.

Through her terror, she had remembered a time before him, though the memory was faint. In that time, before he came into her life, she had been strong and smart and sure. She had been brave. Then she would not have rocked in a corner, timid and broken. She would not have cowered in the dark, watching evil but saying nothing.

Yet she had been silent. She didn't call the police, and this was her sin. Instead, she'd run to the hills, hoping to hide from the monster who'd made her.

It was too late. He'd found her and he would kill her. With the remembrances of family dim, she imagined her life had begun with him.

Would end with him.

Prepared for death, Analise straightened, her chin lifting. "I saw what you did."

"You saw nothing!" Amazed at her temerity, Nathan yelled, "You saw nothing!"

"I saw everything. Everything you've wanted to do to me but couldn't. Couldn't because you needed me." Defiant, dead, she laughed bitterly. "All those times you told me how weak and pathetic I was, how worthless, it was you. Always you."

"You are mine, Analise. I created you!"

The gun smashed into her cheek. Stars danced and she felt reality slipping away. "Created me? You stole from me! My ideas, my words. You took them from me." Struggling to her feet, paying no heed to the gun and the pain, she made her voice strong for her final lie. "I called the police, Nathan. They'll find you."

The confession stunned him. She'd betrayed him, the wretched, pitiable creature he'd shaped into his masterpiece? She dared to defy him? Fury and insanity surged through him and he lunged at her, the gun forgotten. It clattered to the floor between them.

Seeing her chance, Analise dodged the hands that came out to strangle her. She dived for the gun, scrambling to reach it. Enraged, his fist pounded into her stomach, and she felt her rib crack. Clinging to life, she clawed at his arm while her crippled hand closed over the pistol.

Countering, Nathan manacled her wrist, squeezing on the fractured bone. She screamed, and the sound pierced the storm. She struggled not to pass out, to hold on to the gun. Tangled together, they rolled along the ground. He rose above her, eyes gleaming with madness, and he slammed her head into the wooden planks on the floor.

"I'll kill you, bitch!"

Analise refused to die quietly. She fought to turn the gun, whimpering through the shards of pain radiating from her wrist, from her skull. Clinging to consciousness, she vowed, "No!"

There was a cacophony of sound, perhaps a blast or the tumult of the storm. It was then consciousness deserted her. Shame was her last clear thought as pain burst through her skull. Nathan had won and she had lost.

Groggily, she came to. She emerged from the agonizing darkness to find the gun in her hand. The metal felt cool where it rested in her palm. Odd, because she had always imagined searing heat. But Nathan had warned her that her imagination could not be trusted. Her strange mind, trained with precision to see words and patterns and images, played terrible tricks on her. It made her believe the impossible.

Her hand squeezed the gun's grip spasmodically. She shivered again, frozen to the bone. She crawled to Nathan, wanting him to be dead, praying he was alive. The body was still, lifeless. Red bloomed in obscene beauty along his left side. He stared up at her, the blue eyes unmoving and accusing. Her head throbbed and blood trickled down her neck. Dragging herself to the sofa, she managed to get to her feet. She swayed, the room spinning dizzily around her. She blinked, trying to orient herself.

A wink of silver caught her eye, abandoned on the hardwood, where it had fallen from his hand in the struggle. She staggered over to the ring that had left too many marks on her skin. She picked it up, a reminder of the price of freedom.

When the storm cleared, she called Sebastian. Together, they sent Nathan over the mountain, onto ancient rocks and clay that swallowed his body and her sin.

Then she walked out of her life.

CHAPTER 1

Humid dark hung over the boulevard lamplight as a pale moon rose beyond the trees. Cicadas began their nightly chants in concert with the cries of tree frogs. Comforted by the familiar song of spring, Maggie Fordham locked the door to the Alabaster Rose Nursery with ritual flourish. First, she gave three quick turns to the ornate brass key that had secured the store for nearly a century. As she'd been taught by her grandfather, she jiggled the handle three times before smacking the mahogany with the base of her hand. A silly rite, perhaps, but after a hundred years, who was she to tempt the fates?

It was easy to be superstitious in New Orleans, Maggie acknowledged as she hit the sidewalk. Equal parts religion and culture, the ways of the supernatural permeated every breath of life in the city. A fifth-generation native, Maggie understood the call of blood that required spitting on a broom if it swept your feet or the expectation of a windfall when the palms of empty hands itched.

A woman of science, she would never admit to herself that she believed in ghosts or demons or creatures of the night. Still, she instinctively angled her foot on the cobblestone walk to avoid stepping on a crack between the stones. She caught the motion and chuckled softly. Apparently, even science had its limits.

She turned into the alley between her shop and the apothecary next door. Fishing in her purse for the car keys she kept on a separate ring, she opened the door to her new car. The hot red Miata was courtesy of her adjunct teaching gig at Burkeen University. Twice a week, she taught botany to its students, and the check from the university covered the car payments. Not a bad deal, she thought, even if the students were a tad spoiled.

Maggie slid inside the compact car and pulled the door tight behind her. Abandoned coffee pooled condensation in the cup holder. She turned the key in the ignition, eager to get home. Her Labrador puppy, Sadie, would be waiting up for her. Sadie thought she was a guard dog, and Maggie hadn't the heart to tell her different. The car sputtered once, and Maggie pushed down on the gas. The engine revved.

In the next moment, the driver's side window exploded. Before she could do more than flinch, hard hands reached inside the broken window and grabbed Maggie by the throat. Screaming, she raked her nails across the hands that choked her. "No! Help!"

"Shh, Maggie," her attacker warned. "Don't struggle. It will be finished soon."

In response, Maggie's fingernails dug deep but did not penetrate the latex gloves that protected her attacker. Still, a fisted hand slammed into her face in punishment.

"I told you not to struggle."

Blood poured from her swelling nose and sobs tore from her as the pain radiated endlessly from the broken bone. She panted now, breaths coming in short gasps of air through her mouth. "Ah, ah, ah. Ah, God." Her screams and sobs turned to whimpers of agony. "Please, no."

Suddenly the door was hauled open. Maggie lurched forward, trying to escape. Her attacker grabbed her by the hair and smashed her broken face into the steering wheel. Flung into the seat, Maggie struggled to stay conscious, but the searing pain pulled at her in waves, begging her to give in.

Silently, Maggie prayed for the strength to save herself. She could feel herself suffocating. Blood poured into her throat, gagging her. Abruptly the seat belt bit into her neck. *Oh, God, no,* she thought desperately; it wasn't the seat belt. The killer's hands wrapped wire around her neck, the metal slicing through skin, through tissue. Maggie's last pant broke the night air, and the wire pulled tighter, then tighter still. Then the killer turned, face clear in the lamplight.

Why? Maggie mouthed as crimson began to spill onto her pale blue silk blouse, fill her larynx.

In answer, the wire pulled taut and strong. Maggie could feel life ending, and she sought the ethereal light of myth. But only yellow filled her vision, the lamplight above. Yellow and the smile of her killer. The reassuring smile followed her into death, as wire severed the cream column of her throat.

Maggie's lifeless body threatened to fall to the ground, but the killer's braced hip caught her. Methodically, the careful hands arranged Maggie gently against the leather seat. A flick of a side lever, and Maggie Fordham reclined in silent repose. The bloodstained wire was recoiled and laid on the seat beside the empty body. *Without the blood and empty eyes,* the killer thought, *a person might think she's sleeping.*

As before, last touches included removing the crisp bills from the wallet and dropping it into the leather bag that carried all the killer's tricks. Reverent fingers tugged off the tourmaline ring that sparkled green on Maggie's right ring finger.

Staring at the limp, naked hand, the killer paused. The alabaster strip of skin said that she'd worn the ring for a long time. She had probably wished to be buried with it when she died. The ring went into the bag.

After all, if wishes were horses, the killer reflected, *beggars would ride.*

ONE WEEK LATER

The envelope in Erin Abbott's mailbox did not have a return address. As she walked up the stairs to her apartment, she ran curious fingers over the old-fashioned script. Her name had been etched by a calligrapher's pen onto the ivory parchment.

Dr. Erin Abbott
216 St. Bennett Avenue
Apartment 3F
New Orleans, Louisiana

She tucked the envelope into her purse and punched the elevator button for her floor. The entire building was subdued, the lingering sorrow over Maggie Fordham's death, the victim of a brutal, senseless murder. It had been nearly a week since Maggie's body had been discovered.

Her gruesome end shocked the quiet Esplanade neighborhood where she kept a flat and a noisy dog. It forced her next-door neighbor, Mrs. Kemper, to her bed for three days, comforted only by orange pekoe tea and generous shots of Jim Beam. On the first floor, Davis and Shanie Dupree purchased an extra dead bolt to augment their home security system and began searching the papers for condominiums out in Metairie.

She wished she could grieve more, Erin thought as she set her purse down on the trestle table near the entryway. Ignoring the light switch, she held on to the letter and headed out to the balcony to watch the sunset.

Maggie had lived a floor below, and often they'd shared the last minutes of daylight. In silent tribute, Erin watched the sun dip below the edges of the magenta sky. Though the women hadn't been close friends, Maggie had been a good neighbor. In the months Erin had lived in the building, Maggie had been unfailingly kind. She'd shown Erin around the Quarter, helped her haggle over prices in the market. Maggie had told her about the vacant position at Burkeen University.

But while Erin was saddened, death did not affect her as it did others. For one thing, she'd trained herself not to become too attached. Friendly, sure, but never truly a friend. For another, Erin made her living studying death and the dealers in it. A criminal psychologist, she'd seen the worst of the human psyche played out in horrifying detail. She'd learned not to dwell on the passage of human life. She knew all too well how fragile life could be, how easily taken by purpose or accident.

Life was best lived in solitude, she believed. No connections, no recriminations. No one to take notice. No one to tell you who you should be.

It was the only way to survive.

As dusk settled, she turned around slowly, ran critical eyes over the one-bedroom apartment. Potted plants occupied every corner of the postage-stamp balcony. Like the magazine photo she'd patterned it on, inside, buttercup walls held framed prints of Paris and the markets in Senegal. Her furniture was arranged to mirror the glossy pictures from the catalogs. Tacky tchotchkes jumbled onto shelves, more by design than desire. Real homes had the useless things, she'd learned, and she would have them, too. If the sight of them made her wince, it was a small price to pay.

This was her home now. Her life. It was a small apartment but filled with windows and polished hardwoods. Her choice of residence was not a factor of income. A trust funded by her parents' life insurance guaranteed that she would never lack for money. But she spent that money carefully, reluctant to draw attention or interest. No, money was not an issue for her. Freedom was.

For too long, she had lived at the mercy of a madman who controlled her every thought, every move. Now, she had her own space. A life she'd created far away from anyone who cared about the woman she had once been. It had taken more than two years and thousands of dollars, but Analise Glover was gone.

She slid open the French doors and walked into the

apartment, the letter still unopened. Perhaps it was a plea from a student for an extension, she mused, running her fingers along the stationery. Still, a trill of uneasiness crept along her spine.

Erin shook off the feeling and wandered over to the chaise that stretched beneath the wide bay window. She switched on a swing-armed brass lamp and curled her legs beneath her on the brushed cotton. Telling herself to stop being fretful, she slit the seal on the letter and turned it to spill the contents to her lap. Newsprint fell out.

She gasped.

Five obituaries stared up at her. They'd been clipped from the local paper, she realized grimly. Clipped and sent to her. Holding them by the edges, she sifted through the columns, murmuring the names aloud.

"Julian Harris. Burleigh Singleton. Phoebe Bailey. Juan Johnson. Margaret Fordham."

She tripped over Maggie's name and her breathing hitched. Erin forced herself to take a calming breath. *Think rationally,* she commanded herself, trying to ignore the shrill of panic in her head.

Be reasonable. Someone had sent her a packet of obituaries. Strange, yes, but not terrifying. She was, after all, a criminal psychology professor. One who habitually read obituaries and police news to her students to teach them how to look for information.

The envelope was probably a prank by one of her students. A nasty, silly prank to rattle her before exams.

But even as she formed the feeble excuse, her heart thudded against her chest in fierce denial. On her lap, Maggie's grainy photograph watched her with knowing eyes. This was more than a trick.

Hands trembling, Erin shook the envelope again.

A note that had been scripted on a scrap of the same ivory paper fluttered into her lap. Shakily, she lifted it to read. There were only three words.

Analise,
Find me.

For hours, Erin sat in the darkened apartment, lit only by moonlight and a single lamp. She read and reread the five items lined up on the coffee table. A pattern had emerged from the morbid columns and sent her to the computer, fighting the urge to retch.

To an eye trained in more than the nature of crime, the records of the deceased had a connection stronger than the tenuous nature of death.

A killer was on the loose.

Perhaps it took one to know one.

CHAPTER 2

Gabriel Moss loped through the hallway at Burkeen University Monday morning, his loose, confident strides eating up the tiled floor. Though he covered ground quickly, his gait was easygoing. He had learned young that the person at the other end would probably wait until he arrived.

He swung around a corner into another corridor of numbered doors. Since he wasn't in any real hurry to reach his destination, he slowed his steps even more. Genevieve was more than a little annoyed with him, and he couldn't blame her. Her messages had piled up while he'd been away. Messages he'd studiously ignored. As long as he didn't answer, he figured, she couldn't tell him about Mirren Enterprises' latest attack on his fledgling newspaper, the *Bayou Ledger*. And the longer he could wait before he confronted its head rat, Nick Jacoby.

Still, if she was going to be angry, he had a perfect defense. Running the *Ledger* left little time for niceties like returning phone calls. He had to refurbish a dilapidated production center, hire staff, set up a Web site, and convert the fourth-floor administrative center into a place for him to sleep when he could steal an hour. When he was in New Orleans.

Which, as of late, hadn't been too often. For weeks now, he'd been traveling the country, scratching together new investors and allaying fears about the fate of the paper. Luckily, he trusted his managing editor, Peter Cameron, to run the weekly print edition and the daily electronic edition without him. On his last swing through town, he'd hired a business manager to do the day-to-day number-crunching and negotiating that he despised.

He had been and always would be a reporter first. The rest was a matter of survival and revenge.

By his internal clock, he knew he was already fifteen minutes late for their 11:00 a.m. meeting, but he also knew Gennie would forgive his tardiness. After almost thirty years, his baby sister had no doubt grown used to his fluid relationship with time, much as he had accepted her fanaticism about punctuality.

Maybe he should have brought a peace offering, he thought, pausing midstep. Gennie was a sucker for boxed chocolates. He stood in the hallway, debating whether he had time to run out to a drugstore.

Before he could decide, applause, then a dusky laugh like lust draped in fog floated into the passageway from a lecture hall, distracting him. Intrigued by the siren sound, Gabriel walked over to the bright blue door propped on its hinges and peeked inside. The room was set on two levels, with raised auditorium-style seating. From his swift perusal, he figured at least a hundred students had crowded into the class. Every eye was fixed on the owner of the sultry laugh.

Gabriel eased into the classroom, drawn despite the fact that Gennie was waiting for him. Years of training had taught him stealth and obscurity. Looking down at the podium on the first level, he firmly decided that the sexy-sounding professor had at least taken lessons in the second. She earned excellent marks. If he hadn't heard the laugh for himself, he'd never have guessed it had come from the dowdy waif at the lectern.

Boxy brown swathed the woman from shoulder to mid-calf. The ill-fitting mud-colored tweed was out of place in the spring and positively stifling in the weeks leading up to a New Orleans summer. Awful brown shoes encased her feet, and if he wasn't mistaken, misshapen hose bunched a bit at the ankle.

The view got no better the higher his eyes traveled. Glorious black hair had been twisted into a mockery of style. Caught somewhere between bun and ponytail, the length of black silk hung in a defeated hank at her slender neck. To complete the picture, spectacles perched on the bridge of an arrogant nose, one with surprising character. From his position, he approved of lips drawn to a permanent pout and cheekbones that could etch stone. Then she angled her head and glass glinted in the fluorescent light.

She was extraordinary, Gabriel thought, as heat shot through his gut and tripped up his pulse. A face to match the voice. Delicate warred with fierce and resulted in dazzling. And, Gabriel realized as light splintered toward him, the beauty was looking straight at him.

Though she had not stopped speaking, he could tell by the tilt of her head that she was examining him as carefully as he had her. He knew what she saw.

Jeans strained white at the knees and a black T-shirt

that had seen better days. He kept his curly brown hair from reaching too far down his neck and his face clean. He'd inherited his father's slightly square jaw and his mother's long, romantic mouth. He was an attractive man, teetering on the precipice of handsome, and comfortable with the balance.

Watching her watch him, Gabriel held what he assumed were the professor's eyes. Her ability to keep speaking—and his to keep breathing—while she dissected him impressed. And, if the jut of her chin was any indication, she was none too pleased by what she saw. Amused by her irritation and freed by the reaction, Gabriel grinned broadly and winked. With an impudent nod, he strolled back outside.

In the nearly empty hallway, the grin faded and he rubbed an absent hand over an unexpected ache in his chest. The edgy punch of desire had caught him unawares.

Forget it, he warned himself. The husky-voiced professor was certainly striking, but not his type. He definitely preferred the flamboyant to the drab, if beautiful, bookworm. Besides, the *Ledger* left no time for anything else. *I came; I saw; I admired; I moved on.*

It was harder than he expected, though, for Gabriel to banish the temptation to discover what lay beneath the professor's poorly fitted clothes. Shaking his head, he continued his journey along the citrine-tiled hall. Three doors down, he knocked on the faux oak and listened for the exasperated call to enter. Yep, he sighed, he should've brought candy.

"You're twenty minutes late," Genevieve declared from behind her desk. Carefully framed diplomas decorated the faded beige walls behind her. As was his habit,

Gabriel read yet again the gilded nameplate announcing: DR. GENEVIEVE MOSS. Like their mother, she'd chosen the life of the academic rather than that of their father, the journalist. An indulgent smile added warmth to smoke gray eyes that could freeze in an instant.

With a scowl, Genevieve soaked in the sight of her brother. Finally, a feminine echo of his smile curved her lips as she stood up to offer a tight hug. "Would it kill you to be on time once in a while?"

Gabriel shrugged negligently. "Stranger things have happened. Why tempt fate?"

"Live dangerously," she retorted.

"I gave that up when I left the big city. No more intrigue for me."

Gabriel grinned, but Gennie saw that the smile didn't reach his eyes. They rarely talked about his life before he came home to work with their father at the *New Orleans Chronicle*. Before then, she'd faithfully clipped Gabriel's articles from trouble spots around the world. Whether it was the massacres in Uganda or weapons cartels in Kyrgyzstan, he'd been on the ground, in the thick of the action.

For better or worse, those days were gone. Loyalty brought him home to New Orleans, but it was the vengeance that held him here that worried her. A vengeance she was about to stoke. Bracing herself, she pushed him into one of two chairs that flanked her desk. Perching on its smooth surface, she pouted, "I'm starting to annoy Peter."

"Peter is always annoyed. It's his trademark."

Forced to agree about his cranky managing editor, Genevieve tried a different tack. "One might imagine he's the owner of the *Ledger* rather than you."

"Sometimes, he thinks so, too." He leaned forward and stole a sip from the coffee mug steaming near her. The robust chicory flavor settled on his tongue, the essence of New Orleans. He grinned. "Peter's attempted coups are usually my cue to return."

Not to be placated, Genevieve chided, "You've been gone for weeks, Gabe. Perhaps you could take some time between pitches to check in. Say, 'Hello, I'm alive'?"

"Are you going to lecture me on my manners?" He reached out a hand and cupped her cheek affectionately. Sometimes she looked so much like their parents, it broke his heart. To ward off the tendrils of grief, he teased, "If so, I think I have the one from last week on tape, to save you time."

"Very funny." Genevieve wrinkled her nose at him, knowing he'd never change.

At thirty-four, he was six years her senior. It was an age difference he never let her forget. In his eyes, it made him responsible for her. She'd conceded years ago, like many a disappointed suitor, that it was a fool's errand to argue. Just like it had been pointless to argue that he had no obligation to take Dad's place at the *Chronicle*. Or that it wasn't his fault when Mirren Enterprises stole their family legacy while he was at the helm.

They were about to take something else.

Leaning back, she scooped a letter from a disciplined pile on her desk. Genevieve extended it to him, then pulled back before he could take it from her. "First of all, I need you to not overreact. Second, I only opened it because it was addressed to G. Moss and it came to the house."

Smoky eyes darkened to pewter. "Give me the letter."

"Please remember that threatening physical violence is a criminal offense and you don't have bail money. Neither do I," she hurried on, clutching the letter in her fist.

"Genevieve."

The dark, implacable voice that her big brother used to great effect, coupled with the solid, work-roughened hand that swallowed her own, convinced Genevieve to slowly uncurl her fingers.

"They're not worth it, Gabe," she warned as he ripped open the legal-sized envelope.

"Albert Fish eventually confessed to the murders of sixteen children, including the cannibalism of ten-year-old Gracie Budd." Erin tore her eyes away from the empty doorjamb and tried to focus on her final lecture in psychopathology, what her students called Murder 101. But rather than the sadism of Henry Lee Lucas and Edmund Kemper, her mind wandered back to her unexpected visitor.

Impressions flashed in rapid succession. Three words stuck in her suddenly fuzzy mind.

Tall. Gorgeous. Trouble.

Trouble most of all.

Broad shoulders, muscled arms, and narrow hips sketched the body of a rogue. Angles and planes dueled in mahogany, carving a tough, compelling face, ceding curves only to heavily lidded eyes and a wide, seductive mouth. The easy invasion of her classroom said he went where he chose. And the silent, intent observation said he remembered what he saw.

Definitely trouble, Erin concluded firmly. Which she could absolutely do without.

She struggled to put the handsome interloper out of her head; however, faithless memory lingered on a rakish face softened for a moment with an insolent grin.

When she caught her hand on its way to her mouth, Erin wrenched her focus back to the present, but traitorous flutters trembled in her belly.

This is nonsense, she lectured herself sternly. A strange man lurking in the back of her classroom should not be so . . . affecting. She'd seen attractive men before.

Gorgeous, a traitorous voice countered. *The reason heaven gave us denim.*

Muffling a sigh of appreciation for the artisans who first made jeans, Erin returned her attention to her students. With concerted effort, she finished her final lecture for Murder 101. After two more classes and exam period, the summer would begin.

She absently nodded to the students as they filed past, turning in take-home tests. Rather than the quiet murmurs that usually greeted the end of class, pleased chatter filled the room. And they'd wildly applauded her announcement that final papers weren't due until the last day of final exams. Though the semester ended on Friday, she understood students enough to know that most hadn't started their projects and would need the extra time to finish. But with other, more disturbing matters on her mind, she wasn't in a hurry to read amateur rationales for criminal behavior.

Not when she had a real mystery in her briefcase.

Standing at her desk, she quickly accepted the exams, half-listening to the sounds of students in the background as they talked about the evil of finals, summer break plans, and the welcome passage of another school year. As they had all morning, the voices faded in and out, replaced by memories she'd sworn to forget.

"Dr. Abbott?"

Jolted from her reverie, Erin turned her attention to the student waiting for her. She banished the envelope and her past from her mind. "Yes, Ms. Turner?"

Harmony Turner chose a bright, wheedling voice with the honeysuckle tones native to every New Orleans citizen and launched into her spiel. "See, my boyfriend's computer died last night and he had all of my research on his hard drive and I promise I can finish my paper, but between pledging and my other classes, it'll be impossible to meet the deadline and I really need to get a good grade, so I was wondering . . ."

While Harmony streamed through her speech, Erin peeked at the utilitarian clock that hung on the back wall of the lecture hall. She had an appointment at noon. Turning her attention back to Harmony, Erin asked mildly, "Are you requesting an extension on your paper, Ms. Turner?" In notable contrast to the dulcet tones of Ms. Turner, Erin's voice was low and solid.

"Yes, ma'am." The student's blond head hung with a mixture of hope and precious shame. Limpid blue eyes filled as if on cue. "If I do well in your course, I can make the dean's list and then my daddy will let me go to Greece for the summer with Pi Gamma Delta, if I make the house, and if I make it and I can't go then I'll be the only one and I'll just die, Dr. Abbott, I'll just die!"

Casting the specter of imminent demise did nothing to move Erin, but she appreciated the attempt. Summoning up her most stern look, Erin responded, "Ms. Turner,

I just announced that the papers aren't due until the end of the exam period. Were you not paying attention?"

"I tried, but Reggie Clark was talking to me about a party tonight and wouldn't shut up. I don't know why I ever listen to him, because it's not as though he really knows anything except football!"

Coy crossness raised the high-pitched voice a notch, and Erin resisted the urge to wince. "Perhaps when a teacher is speaking, you should work on listening?"

"Yes, ma'am!" Harmony beamed, showing the results of braces no doubt paid for by the daddy who'd be flying her to Athens in a month. "I'll send you a postcard from Greece!"

The bubbly student turned on fashionably nonfunctional heels and hurried to join her friends in the corridor, heading off to class. Classroom empty, Erin packed her notes away and checked the room for stray students or papers. Experience had taught her to be diligent about cleanliness, to leave no trace behind.

Somewhere along the way, she'd failed. The note to Analise said so. Someone knew her secrets, perhaps even her darkest one. *Run,* a shrill voice in her head urged, as it had last night. *Right now, pack your bags and go.*

But she'd sworn never to run again.

Still, bravery didn't mean stupidity, she'd decided. Which was why she wanted to be on her way to the police station before she lost her nerve and gave in to the panic.

She needed to check in with her teaching assistant and grab her grade book, then she'd be on her way. Taking a deep breath, Erin hoisted the bag laden with exams and slung the leather strap high over the thick padding at her shoulder. As soon as she left the air-conditioned confines of the psychology building, sweat would bead on her brow and pool beneath the suffocating tweed. In anticipation, she tugged at the collar with dread but didn't slip the heavy fabric off.

The shapeless, matronly jacket with its silk liner and myriad buttons mocked her attempts. Sometimes she longed to peel away the layers she shrouded herself in and race through the halls naked.

Well, maybe not naked, she corrected. *But cotton would certainly be an improvement.*

"At what cost?" Erin examined the hideous brown that engulfed her arm down past the wrist. She understood what the stranger must have seen, why he'd disappeared as quickly as he'd come. But his lack of interest was what she wanted, she reminded herself.

It was another one of her rules. Survival wouldn't allow for dating or relationships or falling in love. Men rarely looked below the surface, so she made her surface as unappealing as possible.

Gone were the clothes she'd once dressed in. Ones that emphasized her generous bust and shapely hips. The flattering haircut worn by Analise had grown shaggy and unstructured, no longer highlighting the refined bones and drawing attention to unusually pure brown eyes. Rubbing the nubby fabric again, she grimaced, then pulled the jacket more firmly around her. Shapeless clothes and isolation were her only guarantees of anonymity. Of independence.

"Whatever it takes," Erin vowed fiercely to the empty room. If she had to drape herself in worsted wool in the dead of summer, she would. Hadn't she already proven she'd do anything for her freedom?

The chiming of a clock in the university courtyard reminded her of the hour. Her mouth settled into grim lines as she took the steps out of the classroom two at a time. If she didn't leave now, she'd never go. Erin urged her legs into a swift jog and hurried out of the room.

And promptly plowed into a man heading in the opposite direction.

CHAPTER 3

"Oof!" As a brown missile collided with him mid-chest, Gabriel automatically braced himself to keep them upright. A satchel bounced once on his foot, then sprawled at their tangled feet.

Shifting to steady himself, Gabriel saw that his attacker was the dull-looking professor with the sensuous voice. When she swayed, his quick hands slid beneath rough fabric and grasped smooth silk. The span of waist allowed Gabriel's fingertips to meet at the small of her back. He set her on her feet and stared down.

"Hello," he offered, simply because other, more complicated words stalled in his head as he examined her at close range.

Skin the color of coffee skimmed with cream shaped a flawless oval tightened in apprehension. White teeth gnawed apprehensively at a curvaceous mouth, making tiny impressions on its heavy bottom lip. Arresting eyes, a rich, vibrant brown, studied him from beneath a dense fringe of lash. Their shape was slightly exotic, tip-tilted at the corners.

It was the hint of caution mixed with reluctant interest in the clear orbs that nudged his brain into gear. "You have wonderful eyes," Gabriel murmured, the first thought to scuttle into focus. "Do you have a name?"

"Erin," she answered hesitantly, preoccupied by the feel of his fingertips resting at the base of her spine and the currents of heat that rippled there. It had been so long since a man had held her this close, even in rescue from her own clumsiness. *Savor it,* she told herself hazily. *Then walk away.* "Erin Abbott."

Gabriel couldn't tell if the tremulous response was from the impact of their collision or a more personal distress. She barely reached the top of his shoulder, and despite the lean muscle, he definitely overwhelmed her diminutive frame. Suddenly the mix of fear and curiosity took on a different meaning.

He knew he was a tall man, broad across the shoulders and imposing in height, but he didn't often strike fear into the hearts of women. The thought of scaring the woman in his arms disturbed him at his core. He settled his voice into calm tones and smiled gently. "Hello, Erin. I'm Gabriel."

Her muddled wits absorbed that her stranger bore the *nom de guerre* of the guardian of paradise. Like his namesake, this Gabriel commanded obeisance or, at least, attention. Sable hair curled around an angelic face, though not the cherubic, sweet-tempered kind. No, she imagined, this Gabriel would have stood at the gates, righteous sword in hand. She'd already learned he would go where he chose, with or without invitation. "You were in my classroom."

Gabriel noted the wary acknowledgment of their earlier encounter. Erin Abbott obviously did not appreciate unexpected visitors. "Siren's call. Couldn't help it." When she looked at him quizzically, he explained, "Your laugh. Do you often find homicidal maniacs amusing?"

Erin grimaced. "My class was enthusiastically grateful for a reprieve."

"Canceled final?"

"Extension on their paper. One they will undoubtedly squander."

Gabriel chuckled.

The laugh was a mellow rumble of hypnotic sound. Sensing that she could stand and listen to it for hours, Erin wriggled in his grasp and tried to pull away.

A bone-deep refusal to release her speared through him, because he knew if he did, she'd run from him and never stop. In instinctive response, Gabriel firmed his grip on the resilient waist with one hand and lifted the other to her enchantingly triangular chin. His thumb sank into the sexy dent in its velvety surface. Tipping the anxious face up to his, he asked, "Where are you off to in such a hurry?"

"I have . . . an appointment. I'm late."

"Will Alice be meeting you there?"

The slight teasing drew a tentative smile from her. "Not exactly. But it is a very important date."

"It or he?"

Erin's eyes widened at the unexpected intensity of the question. "I'm not sure."

"Good."

The sound of male satisfaction in the gritty voice sank

into her, and Erin resisted the urge to flee. She wasn't completely certain her legs would move anyway. Pulses of heat coursed along her body, rippling out from where determined hands held her waist beneath the jacket, caressed her chin in the cleft in its center. Despite their callused edges, Gabriel's fingers were infinitely careful, as though afraid of bruising with their touch.

Her earlier assessment of tall and gorgeous was woefully inadequate. Hanging inches beneath the strong line of jaw that seemed to be chiseled from granite, Erin guessed he was at least six-three. *Gorgeous* scarcely described the body that also had been hewn from solid rock. Black cotton strained against sinewy biceps and a flat waist.

From a distance, the planes of his face had seemed handsome. Up close, the sweep of lines and hollows, the straight, prominent nose, irises the color of storms, composed a starkly beautiful man. Scattered impressions coalesced into a singular notion.

Danger, she thought dimly. Pure, unadulterated, untamed.

The truth of it seared through her with every breath. Though Gabriel touched her only at her waist and chin, she could feel him. Everywhere.

It was too much.

"I have to go," Erin apologized hastily as she wriggled away. Subtly he chased her and the movement brought her flush against Gabriel's body. Corded thighs, muscled chest, burned along the length of their bodies and she jolted at the contact. "Please," she gasped.

"What?" The heated question demanded a response.

What she wanted, to stay or to go, was impossible to

fathom. Her only lucid thought was of heat and strength. Both alarmed her. Enticed her. "I can't—"

"Gabriel?" Genevieve skidded to a halt beside them and grabbed her brother's arm. "Oh," she said with some astonishment when she saw whom he was holding. "Gabe, what's going on here?"

His eyes still on Erin's, Gabriel answered quietly, "The professor bumped into me. She's in a hurry."

Genevieve looked at her brother and at his less-than-willing captive. "Then shouldn't you let go of her?" she queried lightly. She tugged at his elbow, with no real success. "Let Erin go, Gabe," she chided.

Reluctantly, Gabriel drew his hand away, reveling in the glide of silk and flesh along his palm. He felt rather than heard Erin's quick intake of breath, and a contented grin threatened.

When his hand fell away from Erin's waist, Genevieve draped a friendly arm around the younger woman's shoulders. "The chin, too," Genevieve reminded him.

Gabriel released his hold, his fingers sliding along creamy skin with disappointment. At the peak of the caress, he would have sworn that she leaned into him for a brief moment, loath to end the contact. The telltale gesture made him yearn to trace the pert tip of the nose wrinkled in confusion. But he shoved suddenly unsteady hands into the worn pockets of his jeans. "Is Erin a friend of yours, Gennie?"

Genevieve scowled at the use of her nickname in public but decided to ignore it. "Erin, may I present my boorish brother, Gabriel Moss? Gabriel, this is Dr. Erin Abbott, criminal psychologist extraordinaire. Remember, I told you she took Dr. Fifer's place when she took maternity leave. We were lucky to find her on such short notice."

Gabriel brushed a hand along Erin's arm and captured her fingers by threading them with his own. Normally, he pretended to respect boundaries until he'd built enough trust to disregard them. But contact with her seemed vital, and he was driven to touch. And question. "Why would such a beautiful woman go to such trouble to hide it?"

Erin blanched. "I don't know what you're talking about."

"The disguise, Dr. Abbott," Gabriel explained, holding her eyes as captive as her hand. "What are you hiding from?"

"W-what?" she stammered, prepared to run. Maybe to Sebastian or to London. She hadn't been to London in years.

"Stop prying, Gabe. There's no mystery here," Genevieve said. Turning to her suddenly paler colleague, she wondered what she'd missed. But she didn't pry. Unlike her brother, she fervently believed a person's secrets were her own. Erin wouldn't tell anyway. After months of trying, she'd gotten no closer to her. "Sorry, Erin. It's an occupational hazard of his."

Erin felt a trill of warning frisson along her spine. If he hadn't held her hand, she would have bolted. "Occupational hazard?"

"Didn't I tell you?" Genevieve proudly beamed at her brother. "Gabe is a reporter. Newly the founder and editor of the *Bayou Ledger*."

Panic roiled in Erin's stomach, greasily displacing any lingering heat. *A reporter*. A man paid to ferret out secrets and expose them to light. A man who'd seen beneath her disguise too effortlessly. Erin tugged urgently at her imprisoned fingers. "Please. Let me go."

Genevieve noted Erin's frightened eyes and Gabriel's unyielding grip. "Gabriel," she said as she stepped firmly between them. The movement forced him to release Erin.

Erin hurriedly bent to retrieve the bag sprawled at her feet. Gabriel knelt at the same instant, and they collided, head to chin. He lifted the satchel with one hand and helped to stand with the other. Baffled by the shift from cautious flirtation to utter panic, he murmured for her ears only, "You make quite an impact, Erin."

She flushed and pulled away. "Mr. Moss. Genevieve." Then, dropping any pretense of dignity, she ran.

Gennie followed his watchful stare and considered. Her enigmatic colleague and her curious brother. The match had potential, but she knew better than to interfere. But she could mock. "Gabriel? Hello? Anybody in there?"

Drawing his eyes away from the metal door that had swung shut behind Erin, Gabriel turned his attention to his sister and away from skittish Dr. Abbott. His fingers still tingled, but the sensation would fade. "If you came after me to talk about the paper, you're wasting your time, Gennie."

"Mirren Enterprises isn't worth this, Gabe. You'll go to the offices, they will say something snide, you'll hit somebody, and they'll call the police."

"One time. I hit Jacoby one time." Gabriel shifted with defiant embarrassment. "If he hadn't mentioned Dad—"

Genevieve curled her arm through Gabriel's and led him

inside an empty classroom. She settled on the teacher's desktop. "Sit down, Gabriel." She imperiously pointed to the chair behind the desk, but Gabriel remained standing.

Alert and ready, he balanced his weight on the balls of his feet, as though expecting attack. Unconsciously he angled himself between Genevieve and the open door, able to monitor both the hallway and the world beyond the window. He caught Genevieve's disapproving look and shook his head.

"I can't let them win. They stole the *Chronicle* from us, and now they're coming after the *Ledger*. I won't let them have it. It's all we have left of Mom and Dad." He shook his head in fierce denial. "They can't have it."

"Of course not." Genevieve leaned forward, imploring. "Why not drop the Adams story? That's what they're angry about. There are other stories out there. This is New Orleans."

Familiar temper ripped through him. "Bert Adams' trial is front-page news because I dug it up. I found out about the prostitutes and the real estate deals. I tracked the money. I wrote the damn copy!"

"And Mirren Enterprises bought the paper from the stockholders."

"He fired me for telling the truth."

"He fired you for hounding his old friend, Harmon Turner, after explicitly telling you to lay off," she reminded him brutally. "Your severance package, as I recall, was paid out on the condition that you leave the Adams story with the *Chronicle*." *And sell your soul,* she added silently.

"They've got that prissy snitch Angela Burris on the trial now. First she turns me in to Mirren, and now she's sugarcoating the reports and tainting the jury pool."

Genevieve knotted her forehead in confusion. "I thought the jury was sequestered, Gabe."

He waved a dismissive hand. "This trial is a sham. The DA is going to agree to a mistrial. They'll have a new jury in a few months, and Congressman Adams will be on his way to a fourth term."

"How do you know that?" Genevieve asked, then immediately held out her palms in mock apology. "Forget I asked. I forgot you were not only the best investigative reporter in the country; you're also omniscient." She bounded off of the desktop and bowed elaborately, genuflecting as she approached him. "Forgive me, O Great One. Do not smite me with thy Pulitzer."

Gabriel tried not to smile but failed. Genevieve had always been able to tease him out of the black moods. Even before their parents died, first his mother from cancer, then his father from grief, Genevieve had been the brightest light in their family.

"I can't lose the *Ledger*, Gennie."

"I know. But you've got to drop the Adams story. You have a staff now, and they rely on you. If Mirren Enterprises crushes the paper beneath a lawsuit, where will they go?"

Mirren and his hired gun, Nick Jacoby, had tried to steal the *Chronicle* from Gabriel's father for years. After his death, protecting the *Chronicle* had been Gabriel's responsibility. He'd failed.

Now sales were falling at the *Ledger* and the *Chronicle* was swooping in for the kill.

Perhaps he'd have to drop the Adams story, but scandal was born in New Orleans every day. He'd find a way to beat the *Chronicle* and save the *Ledger*. One way or another.

A cunning light gleamed in Gabriel's eyes.

He knew just where to start.

CHAPTER 4

"Conti and Royal," Erin instructed quietly as she settled into the rumbling taxi. The taciturn driver merely nodded, too tired to make perfunctory conversation or to inquire about why a nice young woman would need to go to the police headquarters. He'd learned to mind his own business, especially when the temperature rose, seeing as how tempers usually flared to match. Spring hadn't bothered to make an appearance this year. Indeed, a blanket of wet heat had settled snugly over the city and aggravated everyone who ventured outside. The blast of frigid air from his trusty unit was a welcome respite, and the cabbie leaned in close for another pass.

Minutes later, the cab pulled up to 334 Royal Street, in the heart of the Quarter. Erin handed the driver his fare. She opened the door, careful to not scrape the curb, alighted from the car, closed the door, and turned.

Marble columns and old-world charm, framed by dogwoods and willows, failed to prepare Erin for her first visit to the Eighth District Police Station. Climbing the shallow curved steps, she eased open the French doors, waiting for the assault of noise and stale coffee she'd read so much about in hard-boiled crime novels. Instead, soft hues of mauve and cream adorned the walls and the carpet. Blue steel doors lay to one side, secured by a keypad. Obviously a waiting area, the circular room boasted a coffeemaker, a water station, and a raised platform that sported a series of flyers and placards. A young man in police blues who staffed the information desk welcomed her with a polite smile.

"Can I help you, miss?" the officer asked in a liquid Southern drawl.

Tentatively Erin approached the high kiosk with its WELCOME TO NEW ORLEANS banner. "I'm here to see Captain Sanchez."

The officer's smile dimmed a bit. "Captain Sanchez is out in the field. Perhaps I can help?"

Erin shook her head, clutching her bag close. She would tell her story only once. To one person. The tidy gold badge identified this officer as Calvin Rochon. "Thank you, Mr. Rochon. I had an appointment yesterday, but I had to cancel."

The polite smile gracefully transitioned to an expression of remorse. "I'm sorry, Ms. . . . ?"

"Abbott. Erin Abbott," she quickly supplied. "I called again this morning, and the receptionist told me I could try to meet with the captain at noon." Unconsciously, nervous fingers twisted the leather strap again and again. Officer Rochon caught the motion and brightened his smile.

"Well, Ms. Erin Abbott, the captain is out, but we'll just have to find someone who can talk with you." He lifted a black handset and depressed a button. "Sylvie? . . . Yeah.

I've got a Ms. Abbott here to see the captain." He flicked a look down her body, then back up to her face. "She looks harmless enough," he added in a low, sympathetic whisper.

Erin caught the description and fought the urge to tug at her starched collar. A warm flush crept up her neck, and she stared determinedly at her shoes. At the sight of the dated pumps, she closed her eyes in dismay.

"Ms. Abbott?"

Her gaze darted up to meet his. "Yes?"

"Detective Iberville will escort you back in a minute. Please have a seat." He pointed to a row of folding chairs lined against the far wall. Their teal paint was chipped in places, and the beige plastic cushions had seen better days.

"Thank you." Erin hurried to the bank of seats, empty but for a few occupants. An older man with a grizzled gray beard snored gently into his chin. At the edge of the row, a middle-aged woman flipped through a magazine, one of several provided on a low, round coffee table in front of the chairs. Erin leaned forward to snag a dog-eared copy of an haute couture magazine. The buxom, sculpted cover model stared up haughtily, secure in her superiority. Erin drew back her hand and instead rummaged through her satchel.

A handful of exams lay at the bottom, and somewhere in the satchel's depths she was certain hid a red pen. Corralling the pen and the tests, Erin started grading. Swiftly she marked tests, speeding through the stack with ease. As she graded, Erin marveled at the ability of some students to answer everything but the question asked. Or the probability of duplicate answers on an essay.

Contrary to the odds, when asked to recount the characteristics of a serial killer, Harmony Turner had recited the exact answers offered by Reggie Clark seven papers before. Likely neither had crafted the responses themselves, given the clichéd intellect of the sorority girl and the student athlete. More the pity, both answers were uniformly inaccurate.

"If you plan to cheat," Erin muttered with annoyance, "at least cheat off someone smart." The red D at the top of Harmony's exam probably torpedoed her summer in Greece. Luckily for Mr. Clark, he had completed the multiple-choice section on his own, so he squeaked by with a C−.

For a moment, Erin thought of failing both students, but to accuse them of cheating would cause a scandal. The most popular girl at the university and her quarter-back boyfriend? With a psychopath sending Erin notes, she didn't dare—a happy coincidence of fate for Harmony and Reggie.

"Ms. Abbott?"

Erin turned in the narrow seat. Standing at the end of the chairs, a woman no taller than Erin beckoned. Sun-kissed olive skin stretched taut across a broad face, capped by tight gray curls. Muscle packed tightly across the small frame, layered by a bit of cushioning. Erin set the papers on the table, rose, and extended a hand in greeting. "I'm Erin Abbott."

"Detective Sylvie Iberville." The detective waited patiently while Erin collected her things. "Come this way, please." They entered the squad room through the metal doors.

Beyond the reception area, silence erupted into fits of

sound. Cubicles and desks crowded a dingy floor that may
have once been a cheery yellow. The detained waited in
cages or sat chained to aluminum chairs bolted to the
floors. Cries and screams drowned the clattering of type-
writers and computers. Here the expected smell of day-old
coffee wrestled with the disarming aroma of the unkempt,
the busy, the overwhelmed. Rapt, Erin's eyes widened in
curiosity and apprehension. She caught the eye of a drunk,
who proceeded to launch himself at her feet, declaring his
love. Erin jumped and bumped into Sylvie.

"Your first time in a police station?" Sylvie asked
kindly, easily bypassing the drunk.

Erin nodded sheepishly. "I've seen them on television,
but the real thing is—"

"Real," the detective finished. " 'Cause we're in the
middle of the French Quarter, life is never dull. It's a
twenty-four-hour party, and all the parents are away on
vacation."

"I teach college students. I can only imagine."

Together, the pair walked to the end of the squad room
and turned down a longer corridor. The hallway muffled
the sounds of the police station, but the din hummed in
the background. Sylvie escorted her into a cramped office, where file cabinets dueled with the desk for space.
Papers leaned drunkenly on every horizontal surface.

"Sorry about the mess," the detective said as they ma-
neuvered inside. She motioned Erin to a spindle-backed
chair that wobbled as she sat. Sylvie swiveled her hips
around to the opposite side with a minimum of effort after years of practice. "As you can see, I'm not much for
the whole cleanliness-and-godliness idea. I figure He'll
take me as I am."

Erin smiled reassuringly. "No apology necessary. I appreciate you taking the time to speak with me."

"But you were expecting an audience with the captain."

Clutching the bag close, Erin shrugged. If Captain Sanchez was unavailable, she'd take what she could get. "I'd rather not do this more than once."

The detective leaned back in the office chair, one hand drumming lightly on the arm. "Captain Sanchez got called into a meeting. It will be a few hours before he's back. I can take down your statement, and he'll follow up." No need to explain that Sanchez had pushed this one down to her in retaliation for a crack she'd made at staff yesterday about the ugly toupee covering his formerly shiny bald head. The man had no sense of humor. "So, what do you have for us that's so important?"

Erin hesitated for an instant, then reached into her satchel and pulled out the album she'd compiled. Setting it on the desk, she marshaled her thoughts. "I'm a psychology professor at Burkeen University," she began. "I teach undergraduates, primarily, but my doctorate is in criminal psychology."

Used to the babbling of the nervous, Sylvie pasted on a patient look and examined her visitor. She wasn't a native, that was for sure. Her crisp tones said money and breeding. Sylvie would bet the Northeast or maybe California. The young woman had the bone structure of the well-heeled, haughty and perfect. A gold strand with a solitaire gleamed at her throat, and actual diamonds winked in her ears.

The suit she wore cost more than Sylvie made in a month. And she'd bet the blouse beneath it was silk. Same with her hair. As a woman, Sylvie understood the vibrant sheen and healthy strands, but with hair like that, a nice cut to shape her face wouldn't have hurt.

The cop in Sylvie listened to her, and she wondered what put the anxiety in Dr. Abbott's cool voice. The woman obviously came from money, but she had brought trouble with her. "What brings you to the Eighth District on your lunch hour?" Sylvie asked quietly.

Erin took a deep breath. "I received a note. And five obituaries." She rummaged in her case and handed the envelope to the detective. She'd cut off the first line, the one that called her Analise.

Shifting forward to take it, Sylvie pinned Erin with a stern look. "You think these deaths were homicides?"

"Perhaps. I mean, yes. I did all the research I could, and they seem to fit a pattern."

Sylvie riffled through the columns and read the note. Running her thumb along the top edge of the note, she murmured, "Five murders?"

"Those are the ones he sent me. D or possibly E and F are missing, but," Erin blurted out, "I think you may have a serial killer operating here in New Orleans."

CHAPTER 5

Sylvie leaned forward. *Why did she always get the crazy ones?* "You want to run that past me again?"

Easily reading the detective's expression, Erin resisted the urge to bolt. What she had seen in the obituaries was an idea so preposterous, she hardly believed it herself. Mouth thinned, she opened the pages of the album. "I'm not insane, Detective. Someone wanted me to see something in these obituaries, and I think I do. I see a killer who wants an audience. He picked me."

"Why you?" Sylvie lifted the album. "Out of the thousands of people in the city, why'd he come to you?"

"Because he knew I'd see the pattern." Because Erin had seen darker passions, had come close to evil before. An evil that may have found her. Her stomach tightened, fear churning like acid. "Will you listen?"

In silence, Sylvie considered the question. A fifteen-year veteran on the force, she knew what crazy looked like. The good professor seemed pretty sane but full of secrets. Dr. Abbott was also terrified. Watching the tug-of-war in her eyes, Sylvie grudgingly admired the sheer force of will that kept the girl in her seat.

Sylvie decided to play along. Her next break wasn't for nearly an hour, and Dr. Abbott's story could pass the time. Dropping the album atop a stack of papers on her desk, Sylvie tapped a magenta-tipped nail on the plastic cover. "What am I looking at?"

Erin took a deep breath, opened the album, and launched into her explanation. "After I got the note and the obits, I researched each victim's death. This chart here." Erin pointed to a table that listed each victim's name, occupation, and date of death, and the murder weapon. Beside each column, she'd added a letter of the alphabet.

"*A*. Julian Harris was a city planner who died outside his office. The police found a plastic cord that had been used to strangle him. *B*. Burleigh Singleton was beaten to death with an object the police officer on-scene identified as a cricket bat. But he couldn't be sure, since he'd never played the game."

Surprised by the detail, Sylvie arched a brow. "You got all this from the paper?"

"I found most of the information online. There's a Web site about homicides in New Orleans."

"Damned Internet," muttered Sylvie. "That's where all the psychos get their tips these days." Shaking her head, she said, "Go on."

Erin pointed to the next item. "Here. The police reported that Phoebe Bailey was found strangled near the Newbern Menagerie. She was a dancer in the Quarter. The assailant used equipment from the horse's stall to kill her. That's *C*." As Erin flipped the page, the words seemed to tumble out. She circled the next entry with a shaky finger. "Police found the body of Juan Johnson, docent for the Heritage Museum, stabbed in the parking lot near the museum. According to the Web site, a chisel was used to kill him. I think he's D or E, but I can't be sure. Last week, the victim was Maggie Fordham. She'd been strangled with a coil of wire, left at the scene. G."

Sylvie heard the break in her voice. "You knew her?"

"We were neighbors. She was kind to me."

Interesting, Sylvie thought, that the young woman sounded surprised by another person's kindness. She'd file that little tidbit away for now. First, she needed to understand the story she was hearing. "Tie it together for me," Sylvie instructed. "You've given me dates and weapons and names. I don't see the connections."

Erin returned to the chart. "See these occupations?"

"Uh-huh."

"They're not exactly accurate. For example, although the police report stated that Mr. Harris was a city planner, according to his obituary he was trained as an architect."

"Who was strangled."

"No, not strangled. Asphyxiated."

"So?"

"The murderer tied a cord around his neck and asphyxiated him. Architect. Asphyxiation."

"That's quite a leap, Doctor." This time, Detective Iberville rolled her eyes in disbelief. "You can't mean to tell me this supposedly brilliant serial killer is that obvious? *A* is for *apple*? Are you serious?"

"Yes," Erin confirmed coolly. "The first one isn't terribly elaborate, I'll grant you, but it was enough to throw your investigators off. Look at this one," she instructed, jabbing at the details on the next page. "Mr. Singleton was a loan officer. A banker."

Not bothering to contain it, the detective snorted her amusement. "Who was beaten?" The full-blown laugh rippled through her. Wait until she told the squad. "Stretching a bit there, aren't we, Doctor? You've been in the classroom too long."

Eyes narrowed and hardened, Erin bit out, "Mr. Singleton was not beaten. The more accurate description for the act was *bludgeoned*."

"Same difference."

"Different difference. The weapon the police officer misidentified as a cricket bat was a short stick filled with lead at one end."

"So?"

Using the tone she generally reserved for obnoxious students, Erin explained brusquely, "A bludgeon is a short stick that usually has one thick or loaded end and is used as a weapon. I believe that would be the connection."

"Enough of this," Sylvie snapped. "I'm sorry your classes are boring you, but I don't have time for conspiracy theories or whatever this is."

The derision stung, but Erin held her temper in check. Detective Iberville had every reason to doubt her tale. Erin barely believed it herself. Still, one word kept her in her chair, kept her voice steady as her stomach trembled. *Analise.*

She tried a different tack. "For the sake of argument, at least consider this: according to what I found, officers discovered the murder weapon at each crime scene."

"Your point?"

"Criminals usually hide the evidence."

Sylvie tried not to roll her eyes. "If you're really a psychologist, shouldn't you of all people know that criminals are mostly stupid, Dr. Abbott?" Her tone left the legitimacy of the title "Doctor" hanging in the abruptly tense air.

Grinding her teeth, Erin explained, "This killer did two things. One, he killed each victim near his or her workplace. Two, he left the most obvious clue at the crime scene." Again Erin pointed to the album. "Whoever sent me the note knew that all I'd be able to find would be vital statistics and the method of murder."

Speaking over her, Sylvie wagged her finger. "Given the number of murders that happen in New Orleans each year, the absence of a criminal mastermind isn't a lot to go on."

Erin slapped the book closed. "This isn't the absence of a criminal mastermind! It's the work of a man who wants admiration and a chase. Admiration because he committed five murders right under your nose. Actually, if I'm right, there have been seven victims."

"Seven murders without anyone but you catching on?"

"I didn't. Not until he showed me. He wants us to see what he can do when we're not looking. Seven murders with no obvious connection. Which doesn't matter as much because it's seven out of twenty-six."

"Why not tell you about all seven?"

"It's all about the chase. He's ready to play, and he wants to play now. So he offers me enough for a quick analysis, but I have to figure the two others out for myself."

Anticipating the next question, Erin asked it first. "Why did he pick me?"

"Got it in one."

Erin did not stumble over her lie, though her throat threatened to close over the words. "I'm a criminal psychologist. He must know this. Moreover, I specialize in serial killers."

"Do you think he's one of your students?"

No, she thought. *I think he's the man I killed two years ago.* "Perhaps."

Sylvie wasn't convinced, but before she decided, she planned to do a little private investigation of her own. "Where are you from, Dr. Abbott?"

"I teach at Burkeen University."

"I didn't ask where you taught. I asked where you're from." Sylvie dug under a pile of folders for a pen and held it poised over a page covered with scrawl. "When did you move to New Orleans? Who gave you your degree?"

"You don't believe me."

Pursing her lips, Sylvie said, "I think *you* believe it."

"But you're not going to help."

"We're tight on resources, Dr. Abbott. These are real murders, and their families deserve justice. I'm not going to go haring off on a wild-goose chase to look for a phantom serial killer." Sylvie patted Erin's arm sympathetically. "A madman killed your friend Maggie. It's natural to want revenge. And in your line of work, I can understand why you'd see conspiracies in every corner."

"I'm not some grief-stricken nut, Detective." She shoved the album forward, angry that her hand shook slightly. From terror. If the police didn't help her, didn't believe her, she was on her own. Desperate now, she insisted,

"Someone sent me these obituaries. Someone wrote me this note. I'm not making this up."

In polite dismissal, Sylvie pushed back from the desk and stood. "Dr. Abbott, your own theory doesn't work." Opening the album, she pointed to the page labeled *"C."* "Flaw in your theory, Professor: Phoebe Bailey was a dancer killed with a surcingle. I've known her for twenty years, and I used to work at a stable. *Dancer* starts with *d* and *surcingle* starts with *s*. Nice try, though."

Erin went still, paralyzed by defeat. The police weren't going to help her. Even if she tried to go around Detective Iberville, she'd probably face the same pitying looks of doubt. Once again, her survival rested in her own hands. Hadn't she learned by now that she couldn't count on others to save her?

Stiffly she collected her things and walked to the door. "It's your prerogative to doubt me, Detective Iberville. I didn't expect you to believe my theory, but I had to try." Opening the door, Erin halted in the doorway. "However, with all due respect, Ms. Bailey's obituary says that she was a dancer from Jamaica, where the native dance is calypso. *Calypso* begins with a *c*. And while you're correct, she was killed with a surcingle, you're wrong about the spelling. *Surcingle* is a word that comes from the Middle French *cengle* and the Latin *cingere,* which means 'to gird,' and both of those words are spelled with a *c*. When the word was Americanized, we adopted an alternate spelling with an *s*. But even the American dictionaries recognize the original spelling: *C-i-r-c-i-n-g-l-e.*"

Head down, Erin rushed from the office and stumbled against someone blocking her way out of the station. A smothered oath sailed over her head as her foot connected with a shin. Then icy cola spilled down the front of her shirt and dripped from the tweed jacket.

"I'm so sorry," she said, mortified. She looked up to repeat her apology. "You!"

Gabriel wrestled with a smile. Luscious brown eyes shot venom at him while his soda soaked into her skin. "Hello, Alice."

The combination of fury and embarrassment on Erin's face amused him. And intrigued him, almost more than the conversation he'd overheard.

He started to offer her his handkerchief, then he thought better of the idea. Fishing into his jacket, he pulled out the square of linen every Southern gentleman of a certain age carried. Instead of handing it to her, as a gentleman would, he personally dabbed the linen against damp silk, his knuckles brushing skin.

Erin stiffened at his touch. After the second accidental grazing of the swell of cleavage, she rudely snatched at the handkerchief. "I can dry myself, thank you."

"Of course." He released the cloth. With his other hand, he crumpled his empty cup and set it on the shabby black cabinets that stood sentinel outside Sylvie's door.

He hadn't expected to find his klutzy professor or the answer to his prayers in the station's hallways. But he never turned down gifts from the fates, especially when they came so neatly and enticingly packaged. Propping his elbow on the cabinet and tucking his notepad behind a stack of files, he drawled, "What's a nice girl like you doing at a police station in the middle of the day?"

"Research for a class," Erin lied automatically. The last thing she wanted at this moment was another conversation with Gabriel. She was sopping wet with cola and embarrassed, and her skin still tingled where his knuckles had caressed.

It was all her fault, she conceded, an accident caused by her tendency to keep her head down. She wanted to slink away, but she owed him an apology.

Gabriel spoke first. "Perhaps you should consider wearing warning bells or a turn signal."

Irritation stopped her apology. She grumbled, "Maybe you could stay out of my way."

Gabriel raised a single sable brow. "As it's you who keep plowing into me, I don't think I'm really the problem here. However, since you seem so distressed, I'll forgive your lack of manners and take the blame."

"Generous of you." Erin could feel cold Coke seeping into her skin, and behind her, she heard Detective Iberville shuffling around. The thought of another one of her pitying looks, particularly at her sodden appearance, spurred Erin into a more sincere apology. "I'm very sorry, Mr. Moss. I will launder your handkerchief and return it to you." She sidled to the right of him, eager to escape. "And I swear I will do my best to stay out of your way from now on."

But Gabriel wasn't quite ready to let her go. It was becoming a habit, he thought as he unerringly captured her wrist. Fragile bones shifted beneath his grip, jerking angrily. Warmth seeped into him. A closer hold seemed essential. When he twined his fingers with hers, the movement felt natural. Right.

"Mr. Moss!"

Flexing his fingers where they laced with hers, he studied her. Sparks shot out from the chocolate brown eyes that glared up at him. Antagonism curled the lush mouth. He wanted to kiss, so instead, he teased. "Call me Gabriel. Since you're a friend of the family."

"I'm a colleague of Genevieve's," Erin corrected between clenched teeth. "And I have every intention of limiting my acquaintance to her alone." Futilely she tried to pull her hand free. Which was a mistake. The slide of skin made her pulse leap.

Feeling her reaction, Gabriel bent closer and shook his head in mock disappointment. "Not very hospitable of you, Dr. Abbott."

Erin scowled as he captured her other hand. This had gone on long enough. "Let . . . me . . . go."

Cops wandered past, nodding in casual greeting. Gabriel responded, but his attention stayed on Erin. Instead of releasing her, he lifted her right hand to his lips. With his eyes on hers, he gave in to impulse and nipped at the rigid knuckles. "Say the magic word."

Her mouth dried and she could feel her knees weaken. Trying to be strong, she replied huskily, "Please . . . let . . . me . . . go." Against her will, her fist pressed closer.

Delighted, Gabriel sampled the ridges of bone and the satin flesh with separate kisses, his eyes holding hers. "Where are you from, Dr. Abbott?"

The sharp tugs of arousal dulled instantly. He was the second person to inquire about her past. Two people that she didn't know anything about except that one was a detective and the other was a journalist. Her natural enemies. Avoiding his question, she repeated quietly, "Please let me go."

Gabriel saw the shutters fall over her eyes, desire

banished. The reporter in him wondered what it was about her former home that she didn't want him to know.

There was a story here; he could smell it. Where his lips met her skin, he could taste it. And he'd enjoy uncovering it. As much as he enjoyed the contrast of irritation and attraction he read in Erin's very wary eyes. The first he intentionally stoked by pressing their palms into closer contact; the second he wanted to explore.

"If you agree to have dinner with me."

"Absolutely not."

He thought he heard regret, faint but real. Real enough to keep him rooted in the hallway. "Then I guess we'll just stand here. Hand in hand. But I don't think Coca-Cola agrees with silk."

"It doesn't and if it stains, I'm sending you the bill."

"Bring it to dinner."

The quick retort startled a laugh from her. "You don't give up, do you?"

"Not when fate intervenes. We've been in the same city for months, and we run into each other twice in one day. *Ma coeur*, it must be destiny."

Too bad she didn't believe in destiny, Erin thought. And she didn't believe in coincidence, either. "Mr. Moss, for the last time, I'm asking you to let me go. If you don't, I will start screaming. We're in a police station. One scream, and several large men will come to my rescue."

Gabriel nodded and turned his head to a burly officer lounging near a coffee machine. "Hey, Jerry? The lady wants me arrested. Think you can oblige?"

"For you, Gabe? Hell, we've always got your cell waiting." Other cops chuckled and called out greetings.

"See," Gabriel whispered. "It's fate."

"Please."

The single word spoke volumes, but he wasn't sure what he heard. But it was enough to make him release her hands and step away. "You're free to go."

Without a word, Erin turned and ran. Picking up speed, she plowed through the bullpen and banged on the metal door to be released. Officer Rochon buzzed her through and watched bemusedly as she raced outside the police station. "Strange woman," he murmured to himself. "Pretty, but strange. But that's not so unusual here in New Orleans."

CHAPTER 6

On Royal, weekend revelers milled about, unconcerned that it was a weekday. They were entranced by the party that was New Orleans. Vibrant jazz danced in the air. The moist heat gave young women and men a reason to shed clothes and inhibitions. Mardi Gras had ended months before, but the festivities had simply shifted focus to summer tourists.

With thick crowds pouring into the Quarter, there was not a vacant cab to be found. Erin cursed beneath her breath. She rummaged in her bag for her phone and quickly dialed her assistant. Noise blared in the background. Erin shouted into the phone, "Jessica? Hi, it's Erin."

On the other end, grading papers, Jessica leaned into the phone. "Dr. Abbott? Where in the world are you?"

An engrossed couple, sharing a Hurricane, wove past the station and Erin. She stepped out of their way and sighed. "Down in the Quarter. Is there a chance you can swing by after your office hours and pick me up? I'm not sure I'll be able to get a cab."

"Sorry, Dr. Abbott," Jessica apologized. "I've got to cover a class for Dr. Bernard. He called in sick today."

Hearing the genuine regret, Erin said, "No problem. I've got a few more exams I can grade while I wait."

"I'm sorry, Dr. Abbott. See you tomorrow?"

"Bright and early."

When Jessica rang off, Erin shrugged her shoulders and examined the low-heeled brown pumps. *Thank heavens for sensible shoe wear,* she thought resignedly. She started walking in the direction of home. Perhaps, if she didn't melt first, she'd luck upon a taxi. Erin crossed Conti and wound her way between drunken college students and wide-eyed tourists.

A long shadow fell into step beside her. She didn't bother to look up.

"This could qualify as stalking, Mr. Moss," she muttered wearily as she shifted to put the width of the sidewalk between them.

Gabriel simply followed. "Why are you always running from me, Erin?"

Erin lengthened her stride, knowing that it was no match for the long legs of the man beside her. If he caught up with her, she'd never escape. "Because I don't want to be near you."

"Ouch." Gabriel rubbed at his chest, not quite joking. "Direct hit." He slowed his pace, hanging back to watch her walk. She moved quickly, almost at a run. Despite her diminutive height, her pace ate the ground in quick flashes of motion. Questions, which multiplied each time he was with her, demanded answers. Was she chasing something or running away from someone? The answer seemed essential, almost vital. Before he could ask, though, he'd have to make her stand still. "Erin." He lengthened his stride to catch up. "Wait. Please."

"Go away."

"Can't."

"Won't," Erin contradicted.

"Okay, won't."

Abruptly Erin stopped and spun toward him. "You don't know me. I don't know you. I don't like you. Why won't you leave it that way?"

"Because I want to get to know you. I get the feeling not many people ever do."

"I obviously prefer it, Mr. Moss."

"And I wonder why that is." In what had grown quickly into habit, he caught her hand and tucked it firmly inside his own. He expected her immediate jerk of resistance and countered it effortlessly. "You don't strike me as the shy, retiring type, despite your disguise."

Damn him, he was right, she thought, staring at the steam rising from the pavement. She wasn't shy or timid. She was methodical, conscientious, and deliberate. She weighed consequences, took careful actions. Having friends was dangerous; therefore, she didn't have them. Sebastian was the only exception, because he knew her before.

"Tell me what you're thinking, Erin."

Erin looked up and into eyes that glinted silver. In sharp contrast to the friendly voice, Gabriel's look was anything but friendly. It was stubborn. Possessive. It was a look she recognized.

Firmly she pulled her hand free and slapped it on his

chest. The shift and play of muscle distracted for a second and she curved her hand into him for a second, but only just. "No, I'm not the shy, timid type, but I've an instinct about men like you. You're attractive, with a full arsenal. Quick wit. Incredible voice. Women are drawn to the charm and the attention. They are readily available to you, and you like their company. Maybe they even enjoy the stalking. I don't. I choose my friends, Mr. Moss, and I've asked you to stay away from me."

Stung, more than he would have imagined, Gabriel took a half step back, and her hand dropped away. Not often had he been summed up so swiftly and found so wanting. An awkward silence filled the air between them.

When she made a move to speak, he held up his palms in surrender. "I'm sorry. I will do my best to stay out of your way." He spun on his heel and stepped into the street. With an imperious wave, he beckoned a taxi turning the corner. The cab screeched to a halt at the curb, and Gabriel pulled open the door, squeaking it on its hinges. "Felix. Please take Dr. Abbott wherever she's in such a hurry to go."

"Sure thing, Gabe."

Silently Erin climbed inside. She started to say something, "Thanks," or perhaps an apology, but she did not get the chance. Gabriel slammed the door shut on her unspoken words and banged the roof once, signaling the driver to go. She watched Gabriel walk away until he turned the corner and vanished from sight.

"Dr. Abbott? I need an address."

Erin flushed. "Two-sixteen St. Bennett. Please." After she gave the driver her address, she settled deep into the leather to think. Yes, she was methodical, conscientious, and deliberate. And, she acknowledged on a fresh wave of shame, she still could hurt another simply to protect herself.

At her apartment, Erin entered to the sound of the phone ringing. She locked the door behind her and snatched the phone from its cradle on the third ring. "Hello?" she asked, teetering on one foot as she slid the shoe over poorly sized hose.

"Are you hiding from me?" asked the gravelly voice on the other end.

Erin froze and terror condensed around her like ice. "Who is this?"

"It's me. Sebastian."

A tremulous sigh escaped and she sank weakly down onto the bowed sofa. "Oh, Sebastian." With a quivering hand, she lifted a cup of tea left over from breakfast from the coffee table. She gulped down the tepid brew, trying without much success to inject steel into a suddenly quavering voice. "You frightened me."

"Why are you scared of a phone call?" On the other end, Sebastian Cain narrowed his eyes. "Has something happened?" he questioned carefully.

"It's been a long week." Erin forced her nerves to settle, knowing he would hear every nuance. Because she loved him, because he'd done the unthinkable one stormy California night, she would do for him what no one had for her. Protect him. She would keep him away from New Orleans and the menace that taunted her. With a quick laugh, she explained, "I guess the phone has static. I wasn't expecting to hear from you while the sun was up. You keep such interesting hours."

"All of the hours need tending, love," he replied. "How's the Big Easy?"

"Hot." Erin sank into the sofa cushions and cradled the teacup in her lap. "Are you in New York?"

"I'm around," was the noncommittal reply. "Now tell me what's really going on."

The whole truth, so rarely told, spilled out. She leaned forward to set the cup down, wincing when the delicate china rattled against its saucer. "Someone knows about Nathan."

The quiet oath singed the phone wires. "Who?"

On the other end, Erin shook her head. "I don't know. I got a note on Sunday, with five obituaries. The note had my name on it."

"Analise?"

"Yes. And there was more." Quickly she explained her theory of the obituaries to a silent Sebastian. "It's a stretch, I know, but I'm certain I'm right. Only a person with an abnormal affinity for words and puzzles would have seen the connections. A freak—"

"Erin," Sebastian interrupted patiently, "don't do this to yourself. Don't let Nathan inside your head."

"He's always there. He never leaves. No matter what I do, he's always inside my head." The sob caught in her throat. "I just want to be free of him. Of her."

Sebastian heard the tears, felt his heart wrench. He remembered a younger Erin, a daring little girl called Analise by doting, if distracted, parents. They had marveled at their brilliant child and despaired of understanding her. Laboratories and institutes and universities had studied the four-year-old brain that absorbed Latin like a sponge. At five, she'd mastered Greek, while his ten-year-old mind grappled with dangling participles.

By fifteen, she was on her own, as was he, her parents and his mother killed in a plane crash in Belize. When he'd traveled to California to reconnect, the girl he'd known had been smothered, but not erased. She'd found the will to break free. Whether she called herself Erin or Jane Doe, she would always be Analise. A survivor.

"You are Analise. Changing your name doesn't change who you are. Who you've always been."

The denial burst out of her. "I don't want to be who I've always been! Meek. Simpering. Useless. But I don't deserve anything better."

"You deserve to be happy. You've paid your dues. No one holds you responsible."

"I hold me responsible."

"What are you thinking, Erin?"

"Could it be him? Nathan? Are we sure he's not back somehow?"

"You've been in New Orleans too long," Nathan scoffed. "He was gone when I got there. We both checked. I don't know who's doing this, but it's not him."

"Then someone else wants to scare me. Control me. I can't be a victim again." She thought of the look of pity in Detective Iberville's eyes. "But I won't be a frightened, mute observer to the world spinning around me. In fact, I'm not going to wait for the police to believe me."

Recognizing the tone from long ago, even if she did not, Sebastian bolted upright. "Now, Erin. Wait a minute."

"For what? For the police to listen to a ridiculous half-truth? They won't." Adrenaline sang in her veins, and she welcomed the new sensation that didn't feel so new. Vaguely, she remembered being fearless once, before Nathan and Callenwolde University. "Maybe if I gather more evidence, they'll have to believe me."

"Or they'll turn their investigation on you. It's too big a risk."

"Oh, I won't do anything rash. I am trained in this area."

"You're an academic, not a sleuth."

"I'm a *criminal* psychologist. Emphasis on the *criminal*. I'll just go by the crime scenes. Check their backgrounds. Draw up a profile of their attacker. Easy, nonthreatening stuff."

"This is what he wants. It's very threatening," Sebastian growled. "Whoever is after you isn't playing a game, Erin. He's already killed seven people, and I doubt they were his first time at bat. I won't let you risk your life to atone for doing what you had to do."

"How do you plan to stop me?"

"You're coming to New York."

"Are you there?"

"That's irrelevant. I'll let my doorman know to expect you tomorrow night."

"I'm not going anywhere. I am the resident expert on language and lunatics."

"Cute."

To mollify him, she soothed, "Don't worry. I'm still me. I won't get into any trouble. I promise. But I need to do something. I have to."

Static crackled for a moment, and then a harried sigh stretched across the wires. Erin echoed the sentiment, albeit silently. "If you don't call me by Sunday, I'm coming to find you. After twenty-seven years of friendship, you know I don't make idle threats."

"I know. I still remember the telegraph you sent when I went off to Bilbao and didn't write."

"I will always find you, honey."

"I love you, too."

Sebastian harrumphed gently. "I didn't say I love you."

"But you do."

"Always."

"Bye, Sebastian." She hung up the phone and walked to the cheval mirror hanging near the entranceway. "Hello, Erin Abbott."

Course set, Erin realized that she'd missed every meal that day. Muttering to herself, she said, "I could write a paper about the effects of threats from a serial killer on the appetite."

As a psychologist, she recognized the dark humor as a defense mechanism. It would be stupid not to be afraid, she decided, but fear would never control her the way she'd allowed in the past.

And she'd fight back by ordering dinner.

Thirty minutes later, she stood on her balcony, watching evening traffic. Down below, she saw the deliveryman from Thai Palace in his familiar Jeep, baseball cap pulled low over his hair. Anticipating him, Erin pressed the buzzer to open the door. "Come on up," she instructed.

She counted the bills for payment as she waited for him to make it up to the third floor. The elevator was notoriously slow, which was why she often took the stairs. Thinking of the worn cap, she added a healthy tip. When the knock finally sounded on her apartment door, she absently opened it. "You have the fastest delivery in town."

"I aim to please," drawled a voice that did not belong to the deliveryman. Erin confirmed her suspicion by turning to find Gabriel in the doorway. He removed the cap, tucked it into his back pocket, and extended a gather of flowers. Jasmine.

At the sight of the tiny purple blooms, something in the region of her heart melted, and she considered inviting him inside. "Thank you," she murmured, accepting the flowers.

"A peace offering," he explained. "You are a beautiful woman, Erin Abbott."

Surprised by the compliment, Erin cast a furtive glance down. She wore a black tank and shorts. Chagrined, she swept a hand over the hair she'd piled into an unruly heap atop her head, forgoing the tidy bun or taut braid.

Female vanity urged her to rush into the bathroom and at least bundle her hair into a band, throw on a pair of jeans. Self-preservation warned her to keep Gabriel Moss outside her apartment at all costs.

Gabriel stared, taking his time. Thin black straps suspended a scooped neck that framed the expanse of skin and appealing swell delightfully. Beneath the abbreviated hem of the shorts, he saw the roundly molded shape and lithe legs that had been successfully hidden by the morning's unpleasant suit. It had been worth the risk to his pride to have his expectations proven true. He whistled under his breath. "I was right."

"About what?" Erin asked, against her better judgment.

"Fabulous body." He paused a beat. "And you're hiding something."

Abruptly the warning became a blare and she remembered anew why she couldn't let him inside. *Reporter.* She ignored the stab of disappointment, dismissed the sensation of loss. Gabriel Moss might be gorgeous, charming, and oddly appealing, but she barely knew him. "You have quite an imagination, Mr. Moss."

When Erin moved to slam the door, he easily blocked the move. Then he added silkily, "Honey, uncovering secrets is my specialty."

"I don't have any secrets. And don't call me *honey*," she returned testily. Suddenly the endearment scraped at her nerves in a reminder of what she couldn't have. With renewed determination, she tried to keep him out, wanting only to let him inside. But as she'd learned in the station, Gabriel Moss was not moved without effort. Despite her pressing against the door, it remained stubbornly open, due entirely to the muscled arm he braced against its frame. Refusing to concede defeat, Erin shoved against the immobile wood and huffed, "Get . . . out."

Gabriel flattened his hand against the door and leaned against the wooden frame. The sight of the determined diminutive professor, five-three in her bare feet, he guessed, amused him. Aroused him. She had no hope of removing him, yet she persisted. He'd always admired tenacity.

It was one of his best traits.

"Dr. Abbott, I came to apologize. I think you owe me an apology, too. But I'm big enough to forgive you without one."

Wheezing slightly from her fruitless exertions, Erin swept damp ebony curls back from her forehead. "Apology accepted. Go away."

"I cannot tell a lie. I have another motive." Gabriel relaxed a bit more. The little engine seemed to be running out of steam. "I want to see the note, Erin."

"I'm not talking to you." Erin sagged against the door. "I'm expecting company."

"In this?" He trailed a finger along a narrow strap that had fallen off her shoulder. The tingle skating along his skin eased away more of the sting from her barbs. Her nearly imperceptible shudder at his touch brushed it completely aside. She was fighting something, but it wasn't him. Knowing that was enough. "I like the attire, but it is a bit informal for entertaining. Who is he?"

"Um. His name is, uh . . ."

His lips twitched in delight. "Cat got your tongue?"

Erin blurted out the first name she could think of. "His name is Sebastian. And he'll be here any minute."

At that moment, the buzzer mercifully sounded again and Erin dived for the intercom. Punching the buzzer, she prayed Gabriel would leave before he met Pao, the weekly deliveryman. "Come right up," she urged into the box.

No longer amused, Gabriel straightened from his position in the doorway.

His eyes, as Erin watched in fascination, transformed from a calm winter gray to the angry color of hurricane storms. The chiseled jaw hardened into granite, and the grinning mouth thinned into a flat line of disapproval. The result was terrifying. Thrilling.

"You're just full of surprises, Dr. Abbott," he said in a low voice that reminded Erin of Sam Spade movies and antiheroes. "Lurking in police stations. Late-night trysts."

Erin cast a desperate glance into the hallway. She needed Gabriel to leave before the real deliveryman made his way to the landing. "Please leave."

"I'm not going anywhere, Professor." Gabriel barred

the doorway. Their bodies brushed, and he could feel her inhale. He, too, took a breath, absorbing the scent of jasmine and woman. "You can't pretend there's nothing more between us."

"There's only murder." She schooled her features into cool disinterest, ignoring the drumming of her heartbeat. "And I don't need your help. I thought I made myself clear."

In response, he twirled a lock of hair around his finger, trailed it to the place where her blood pounded against the skin. "What you've made clear is that I disturb you. Your pulse doesn't lie."

She sputtered, but he continued to speak. "Pushing me out of your apartment is usually a good signal. And for most men, your words are enough of a kick to the ego to have them backing off. Hell, it almost worked on me. Then I remembered something."

Erin steeled herself against asking the question. Instead, she thinned her mouth into a firm line of disapproval. It normally quelled the most fractious student.

It had no effect on Gabriel. He watched the pout attempt to firm, and he fought the urge to kiss the rich curve of lips, enchanted. "What? you ask. Well, I remembered your hand."

"My hand?" she repeated involuntarily.

Gingerly he lifted her right hand, examining the slender bones, the flawless skin. "For a second there, when you tried to push me away, your fingers curled into me. Like you wanted to hold on. Then you made yourself let go."

At that moment, the Thai Palace deliveryman rounded the corner. Smiling at his familiar patron, he greeted her by name. Erin responded shakily and made the exchange of cash for the plastic sack. As the young man descended the stairs, she looked everywhere but at her uninvited guest.

Gabriel moved toward her, lifting her chin, forcing her eyes to his. Now he grinned, a curve of lips that was anything but reassuring. "Why do I get the feeling, darling, that you're an expert on the subject of lies?"

She forced herself to hold his gaze. "You're not entitled to the truth."

"No, I'm not." Delicately he traced the slim lines of her collarbone, exposed by the tank top. A faint shiver crossed her skin, and he smiled slightly. "But I will have it. You can tell me now, or I'll find out."

"I don't threaten well." She lifted a hand to capture his. Brown eyes bored into gray. "I may want to hold on sometimes, Gabriel, but I've learned to let go. Sometimes holding on too tight can kill you." With that, she dropped his hand, entered the apartment, and quietly closed the door.

CHAPTER 7

Erin stood outside the address listed as Julian Harris's. His townhome nestled in the Lower Garden District, a neighborhood celebrated for its quaint cottages and stylish town houses. The home she identified as his jibed with the brief profile she had in her bag. Thinking about the outline she'd made at dawn, Erin rummaged in her bag for a steno pad. She uncapped a pen and wrote, "Refined. Elegant. Precise. Compassionate."

Articles about successful auction bids and civic awards drew a portrait of a young architect who'd left the private sector to serve the city he loved. And the devotion showed, she thought.

Julian had obviously refurbished the narrow building, choosing golds and greens to complement the stucco façade. Stained-glass panels graced the asymmetrical windows of the three-story American townhome. On the second floor, wrought iron had been polished to a high gleam, catching the afternoon sun. In contrast, the houses on either side showed their age.

"He was meticulous about historical accuracy," she noted aloud, jotting the phrase down in her notebook. "I could swear I was in Paris."

Why would the killer have chosen Julian as his first victim?

Architect, accountant, archaeologist, anthropologist. Language offered dozens of occupations for a killer to start with as a first target. But either horrible luck or terrible design had selected Julian Harris. Erin hoped that by sneaking into the house and poking around, some clue would show her which one it had been.

Sweltering, she rearranged the gray collar and wiped at her forehead. Then she took a deep breath and hurried across the street. On the low stoop of the house next door, she knocked briskly. No one stirred. Since it was early afternoon, she wasn't surprised. Normal people were still at work or out on errands. They weren't likely to be at home or, she acknowledged with a touch of morbidity, invading the homes of the dead.

With a grimace, she crossed Julian's lawn and repeated her peremptory summons. This time, a man stepped out onto the cluttered front entrance. Her years among students pegged his age at eighteen, maybe nineteen. A dissolute, pampered nineteen. His outfit certainly fit the bill. It consisted of the bottom half of a pair of expensive silk pajamas. Greasy blond hair drooped down over bloodshot eyes and stopped above a reddened nose that had been broken at least once. Or, at least, the capillaries had.

"You one of those church people?" He squinted at her, despite the shaded overhang of his balcony. "'Cause I'm an aesthetic."

Erin winced at the mangled declaration. "I believe you mean you're an atheist."

"Yeah. Whatever. Look, lady, I don't want to buy anything." He leaned in, leering. "Unless you're selling something good?"

She took a hasty step back as fumes assaulted her. He apparently hadn't brushed his teeth since classes ended. "I was just wondering if you knew my cousin?"

"Your cousin?" The man looked around suspiciously. "Who's your cousin?"

Erin pointed hurriedly at the next house. "He lives there. Julian Harris."

He guffawed loudly, bathing her in a foul aroma.

She took shallow breaths and waited for the stench to pass. "Do you know him?"

"I know you're not his cousin." Dubious, he scratched at a furry chest. "Mr. High-and-Mighty was a lot lighter than you."

Thinking fast, she stiffened and pretended to be insulted. "He was from my mother's side of the family."

He studied her afresh, looking for evidence, but he couldn't really tell the difference anyhow. "Oh. Well." Bored by the interview, he jerked his thumb toward the house. "Doesn't matter anyway. He's dead. Cops found him at work."

"Dead?" She gulped as though the news were new. "Do they know who killed him?"

Interest renewed, he shifted toward her. In a rough whisper, he offered, "I heard it was drug related. Like the Mafia. They strangled him and everything." He scanned her face. "Your mom Italian?"

"No. She's not." In fetid proximity, odors from body and mouth attacked with coordinated, military precision. She pressed her hand to her stomach and tried not to retch. "When did he die?"

"Weeks ago. House has been closed up since then. They said he had no family." As he spoke, his eyes narrowed suspiciously.

"We're distant cousins," explained a familiar voice from behind her. "Related by marriage."

Erin spun around to face a smugly mournful Gabriel. It only needed this, she thought. It wasn't enough that she was lying to neighbors and skulking around a dead man's house. No, she supposed, her life of crime wouldn't be complete without Genevieve's loathsome brother to record her fall. "What are you doing here?"

"Where else would I be, honey?" He fairly purred the words, daring her to challenge him. She couldn't see the young man watching them as though he couldn't decide whether to call the cops or not. Gabriel could. If the chips fell, he had the First Amendment to hide behind. She was on her own. Right now, the independent Dr. Abbott needed him.

A similar thought occurred to Erin. There was no way to expose Gabriel without painting a bull's-eye on her chest, too. Resigned to play along, she managed to say with saccharine sweetness, "I thought I asked you to wait in the car."

"You were taking too long, darling." Enjoying himself, Gabriel snaked an arm around her and pulled her to him. His fingers pinched her waist in blunt warning. "Plus, I haven't seen your cousin Julian in forever. Sometimes I forget I married into such an extended family."

"Big families are like that." Trapped, Erin could do

nothing but stand there and seethe. And try not to acknowledge how distressingly right his arm felt around her. Strong, steady, secure.

"Why don't we let our friend go inside? You and I can take a last look at Julian's home?" When Erin nodded testily, Gabriel extended his hand to the young man. "Thanks for your help."

Suspicion gave way to lassitude. "No problem, man."

In silence, Gabriel guided Erin across the unkempt lawn to the nearly immaculate Harris property. Weeds had sprouted up along the sidewalk, poked through the bed of tulips at the front door.

Reaching past Erin, Gabriel tried the doorknob, which refused to turn under his hand. He shook the polished brass, to no avail. Looking around, he figured they'd get inside faster through a window. "I'm going to look for an open window," he explained. "Stay here until I get back."

Once Gabriel rounded the corner, she checked over her shoulder. Seeing no one, Erin removed her jacket and reached into the pocket. She removed a slim length of wire and crouched beside the lock. Using tricks learned from Sebastian years ago, she slid the wire into the opening. After testing the lock, she bent the wire and reinserted both tips. Soon the lock released with a slight click. Bingo.

She turned the knob and walked inside. On a side panel, an alarm blinked green. The police had apparently not bothered to reengage it after their investigation. It made sense. There was no one to protect. Julian Harris had lived alone and had no family to speak of. In a few more weeks, the courts would declare his estate property of the city because there was no one to claim it. Erin understood the isolation.

Quietly she wandered down the hallway he'd lined with jazz legends. Etta, Duke, Louis, Dinah and others greeted visitors from framed black-and-white photos. A couple even sported autographs. At the end of the short gallery, dust motes floated in the air, dancing on streaks of colored light. As she took measured steps, original hardwoods creaked beneath her feet. The townhome had the musty smell of abandonment.

She poked her head into the main room on the ground floor. Shaker-style furniture contrasted nicely with lush accoutrements such as a vintage Chesterfield sofa in deep rose. Tiffany lamps perched on high pedestals of oak. Their motifs mirrored the pastoral scenes in the glass windows. Outside of which, Gabriel fumbled with the onerous locks that secured the windows.

Erin reluctantly unlatched the heavy casement and lifted the hook holding the window in place. The glass swung out on its hinges, and behind the pane she heard a muffled curse.

"How did you get inside?" Gabriel demanded as he hoisted himself over the side. Luckily, most of the town-homes had been built at ground level. The climb inside required only a short fall.

"Through the front door." She graciously helped him to his feet, pleased to have bested him. Gabriel seemed to be the type of man who was used to winning. He could stand to lose on occasion, she decided. Lifting a brow, she shrugged. "Seemed easier than the window."

"You had a key?" He advanced on her, equal parts amazed and maddened.

Erin took a healthy step away. "No. I'm just good with locks." Unwilling to say more, she whirled around and headed for the stairs. The damp heat inside mimicked the atmosphere beyond the door. In deference, she shrugged off the gray jacket that matched his eyes and hung it on the newel post. It amazed her that the color could be the same and yet so dramatically different. "I'll be upstairs," she announced, climbing quickly.

"I'm coming with you." Gabriel fell in step behind her.

Erin halted on the step and turned to face him. "Let's get one thing clear. We're not here together. I'm here and you're here. That's all."

"That's garbage," he snapped. "I got you past Junior."

"Thank you. Now go."

"I'm not leaving, Erin. For a reason you don't care to elaborate on, you've been able to spot a pattern no one else has seen. I heard you explain it to Sylvie. She's too cynical about the lunatics in New Orleans to bite. But I'm desperate. So rest assured, I'm going to dog your steps until I find out what you know. You could save us both a lot of time if you cooperate." He straightened his arm to cover her hand on the wood, and then he pounced. "Are you the killer?"

The stark accusation almost made her lose her footing. "Of course not!"

Gabriel grabbed her before she completely lost her balance. In a single, smooth motion, he towed her close to him. Certain she'd regained her equilibrium, he lifted his hands in apology. "Sorry. I don't think you're a homicidal maniac, but it had to be asked."

Catching her breath, she muttered, "I could learn to hate you."

Grinning at the straightforward announcement, Gabriel resisted the urge to kiss the angry mouth. "You have only yourself to blame, Doctor." When she looked confused, he explained. "Your visit to the police station. Criminals like to confess in order to clear their consciences."

"I went to the police because I wanted to help. Not to confess or be laughed at by Detective Iberville or hounded by you." She left no doubt as to which outcome irritated her more.

She mounted the stairs with speed, having hiked the narrow skirt up to her knees. From his vantage point, he admired the curve of subtly muscled calves and the rise and fall of the pert bottom. What else, he wondered heatedly, was Erin hiding?

The mystery tugged at him, and each encounter added a new layer. Like how a prim professor had learned to pick locks. Or why she had been chosen to find a killer. Any answers, he would have to discover on his own. He was looking forward to the search.

He'd learned one thing already. Erin had a prickly conscience, one that wouldn't permit injustice but allowed for breaking and entering. The malleable code intrigued him, but not as much as the story it would uncover for him.

At the landing, an unaware Erin glanced down the hallway. To her left, the stairs led up to the third floor. Four doors were arrayed on the second floor, two along the opposite wall and a third on the other side of the stairs. The fourth door stood ajar at the far end, and she glimpsed the corner of a bed in the center. She didn't know exactly what she was looking for, but the master bedroom seemed like a good place to start. If she didn't find anything of interest, she'd move on. Going with her gut, she turned to the right.

Gabriel caught her arm to stop her. "What is the plan, exactly?"

"*My* plan—" She stressed the *my*. "My plan is none of your business." Erin dragged her arm free. "I didn't ask you to come with me."

"I think we just had this argument. You don't want me here. Too bad. I'm here." He circled in front to block her. "I'm not leaving without the whole story. Like why you think Julian Harris was murdered. And why you're lying to his neighbors to get inside his town house. And how you got inside his townhome."

Erin jutted her chin out defiantly. "Why are you here?"

"For the headline," Gabriel answered without hesitation. "I need a big story to boost the *Ledger*'s sales, and I think your serial killer theory might be the ticket." He smiled, that slash of white that made it hard for her to breathe.

Disarmed by his candor, Erin faltered. She hadn't expected the truth. More to the point, she had no idea what to do with it. She understood subterfuge and lies. Honesty stumped her. "How did you know where to find me?"

"I take good notes. Plus, I followed you."

Erin folded her arms and narrowed her eyes. "You followed me?"

"From campus after you'd finished giving that social psych exam. The cabdriver dropped you off and you spent a good fifteen minutes building up the courage to cross the street. Good move, to canvass the neighbors first." He chucked her chin to close the mouth that had fallen agape. "You work like a pro, Dr. Abbott."

Despite the sincere compliment, Erin considered the implications. Gabriel—no, a reporter—had lurked around the school, unbeknownst to her. He'd spied on her for nearly an hour and she had been none the wiser. The thud in her stomach echoed the pounding at her temple.

When she decided to investigate and gather clues, it hadn't occurred to her that the quest could be her undoing. Gabriel may have only come for the murder story, but if he stayed too long, he could uncover more.

Glaring, she muttered, "I don't like being followed."

Gabriel shrugged. "Next time, invite me along."

"Don't hold your breath," she said.

He had already come up with a better way to spend his time, Gabriel decided. "Tell me why you came to Julian Harris's house."

"To find the truth." She stalked ahead of him into the main bedroom. An ascetic's bed with a plain black comforter took up little space. Ruthlessly organized books lined the walls. An armoire in the same Shaker style as the bed frame stood partly open. Curious about its contents, Erin peered inside. It was, she determined, like looking into a satellite of Banana Republic. Cashmere sweaters, oxford shirts, and multiple slacks in muted, fashionable shades hung from cedar hangers. Accessories were in drawers that smelled of cedar chips. A perfect replica of a perfect life.

Erin took note.

"What are you writing?" Gabriel asked.

"A profile."

Gabriel looked around. He, too, had been considering the simplicity and starkness in Julian's bedroom. "What do you see?"

"Julian Harris was a man who cared about appearance, hence the trendy address and the expensive townhome.

He also desired uniformity, as signaled by the ready-to-wear wardrobe. Comfort meant less to him than style."

Impressed, Gabriel asked, "How do you figure?"

"The bed. All the furniture, actually. The Shakers were known for craftsmanship, not comfort, and the full bed couldn't have been long enough for a man with a thirty-four-inch inseam."

Gabriel pointed to the rows of books. "What do those tell you?"

Erin crossed over to the bookcase. With reverent hands, she thumbed through first editions, caressed embossed spines.

Julian had organized his collection by topic, in a modified Dewey system. Botany sidled up to biography. Geometry nestled alongside hermeneutics. Her eyes skimmed over topics and stumbled over a dust jacket that stopped her heart.

There it was again, Gabriel thought, watching her remove a book from the shelf. An emotion that wasn't quite panic, wasn't quite guilt, clouded her beautiful eyes. It trembled her hands until, as he looked on, she willed them into steadiness. Control and what he could only describe as grit displaced the shocked look.

"What's the book?" he asked.

"*The Language of Discovery* by Nathan Rhodes." The name emerged without a hint of the turmoil raging inside her. She was proud of the deception. "A linguist from California."

"I thought our Mr. Harris was an architect?"

"He appeared to have a wide range of interests." The explanation did nothing to quiet her anxiety.

Gabriel lifted the book from her nerveless fingers. He

flipped through the pages, hoping for a clue to why the tome had frightened her. On the inside flap, a distinguished older gentleman with black hair winged with silver gifted the camera with a haughty half smile. "Looks like a pompous ass."

For that alone Erin could have kissed him. Instead, she managed a smile. "Academics often are."

Gabriel shoved the book into its space on the shelf. "Are you?"

Erin shook her head. "I don't think so. However, you'd have to ask my colleagues. What was it Robert Burns said about perception? 'Wad some power the giftie gie us—' "

" 'To see ourselves as others see us.' " Gabriel finished. At her look of admiration, he comically bowed. "I'm a layered man, darling. Surprise after surprise."

"Amen." The impassioned whisper carried no farther than her lips, but he heard it.

"Give me time." Promise glittered in his pewter gaze, darkened the midnight voice.

When she tamed her skipping pulse, Erin returned to her task. "Time is in rather short supply."

"How much do we have?"

"From the dates of the obituaries, I'm sure he'll strike again soon. Ten days, maybe. Two weeks at most." She slid another book into place. "If I'm right."

"I think you are," he replied evenly. "I think you see something in those obituaries that most people can't. Though I wonder why the killer knew you would."

A flush crept to her cheeks. It was difficult to lie when silver eyes held hers captive. They seemed to reach out to her, to offer a haven where she'd be safe and secure. *An illusion,* she chided herself. *Just an illusion. Nothing more*. She shrugged, dismissing his question. "I explained it to Detective Iberville. I'm a criminal psychologist."

Gabriel felt the sudden burn of anger at her obvious lie. He didn't like it. So he pushed. He crossed the room in two strides, crowding her against the bookcase. "Try again. Most criminal psychologists don't know the Middle French spelling of *surcingle* and the proper description of a bludgeon."

"I like crossword puzzles," she snapped impatiently. Shoving at his chest, she added, "And my space."

"More than the truth, I see." Gabriel had sparred with her enough for one day. Turning away, he moved to the doorway. "Let's check the next room."

Aware she'd made a narrow escape, Erin quietly followed.

CHAPTER 8

By nightfall, they had checked every room and Erin had read every scrap of paper in the townhome. She was no closer to a motive or a connection or the identity of the killer.

The sum of her discovery was Julian's passion for reading, his unremarkable taste in clothing, and his fondness for solitude. She'd found no letters, no correspondence of any kind. Gabriel had taken the lower level, but she doubted he'd be any more successful.

She dropped onto the lower steps of the staircase, chin in hand. What had she expected? A signed note from the killer? If her theory was right, she was dealing with a brilliant, twisted mind, one that wouldn't reveal itself until it was ready. Until the audience was ready.

"Thirsty?" Gabriel handed her a mug of steaming coffee. When she hesitated, he said in a dry tone, "I don't think he'll mind."

She took the cup and sipped. Warmth spread through her, banishing a cold she hadn't been aware of. "Thanks."

"You're welcome," Gabriel replied as he squeezed onto the step beside her.

The narrow steps pressed their bodies into contact. Erin tried to scoot away, only to be stopped by the banister. She smothered a sigh. Personal space appeared to be a foreign concept to Gabriel, but she was too tired to argue. Instead, she asked, "Find anything?"

"Nope. Nothing in the cellar." He looked at his notepad. The pages were still blank. "You?"

Erin shook her head and set her cup on the step above them. "I'm not sure I know what I'm looking for."

"Serial killers have patterns, don't they? A reason for the victims they choose." Gabriel placed his mug beside hers. "Like Ted Bundy or Albert Fish. Psychopaths target their prey because of what the person represents."

She thought of the book upstairs, of Nathan's photo on the dust jacket. "Sometimes, the victim isn't the target. He's just a means to an end."

"A way to get to you," Gabriel said flatly. Before she could lie to him again, fob him off with a nearly plausible explanation, he continued. "I don't believe he picked you because of your training. With all the cops and profilers here in town, he has other options. But he picked you. The note was personal."

"You think 'find me' is personal?" Erin scoffed. "I'd hate to get a love letter from you."

Without warning, Gabriel twisted to face her, irritation fighting with worry. He grabbed her shoulders to draw her close. "I'm not Sylvie, Erin. I can see that you're terrified. You know he's baiting you, and you know why." He lifted a hand to her cheek. "If you don't talk to me, I can't help you."

Shoving his hands away, Erin struggled to her feet. She brushed against the banister and clamped onto the railing. "I didn't ask for your help. I don't need you." The last came out breathless.

"You need someone."

"No. I don't." She took a deep breath, calming herself. Letting him come inside with her had been a mistake. If the police wouldn't help, she'd do this alone. "I can find the monster on my own."

Emotion flickered in luminous brown, an edgy emotion he'd seen before but couldn't quite place. The same emotion quavered in her smoky voice. He didn't like it. "How? By poking through the victims' closets?"

Erin pushed past him and walked to the front door. "I'll find him by doing what I know how to do. Profiling."

"You said you didn't know what you were looking for."

She paused in the doorway. "He does. Lock up on your way out."

Gabriel followed her out of the house. "How will you get home?"

The same thought had occurred to her. A taxi would take nearly half an hour, and the bus would take longer. "I've made arrangements."

With a snort of disbelief, Gabriel steered her toward his car. He fairly threw her inside, and slammed the black door with its deep gouges revealing gray primer. The force was necessary, both as a vent to his frustration and as a counter to the stubborn fifteen-year-old hinges that occasionally resisted the instruction to close. The buyout from Mirren and a modest inheritance certainly afforded him the luxury of reliable transportation, but Gabe had plowed every red cent back into the *Ledger*. "St. Bennett, right?"

Sulking, Erin refused to answer. Instead, she turned her face to the dirt-clouded window. "Car washes are legal in this state," she said.

"Then buy your own car." To drown out her response, he flicked on the radio, allowing Thelonious Monk to fill the cramped space.

At her apartment, Gabriel dogged her steps and followed her inside. He'd check out her apartment, guarantee she was settled for the night.

Erin Abbott had a protector, whether she liked it or not.

He blocked her attempt to shut the door and this time came inside. "Nice place," he murmured as he surveyed her home, quickly cataloging its contents.

A wide navy cotton-upholstered chair had been placed perpendicular to the pristine matching sofa, whose brushed linen appeared untouched. Bay windows opened onto a tiny balcony she'd crowded with plants of every variety.

The kitchen was ruthlessly clean, not a bowl or cup out of place. Behind the sofa, a badly lit hallway led to what he assumed was the bedroom. He strode down the hallway, flipped on the lights. Erin chased him, protesting.

"What are you doing?" she asked.

"Looking after you. Somebody has to." Gabriel hid a smile at her inventive description of his body parts.

Returning to the living room, he moved to the far wall. The mantel gleamed in polished mahogany flanked by bookcases filled to overflowing, but scrupulously organized.

"Rent or buy?"

"Buy," she answered automatically. Erin snapped her teeth shut with an audible click. She was not going to engage in conversation with him. First he kidnaps her; then he prowls around her home, as though he had every right. Any relief she felt was buried beneath righteous indignation.

"Nice digs," he said. The apartment spoke of quiet wealth and impeccable breeding. It explained the aristocratic tones and the arrogant manner. He understood, as a product of both himself. He recognized the Limoges on the mantel, the Persian on the floor. The lithograph by Jacob Lawrence drew a twinge of envy.

Suddenly he noticed something peculiar. In spite of the remarkable lack of clutter, tawdry knickknacks jumbled on the mantel's surface. On first glance, the collection of mismatched trinkets screamed of comfort and home. Upon closer inspection, Gabriel discovered, the mélange was a dogged grouping of commercial tchotchkes and bric-a-brac designed to trick the untrained eye.

If he had to guess, local merchants had made a killing off of the fair Dr. Abbott during her short tenure in the bayou. He lifted a squat gnome grinning with ivory teeth. These weren't items lovingly accumulated over the years. These were the mementos of other families, the creations of shopkeepers, calculated to sate the nostalgia of tourists.

He didn't know her well, but he was willing to bet good money these items weren't Erin's keepsakes. Not unless she harbored an unusual fascination for the cheap and grotesque, a possibility belied by the showroom quality of the rest of the apartment.

Intrigued, Gabriel set the gnome beside a porcelain ballerina, *en pointe,* and dropped into the great chair without asking permission. He could tell from the gentle indentation of the cushions, the massive chair was her favorite seat.

Standing over him, Erin seethed at his easy usurpation of her place. *He,* she thought dourly, *has no manners.* "Feel free to sit wherever you want," she muttered.

"You say something?" he asked with a smirk. "You tend to mumble when you're angry." Without waiting for an answer, he lifted the album she'd set on the table and began to flip through the vellum pages.

"I'm not angry. I'm irritated. A condition that is easily satisfied by having you not here." Flouncing a bit, she perched on the end of the sofa. She didn't sit back, deciding that if she made herself comfortable, he'd take it as invitation to stay. Instead, she scooted forward farther, perched on the edge of the cushion. Her knee brushed his, and she quickly shifted away.

Gabriel moved forward as well, until their knees brushed again. Lifting a hand to the curls lying against her temple, he murmured, "You still don't like me, do you, Erin?"

Rearing away from his heady touch, she said bitterly, "What gave it away? The many times I've told you?" She'd be fine if he'd stop touching her. Light, undemanding points of contact designed to rile and disturb. "In case I've been vague, I don't like you."

"I'm crushed." He angled closer, caging her legs between his powerful thighs. His eyes captured hers as he stroked a finger along the fist she'd been unaware of making. "However, in all fairness to me, you've only said you don't like me once."

Though only her legs were imprisoned and a single fingertip touched suddenly sensitive flesh, Erin felt surrounded. Invaded. What disturbed more was the feeling of safety. "I don't want you as a partner. I don't want you in my house," she said. "But you keep crowding me." Easing back along the cushions, she stared pointedly at his position. "Like now."

Gabriel moved forward, following. "You think I'm crowding you? I'm sitting in a chair, darling."

"Take your hands off of me." She flicked a disdainful gaze at the hand that now covered her own. "I choose who touches me."

The haughty sneer pulled at him, stiffened his spine. Whenever she chose that lady-of-the-manor tone, he was hard-pressed not to snarl. Gabriel wondered what it was about the determinedly isolated professor that made him so determined to antagonize her. "Don't push me, honey. I don't like games."

"I'm not playing games with you. I'm being as honest as I can without calling the police." Erin stood, studiously avoiding contact. She opened the door and shot him a pointed look.

Duty completed, Gabriel walked to the door. He paused in the doorway, his body brushing against her. "I'm going to figure you out."

The words, intended as a promise, sounded like a threat even to his ears.

"Peter, get me everything you can find on a Dr. Erin Abbott!" Gabriel shouted as he stormed into the *Bayou Ledger* thirty minutes later.

She was the key to everything. The murders weren't about the victims, she'd told him. They were about the audience. Which meant he needed to know more about Erin.

The curiosity was more than professional, he knew.

Since the moment he heard her laugh, a connection had linked them. One that she refused to acknowledge and that he couldn't ignore.

Just as he couldn't ignore the way he behaved around her. He had never been a bully. Or a lecher. If a woman said no, then the answer was no and he was on his way. Despite the fact that *no* was a word he rarely heard, he still respected the right of a woman to use it.

Still, whenever he found himself near Erin, the part of his brain that recognized boundaries clicked immediately off.

Certainly she was stunning, but he knew women who were more beautiful. Striking, gorgeous women who understood the value of a good hairdresser and the subtle uses of makeup.

Yes, she had eyes the color of dark brandy, but he'd seen prettier eyes. Eyes that didn't flash distrust at him, alternating with fear. Eyes that didn't accuse him of treachery simply for being alive.

Perhaps she had the legs of a goddess, but he'd been in closer contact with perfect legs before. Legs that had never been draped in worsted wool and protective hose.

What drew him, he thought, what made him refuse to walk away, were the secrets. He'd always been compelled to find the answers. And Erin Abbott's lovely eyes and smart brain hid dozens of secrets.

Making his way past scattered tables, reams of paper, and cartons of ink, Gabriel didn't spare a glance for the warehouse that was now the home of the *Ledger*. The cavernous space had seen better days, most of them before the turn of the century. Exposed red brick trickled with oxidization and age. Metal pipes vibrated with the sound of the tugs approaching the river. Thousands had been spent to remove, rewire, and refurbish.

Gabriel poked his head into the office next door to his. There Peter hunched over a computer in the makeshift managing editor's office. Dreadlocks bound in a leather thong fell from a high forehead. Eyes the color of chocolate and with all the warmth of a glacier shifted swiftly across the screen. A black mustache slashed across the rough-hewn face, dividing a pirate's nose from a perpetual sneer.

Peter Cameron had been a reporter for more than two decades. He could track a rat through the sewers, beat the rodent to the other side, and never get dirty. And he never stopped working.

"Did you hear me?" Gabriel asked, his tone rough.

"The whole staff heard you," Peter said mildly. "Erin Abbott. Got it. Want to tell me what I'm looking for?" Before taking on the project of starting up the *Ledger,* Peter Cameron had been the best investigative reporter in the Southeast.

From anyone else, such insolence would be unthinkable. But Peter didn't have to worry. He'd trained Gabriel as a cub reporter at the *Chronicle,* helped get him his first job as a foreign correspondent. "I've had a long day," Gabriel said. "She's a part of a story I'm thinking about."

"Good enough." Peter pulled up a new screen on his computer. Gabriel Moss, like his father, had a sharp eye for hidden headlines. "I'll see what I can find."

With a nod, Gabriel walked next door to his office. Swinging inside, Gabriel surveyed the neat stacks on the desk he'd left behind for more than a month. Correspondence. Copy. Bills. Contracts.

He lifted the first stack of bills, took a seat, and started reading. When the words "Past Due" morphed into "Find me," he dropped the letter. To distract himself, he dialed his business manager.

"Yeah, boss?" she answered on the first ring. Despite the late hour, the staff of the *Ledger,* twenty in all, understood the nature of a start-up. They worked long hours for meager pay and little recognition.

Gabriel had plans to change all of that. "I've seen the past due notices," he drawled.

"Be right there."

A few moments later, a gangly woman in torn jeans and a faded Grateful Dead T-shirt rushed into his office and dropped a folder on the teak desk. She moved quickly, not out of concern but because her body had no other speed. Neither did her mouth.

"I bought us another couple of weeks on the bills. And I got us an excellent deal with Tetrick Airways. Three-month spread, two-page color copy, and six weeks online. Nice deals. Cute guy is the sales rep, but he's got a girlfriend. They always do. Scored an even better deal with DeLoach Tires and Treads. He's up for a six-month weekly and Web site, with a bonus tied to sales. Customers bring in our ad enough, and he'll make it a year. Take that, *Chronicle*. Plus, I'm meeting with the Chamber on Monday. Gonna pitch a package deal to members. Revenue report's in the file. If the summer picks up, we might break even this month."

"We *will* break even," Gabriel corrected.

She lifted a paperweight from a pile of copy and began to toss the tourmaline rock into the air. "You've got to talk to Peter. He's playing business manager again. I told him I was going to squeal on him, but who has time to argue with a curmudgeon? I think he just likes being ornery. An ornery Captain Hook. Just needs an eye patch and a foul-mouthed parrot."

Gabriel stretched long legs beneath the desk and laced his fingers behind his head. He fixed the chattering woman with a look. Then he grinned. It was good to be home.

"Hi, Kelly."

"Hi, yourself." Lifting a rubber ball in iridescent colors and a bottle of Liquid Paper, Kelly began to juggle the objects in the air. "We've got a meeting Friday with the bank. Our cash flow projections aren't looking too healthy, and they may decline the loan."

Gabriel slid a letter across the polished surface. "Too late. Already done. At least they had the decency not to laugh."

She set the objects back on the desk in their appointed spaces. As she skimmed the brief missive, she thumped the letter. "New businesses take time. Any banker knows that. 'Negative cash flow.' Of course it's negative. We've only been up and running for six months. Budget projections don't have us breaking even until the fifteenth month of operation. Morons."

"Without a doubt," Gabriel agreed. "But they have a point. Even if we break even this month, the *Chronicle* has steadily eroded our advertisers. If we don't increase readership, we won't get them back."

"More morons. If people read us and the *Chronicle,* they'd see who has the superior paper."

Gabriel didn't disagree. "The *Chronicle* is a daily. We're a weekly."

"We change our site every day," Kelly sulked, tapping

her foot on the chair opposite her own. "Besides, we're much better."

"Yes, we are." Gabriel motioned to a leather chair angled across from his desk. Picking up the phone, he summoned Peter. When the older man trudged in, he scowled at Kelly and Gabriel as though their presence offended him.

"What?" he demanded, taking the seat next to Kelly.

"Good evening, sunshine," Kelly responded in a bright voice.

He merely grunted. To annoy, Kelly smiled and tapped a pink sneakered toe on the bottom rung of his chair. Peter stared at her, then at the tapping foot with a mix of incredulity and exasperation. When the stare failed to have any effect, he growled menacingly, "Cut that out."

Unperturbed, Kelly continued to tap. "Ask nicely."

In response, Peter shifted his chair.

The tapping paused for a second, then returned as Kelly stretched her leg out farther, playing the cadence of the "Battle Hymn of the Republic."

Gabriel stifled a laugh when Peter barely restrained himself from lunging. "Children. Behave." Peter scooted his chair beyond the reach of Kelly's foot, and in retort, Kelly began to hum beneath her breath.

"Kelly."

The stern tone immediately cut off the tune. "Sorry, boss."

Gabriel looked at the pair helping him keep his dream alive: the grizzled veteran and the business whiz kid.

Kelly Cole was a more recent find. Fresh out of business school, she'd shown up at Gabriel's doorstep on the second day of the *Ledger*'s existence. She showed him financial models, revenue projects, and sales pitches designed to make the paper a success. When he asked why she'd gone to all the trouble for a fledgling newspaper no one had ever seen, she answered simply, "Because I like to read and I like to win."

Unlacing his fingers, Gabriel folded his arms across his chest. "I've got good news and bad news."

"Bad news first," Kelly decided.

"I was served with a cease and desist order from the *Chronicle*. We continue with the Bert Adams story, we go to court."

"But that's your story!" Peter said, bellowing. "You did the digging. You wrote the copy. Now that kiss-ass Burris will turn it into a fluff piece about Armani suits and Prada shoes."

"I agreed to leave all stories behind when I left the paper. I fight, we'd probably lose."

"So?" Kelly asked.

"So we can't afford the legal fees or to pay a judgment. The story's dead."

"The story is the front page of next week's edition and the teaser was going to run on the site tomorrow," Peter said sourly. "Hell, it's pretty much the whole paper. All we got left are the police blotter and the wire stories."

Gabriel smiled slightly but did not respond.

Kelly imagined the calls asking for ad copy refunds and expanding pools of red ink and asked glumly, "You said there was good news?"

"There is. We're moving to a daily edition."

Silence greeted his announcement.

"No questions?"

Peter erupted first. "Have you lost your ever-lovin' mind, man? You just told us we've lost the Adams story. Little Ms. Perky never ceases to remind me that we're broke. How in the hell do you plan to increase our production with no stories, no circulation, and no money?"

"Especially with no money," Kelly added, lifting the denial letter from the desk. "The bank said no, boss. Not *Maybe*. Not *Come back and see us next week*. They said no."

"I haven't been on vacation, guys. I've been raising money. Finding investors." Gabriel lifted the rock Kelly had played with earlier. The gleaming stone had been a gift from his father. Holding it, he knew his dad would approve of his next move. "No one wants to invest in a weekly. Not when there is a viable daily in the community. However, Mirren Enterprises has created a raft of enemies around the country. Small papers, midsized dailies, all wiped out by the Mirren machine. They come in, buy out the strongest paper, and fire the troublemakers. Then they relegate local news to a couple of pages in section B and clone the headlines from everywhere else. Mirren won't run the Adams story because Adams is voting on antitrust rules in the next session. The vote goes their way and Mirren will be able to buy radio and television stations. One source, one story."

Kelly stopped tapping her foot. "I hope this is somehow leading to the good news, boss, because I'm getting more and more depressed."

"When I was up in New York, I met with a group of investors who want to reclaim local news. They are willing to pour money into papers in major urban cities, as test cases. But there's a catch. They only fund dailies."

"Which we're not," Kelly reminded Gabriel.

"Which we're going to become," Gabriel said, ready for Peter's explosion. He didn't have long to wait.

"Which brings *me* back to my original point. We don't have the stories. No big headlines. Sure, I can fill the pages with local interest, but that doesn't bring in readers. Scandals do."

"So does murder."

Peter watched his old friend and suddenly relaxed. "You've got a story. And Dr. Erin Abbott is a part of it."

"I can feel it."

"I ran a quick make on her. She's a criminal psychology professor from Mississippi. Graduated with her Ph.D. two years ago. Bought a place on St. Bennett. Teaches at Burkeen."

"She's not from Mississippi."

Nodding in agreement, Peter scooted forward. "Probably not. According to what I could find, which wasn't much, she didn't do anything but go to school. Published an article on profiling serial killers, but that's it. Then the job here at Burkeen came available, and she slid right in."

"Family?"

"None on record."

"Is she a murderer?" Kelly asked.

"No," Gabriel said in a tone that brooked no argument. Realizing how his vehemence sounded, he explained, "However, our professor has an interesting theory about recent deaths in the area. I'm calling it the New Orleans ABC Murders."

Aghast, Kelly stared at Gabriel. "You can't print that story. It sounds like Sesame Street after the Mansons have moved in."

"It will sell papers. And ad space." He lifted a pen and

his notebook and began to issue orders. "Peter, I need you to keep digging on Dr. Abbott. Also, assign a reporter to gather information for me on these deaths." He ripped out the page where he'd scribbled the names Erin had read aloud to Sylvie. Gabriel handed Peter the list. "Pull their obituaries, too."

"I'll have it by tomorrow." Peter studied the list of names. "Who's our police contact?"

"Don't have one. The police weren't interested in Dr. Abbott's theory," Gabriel mumbled. He had been dreading this part of the conversation.

Peter looked up sharply. "I don't do tabloid. *We* don't do tabloid. That's Mirren's shtick."

"I wouldn't besmirch your ethics, Peter," Gabriel said soothingly. "I overheard her explanation to the NOPD. It didn't sound like fiction to me. Today, she and I did a little investigating. I found enough to know there's a story here. One the *Chronicle* has no hint of."

Gabriel had an instinct about mysteries, and this one sank its teeth into him, down to the bone. The lovely professor was on the trail of a killer, and she had personal skeletons she desperately wanted to hide. Whether the two were connected or not, he intended to discover.

If he saved his paper in the process, so much the better.

"Kelly, run the numbers if we move to a daily. I need to send a revenue projection to the investor group by Monday. Calculate the likely circulation increase if we ran a story about a serial killer, with teasers on the Web site. If we can sell one hundred and fifty thousand copies, that's the proof we'll need for the investors."

"One hundred and fifty thousand?" both Peter and Kelly repeated in unison.

"To start." Gabriel paid no attention to the incredulous looks. "We don't have a lot of time here. If the doctor's theory is true, then we'll have the *Chronicle* for lunch."

"Or start a panic."

He didn't disagree. But sometimes, the ends and the means had to learn to get along. "Or maybe, we'll catch a killer."

CHAPTER 9

Like any grand old dame, New Orleans showed a properly powdered face to company and rouged and bawdier side to relatives and bosom friends. The French Quarter embodied her delectable, if misspent, youth. But when she had a mind to, she'd share a glimpse of her majestic past or regale with epic tales.

She'd chosen her more refined side today, Erin decided. Esplanade Ridge teemed with early weekend tourists, eager to view the contents of the New Orleans Museum of Art or tour the half-remembered glory of Faubourg Tremé. The area, known as Tremé to its inhabitants, had been the site of great civil rights victories. Their triumph faded as the struggle moved east to Selma and Atlanta, but New Orleans remembered her sacrifice.

It was difficult, Erin thought, to reconcile the pieces of New Orleans into a whole. It was a difficulty she recognized in herself. Perhaps that's what had drawn her to the city, when she and Sebastian were creating her new life.

New Orleans was more than a survivor. The city reveled in its contrasting sides, in its rebellious youth and horrible missteps. Maybe, Erin hoped, she could find redemption here, too.

She'd begin by retracing the lives of victims Burleigh Singleton and Phoebe Bailey.

Mr. Singleton had been employed at the First Bank of New Orleans, which had a branch on nearly every street corner. Erin kept an account at one near the school. Standing in the marble atrium, she looked around to get her bearings.

"Welcome to First Bank. May we help you?"

Erin turned. The chirpy voice matched the speaker. Sunshine yellow had been whipped into a froth and poured into a snug suit that stopped midthigh. Pale golden skin, bright blond hair, and a toothsome smile completed the picture. Her name tag introduced her as Amber.

"Hello . . . Amber." Erin glanced around the bank. "I'm looking for an old friend of mine. Burleigh Singleton?"

Amber's good cheer evaporated. Suddenly somber, she said, "Mr. Singleton is no longer with us."

"He's not? Do you know where I can find him?"

"Excuse me, what was your name?"

"Erin Abbott."

"Well, can you hold on a sec? Just a sec?" When Erin nodded, Amber hurried away toward the offices in the rear of the bank.

Hopefully, Erin thought, Amber would introduce her to a co-worker or preferably his secretary. She wanted to get a picture of Mr. Singleton's life and check for connections to Julian Harris. A night on the Internet had revealed little about Singleton. She had found a brief bio and a mention of his recent promotion to the branch's chief loan officer position. He was beloved by his alma mater, where he gave annually and often recruited graduates to work with him. The alumni association had named an award after him, which was the angle she planned to use.

The bank interview was her best shot, because, according to his obituary, he left a wife and two children in a tony home in Lakeview. She thought about talking to Mrs. Singleton, but she doubted she'd get past the front door. There would be no repeats of the Harris B and E.

On the plus side, that meant no Gabriel to ask questions he knew she wouldn't answer.

He was a liability she could not afford. Self-preservation demanded that she resist the lure of good looks and good humor. She couldn't risk an attraction to a man who'd been able to see through her painstakingly fostered image of the distant, fashion-challenged professor.

Though her skin heated at the memory of him calling her beautiful, she couldn't ignore the rest. Anyone who paid too much attention was a hazard, especially if her heartbeat scrambled when she was near him.

Her precarious situation posed enough danger without upping the ante by inviting the enemy to find her. Gabriel Moss was a reporter, the last person a woman with secrets should know.

"Ms. Abbott? I'm Delilah Weems, Mr. Singleton's secretary." An older woman with clothes as dark as Amber's were bright motioned Erin to follow. They wound through the bank to a suite of glassed-in offices. Ms. Weems ushered her into one and firmly shut the door. "You're here to see Mr. Singleton?"

"Yes. I'm in New Orleans for a conference." Erin smiled reassuringly. "I didn't have an appointment, but Burleigh always told me to just stop by when I was in town."

"Are you from San Cabes?"

"California?" Erin felt her blood run cold. "Wh-why? Why do you ask?"

"Amber indicated that you were an old friend. I assumed you were from his hometown." Ms. Weems gave her a narrow, suspicious look. The young woman was half-again Mr. Singleton's age and dressed entirely too casually. "Exactly how did you know him?"

Erin was prepared for the question. "Business school. The alumni association. Burleigh was great to younger alums. He got me my first job in New York. Told me if I was ever in New Orleans, I should look him up." Then she frowned and bent toward the dubious Ms. Weems. "You used the past tense. You asked me, 'How did you know him?' Has something happened to Burleigh?"

Tears pooled in Ms. Weems's eyes, and she choked out a sob. "Mr. Singleton died not long ago. He was murdered."

"I'm so sorry," she said sincerely. Erin shifted to pat awkwardly at the woman's sleeve. "What happened?"

Ms. Weems hiccupped. "The police said he was attacked behind the bank. They think it must have been a mugging."

Comforting the woman, Erin gently probed for information. "Had you worked for him long?"

"Nearly fifteen years. He was such a kind soul. And an excellent boss. Punctual. Polite. Never a cross word." Ms. Weems covered Erin's hand with her own. "I miss him so."

Erin stayed in the office for another twenty minutes, listening to Ms. Weems recount stories of her time with Mr. Singleton. According to her, he'd been a generous man who hadn't an enemy in the world.

Except a mugger no one could find.

She left the bank, her thoughts turning to the links she'd found between her life as Analise and the two victims. A dust jacket and a tiny mountain town in California. Two strangers living in a city of thousands whose lives shared eerie connections to her past. A past she couldn't reveal without jeopardizing her freedom.

It was one more terrible decision she would be forced to make because of Nathan Rhodes. One more in a series that had begun more than a decade before.

Callenwolde University, tucked along a curve in the San Francisco Bay, had been training exceptional students for more than a century. Mornings in September were crisp, with the bite of fall in the air. The semester was in full swing, and students had resigned themselves to another bout of classes.

In marked contrast, Analise tried to tamp down her excitement as she parked her bike outside the Linguistics building. The clear, brisk weather matched her mood perfectly. She jogged across the lawn and took the stairs two at a time. Students filed out of the building, but few spoke to her. She'd been on campus for more than a year, but her reputation kept her isolated, even among those like her. Orphaned weeks after coming to campus, she was accustomed to the loneliness. Welcomed it.

Today, though, she didn't notice. She'd called Dr. Rhodes last night, asking for an appointment to show him her draft text on the linguistic similarities in a Malaysian dialect and one found in the jungles of Brazil. After working hard on it all summer, she was so excited to show him her discovery, she'd e-mailed the document at midnight. If he found it persuasive, perhaps he would agree to co-author the final paper. To publish with Dr. Rhodes would be an honor, one only select graduate students experienced, let alone a college junior. At sixteen, she was younger than many of them, but she had been studying language her entire life.

She keyed in her access code for the laboratory wing and, when the panel coded green, she heaved open the thick glass doors and rushed through. It was her finest work yet, she thought. Her parents would have been so proud. A wave of grief caught her and she stumbled to a halt. Bodies pressed past her, but she didn't move.

Guilt overwhelmed excitement. She couldn't blame them for sending her away. Though she'd fought them, she had required closer supervision than either of them could provide. She could finally admit that their difficult decision to leave her in California had been the best choice for all concerned. It wasn't as though they'd abandoned her. No, Callenwolde and the famed Dr. Nathan Rhodes were the only choice. He had promised careful attention to the brilliant but troubled teen.

Still, she wondered, if she'd been a better daughter, would they still be alive? Would they still be with her? Every day, she missed them. Missed her life with her parents and Sebastian and his mother, Mrs. Cain.

"No more wallowing," Analise muttered to herself. "Dr. Rhodes is waiting."

He was an exacting man who had little time for social

niceties with a teenager. Quickly installed in a dormitory, she only saw him during their monthly meetings. He didn't approve of the way she'd used her talents before Callenwolde. A regular on the gameshow circuit and on talk shows, all that had ended.

Today she'd prove that she was more than a sideshow attraction. The paper she'd worked on in secret would make her a scholar.

Beyond the communal laboratory, the professors maintained their offices, which increased in size depending on the length of tenure. She halted outside Dr. Rhodes's office, suddenly stricken with worry. He was an academic marvel, a renowned scientist, like her mother. He was also a writer, like her father. She'd read every one of his books, and longed to see her name imprinted on a monograph one day soon.

However, her hesitation was as much feminine as it was intellectual. In addition to his remarkable intellect, Nathan Rhodes was quite handsome.

At forty-three, he had no physical interest in her, she realized, but basic vanity prompted her to touch up her lipgloss and run nervous fingers through hair that tended to escape its confines.

Inside the office, Nathan Rhodes waited for Analise. The child was infuriatingly prompt, another of the imp's perfections. The currently maddening example smirked up from the bare surface of his desk. No other papers cluttered the top, but not because of neatness or a pursuit of order. Nathan doggedly locked all of his personal work in the filing cabinets behind him until he required a document. The more important documents were safeguarded in his desk.

The world of academe was brutal, filled with cutthroats

and thieves; and, he acknowledged dryly, he was among the more creative. His peers, such as they were, harbored bitter resentment against him. He was famous, popular, and prolific, the stuff of fantasies for the administration. His spacious office, inflated salary, and five teaching assistants proved his worth to his struggling contemporaries. He was one of the most admired men in his field. As a particularly astute journal article had phrased it, he was a creature of talent envied by all.

Nathan drummed thin, tapered fingers on the paper on his desk. He had once toyed with the idea of becoming a concert pianist. At his Juilliard recital, when he'd placed second, he had stormed from the concert hall and enrolled at NYU the next week. Staring at the slim lines of bone and flesh, he remembered the vicious pulse of disappointment. Second was unacceptable.

Which raised the issue of Analise Glover. Again, he thumbed through the sheets of white, with their black text. She had done a magnificent job. Using source texts and fables from two cultures, she'd linked them together. Others had postulated the travels between ancient worlds, but the child who sat in his social linguistics class had proven it. Her writing was crisp, eloquent. It brought the academic reader to the point quickly and thoroughly, but would not alienate the amateur. It was a brilliant document. Too brilliant.

"Dr. Rhodes?" Analise called out, following a light tapping on the door. Nathan did not respond immediately. One waited for greatness; greatness did not hurry. She said his name a second time, her voice growing less certain.

Nathan understood nuance, and he understood Analise. He wanted her intellect because it would suit his goals. He needed her idolization because otherwise, she would surpass him. The trick would be to cultivate them without losing control. Her third, more timid request for admission assured him he could have both.

"Come," he instructed. The heavy wood swung silently on its hinges, and she peered inside. "Ms. Glover. Please sit."

Erin moved to the leather chair opposite his desk and sat, legs crossed. The floral summer skirt covered her knees, but left toned legs bare. Glancing up, Analise thought she caught him staring. For an instant, she felt self-conscious, then dismissed the feeling. She may have a crush on Dr. Rhodes; however, he was too worldly, too handsome, to think of her in that way.

Nathan pushed the pages across the desk to her. "Would you consider this your best work, Ms. Glover?"

Analise reached for the paper, but he did not release it. Instead, she rested tentative fingertips on the title page. "I think this is the most thorough research I've conducted. The idea is novel. I couldn't locate other texts on the matter, besides supposition."

"Is this your best work?"

"Yes, sir."

"Then I will kindly ask you to leave my program!" he bellowed suddenly, ripping the pages from her. In an instant, he reduced the hours of research to narrow shreds of paper. "How many times must I tell you? I have no time for dreamers. Either do the work or get out! Do you understand me?" Nathan's fists pounded the table, close to her hand. The edge of his ring caught her skin, leaving a small mark.

"Yes, sir," she stammered. The cut from the ring stung; less though, than the destruction of her work. Language was all she knew. She'd been bred to understand it, trained and studied because of her rare facility for words. She wanted to protest, but anxiety crowded into her throat and she did not move. If he sent her away, where would she go? "What's wrong with the research?"

"It's drivel! Who cares about the ties between two communities no one has ever heard of? Do you really think you are the first person to unearth this great find? Of course not! But others had the good sense to see it was meaningless. Meaningless."

"I—I didn't realize." Tears burned behind her eyes, and Analise struggled not to weep. *I'm too inexperienced,* she thought desperately. *I have nowhere else to go.* "My folk tales professor—"

"Is a moron!" Nathan finished. "We have a waiting list, Analise. A very long one. While your story is tragic, there are others who are willing to work hard. I'm sure the courts will find you a nice home until you're eighteen."

"Dr. Rhodes—" Her heart pounded, echoed in her ears, and she fought not to cry. He was going to make her leave. "What—what can I do to stay?"

Pleased by the fear, Nathan smiled sympathetically. He had expected her groveling response, had counted on it. He had plans for her. Plans that would keep her close, and keep him on top. As abruptly as the explosion began, he subsided. "I think we have made a grave error with your studies here. You have focused your entire life on one area. It has blinded you."

She swallowed hard, twice, before she could speak. "Yes. Sir."

"We can salvage the situation, but you must agree to follow my instructions. Can you do that?"

Hope bloomed inside her, an unfamiliar sensation, and she felt a tremulous smile begin. "Yes. I can do that."

"Good. Good." Nathan rose from his chair and stood near the window. In the bright morning, he knew the image he cut. Tweed jacket, collar open to reveal the strong line of his throat, the proud angle of his chin. On dust jackets across the country, the ascetic profile of the eminent Dr. Rhodes was knowingly the same each time. The pose caught him as both striking and austere.

Nathan walked over to her and patted her hand. The slender fingers were elegant, lovely actually. She too could have played. Perhaps he'd teach her. Nodding sagely, he twisted the screws. "You don't have too many friends here, do you, Analise?"

"No, sir. I haven't had much time."

He sniffed with disdain. "I doubt you've ever even had a boyfriend like normal girls."

"No," she whispered, doubts swirling.

"Yet, you've been here for a year and a half now." He patted her shoulder. "It is to be expected, given your freakish upbringing."

"Freakish?" She'd called herself a freak a million times, but the taunt from him felt like a blow.

Enjoying himself now, and the glazed look in her eyes, Nathan continued, "Semantically speaking. You have abnormal linguistic skills. You were reared by two intellectually abnormal parents. By any definition, you are a freak."

When he explained it, it seemed less like an insult. "I–I never thought about it."

"I have. So did your parents. I have taken this past year to observe you, and while I am still willing to work with you, I must set rigorous conditions. I will expect hard work, no excuses. Under my guidance, I will introduce you to the finest minds in your area."

"Thank you."

He approached her chair, laid an affectionate hand on her shoulder. "Leave everything to me. You have a good mind, Analise, I'm sure you know. But perhaps you've spent too much time studying only language. You are too close." Carefully, Nathan swept the shredded pages into the wastebasket by his feet, secure in the knowledge that the original was secured in his hard drive. A few tweaks, he thought, and it would be ready for publication.

Another triumph for Dr. Nathan Rhodes. He easily smiled at her then. "I think it would be best if you selected another major, and chose linguistics as your minor. Keep your options open."

"I'm already a junior," she protested, a spark of resistance flaring. "It's too late to change my major. And I'm good at it." Years spent traveling to universities to be tested and studied had demonstrated that at least. "I want to be a linguist."

Smiling beneficently, Nathan nodded and lied. "It may not be your forte. Your parlor tricks with words might amaze the pedestrian crowds who watched you when you were a child, but this is college. This is serious."

Analise flushed miserably. Images of late night talk shows, where she'd stunned the audience with obscure lexicon drawn from dead languages, of game shows where adults bowed in defeat, suddenly embarrassed her.

She had once reveled in being different, but now, she wanted something different. Though she'd fought her parents, part of her welcomed the stability of college. She'd come to Callenwolde to become a scholar, no longer a *rara avis,* a freak show for the college crowd. "I want to study linguistics. I want to be taken seriously."

"We set others' opinions of us early. You chose to exploit your talents for profit and fame. It will take more than a shallow analysis like that," he gestured to the discarded scraps, "to compel anyone to take you seriously."

"This is what I know."

"Form cannot prevail over substance in the academy." His capped teeth snapped together into a condescending smile. "You'd do well to think of other options, my dear. Eggs and baskets. You know the saying."

Hearing dismissal, Erin grew afraid. Fear, unfamiliar and oily, smeared her voice. She couldn't go back onto the circuit, an object of curiosity for the public. He had to let her stay. "If I change my major, I can remain in the program?" She threaded icy fingers together in her lap.

"Yes." Gratified that she'd followed his lead so quickly, he pounced. "What would you study?"

Stunned by the reprieve, she searched for an answer. It would not do to have him think her limited. Then she knew. "Psychology."

"Why?"

Analise didn't answer aloud. How could she explain the need to understand the people around her, hoping she might understand herself?

"No matter. Psychology it is."

Erin rode her bike along the mid-day street, shaken by the memory. It would be a small victory if Nathan's tyranny helped her save another person's life. A small but vital balance to the scales of justice.

Phoebe Bailey's digs were a far cry from the historical

charm of the Lower Garden District or the tony mansion Singleton's family had inherited. She lived in a shotgun cottage on the outskirts of the neighborhood, where seediness nipped at the historical legacy. The home that had been the dancer's had been quickly turned over to new, taciturn occupants.

Moving to the next bungalow, Erin introduced herself as a reporter and found herself ushered inside a dimly lit parlor that smelled of peppermints and biscuits. After making small talk, Erin broached the subject of Phoebe Bailey's murder.

"The police aren't trying hard enough," Mrs. Caroline Littlejohn complained, a wizened old woman with skin the color of maple leaves in autumn. The ancient voice shook in outrage. "It's because she was a dancer. Not a hoity-toity hotshot."

"I understand they found her at the menagerie." The stabled horses were rented out for carriage rides. Erin had been to the stables in the Quarter a few times, as her own version of therapy.

She remembered how horses had terrified Nathan, which had been reason enough for her to sneak out of the house when he was in class. She'd learned to ride in secret, a tiny triumph over his tyranny. The sorrel mare called Willow had become her confidante. Until the day Erin's riding instructor passed her and Nathan at a play and complimented her on her improvement.

That night, he had locked her in her room. After he released her two days later, she never rode again.

Refusing to succumb to memory, Erin sipped at the glass of thickly sweet tea pressed upon her by Mrs. Littlejohn. "Do you know why anyone would want to harm her?"

"Absolutely not! Phoebe was a darling, with that lovely accent. She was from the islands, you know." Mrs. Littlejohn swelled with pride. "My family was from Barbados. Nicer than Jamaica."

Erin smiled weakly. "Barbados is a beautiful country. Do you ever visit?"

"Shucks, no. I took a boat over here. I'm too old to return by boat and my feet ain't left the ground in eighty-two years. The Good Lord wants me home, he'll send me there like they do on that *Star Trek* program. Beam me up." She chuckled over her witticism.

"I never had the pleasure of seeing Phoebe perform. I understand she danced calypso."

"Down in that devil's lair, yes." The lady sniffed. "But on Sundays, she played for the Antioch Baptist Church. You know, she first came over to the United States to attend that fancy school for music in New York."

"Ju-Juilliard?" Erin stuttered out the question, but Mrs. Littlejohn failed to notice.

"That's the one. But she broke one of her fingers on the subways there, and that was the end of it." Fierce with loyalty, she added, "I still think she played like a dream."

Erin barely heard the passionate defense. She concentrated her energy to fight off a smothering blanket of panic. Out of hundreds of books, she'd found one written by Nathan. His last one. Burleigh Singleton had grown up in San Cabes, a remote town where Nathan kept a cabin. And now, she found that a calypso dancer named Phoebe Bailey had once attended Juilliard. Like Nathan.

It couldn't be coincidence.

Gulping down the rest of her tea, Erin got to her feet.

She set the glass on a coaster decorated in butterflies. "I appreciate your time, Mrs. Littlejohn."

Erin helped the older woman to stand. They walked together to the front door. "No bother a'tall. Don't get many visitors at my age."

"That's a shame. You're a wonderful lady." On impulse, she kissed the woman's wrinkled cheek.

Outside, Erin grappled with the implications of what she'd learned. Nathan Rhodes was dead. She'd shot him, felt his blood thick and cold on her hands. Together, she and Sebastian had tossed the body into the canyons of San Cabes.

Someone had seen her do it.

Someone who had tracked her to New Orleans. Lost in bleak thought, she retrieved her bicycle and pushed it forward. The notes, the obituaries and clues that pointed to Nathan. Clues only she would understand.

The murderer wanted her to see him. To find him.

Murder, to him, was a means to an end. A means he enjoyed. For all the linguistic maneuvering, at the core, she thought, he was just a killer. Julian Harris, she'd bet, hadn't been his first victim.

Then there were the clues themselves. Burleigh and Phoebe had natural ties to Nathan. But Julian's link had been manufactured. A book slipped onto a shelf, waiting for her to stumble across it.

Nathan Rhodes had terrorized her, controlled her. She'd broken free, and the killer hated her for it.

Who are you? Erin wondered. *What do you want from me when I find you?*

"Why don't you drive, Erin?" Erin heard a voice say beside her.

Jolted from her thoughts, she stopped the bike and took a fortifying breath. Certain she wouldn't curse, she turned to glare at her shadow. "Go away, Gabriel. There are thousands of other women for you to chase."

"They wouldn't be nearly as much fun." Like the sight of Erin in an outfit that didn't swallow her whole. Today the horrible suits had disappeared. In blessed contrast, she wore sleek black track pants and a white T-shirt. Curves he'd only speculated about were terrifically displayed. "Much better outfit today."

"Excuse me?"

Gabriel touched her shoulder, pleased by the absence of shoulder pads. "I hate your suits. The lines are all wrong for you."

"They're Chanel," she protested, though she agreed with him. But the idea of admitting even the obvious galled. "My suits are classics."

"Maybe at Harvard in 1953."

Impossibly, Erin's ramrod-straight shoulders stiffened further. The voice he'd described to himself as sultry emerged on a river of ice. "Mr. Moss, I do not take fashion advice from a man who thinks denim lasts forever." The cutting glance at the frayed waistband and thinned fabric should have brought him to his knees. Instead, the obvious scorn enchanted.

"Touché." Duly chastened, he skated a hand down her forearm to cover hers on the bike. She tugged at it, discreetly, but Gabe pretended not to notice. He lifted her left hand and examined the graceful lines and the absence of jewelry. She wore a wide band of silver on her right ring finger, with a raised onyx in the center. Indecipherable inscriptions surrounded the band. "What does this say?" he asked, tilting the ring into the light.

This time, her sudden jerk was successful. "It's nothing," she insisted, too forcefully. "Just a pretty design I liked."

"In the spirit of partnership, I won't call you a liar. Plus, I'm hungry. Any interest in having lunch with me? I spar better after I've been fed," Gabriel teased.

Erin struggled against laughter and, he hoped, caring more than he should, against saying no. Laughter wrought a transformation in her that captivated him. The soft brown eyes danced with merriment. The lovely, haughty face transformed into beguiling. Again he thought of fairies and angels and other unearthly beings of loveliness. "Have lunch with me," he repeated softly.

"Mr. Moss," she began.

"My name is Gabriel. Gabe to family, a few close friends, and those who think I owe them money."

Sidetracked and unwilling to break the fragile concord, she inclined her head quizzically. "Are you a gambler?"

"Depends on the stakes. And the prize." Gabriel studied her then, his eyes running over her in an almost physical caress, a look that promised delights she could scarcely fathom.

Beneath his silver gaze, her blood quickened and her breathing stuttered.

"Have lunch with me, Erin."

Captivated, she moved toward him. It was a single step, taken despite logic and consequence.

It was folly.

Erin halted. Nothing had changed. The handsome, tempting man who entranced her with laughter and kindness could never be more than the brother of her friend. "I can't," she declined with genuine regret.

"Why not?" Gabe worried that his insistent demands bordered on the frantic, but he could feel her slipping away from him. In the space of a breath, she'd altered again, from lighthearted angel to stubbornly earthbound woman. Damnably, he was fascinated by both women.

He was a man who appreciated women, in face and form. He enjoyed the challenge of their minds, the intricacies of their emotions. Yet in thirty-four years he'd never felt such a powerful, immediate connection to one woman. He was lured like Odysseus by her husky laughter; the compulsion had begun in a heartbeat. Gabriel couldn't imagine it ending without their full and sated exploration. "My car is in the lot. I'll pack up your bike; then we can grab a late lunch."

"I need to go to the museum where Juan Johnson was attacked." *And I can't be alone with you.*

"Then we'll go together. I've already missed Singleton and Bailey."

Immediately her hackles rose and her eyes narrowed. "I don't have to report my movements to you. I am free to do as I please."

"Yes, you are," he replied evenly. "But I thought we were partners on this."

"I never agreed to that." Erin toyed with the handlebars. "How did you know where to find me?"

Gabriel noted that she hadn't said *no* to partnership. That was a huge step with someone as prickly as Erin was. He'd worm an affirmative out of her later. "I'm an investigative reporter, Erin. I tracked you. When you wouldn't answer your phone, I went to the bank. The distraught Ms. Weems told me you stopped by. I checked his house and you weren't there. This was the next logical place."

She hated to admit it, but they'd made a good team before. Without knowing what she was looking for, she might miss an important clue. But it wouldn't do to give in so easily. "I told you I didn't want to help with your story."

"I'm the only one who'll listen. Why don't we see what we find, then we'll argue?"

Erin's shoulders dropped. She was in no mood to wrestle with Gabriel and the unwilling sensations he inevitably evoked. "I assume you'll follow me to the Heritage Museum whether I want you to or not."

When he took her hand, Gabriel whispered conspiratorially, "It's like you're reading my mind."

CHAPTER 10

Erin and Gabriel entered the African Heritage Museum together, and Erin wondered how he did it. How he had so deftly inserted himself in her life that she couldn't dislodge him. This morning, she had been bound and determined to finish this without him. It was only midafternoon, and he stood next to her in the lobby, chatting with the new docent.

How did he do it?

"Come on, Erin." Gabriel nudged her with his elbow. "Ms. Young has graciously agreed to let us see the gatehouse." When Erin frowned, he explained, "Where Mr. Johnson resided."

A guided tour of the home of a possible victim? "Coming."

Gabriel walked beside the docent and thought of the puzzle that was Erin. Partnership frightened her, he realized. What he didn't know was the origin of that fear. They wound through the exhibits, where Bantu ritual masks mingled with twentieth-century paintings. He remembered coming to the museum as a child, pulling Gennie along as they trailed behind their parents. A memory of an older gentleman with shocking white hair and a patient smile surfaced. "Lynnette, how long had Mr. Johnson been the docent here?"

"He became docent in 1982. Trained me when I was a student at Xavier. We all miss him terribly."

Erin caught up with the pair. "Had he worked here before then?"

Lynnette shook her head, smiling sadly. "No, though it seems like it. Mr. Johnson loved to talk about his adventures. He served in the army during World War Two and came back to New Orleans. Put himself through Burkeen on the GI Bill. Before he became chief docent, though, he was proudest of integrating the elevator operators' union in New Orleans in the nineteen-fifties."

Erin felt her pulse trip. "He was an elevator operator?"

"To pay for school. He worked in the Grammercy Hotel in the Quarter."

Gabriel glanced at Erin. He could see her mind working. The trio emerged into the sunlight, and Lynnette led them to the small carriage house behind the museum.

"Juan lived on the grounds of the museum for decades. Said it made it easier to get to work." The air was stale, the interior gloomy, when she unlocked the door. Lynnette flicked on a light and backed away from the entrance. "I haven't had the heart to clean it out. I can't even go inside." She touched Gabriel's arm. "You'll help find the person who did this to him, won't you?"

Gabriel patted her hand reassuringly. "Yes, ma'am. I promise." Looking at Erin, he corrected himself. "*We* promise."

Satisfied, Lynnette left them, after they agreed to secure the door and return the key. Erin poked her head inside, then entered. The house was small, a single-bedroom with the door ajar. They stood in the living room, where he'd decorated the space with more art. Erin wandered over to a corner area near the kitchen. A half-finished sculpture stood on a pedestal that rested on a drop cloth. Work tools gathered dust on a table nearby.

"He was an artist." On her heels, Gabriel whispered, "Do you have any idea what we're looking for?"

Erin turned and put distance between them. "The police found a chisel at the scene. The type of chisel they found is probably an *ebauchoir*."

"To rough-hew sculpture."

Erin's gaze flew up to meet Gabriel's amused look. "You're not the only one who knows obscure facts, Dr. Abbott." Running his hand along the unfinished piece, he said, "The killer knew about his job in college."

"And about his hobby." The grisly conclusion had occurred to both of them. Erin gave it voice. "He stabbed him with his own *ebauchoir*."

Erin pointed at the implements lying on the table. "The police blotter described it as a chisel. I wasn't sure about the link." She wrapped her arms around her waist and stared at the sculpture. "*C* was taken, so it had to be *D, E,* or *F*. Elevator operator . . . *ebauchoir*. He's making it easy."

Dropping a hand to her shoulder, Gabriel snorted. "There's nothing about this that's easy, Erin. Five, no, seven people have lost their lives because of a madman. And he's sprinkling bread crumbs around the city that only you can see."

Erin spun around. "But I can't see it! I can't see what he'll do next! Who he plans to kill!"

To calm her, Gabriel said, "You're working as fast as you can."

"I don't know how long we have. And it could get someone killed." Erin rushed out of the house to the court-yard where flowers bloomed in wild profusion. A magnolia tree stood in the center of the cobblestones and she stopped at its trunk.

Gabriel followed. Unable not to, he pulled her to him, compelled to soothe. She struggled in his embrace, but he refused to loosen his hold. "Accept it, Erin," he murmured against her temple. "Accept that you've got someone who cares about you. That for a minute or two, you have someone to lean on."

"I can't," came the tortured whisper. Still, she wound trembling arms around his waist, rested her head against his shoulder. *One minute*, she thought. Then she'd be strong again.

"Tell me what's going on, Erin." Tension simmered in his voice, and he didn't bother to disguise it.

"I can't. You don't understand. I simply can't."

"Won't." He shifted his hands to grasp her upper arms. "What are you afraid of?"

You. Him. Everything. "Isn't a serial killer enough reason?"

"There's more. And you and I both know it."

She lifted her head and met his insistent look squarely. Courage, a recent addition to her armory, demanded she protect him from the nightmare that had tracked her across a continent. "I don't want to spend time with you."

The pronouncement, so baldly stated, neatly pricked

his impenetrable heart. But he hadn't become a seasoned reporter with a Pulitzer under his belt by accepting rejection without probing for more. "Why not?"

If we spend time together, I'll probably want to know more about you. Erin remained stubbornly mute.

Despite the growing ache, Gabriel smiled. "Strangely enough, relationships often grow with such treacherous knowledge."

She spun away from him, staring at the tender white petals of the magnolias in bloom. The flower, a staple of the region, was foreign to her. As foreign as buying groceries on her own and renting an apartment and feeling safe.

It had taken nearly her entire lifetime to accomplish the first two, and now a specter from her past, determined to strip safety away, had found her in New Orleans.

Gabriel made her feel a million things, but safety wasn't one of them. "We don't have a relationship. We've just met."

"Doesn't matter." Gabriel closed the distance between them and turned her to face him. The look of abject misery compelled him to tease. "Is it my hair? I usually get it cut more often." He brushed his thumb along the edge of her jaw, savoring the glide of velvet flesh.

Laughing sadly, Erin shook her head.

"Then what? Why are you so determined not to push me away? You like my sister. We're practically the same."

"Your sister doesn't make me nervous," Erin said dryly. "She doesn't insist on touching me."

"My sister has poor taste in women."

"Why are you pushing this? I'll give you your story, but you have to let me investigate on my own."

"No."

"Why not?" Erin demanded. "You'll have what you want. A way to save your paper."

"I want more than the paper. I want you," Gabriel said before he realized the words had formed. Abruptly he dropped his hand from her skin as though singed, and this time, it was he who widened the distance between them. He paced off the walkway, his hands shoved deep into his pockets. He returned to where she waited silent beneath the magnolia. He ground out, "I know you. I don't understand it, but I know you, Erin Abbott."

At the sound of her name, Erin recoiled. There it was, lying between them, and he had no idea. How could she talk with him, laugh with him, dream of him, when he had no idea who she really was?

And by his very nature, he would need to know. When she continued to resist, as she must, he would ferret out the truth of it. All of it. But she wouldn't allow that to happen.

The woman she'd once been had disappeared into the California mountains, and she would do anything to leave Analise Glover there forever. She had already possibly committed the worst act imaginable, and she wore his ring as a constant reminder.

No, Gabriel didn't know her, but if she pushed him away, he'd try to find out. She had one hope of protecting her secrets and protecting him from her past. "You can have the story, Gabriel. But that's it. I have nothing else to offer."

"What does that mean?"

"It means I give up. It means we're partners until I can get enough evidence to make the police pay attention. Then we're through."

Gabriel watched her, watched the grim determination thin her mouth. Her eyes were flat, though an emotion flickered in their depths. Carefully, he cupped her chin. She jerked at his touch, but he ignored the movement and tilted her scowling face into the sunlight. The banked temper flashed, and inwardly he relaxed. It wasn't over, he thought. Didn't she know whatever was between them had barely begun? "Let's finish going over Mr. Johnson's apartment; then we'll go somewhere for dinner."

Too drained to argue, Erin mutely followed him inside.

A thorough search of the house turned up little of interest. She rechecked Johnson's bedroom, where Gabriel had looked earlier. Photos of family members lined the dresser. "I know you've left a clue for me," she murmured. She opened drawers, peered under the bed. She didn't see it until she walked into the bathroom.

The frame hanging on the wall was unremarkable. But the print inside frayed her already-taut nerves.

It was a picture of the cabin in San Cabes. Nathan's cabin.

Shaken, she returned to the living room. Gabriel sat hunched over on the couch with the familiar notebook balanced on one corded thigh while he scrawled illegible notes across the page.

"I'm ready to go."

"Gimme a second. I'm nearly done."

Impatient, uneasy, Erin tried to get a look at the tablet. "What are you writing?"

"Copy for our lead," he replied absently. "I need to run a first draft past my editor tonight. With any luck, it will be in our online edition tomorrow." He glanced up at her. "Where did you learn about language?"

Erin stiffened. "Why do you want to know?"

"Keep up." He pointed to the album. "I told you, I've got to get a rough copy done." Mind whirring, he said, "I'll need to bump Riggall's piece on photojournalism, but that's an evergreen. I'll have to ask Kelly about how many SAUs we're holding."

"Evergreen?" Distracted, Erin puzzled over the foreign jargon. "SA who?"

Tapping his jaw absently, he explained, "An evergreen. A piece that isn't time-sensitive. SAUs are spaces we hold for advertisers' copy that hasn't come in yet." He focused abruptly on their conversation. "But none of this applies to our story. We're running this front-page, above the fold. I'll need some quotes. We'll have Michael Riggall take photos of you here, and—"

"No pictures."

The firm rejection stopped him mid-sentence. He shrugged, willing to make concessions on the eve of victory. "All right. No photos. But out of your suit of armor, you're incredibly photogenic. With the sexy bone structure and that gorgeous hair, Michael could do wonders."

Erin refused to be swayed by the offhand compliment or the skitter of her pulse. She repeated, "No pictures."

Gabriel exhaled sharply, trying not to be annoyed. Had they circled back to suspicion already? To stop himself from exploding, he set the pad and pencil on the low table at his knees. He reclined on the sofa, draping his arm along the curved back. He wouldn't push, he promised himself. Lightly cajole, maybe, but he wouldn't make her run.

In a conciliatory tone, he agreed, "No pictures. Gotcha. But there is a story here, Erin. I plan to write it."

"I understand that. I agreed to help you, but I don't want my name mentioned." Erin gestured to the album lying open on the table. "We have the obituaries and the note. I've drawn a preliminary profile of the killer. That should be enough without bringing me into it."

Gabriel sprang to his feet. "You are the story, Erin. The killer wrote to you. The language connection was invisible to everyone but you."

Survival demanded that she remain invisible. "That's my condition, Gabriel. Mention me, and the story's through."

The threat grated. He was tired of having the same fight with her with one hand tied behind his back. She could keep her damned secrets, but she wouldn't ruin the story of his career. He approached her. Towering over her, he taunted, "Freedom of the press, darling. You can't stop me."

"I'll deny it."

"Then Sylvie will corroborate. Face it, Erin. You don't have a choice." Frustration curled his fingers as he tried to moderate his tone. "Stop whining. This has to be done."

Erin saw his fist clench, felt anger transform into panic. In a blind flash, all Erin saw was Nathan. All she heard was cold, male anger and disappointment. All she knew was that she had to get away. Now. Clumsily, she edged out of range. "You can't force me," she accused haltingly.

The transformation startled him. Her pupils had dilated, the brown swimming with fear. Her skin held a thin sheen that alarmed him. Gabriel took a concerned step toward her.

Erin nearly fell as she tried to put distance between

herself and certain retribution. The wall pressed against her spine, a barrier to escape. Braced for the blow, she turned her head. Lost in nightmare, she declared in a flat tone with none of its usual smoky depth, "Don't!"

"What the devil is going on here?" Stunned by the pallor sweeping her skin, Gabriel gripped the icy hands. Delicate bones shifted beneath the fine skin. He felt her shudder and lifted her head so her eyes met his. The stricken look in their brown depths rocked him. "Erin, honey, what's wrong? You're petrified."

She swallowed, trapped in a past where rebellion could be punished by a fist, or words that struck as cruelly. "Please," she whimpered.

"All right, honey." He chafed her skin to warm it. Using his softest voice, he pledged, "I won't write about you, Erin. Not until you're ready. Okay?"

Her voice was thin, plaintive. "I don't want to help you."

"You don't have to. You don't have to do anything you don't want to." Needing to hold her, Gabriel folded her into his arms. "Erin. It's fine, honey. You don't have to help me."

As the reassuring strength of his hold surrounded her, reality flooded in in a rush. Mortified, Erin twisted against him, desperate to escape. Still, the wall at her back and the large man in front of her had her trapped. Sinewy arms held her tight to his body and the melodious baritone crooned in her ear. Warm breath whispered over suddenly fevered skin, and Erin succumbed, too exhausted to fight herself and comfort. She lifted her arms to wrap them around his waist.

When he felt her capitulate, Gabriel sighed in bemused triumph. He tenderly kissed her temple, then her forehead. As she calmed, he pressed his lips to the crown of silky black hair. "I think we've done enough for today. Why don't you let me take you home?"

Mutely, she nodded, unwilling to break their embrace.

Still holding her, Gabriel gathered her jacket and his notes and led them out to his Jeep. He drove to her apartment, wisely not asking for an explanation. But after he helped her alight, he blocked her exit. "Hold everything inside, Erin, and one day it will simply explode, ready or not."

"Gabriel, I—"

What she started to say got lost beneath the kiss that glided over her mouth. He was careful to taste but not take. Erin leaned into the kiss, lulled by its charm. There was no urgency to sink inside, no frantic mating to tie her stomach into knots. But how could she have expected that a first kiss could settle nerves and arouse desires at the same time? Wonder blossomed and she parted her lips to invite more.

Gabriel refused the invitation to sink deep, to explore the countless flavors he sampled with the gentle glide of mouth to mouth. Desire had replaced the earlier horror, but until he understood its source, he wouldn't rush. But he would tempt. For now, he concentrated on learning the dip and curve of her lips, the soft velvet of their surface. For now, he restrained the excitement that beat in his veins, determined to memorize their pliancy without plundering.

When her scent rose and wound itself inside him as though she would always be there, when a low moan

escaped and he couldn't tell from who, when desire and
care and destiny seemed inseparable, he ended the kiss.
And before she could respond or question, he ushered her
inside her apartment and disappeared.

CHAPTER 11

Revenge. Obsession. Domination. Control.

Erin read over the words glowing on her computer screen. She had been up since dawn, unable to sleep with thoughts twisting themselves in her mind. Her final class of the semester began at nine, which gave her another hour before she left for the university. Time enough, she thought, to examine the mind of a killer.

Already she'd printed out profiles of the victims. A fastidious architect who believed in order and discipline, as well as beauty. A fiercely loyal banker. The calypso dancer who danced for men at night and played for her church on Sundays. Mr. Johnson, the docent who had been beloved by all who met him. Maggie, the kind soul willing to help anyone, friend or not.

She typed in another set of words: *Discipline. Loyalty. Duality. Popularity. Selflessness.*

Leaning over the keyboard, she studied the list on the screen. Her eyes widened when her mind made the link. Nathan. It all came back to him.

The killer had selected victims who shared more than the eerie reminders she'd found. A decade ago, Erin would have used mostly the same adjectives to describe Nathan Rhodes. Until the day he'd shown her how twisted words and their meanings could become.

Analise sat on the window seat in her new room, jean-clad knees hugged beneath her chin. A glossy brass latch held the panes closed, and the metal gleamed in the sunlight. She loved the old-fashioned seat and the view it displayed, which was still so unexpected, though she'd been looking at it all morning. Beyond the glass, blue sky met mysterious gray mountains, far off in the distance. From her dorm room, the best view she'd ever enjoyed had been of the student parking lot. But not anymore.

Graduation had passed a week ago, and today was her second day as Nathan's guest. At his gentle urging, she had agreed to move in with him while in graduate school. He'd been right, she decided. She was only seventeen and not quite ready to be on her own.

The other students snickered behind her back about her relationship with him, she knew, and she had seen the disapproving looks from the faculty. She knew what they thought, but they were wrong. Nathan didn't think of her *that* way. He was her mentor.

Nathan—or Dr. Rhodes, as she still thought of him, despite his many admonitions to call him by his first name— had become everything to her. Parent, teacher, and friend.

He'd guided her through her minor in linguistics, allowing her to secretly co-author articles with him. Sure, she would have preferred to see her name in the journals, but she understood Nathan's fear that to do so would undermine the credibility of their work. Most journals would refuse to publish them if they thought a college student had written the articles. It was an honor to be the ghost writer for the great Dr. Rhodes. When he accepted the DiSantis Prize for contributions to the field, she'd thrilled with the knowledge that they'd both won. That night, he'd sent her yellow roses in celebration.

With his help, she'd been able to finish her degree in psychology with honors. Maybe she'd been given preferential treatment when they allowed her to take the extra courses to finish on time, but she'd put in the hours and gotten the work done. Besides, she had nothing else to distract her. It had been months since there had been any word from Sebastian. She had all the time in the world, and Nathan thought it was best if she put it toward her studies. Discipline and determination were the keys to success, he told her time and again. Didn't he spend twelve hours a day on his publications rather than gallivanting around campus like a child? Brilliance demanded sacrifice and did not allow for distractions. Study now, friendship later.

She refused to dwell on the lack of invitations to graduation parties or the tepid applause when she'd crossed the stage. It didn't matter. In the fall, she would start her doctoral studies in psychology. In a few years, she'd be a renowned criminal psychologist and linguist. Nathan had promised to let her continue to work with him, and possibly publish with him, once she was more seasoned.

The question was how she would spend her summer vacation, or at least this first day. She twisted on the bench to look at the pale pink bedroom that was now hers. She'd told Nathan that she didn't like pink, but he had been too busy to notice the color selected by the decorator. It wouldn't do to complain, she decided, when he'd been so unfailingly kind to her. Even his harsher words were all for her benefit. He wanted to make her special. He wanted to make her room special. If she hated pink, it would be immature to grouse about it.

So she'd repaint it herself.

Hours later, Analise wiped away splatters of the ice-blue paint that had reminded her of Nathan's eyes. A fresh breeze blew through the open windows to circulate the air. She propped her arms on the roller handle and surveyed her creation. The ivory linens and the antique furniture were a lovely contrast with the new paint. Nathan would be impressed. The sound of the door closing had her rushing to clean up. Plus, she had yet to start dinner, which she'd promised that morning. She hurried into the bathroom.

Downstairs, Nathan cursed beneath his breath as he stalked into his office. He slammed his briefcase on the surface, and the letter from the *Yale Journal of Linguistic Studies* fell to the floor. He bent to pick it up and studied the offer for a permanent section in its hallowed pages. Crumpling it in his fist, he threw it across the room.

Rather than celebrating his coup, he'd spent the better part of the afternoon being chastised by the dean about his houseguest. The rumors and the chiding were all Analise's fault, he realized. If she didn't look like such a damned ingénue, no one would care. But instead of lauding his latest triumph, the dean had accused him of corrupting an impressionable minor.

The arrogant old prick refused to understand that Nathan didn't need the awkward Analise for physical pleasure. He only wanted the fecund mind, ripe with innovative ideas and eager to please him. Now that he had a quarterly column to produce, having her close by would be invaluable. As long as she remained quiescent, dependent on him for everything but her next breath. And perhaps even that.

He smiled when he heard her timid knock at his door. The smile turned to a scowl when he saw her disheveled appearance. Paint caked to her hair, streaked across her shirt. "What the hell have you been doing, Analise?"

She twisted her hands together. "I painted the bedroom. It was a horrible shade of pink, but I fixed it."

Of course it was pink. The fact that she specifically mentioned hating the color was precisely why he'd instructed the decorator to choose that particular color. Analise would have to learn that only one person's wishes were fulfilled. "You painted the room today," he repeated quietly.

"Yes. I bought the paint this morning. I didn't want to bother you." Analise could sense the anger in him, but she was baffled by its source. "I paid for it myself, out of my accounts."

"Your accounts." Nathan reclined in his chair, his voice pitched low.

The width of the desk separated them, and, instinctively, Analise leaned closer to hear him. To explain. "I know we discussed whether I should talk to you first before I spent money, but the paint and supplies weren't expensive at all. I only painted my room."

When he leaned forward, she was unprepared. In a flash, he grabbed her by the collar of her shirt and dragged her across the desk. Her knees struck the sharp edge of wood; her belly scraped over the discarded briefcase. Stunned, she barely registered the crack of bone as she fell to the ground. She lay at his feet, dazed and whimpering. When he hauled her to her knees, her head lolled backward, and he shook her fiercely.

"Look at me!"

She pried open her eyes, afraid to see the face she loved twisted in anger. But it only smiled at her. "Nathan? What did I do?"

The answering blow to her cheek sent her flying into the credenza. Her lip split from the smash of his hand.

"You need to understand your place." He came to stand over her, striking and kicking over and over until she curled into herself. "You're mine, Analise. Mine."

To hide from the pain, she thought of words, soothing, predictable words. The poetry of Greek. The steadfastness of Latin. For what seemed an eternity, his hands and feet battered her body, and she thought of Swahili and Mayan, of safety and protection.

When he was finished, Nathan lifted her nearly unconscious body and carried her up the stairs to the freshly painted room. The fumes had thinned but still hung in the air. After gently placing her on the bed, he shut the windows and locked them tight, shoving the key into his pocket. It was time for her next lesson.

Carefully, he knelt beside her, pressing his lips to her ear. "This is my house, Analise. Mine. You have no room. You have no home. Nowhere else to go."

She cringed away from the gentle whisper, the harsh truth. Despite the pain, she defied him. "I can move back on campus."

Nathan shook his head. "Not if I tell them to say no.

Not if I tell the judge that you are too unstable to have control of your own accounts. I'm a respected professor and you're an oddity, Analise. You have no parents, no friends. No one in the world who loves you, except for me."

She refused to believe that love could be responsible for the aches that pulsed along her body and throbbed in her head. "Why did you hurt me?"

He stroked her hair tenderly. "Because I love you. You need discipline, Analise. Structure. Only I understand you. If you obey me, I won't have to hurt you again. I won't have to protect you from yourself."

Through the haze of pain, she knew he wasn't making sense, but the waves of agony muddled her mind. The air grew thick with the smell of paint.

The next day, her mind was still foggy when he pressed a paper into her bruised hand, when she signed over to him power of attorney for her trust fund. Soon, she'd stopped thinking for herself, stopped making all but the simplest of decisions. Nathan had become her world. His thoughts were hers; his desires all that mattered. Soon, she believed that this was as it had always been.

Would always be.

CHAPTER 12 ·

Bzzz. Bzzz. Bzzz.

The intercom's summons dragged her to the door. "Hello?"

"I'm here, Erin!" Genevieve's lilting voice greeted her.

"Why?" she asked baldly. "Did we have an appointment?"

"No. I'm your ride for today, compliments of my brother."

"Gabriel." Erin ground out the name, torn between exasperation and gratitude. Genevieve thought she was being helpful. "I appreciate the offer, but I have a way to the university."

"The bus? Oh, come on down, Erin. Gabriel will be angry if I don't do this; plus, I'm double-parked."

Drumming her fingers on the wall, Erin tried for a better excuse. Before she could give one, she heard Genevieve speaking faintly: "Yes, Officer, I see that I'm not actually in a parking space." The voice grew louder and more insistent, designed for Erin's hearing. "I'll move my car in a twinkling, sir. As soon as my teacher friend comes downstairs. Why, yes, sir, I am a teacher, too." The soft sounds of Creole and woman made the officer stammer out his admiration of Gen's dedication to her students.

Erin couldn't let her Good Samaritan get a ticket, regardless of Gabriel's role in the matter. Resigned, she crossed back to the sofa to retrieve her briefcase. She slid the album into her bag, flicked off the lights, secured the door, and headed downstairs.

Outside, in the warm morning already edging toward sultry, Genevieve leaned against a silver two-seater, one finger tracing the officer's shield. Seeing Erin, he tucked a scrap of paper, which she guessed contained Gen's phone number, into his pocket. A deep flush crept up his cheeks, and he stepped away reluctantly.

"Morning, ma'am," he offered politely.

"Good morning, Officer," Erin replied, barely repressing a laugh at the young man's chagrin. "Thanks for watching over my friend."

"My absolute pleasure, ma'am." The officer tipped his hat and gallantly opened the door for her. He escorted Genevieve to her side of the car and whispered something Erin couldn't hear. Smitten, the officer watched as they pulled off and made their way toward the school.

Genevieve zipped along Esplanade, taking side streets at a terrifying speed. Erin clutched the door handle tightly, praying for a traffic light or a cop. "We're not that late. And we *are* the professors."

"I haven't had a single accident in three years," Genevieve protested. "My insurance rates are starting to go down again."

"Oh, God," Erin moaned.

"Don't worry, Erin. I took a defensive driving course. I drive like a nun these days."

"You drive like a maniac."

Cupid-bow lips twitched in restrained laughter. "That's not very polite. I've never heard you not being polite."

"Teetering on the edge of death can do that to a person," Erin explained, squeezing her eyes shut as they cut off an angry semi. She pried open one eye, afraid to miss her own demise, and gasped, "Watch it! A streetcar!"

Genevieve gunned the engine and leaped the tracks, barely avoiding a collision. "That was a close one," she commented as she checked her rearview mirror. The raised fist of the conductor merited a friendly wave.

"Stop the car!" Erin clutched at the door handle. "I'll walk!"

"Can't. Gabriel gave me strict instructions. I'm to pick you up and drive you home today. No arguments."

"I don't take orders from your brother."

Genevieve smiled softly. "Neither do I. However, for some reason, he's worried about you."

Erin's lips warmed at the memory of their kiss, of the utter lack of pressure for more. That almost disturbed her more than the killer who stalked her. Which was absurd. "Do you always do what Gabriel wants?"

"If I agree." Gen tapped her fingers on the steering wheel. "I saw the headline on the *Ledger* this morning: 'ABC Killer Stalks New Orleans Residents.' "

"Oh."

The silver car turned into the parking lot for the social science building. Genevieve cut the motor and turned around to look at Erin. "Gabriel told me about as much when I asked him about his sources. In the next breath, though, he asked me to pick you up and take you shopping."

"Shopping?"

"He's a guy. They think the mall is the cure for every ill that a woman faces. I agreed because I care about you, Erin. I know we haven't been close—" Neither had to point out whose fault it was. "But I would like to be your friend."

Nathan had taken too much from her, Erin thought. Even friendship. Enough was enough. "I hate malls. And I hate shopping." She talked over Gen's appalled reaction. "But I would love to learn to drive."

"You could take classes this summer. Or I could teach you. Though I don't understand how anyone could reach the age of twenty-nine without learning to drive."

"I traveled a lot." Wistfully Erin gazed out at the tree-lined streets that graced the university. The fragrance of wild azaleas mixed with the scent of jasmine.

There'd been a plot of jasmine on the balcony at their pied-à-terre in Paris, right outside her bedroom. That was when her parents had taken her to the Sorbonne.

Sebastian had explained the medicinal uses to her, and she'd tucked sprigs into her suitcase, the evening they left for Amsterdam. Or was it Lisbon?

The schools, the labs, had eventually run together, leaving no time for teenage rites of passage like earning a license.

When she lived with Nathan, he had refused her request to take classes. He preferred that she depend on him for transportation, for everything.

As though aware of the dark thoughts closing in on her, ones she didn't understand, Genevieve offered gently, "If you really want to learn, maybe we can do a lesson this weekend. But it will have to be in my brother's car. You're not getting behind the wheel of my precious Audi." She stroked the dashboard lovingly.

Erin nodded as they got out of the car. "I'd like that, Genevieve. Thank you."

"So, no shopping."

Hearing the longing, she relented. "Shopping today, driving lesson tomorrow." Erin tucked her briefcase firmly under her arm. Together they walked to the building. "Hopefully, you teach more safely than you drive."

"You'll see," Genevieve teased. "I'll meet you at my office at one." With a friendly wave, she sailed down the hallway to her office.

Erin headed for her office, her heels echoing in the nearly empty corridor. In ten minutes, students would fill the space, eager to finish tests and head off for the summer.

At her office door, Erin turned the knob and entered. And jumped. "Oh!"

Erin looked down at Jessica, her teaching assistant, who sat in the single office chair that faced the desk. The computer screen was filled with text.

"Dr. Abbott, you okay?"

"I'm fine." Erin set her briefcase on the credenza. "You just startled me. I wasn't expecting anyone to be in here."

"Didn't mean to scare you," Jessica apologized as she cleared the screen. "I've been working on this for hours, trying to get a jump on my project. You said you didn't mind if I used your computer. The one in the TA office is on the mend. Again. Someone downloaded a virus from the Net."

Jessica popped the CD from the drive and came from around the desk. In the cramped quarters of her office, Erin bumped against a sheaf of papers stacked on the desk's surface. The pile tumbled to the carpet in a flurry of white.

Jessica quickly knelt to gather the scattered pages, and Erin bent down to help.

"I've got it, Dr. Abbott." Jessica hurriedly shuffled pages into a pile. "I'm so sorry about this."

"No problem." Erin shifted to help. "I remember dissertation proposal time. Back then, though, we used a chisel and hammer to etch out our papers on slabs of granite."

Jessica chuckled appreciatively. "You're funny, Dr. Abbott. I don't care what the students say." The TA glanced up, her mouth a moue of embarrassment. "I'm sorry. I didn't mean to say that out loud. Uh, the students love you."

"You don't lie well, Jessica," Erin admonished, handing the young woman the last of the pages. Then Erin rose from her crouch on the ground and reached down to help the younger woman stand. "I know they think I'm hard."

"They just haven't gotten a chance to know you." Silently, though, she had to agree with the students. Despite the woman's fairy looks, Jessica knew there was nothing soft about the strict, style-challenged Dr. Abbott. The woman reminded her of one of those spinster librarians in bad commercials, the ones with the stodgy buns and boring spectacles who hissed at patrons for silence, then transformed into sex goddesses behind closed doors.

"Jessica?"

Dragging her attention back to the moment, Jessica smiled sheepishly. "I'm sorry. Late nights."

"I asked if you had the tests ready. I left them in your box to be copied."

Jessica lifted a smaller stack of papers from Erin's desk. "Here they are. I had them collated and stapled."

"Good." Erin accepted the tests. "Hopefully, I won't have a repeat of Murder 101's tests," she muttered.

"What happened?"

"Oh, I have a couple of students who don't comprehend the idea of cheating as bad."

Frowning, Jessica returned to gathering her things. "Who was it? If you don't mind my asking?"

"Ms. Turner and Mr. Clark seem to believe in share and share alike. Not that I can prove it."

"Are you going to fail them?"

"Not this time. But they'll be getting a strongly worded lecture." Erin loaded the tests into her arms. "Will you be around to help me grade?"

"I can't, sorry. I'm living in the library getting ready for the committee meeting."

One of the perquisites of being a professor at a university was service on dissertation committees. Jessica had sought Erin out within days of her arrival at Burkeen, and the grad student had convinced her to oversee her dissertation. Proposals were due. Two others had been able to con Erin into service as well.

"Do you know if Neldra or Walter is presenting next week?"

"Walter is. I think Neldra postponed."

"Will you let them know I'll be around?"

Jessica nodded. "Absolutely."

"Good." Erin shifted the exams into one arm. "Make sure you take some time to enjoy your break."

"I will, Dr. Abbott."

Erin walked out with Jessica, scanning the exams. Five pages, fifty-five questions. Challenging but not impossible.

She entered the lecture hall and set the pages on the desk. Students had already entered and filled the seats, ready to finish the exam and move on. The test asked her criminal psychology class to speculate about the composition of murder. What drove man and, less often, woman to take human life? What churned inside a psyche and erupted in such irrevocable destruction? The harsh, pungent nature of violence drew the class's imagination in a way little else did.

While the students pored over questions, her encounter with Detective Iberville replayed in Erin's mind, and she wondered if she'd tried hard enough to convince her. Maybe if the detective knew about her previous life, where she'd been a master of language, the woman would believe. But to reveal that would be to reveal all, a chance Erin wouldn't take. Not her life for a stranger's, not when there was still another way: working with Gabriel.

After the room emptied, Erin remained behind to grade their tests, grateful for the distraction. She plowed through the stack, impressed by the responses. It seemed this class proved slightly more attentive than her psychopathology students and less prone to sharing answers.

"If you'd been my professor, I'd probably have been a better student."

The sudden announcement startled Erin and she clutched her pen like a dagger. Looking up, she met the mildly lecherous smile of Dr. Kenneth Bernard, chair of the psychology department. She was doing her best not to overreact to every sound, but the emotion always hovered close to the surface. Slowly she relaxed her fingers. "Kenneth. I didn't hear you come in."

"I was passing by and saw you inside. Getting ready to leave?"

Hooded eyes watched her with a sharp gaze. His narrow face was pale from its infrequent adventures out-of-doors. Of medium height, he tended to favor hand-tooled leather boots. He worked out precisely thirty minutes per day, never in a gymnasium. The stench of sweat and body odor did not settle well on his stomach. He preferred the artificial lights of well-air-conditioned buildings to the oppressive heat of actual sun and the privacy of his treadmill to public gyms. In both places—outdoors and in gyms—too many of God's inferior creatures prowled their restless bodies over every spare inch of earth to suit his urbane tastes.

He favored the refined and aloof city dweller to the tumescent average local resident. Erin Abbott had the bearing of someone who understood the distinction. Lightly tapping the test she had graded, Kenneth shook his head.

"Such dedication, Erin." He balanced on the edge of the desk and casually draped his arm across a thigh muscled from Pilates and yoga. He wore loose linen pants in a soft burgundy and an elegant ivory shirt of the same fine weave. Against the linen, the muscles were outlined nicely. "You'll wear yourself out."

"I have miles to go before I sleep," she quipped. She

assigned a B+ to the exam and conceded silently that her respite had evaporated. Apparently, the rest of the papers would have to wait for the quiet of her office or her home.

"I thought I overheard you telling your teaching assistant you'd caught some students cheating." At Erin's raised brow, he lifted his hands in apology. "I wanted to ask you to lunch, but you were obviously occupied. We really don't tolerate academic dishonesty at Burkeen. This must be reported."

"I'd rather not." She folded her hands, dismayed at the thought of Kenneth running to the dean with a complaint about cheating. Academic investigations were never secret, and too much hinged on the outcome. Cursing herself for even mentioning it, she explained, "I will speak with the students directly. There isn't enough evidence for an inquiry." To change the subject, she asked quickly, "I thought you were already off on vacation? A conference in Versailles."

"Excellent memory. I didn't think you listened to me." Leaning close, he caressed her temple and pretended not to notice her subtle flinch. He'd startled her, that's all. Deliberately, he repeated the caress. "You always seem so far away."

Instinctively Erin inched away. "I'm right here," she demurred.

"So it appears." Kenneth sidled closer, his hip just brushing her fingers where they rested atop the exams. He cocked his head, studying her. "We haven't had much of an opportunity to talk since I hired you, Erin. I think we'd like to get to know each other, colleague to colleague." A cool, smooth hand covered hers where it lay atop the papers. "Don't you?"

Frissons of distaste wound through her, but she didn't dare move her hand away, lest she openly insult him. Men seemed unusually preoccupied with her hands, she thought with exasperation. But where Gabriel's unwanted caresses catapulted her stomach into somersaults, Kenneth elicited only a sensation of oily distaste. If this groping trend continued, she'd ask Madame Bee Dowdell on Bourbon Street for a wart-causing potion.

"Maybe lunch, when you return?" she suggested casually. "Genevieve and Dr. Meyers mentioned that we should try to get together over the summer before the students return."

"That would be nice." Kenneth restrained a surge of irritation with effort. He had little to no interest in sharing air with the coarse Anthony Meyers, and his flirtations with Genevieve Moss had proven fruitless years before. His sights were solely focused on the dreary little Dr. Abbott. She appeared to be as fussy as he, and malleable.

Unaware of his thoughts, Erin asked, "When do you leave for the conference?"

"Next week. Morning flight. First class." He preened a bit. "As a featured speaker, I insisted."

"How nice for you." Unobtrusively Erin increased the distance between them. Though Kenneth had been nothing but gracious since her arrival, his unabashed contempt for their young charges, coupled with his constant chastely lurid attention, disturbed her. And, if she was honest, so, too, did his faint resemblance to Nathan. Perhaps it was the profession or the palpable disdain for the less-gifted, or even the slick charm coated in brilliance, but whatever the cause, she studiously avoided prolonged conversations with Kenneth.

She discreetly removed her hand to lift her satchel and she shuffled the papers inside. "Which paper will you deliver?"

"I evaluated the response–reinforcement correlation during modeling phase to determine the acquisition of novel responses by observers' subjects."

"Fascinating." Erin stood and slung the strap over her shoulder. "I look forward to hearing all about it."

Kenneth rose to his feet and shifted to block her departure. Another habit of men she had quickly grown to despise. Gabriel seemed to make it a point of honor to get in her way. Incensed by the way her thoughts invariably returned to him, she smiled recklessly at Kenneth. "Have a wonderful trip."

"Rushing off so soon?" he asked, encouraged. "I thought we might have time for coffee."

A headache began to thud dully, and Erin shook her head, unconcerned about appearing rude. She needed to be alone, away from disturbing men and their unwanted attentions. Away from killers and their byzantine clues. Away from guilt and sacrifice.

Before she could make her excuses and dash, Jessica appeared in the doorway. "Dr. Abbott. Oh, Dr. Bernard," she stammered over her greeting. "I didn't mean to, that is, I didn't know you were—"

"We were just talking about Dr. Bernard's trip, Jessica." Erin motioned her inside, grateful for the interruption. "Can I help you?"

"Actually, I wanted to ask you both about our meeting next week." Jessica smiled sheepishly, her eyes darting adoringly at the head of the department. "Would it be okay if some of the other students heard my presentation?"

"Certainly," Kenneth responded, without looking at Jessica. "I may make attendance mandatory."

Jessica beamed. "It would be a great learning experience for us. With defenses next year, a lot of us could use the coaching."

Kenneth nodded.

"Send me an E-mail with the time." Erin grabbed onto the date like a lifeline. "Sorry, but I have to go." Moving past him to the door, she ignored his sputtered protest. She hurried through the open door and into the hallway, careful this time to check for occupants. She saw no one. With unseemly haste she rushed out of the building and out to the curb. Genevieve would have to forgive her, but she didn't want to hang around the school, in case Kenneth tried to corner her again. The street promised no assistance by way of a cab. As she was condemned to walk home, the humidity mocked her and the confining suit.

In rebellion, she tugged at the buttons of the sweltering suit and fairly ripped them from their moorings. She removed the satchel, thrust the jacket off, and bundled it into a crumpled ball of fabric. If wearing the horrid clothes didn't manage to keep Gabriel or Kenneth at bay, she could see no good reason to sweat to death in vain protest.

Rolling with the liberating wave of defiance, Erin unfastened the cloth-covered buttons at her throat, not stopping until her fingers encountered the edge of lace at her chemise. There her rebelliousness faltered, and she managed a ragged grin at the image of herself stripped down to chemise and skirt hiked up over naked thighs.

She settled on a slight hitch in the calf-length skirt and the pleasure of an itinerant breeze occasionally wafting over her skin. As she strolled along the boulevards, beneath a canopy of verdant green and cloudless blue, and inhaled the scent of honeysuckle, the drumming headache disappeared. For the first time, in too long a while, she thought, she might one day be happy. Or at least content.

CHAPTER 13

Her good mood lasted until she opened her mailbox. She saw the ivory parchment envelope poking up between the flyers and bills, felt the spurt of terror. Concentrating on each breath, she mounted the stairs to the third floor.

Later, she would not remember unlocking the door or slamming it shut. She wouldn't recall drawing the safety chain across before she sank to the floor. For her, it was a series of sounds: the rip of thick paper, the sibilant hiss of the note that fluttered onto her lap. Then elegant script that mocked her with its beauty.

Analise,

You disappoint me. Days pass, and you are no closer to my goal. To finishing what started in the cellar. In the mountains.

Now you have an ally. How soon before he seeks the truth about you? How soon before I tell him?

You know the words. All the lovely letters arranged to tell the truth. Twenty-six letters. Not a second to waste.
Find me.

Erin scrambled to her knees, knocking the note and envelope to the floor. She snatched the phone from its cradle and called information. "Gabriel Moss, please."

Soon the operator connected Erin to his line. After several rings, she heard the subtle click. "Hello?"

"Gabriel?" Erin willed her voice to be strong, but it wavered slightly.

"Erin?" Gabriel heard the thread of tension. "Where are you? Where's Gennie?"

"She's still at the university. I walked home." The panic rose higher, choking her. "Can you come to my apartment? It's important."

"I'm on my way."

Erin replaced the phone, staring at the note. Calling Gabriel had been instinct. What she had to do next was purely self-preservation. She circled the breakfast island and entered the kitchen. Coolly, she reached into the kitchen drawer for a pair of scissors. The strip of paper with her name on it floated down into the sink. The rush of tap water blurred the ink before the compactor ripped the sliver to shreds. She filled a glass, drinking to soothe her tight throat.

Erin paced beyond sight of the window, able to see out without others seeing in. At each creak and moan of the old building, she shivered in the evening heat. She should be terrified, she imagined. But there was no room for terror, only survival.

There was no question now: The killer wanted revenge.

Revenge for the death of Nathan Rhodes. Because she'd chosen her life over his, knowing she had no choice.

It had been months before she could sleep in Sebastian's apartment with the door closed, the lights off. In the dark, the dreams waited.

If the killer knew of Analise, knew of Nathan, then he knew of the dark room and what she'd seen. He knew that she had run to the mountains to escape. Horror forced her to run. But she'd run as far as she could, and Nathan had found her. She'd run again, only to wind up in the middle of a nightmare. This time, she had to take a stand.

She would not run again.

So she was calm when Gabriel's battered Jeep screeched to a halt at the curb. As she pressed the buzzer to admit him, she thought about how much of the truth she could give him.

"What happened?" Gabriel demanded as he rounded the corner, seconds later. "Are you okay?" Without waiting for a response, he pushed past her into the apartment.

Erin closed the door and secured the latch. She handed him the doctored note. "It was waiting for me this afternoon."

The words on the paper skittered nerves Gabriel thought long since deadened. "Where did you find it?"

"My mailbox. Just like the first one." She took a seat on the couch, sipped from the water she'd poured. "The next victim is coming. Soon."

Gabriel leaned against the mantel, which gave him a clear view of the windows. "Tell me about the cellar, Erin." It was a command. His hard voice contained no compassion, no hesitation. Just certainty that his orders would be met. "What happened in the mountains?"

She stared at him for infinite seconds. Tall, solid, with skin burnished to a copper sheen, he reminded her of a sculpture of a modern god. His smoke gray eyes, so unexpected amid the shades of brown, seemed to burrow into her. They demanded her secrets, every story she could tell.

She shifted forward. "Metaphors. Heights, depths."

"You're lying, Erin!" Gabriel stormed toward her, mouth tight with anger. "Seven people are dead. And you know why."

"I'm trying to stop him!"

"Try harder! Tell me the truth." Gabriel slapped the manila folder on the coffee table. "You knew all of them, Erin. All five of the victims."

Erin recoiled as though struck. "I didn't," she whispered.

He squatted beside her, caging her in. With one hand, he opened the file. "I had my reporters run a cross-check. Everything they could find out about you and the victims." Jabbing a photo of a man. "Julian Harris attended your gym. He asked you out on a date once."

The photo watched her with damning eyes. Eyes she recognized now. The 6:45 A.M. treadmill. "No," she murmured, touching the glossy print. "I didn't know his name."

Relentless, Gabriel ripped out a second page and laid it beside Julian's photograph. A familiar name had been scrawled across the bottom of her loan papers with First Bank. "Burleigh Singleton approved your loan for this condo. Did you forget him, too?"

"Oh, my God." Erin reached for the next sheet, fingers trembling. Another photograph of a face she'd seen but never looked at. "Phoebe worked part-time at the Newbern Menagerie? I never paid attention to her. I try not to notice other people, hoping they won't notice me."

Gabriel rose from his position on the floor. "You're not invisible, Erin. We touch the world, and the world touches us." He joined her on the sofa, lifting her hands to hold them. "What did he do to you?"

"Made me a shadow. A pathetic shell. I don't want to become that woman again."

"We won't let him win. Let me help you."

The words, as rough and potent as whiskey, sped through her like lightning.

Gabriel gently traced her widow's peak and the curve that flowed from it. "What are you afraid of, Erin? Tell me and you're safe with me."

"Rubbish," Erin whispered. The tension tightened and the churning in her belly became a flutter.

"True," he agreed immediately. "But your secrets will be. Trust me."

"He wants me to tell you. To pull you inside."

"I'm already there. He knows we're working together. This note intends to make us weak. You won't let him."

The guilt burned through her like acid. "I didn't mean to harm those people. I thought it was finished."

"You didn't do this." Driven to comfort, Gabriel tugged her closer. "I want to know what's going on in that complicated head of yours. I want to know you, Erin."

"If you do, he'll come after you as well."

"Haven't you noticed I don't frighten well, darling?" Gabriel shifted forward until Erin bumped against the sofa back.

He lifted a hand to cup her cheek, and she shook her head in fierce denial. "Yes," he corrected.

"Don't." Erin's mind swirled with possibilities. Push

him away. Keep him at arm's length. It was the only way to protect herself. But a traitor's voice whispered louder than logic. It demanded action. Pull him closer. End the ache and taste. "Please don't," she whispered, and turned her hand beneath his, palm to palm.

"I don't seem to have a choice." He slid the hand cupping the soft cheek in search of the slender nape of her neck. On his way, he became distracted by the pins holding the dreary bun in place. With slow, deliberate movements, he drew pins from the black, silken mass. Drawn down by its weight, it spilled over, caressing his fingers as he tangled them in its skeins.

The cool strands burned like separate flames, and his hands tightened. "You make me wonder why you bind this beauty so close. Why your clothes don't fit you. Why you have keepsakes you'd never own."

"I don't know what—"

Gabriel shook his head once, unable to trust his temper. Understanding, she fell silent. So close to her, able to read the wide brown eyes, his fury rose. "I don't know you, but I know lies. This," he lifted a handful of glorious ebony hair between them, "is a lie." With his thumb, he smudged away the last remnants of the bronze gloss she painted upon her lips. "You wouldn't wear this color. It's too innocuous. Your mouth needs a deeper hue, earthy. Hot. You know this."

"I can choose my own—"

"Shut up," he said quietly. "I don't want to hear another lie from you. From your mouth. When I kiss you this time, I want only the truth between us."

Inexorably, Gabriel drew her to him. Desire fisted inside him, demanding he take. Still, he denied himself speed, wanting only to savor. Mysteries caught him this way. He peeled away at layers, at a leisurely pace. Eventually, he would get his answers, and he would enjoy the journey.

A breath sighed out between them, and he breathed deep. It told him of need. Of craving. Her sigh, he had to believe, was the truth. Needing to be convinced, he closed the distance between them. As his lips met hers, a broken moan rose between them.

He couldn't tell whether it was him or her.

In the next instant, he didn't care. The kiss thundered through him, hard and fast, though his mouth barely moved. Then her lips parted, and he could do nothing but sink inside. Exploring, he found the serrated edge of teeth a spur, the satiny tongue a revelation. It danced with his, and he dragged her closer, diving inside. Soft, wet, perfect, her mouth met his every thrust, parried with delight. Flavors so exotic they could only be called Erin burst inside the kiss, and he reveled. Turning her, he pressed them together, not daring to separate.

Erin felt herself falling. Tumbling, she thought dazedly, into nothing. Into everything. As she searched his mouth for safety, she found only danger. A stunning, seductive danger that called out to her. Demanded she join. Heat suffused her, and she could only reach out for anchor. Unable to not, she stroked her hands along the chest that loomed over her, across the broad back that tempted her. When the feel of cloth tormented, she searched for more.

Her hands skimmed along beneath his shirt, and Gabriel arched with pleasure. He rewarded the discovery with tender kisses pressed to her temple, gentle nibbles along her throat. Tracing the collar of her shirt, he pushed the wide band aside and traced the bared flesh with warm licks of fire. Down, over her shoulder, the shirt fell, and he followed, unwilling to miss even a taste.

Not to be outdone, she shoved buttons from plackets, eager to feel. To know. When the white cotton fell open, it draped them both, cocooning her from the outside world. Shrouded in the scent of him, Erin tested corded muscle at his neck. Unsatisfied, she nipped at his chest, soothing small wounds with delicate flicks of tongue. He tasted mysterious and familiar. She feasted.

"Who are you?" he demanded, the question a groan. "I need to know."

Erin surfaced. Remembering, she scrambled away from him, until she reached the arm of the sofa. Clumsily she closed her shirt. "We can't do this now."

"Now," she'd said. Not "ever." Hearing the promise, even if she didn't, Gabriel sat back against the opposite arm. His blood beat hotly in his veins, but he kept his unsteady hands to himself. He didn't like the feeling that if he continued to touch, he would want to take. "Fair enough."

The simple agreement threw her. "I don't understand you." She fumbled the buttons into place.

With a harsh laugh, he reached out and gently rearranged her collar. "Liar. You do understand me. And it's scaring you to death." Retreat won more wars than people realized, Gabriel thought. He'd pushed her as far as he could without breaking one of them. Instead, he twisted on the sofa and lifted his file and hers. "Have you made any progress on the profile?"

Erin inhaled sharply. Her pulse might be pounding, but she could be clinical. Detached. She'd explain the profile and the desire would go away. It had to. She lifted the photograph of Julian, the implications suddenly clear. "Julian's murder was the trigger." When Gabriel frowned in confusion, she explained. "The first murder was emotional, but it gave him the rationale he needed. He wanted vengeance, and he found satisfaction in hurting Julian. But his ego needed more. It had to be complicated. He had to convince himself that it was part of a larger plan."

Gabriel picked up the thread. "So he researches his victim and finds out he's an architect. He has asphyxiated an architect. Straightforward. Simple, really. This one was the one that determined what became his calling card."

"It took him ten days to find the next victim. He wanted to draw attention to his crime, but he knew it would be a while before the links were made. I closed on the condo a couple of weeks later."

"At the bank?"

"No," she answered. "I did most of the paperwork electronically."

"From here?"

"Here and from the office. That's why I didn't remember Mr. Singleton. We never met." She lifted the loan contract. "I mailed in my paperwork, after I signed it."

Unable to sit any longer, Gabriel wandered over to the window. "But someone knew he was your loan officer. The banker. Bludgeoned. Again, simple clues, but not dispositive until someone noticed the pattern."

"Now he's in the thick of it. Two dead bodies. Neither kill is spectacular, though. With number three, he wanted to demonstrate his cleverness and his education. He used an obscure Middle French spelling and the cultural knowledge of a native dance to make his association." Another thought clicked. "Maggie was G because he was watching me and her. The wire, the violence of it, it was about emotion again. Rage that she could show me kindness."

Gabriel heard her voice break, could hear the coating of shame. *Not yet,* he thought. *You won't get her yet.* "D and F are missing."

Looking up, Erin nodded. "I know. Without access to police files, I can't make the connection."

He dug in his pocket for his car keys. "That's where I come in. I'll get you inside the police station. We can locate the files from the right time periods and see what we find."

Then he jerked her close, and his mouth closed over hers in a searing kiss. When neither could breathe, he lifted his head. "Be ready to go when I get back."

Sylvie Iberville motioned in her late-afternoon visitor. "Look who finally decided to stop by. Been too busy stirring up trouble to return my call?"

Gabriel ignored the chair to lean against the filing cabinet, long legs crossed at the ankles. "Something like that. How are you?"

"Fit to be tied. And you?" Sylvie answered as she settled into her chair, stifling an angry sigh. Men like Gabriel Moss tripped the heart and accelerated the pulse. But they rarely stood still long enough to grab hold of. In her younger days, Sylvie had enjoyed a brief romance with Lincoln Moss, Gabriel's daddy. Then Lincoln had met her best friend, Nadia, and Sylvie became an aunt to their two kids. Still, one look at Gabriel reminded her of a young Lincoln and a time she'd never forget.

"Don't be mad at me, Sylvie. Who else can save the world and make the best beignets outside Café du Monde?"

Boy had always been a charmer, working his way around justified anger. She could feel the heat settle, but she wouldn't smile at him. "Better, boy. Mine are better."

"Absolutely right. I'm obviously an idiot."

"You won't get an argument from me today."

Gabriel had the grace to look sheepish. "You're angry about the article."

"Damned right I am. More's to say, I'm mad that you'd write a piece like that without talking to me first. We have enough real killers prowling the town without you starting a panic about a serial killer." She fixed him with a stern look. "You owed me a heads-up, at least."

Like a schoolboy, he tried to worm his way out of trouble. "I heard you tell her you didn't think she had a case."

The anger that had begun to fade flared again. "You eavesdropped on my conversation, boy?"

Recognizing quicksand when he stepped in it, Gabriel said, "I fouled up. I should have talked to you first."

Sylvie huffed. "Damned right. We've been fielding tons of calls because of your stunt. Captain's been all over me to find some reason to arrest you."

"It wasn't a stunt." At her raised brow, he corrected, "It wasn't *just* a stunt. I believe that there is a killer out there who wants to harm Erin. Five have already died that we know of. I need to find out about two other possibles. Any chance you'll let me look through the homicide files for our next installment?"

"Can't do it," Sylvie said. "Orders from the captain. The official line is that it's a crazy woman's story without an ounce of truth. After she ran, I took her theory to the top. No dice."

"You explained what she received? The note? The obituaries?"

"I did. Captain Sanchez didn't bite. Your friend said the murderer had killed Phoebe Bailey who danced in the Quarter. Evidence points to one of her more enthusiastic clients, who followed her to her job at the menagerie. A john strangled her, not a serial killer."

Gabriel shook his head. "I heard enough from Erin to start following my nose, Sylvie." Gabriel took the three steps to Sylvie's desk and bent close. "She's on to something. And he's coming after her. Let me take a look at the homicide files from the past few months."

"I don't want any trouble, kiddo. You start writing about this like it's real, and the loonies will really go over the bend. Copycats and whatnot. Plus, the captain will have my badge."

"Or I can dispel the theory. Give us four hours, Sylvie. Please?"

"This could get me in some deep trouble, Gabriel. Bad enough if I let you in, but you want to bring the doctor?"

"I'll make you a hero, Sylvie. You know I won't let you down. That's why you love me."

Sylvie grunted. "I love you 'cause you're the spitting image of your daddy. And 'cause I promised Nadia I'd look after you."

"And you've done an excellent job."

She considered her options, which weren't many. If she ignored the possibility of a serial killer and more died, she'd have to live with that for the rest of her life. That would be harder than unemployment. "I get first look at what you find?"

"Absolutely."

Sylvie studied him, weighing the possibilities. She could say no, and Gabriel would simply find another person to get him his information. Or she could say yes and maybe make the biggest collar of her career.

"Tonight. Nine p.m. If you're a second late, boy, the deal is off."

"Gotcha."

"Then get."

CHAPTER 14

"Come down, Erin. We're going on a trip." Gabriel leaned against the apartment building's redbrick sidewall and spoke into the intercom.

"I'll be down in a minute," came the quiet response.

He could hear the hesitation in her voice as it emerged tinny from the metal box. More subtle was the undertone of defeat. He wouldn't allow her to cave in, Gabriel thought, to let a madman win.

Alert, Gabriel turned as Erin pushed open the lobby door. She stopped and double-checked the security plate for the red light to indicate the door had locked behind her. She'd changed clothes from earlier, he discovered quickly. The oversize outfit had been replaced by slim-fitting black pants, black shoes, and a black T-shirt that snugged over generous curves. The silky ebony hair he longed to dip his hands into again had been confined once more, but this time into a tumble of curls secured at her nape.

The transformation was breathtaking. When he realized he'd been holding his own, he forced himself to speak. "You look like you're ready to scale walls or break and enter."

Pausing beside him, she said, "I decided I should dress for anything." She reached the derelict Jeep and lifted the handle. Once. Twice. After the third failed attempt to open the door, she shot a glance over her shoulder at an attentive Gabriel. "I assume there's a trick to the door?"

Gabriel pushed away from the wall and ambled forward. Around him, night had settled over St. Bennett, but the lamplight splintered golden over Erin's sexy face. The arched brow spoke clearly of her disdain for his vehicle. He jangled the car keys gripped in his hand beneath her nose. With deadpan delivery, he explained, "A trick to the door? Well, unlocking it seems to help."

Erin bit back a retort and tried to step aside to give him access. Simultaneously Gabriel moved closer and reached past her to the lock. His arm caged her between him and the frame, and their bodies brushed for an interminable instant. Then the key turned easily in the slot and he opened the door. When he grasped her elbow to help her inside, she started at the touch.

Heat radiated everywhere, reminding her of their earlier embrace. Spice and sandalwood teased her senses and she remembered the piquant flavor of his kiss. The strength of his arms arching her into him. Forcing herself to ignore the cascade of sensation, she slid quickly across the cracked leather seat, snatched the seat belt across her shoulder, and primly folded hands that itched to touch in her lap.

Giving in to the appeal of Gabriel Moss was a mistake she did not intend to repeat.

He closed the door and circled the bonnet. Once inside the Jeep, he echoed her movements. The engine roared to life with a rumble of sound. Plumes of smoke spurted out behind them, and the smell of gas and carbon monoxide seeped inside.

"I don't think I've really noticed your car before." Erin looked dubiously around the battered interior. Duct tape stretched in patches across the seat. Plastic peeled from the console and, if her eyes didn't deceive her, dental floss held the radio faceplate in place. "Does it pass emissions tests?"

"Her name is Betty and she's as trustworthy as an old hound." Deciding not to take offense, Gabriel deftly levered the gear into drive and headed toward the Eighth District Police Station. Betty purred, then coughed. He fed a little more gas, and the coughing subsided. The Jeep gained speed as he whipped through the thoroughfares that separated neighborhoods from the center city. "I talked to Sylvie. She'll let us look at the homicide files."

"Exactly how close are you?" Erin's tone left little doubt about her thoughts on the matter.

Gabriel chuckled softly. "I've known her since I was a baby. She was my mother's best friend."

"Was?"

"Gen and I lost both our parents last year."

"I'm sorry," she offered awkwardly. "I didn't know."

"I still miss them. They were remarkable. Strong, sturdy. Mom had the business skills. Dad was a dreamer. They met at the *Chronicle*. Mom ran the ad department, and my father edited the arts section. Somehow, he became the managing editor."

Companionably, he covered her hand, toying absently with her fingers. She didn't pull away. "Like father, like son."

Gabriel smiled, watching the road. "Not quite. Dad enjoyed the pace of New Orleans. The familiarity. Tourists flowed in like flotsam, but the real people of the city were his favorites. I preferred to roam. Had notebook, would travel."

"Did they mind?"

"No. They clipped every article. Kept a scrapbook. One on me and one for Gen."

"Your family sounds lovely."

"I miss them." Shaking off the melancholy, he stopped at a red light and asked, "What about you, Erin?" He wondered if the reticence was the result of a cold, isolated upbringing. Or maybe a tempestuous marriage ended by bitter divorce. "Where's your family?"

It was astonishing to see the shades fall over the toffee-colored eyes, any trace of expression banished.

"I don't talk about my family," she said evenly. Calmly she removed her hand and folded her arms across her chest. Out of his reach. "Detective Iberville believes me?"

"Where did you go just then? When I asked you about your family?"

"Did you tell her about the second note?" Erin replied stubbornly.

"Erin Abbott as Athena." At her quizzical look, he went on, "Popped into the world fully formed. No parents, no past. Except that a killer wants you dead and I know you came from somewhere."

"For tonight, Gabriel, please just leave it alone."

He watched the road ahead with his mouth thinned. "I've taken a great deal on faith here, Erin."

"I didn't ask—"

He cut her off, anger boiling over. "No, you wouldn't

ask, would you? But you do need. You need friends, you need protection, and you need help. And I don't have any choice but to give it to you. Because he will kill you if we don't find him first."

The truth hung between them, and he decided she would have all of it.

"I'm falling in love with a woman I barely know. A woman with a secret in her past so terrible, she can't allow herself to live." He skimmed his eyes over her profile for an instant, hoping to see some response. Some sign that he wasn't falling alone.

Through the windows that never quite shut, he could hear the first beats of the nightly party unfolding on Bourbon Street. Sultry trumpets dared hard percussion to perform the rhythms that coursed through human veins like heady wine. The same rhythms called out to him from Erin, he knew with absolute confidence, but she was having none of it.

"I have nothing to offer you, Gabriel. That is the truth."

Methodically he curled his fingers around the steering wheel, easing the violence coursing through him. Because, beneath her icy rejection, he heard the longing. It was reflected in the way her muscles melted like wax beneath his touch, the way her husky voice caught.

But, regardless of their connection, a more sinister song played its cadence to her.

He had every intention of learning its history.

In silence, they rode the remainder of the distance to the station, each occupied by thoughts of the other. Gabriel parked in the police officers' lot and killed the engine.

"This lot is restricted," Erin felt compelled to point out. "Police only."

Gabriel shrugged. "They won't tow me. They know my car." He led her inside the station and was greeted by the on-duty desk clerk. The young man pointed to the secured entryway. "Jeep's out back, Calvin. Make sure it stays, will you?"

"Sure thing, Gabe. Detective Iberville said to send you on back."

Erin trailed behind Gabriel as he wound his way through the cacophony of the floor. Criminals and police alike called out friendly greetings, which he cheerfully returned. A particularly attractive lady of the night cooed with pleasure at the sight of him.

He halted beside where the woman, who appeared scarcely out of her teens, sat in a folding chair beside an officer's desk. Bending, Gabriel gallantly kissed the slim hand she offered. Ugly bruises marred café au lait skin stretched taut over fleshless bone. "Lindy, love, what happened to the job as a stenographer? I thought we'd gotten you fixed up with Jim Anderson's shop."

"Nine to five isn't really my thing, you know." She dropped her head to stare at gold sandals, one missing a heel. The short cap of curls left her neck bare, and Erin started at the sight of finger marks around the slender throat. "Plus, Donovan didn't like my change of occupation."

"Did he do this?" Gabriel tenderly brushed at the purpling welts across her jaw. "Where is he?"

"Mr. Donovan is in lockup," Detective Sylvie Iberville, who had joined them, explained. She covered the hand he'd fisted out of Lindy's sight warningly. "He'll stay there if Ms. Nicollo decides to press charges."

"How about it, Lindy?" Closing off rage, he knelt beside

the girl, bringing their eyes level. "We talked about this. You can't let him treat you this way."

Defeat glimmered behind tears she was too tired to shed. "I don't deserve no better, Gabe. It's not like I'm gonna find a man like you." The self-mocking laughter shook narrow shoulders. "Like Donovan says, I'm his."

Echoes of Nathan's tirades filled Erin's ears. She'd listened and believed. For too long.

"No, you're not." Erin bent at the waist, her words sharp and insistent. "No one owns you. You are nobody's property."

Lindy cocked her head and sized up the lovely young woman wearing real sapphires at her ears. The sheen of class was almost blinding, and one look at how Gabriel watched her made Lindy ache with longing. Here was a woman who'd never had to scrounge for a meal or a man. Envy rippled through Lindy and she asked bitterly, "What do you know about it, lady?"

"As much as you," Erin replied quietly, staring at Lindy's angry, battered face. She missed the looks exchanged over her head and the dangerous sparks in stormy eyes. Her only thought was rescue. In a low voice, she spoke only to Lindy. "He tells you you're nothing without him. That you'll die without him. And when you try to leave, he finds you, doesn't he? Hauls you back inside and punishes you for trying to leave." *Until you don't think there's anywhere else to go.*

Lindy cradled her throbbing cheek in her hand. Tears pricked eyes that hadn't cried in too long. "So? I owe him. He made me."

"He made you a whore." Lindy flinched at the description, and Gabe moved forward in protest. A single glare from Erin stopped him. She knew every word she spoke to the battered girl risked exposing her secret to Gabriel, but once more, it was about choices. Someone had to make Lindy see hers, to loan her the courage to decide what she wanted from her life.

"He made you a whore," she repeated. "But you're better than that."

"What? Being a typist for some lawyers who'll make fun of me?"

"No. By being a woman who can take care of herself."

"What do you know?"

"I know Gabriel is a good judge of character, and he sees something in you. Sometimes, we can't trust our own vision. We have to see the good another sees in us." Like Sebastian had done for her. "Gabriel sees the good. Trust his sight until you can trust your own."

Lindy's eyes filled with tears. "I don't know how to do it."

Urgent now, Erin brought Lindy to her shoulder. "If you don't let them help you, he'll take everything from you. Not just your dignity and your courage and your self-respect. He'll take your life, Lindy."

The appeal was muffled against her shirt, but Erin could feel the plea. "But how can I—"

She straightened her arms to hold Lindy upright. "File the report. Let the detective help you. Let Gabriel help you." Erin fished her wallet from her purse but saw only credit cards. Without a second thought, she unclasped the sapphires from her lobes and held them out. "Let me help you."

"My God, lady. I can't take these." Lindy balled her fingers to keep from snatching at the earrings.

"Fine," Erin said. "Then I'll buy your services with them. One," she clarified as she set the stone in the trembling palm, "is for tonight. File the police report."

Detective Iberville interrupted. "You can't buy a police report, Dr. Abbott. It's against the law."

"Then turn around and pretend you don't see us," Erin said. Turning her attention back to Lindy, she swung the second blue drop in front of her. "Bring me a copy of the report to Burkeen University, and this one is yours. Do we have a deal?"

Lindy hesitated.

"Right now, Lindy. Yes or no. Do we have a deal?" The tone brooked no arguments.

The girl nodded shortly, then bobbed her head in quick agreement. "Yeah."

"My office." Erin slid a business card from her wallet. She gracefully rose and extended a hand. Lindy clasped it between both of hers.

"All right."

Detective Iberville motioned to a uniform. "Take Ms. Nicollo's statement and drop her off at home. Move Mr. Donovan to the violent offenders' holding pen." The uniformed officer shifted behind the desk and pulled up a program on the computer. The detective motioned at them to follow her. Erin fell in step behind her, and Gabriel stooped and pressed a kiss to Lindy's cheek.

He followed behind Erin, perplexed. Who was this woman who had collided into his life? The lady kneeling beside the prostitute, sharing a pain he could never comprehend. The contrasts intrigued him. The vulnerability frightened him.

Gabriel breathed deeply and tried to quiet the fury

seething in his belly. Like his next breath, he wanted to find the man who'd put such terrible knowledge in Erin's voice and beat penance from him. But it was too soon to demand answers, though the need snarled inside him. He wasn't sure it wouldn't spill out and maim them both.

Sylvie led them past her office and down a flight of stairs. In the basement of the building, rows of locked doors waited with alarm panels. She keyed in a code at the second door, marked: CENTRAL FILES, and ushered them inside. Overhead, the naked bulb of the file room cast gloomy shadows, an atmosphere not at all lightened by the nature of the room's contents. Organized by date, open homicides stood sentinel in silent rows.

"You've got two hours, Gabe. I'm off at eleven-thirty."

"Gotcha."

"And everything stays down here. Take notes but nothing else," she warned.

"It was one time, Sylvie," protested Gabriel. "And I brought it back."

"Nothing leaves here, Gabe." With that warning, she exited the room, locking them in alone.

CHAPTER 15

Gabriel set his bag on the single table in the room and surveyed the space. Years of hunting through these files made delegation easy. "I'll pull the files on the murders we have. Take March," he instructed, pointing at a wide horizontal cabinet four stacks deep. "Look for the missing murder victims. The files contain police reports, photos of evidence, and miscellaneous information. Because most of it is on computer now, they use these files as backup only." He met her eyes for the first time. "You did good with Lindy. Thank you." Then he walked over to his cabinet and began to read.

Erin exhaled, not ready to answer questions about what she'd revealed in the bullpen. Instead, she pulled her assigned drawer open and began thumbing through the maroon folders. Thirty minutes later, she was no closer to finding their answers. Frustrated, she asked, "Can't we get access to their computer system? This is archaic."

"This is as good as it gets. Sylvie's taking a huge risk letting us come down here."

"Why? She doesn't believe me."

"Not yet," he acknowledged. "Which is why we have to work down here. The captain doesn't buy the story, either, and she's under orders not to be cooperative."

"Why is she taking the chance of getting caught?" The idea of such a sacrifice seemed alien to Erin. "What changed?"

Gabriel's sly grin, which she was fast learning to distrust, cut through the badly lit space. "You have to know how to sell a story, darling," he drawled. "And I do."

Erin snapped the folder shut and moved on to the next cabinet.

Swigging from the can of Coke resting atop the black steel, Gabriel studied Erin. She worked hard. In seconds, she skimmed reports and moved ahead. He might have suspected she wasn't really reading, but for the tiny wrinkle that appeared on the smooth forehead when something struck her as odd. Then the quick, lustrous eyes would narrow in concentration.

While he watched, she propped a negligent hip on the conference table, which dominated the center of the cramped, airless room. Black pants bagged at the waist and revealed a strip of creamy skin. Angling for better light, she flipped through the pages of the police report, and the black cotton top rode higher as the waistband dipped lower. The slow striptease of inches of flesh mesmerized Gabriel like he was a randy kid. Passion flared in silver heat, so blistering, it would have shocked Erin had she turned.

When she absently yanked the shirt down, he grasped

slickly at control and forced his attention to the report in his hands. Hands that were not quite steady. Desire hummed over his skin, punched his gut, scrambled his brain whenever he was within arm's length of her.

Not since his return to New Orleans had a woman called to him, blood to blood. Whether she liked it or not, fate intended Erin Abbott to be his.

Soon, he decided, as hunger coiled tight and treacherous. *It will be soon.*

"Oh, no." Erin dropped the blue-tabbed file to the table between them and buried her face in her hands.

Gabriel picked up the file. "Officer Rose Young."

"She audited one of my classes. When she dropped out, I assumed she didn't have time to attend." Remorse rubbed her conscience raw. "I didn't call to check on her. All this time, and I didn't bother to ask."

"She was a grown woman, Erin." Seeing the glaze of pain, Gabriel tried to focus her attention. "Why did he choose her? What's the connection?"

Erin forced herself to read the file. "She was assigned to intake. Murdered on March twenty-fifth," Erin murmured, a theory spinning. "The police report says she was mugged."

"'Stabbed,'" Gabriel read aloud. "With a short, serrated blade left at the scene."

Erin pointed to the photo of the weapon taped inside the jacket. "A dagger. Ceremonial. Late twelfth-century China." Nathan had loved Chinese artifacts.

"What's the connection?"

She lifted her troubled gaze to meet his. "Intake at a jail, that includes fingerprinting, right?"

"Yes." He waited a beat. "And?"

A grave sigh preceded her answer. "The Greek word *daktylos* literally means 'finger.' In Latin, the word is *dactylus*."

"And in English, the word becomes the description for fingerprinting."

Impressed by his swift comprehension, Erin closed the file. "Dactylographer. Fingerprinter."

"He's good." Gabriel took the file and laid it on the table. Her chin jerked when he tipped her eyes to meet his. He caught the flicker of horror and wanted to cradle her to him. "You're brilliant. I'd guess you're a bona fide genius."

"I'm responsible." She automatically tugged at his wrist, but he did not release her, as had become his habit. Erin didn't fight too hard, grateful for the warmth, however fleeting. For weeks, for months, she'd been so cold. But when he touched her, heat curled in her belly. At this moment, she needed it. Needed him.

"You didn't do this to her or the others. But you'll find him. Only you."

"I know some words," she said softly.

"I'm a writer, darling. I know some words." Gabriel stroked the dark curls resting along her temple. "You know all of them, don't you?"

"And he's using that to pick who he kills next," she said.

"Their deaths aren't about you."

"He's choosing them because of me."

"His choice. We all make them. Hell, you just chose to give thousands in jewels to a complete stranger. Like it or not, you're here with me because you chose to come. We're not puppets, darling. Human beings act with free will."

"Not all of us," she whispered. "Not all the time. If you've never known you had a choice, how could you make one?"

Gabriel wondered how long it had taken for her to break free. He stepped toward her, and she shifted away. He tried not to be hurt by the reaction, remembering what she'd said to Lindy. "Don't help him by becoming a victim, too. Use what you are."

"What am I?"

"Better than he is." With that, Gabriel handed her another file.

In silence, they read through reports of murder. Finally, Gabriel spoke. "Take a look at this one," he said.

Erin flipped the cover and stared at the photo of a middle-aged woman lying in a pool of blood. Beside her, the same blood drenched a tapered bit of wood. The face tugged at her memory, but in death, it was slack and terrified. Recognition dawned, and her shoulders slumped, overwhelmed. Another face in the crowd she had made herself oblivious to. Another kindness she hadn't noticed, had not acknowledged. "She used to wait for the bus with me. Every Thursday. Told me about the children she worked with at a school. She'd chatter on, but I never spoke to her. I was too busy keeping myself isolated. For all the good it did her."

Hearing the grief that was about to overwhelm her, Gabriel covered Erin's cold hand. "Focus, Erin. She needs your help now. Do you think she's one of them? Could she be F?"

Taking a deep breath, Erin scanned the police report. She read aloud, " 'Mrs. Harriet Knowles. Lived near the college. She was the assistant to the head of St. Ignatius'

Academy for more than thirty years. According to his affidavit, she did everything for him.'" The word revealed itself, but she tapped the picture of the weapon. "I think it's famulus."

"Fabulous?" Gabriel's head shot up. "Did you say 'fabulous'?"

"No. *Famulus*. It's German, from the Latin. It means private secretary or attendant." She examined the date. "Mid-April. It fits. But I don't recognize the weapon."

Gabriel stared at the strip of wood. "It's called a fid. Sailors use it to open the strands of rope on a ship. Or a shrimping boat. He used it to stab her."

Very slowly, she closed the file. "So much death," she whispered. "How can he do it?"

Gabriel fought the urge to console. Right now, she needed to talk, not be coddled. And she needed logic, not sentiment. "You know why. Murder isn't unnatural. It's an innate part of the human condition, whether we like it or not. Gruesome but real."

"I know. But taking a human life tears at you. It can eat you alive."

"Murderers don't care about human life. I doubt they feel a thing."

"You can't know that." Erin thought of that night, the way the gun had kicked and emptied its bearings into Nathan. "Maybe they feel everything. Too much."

"A killer isn't a tragic hero," he chastised. From experience, he knew there was nothing beautiful or lovely about the violence of murder. Nothing poignant in apprehending the brutal, the vicious. "They take something that can never be returned."

"What if they have no choice?"

Gabriel snorted. "I told you. There's always a choice. Sometimes it's not one we'd like to make, but it's a choice." He watched her thoughtfully, then added, "But murder is not the same as protecting yourself. I think taking another person's life can be necessary to save your own."

"Sometimes it's the only way." Indeed, Erin knew it had saved her life. But the police and a jury of her peers would not be as sympathetic as Gabriel. More likely, they would share the killer's blood thirst. "He isn't motivated by self-protection."

"What, then?" Gabriel rose from his seat to prowl. "Revenge, certainly. Rage at those who show you mercy. He's also deeply jealous of your mind. Envious, in fact. Look at the obits he sent you, versus the ones he hid. It's taken us three hours to find the victims. And only because we had to weed through so many files. Once you had the files, you instantly recognized the words."

"He's smart, too." The famulus connection had been tricky, made harder because of the shipping tool. "I didn't know what a fid was. He knew, and all the other words."

"It took him ten days to kill after Mr. Johnson. Time to research. He was ready to kill again, but he didn't know the words. He's very intelligent, but not a genius."

"Not a freak," scoffed Erin as she glanced at the names and dates on the conference table. "And perhaps not a he."

The announcement stopped Gabriel. "A woman did this?" He lifted the crime scene photo of Burleigh Singleton. "He was six-two. Julian Harris was just under six feet."

"I'm not saying the killer is a woman. Traditionally, yes, serial killers are male. But when the motive is revenge or jealousy, the killer targets the same type of victim.

Aileen Wuornos chose johns. John Wayne Gacy strangled young men because he thought they represented the inadequacies his father saw in him. Ted Bundy killed women who resembled his fiancée—women with long brown hair. At the most superficial level, serial killers attack the vulnerable. Children or women are their prey."

"He or she is killing men *and* women."

"The crimes are not sexual for the killer. He kills quickly. No torture, no perversions."

"And that sounds like a woman to you?" asked a dubious Gabriel.

"The murders are clinical, almost dispassionate, except for Julian. He could be a she."

"Damn." Gabriel flipped the cover of the manila folder shut and stretched cramped arms to push away from the low table. He got to his feet, his bones stiff, his stomach growling. He could practically hear the gears turning in her brain. Gears that he doubted ever shut off.

Outside the single narrow window, evening had succumbed to a deep violet midnight, long past Sylvie's deadline. Though she didn't say it, Gabriel could tell that the normally gruff Detective Iberville had relented solely because she'd been impressed by Erin's care with Lindy.

But a murderer was prowling the streets of New Orleans. He glanced over at Erin, but his companion didn't seem to notice or care. Hunched shoulders hovered below her ears, and he understood the concentration. She was determined to find a clue to the person's identity, a predictor for his next act.

Regret flared inside Gabriel as he watched her strong, elegant profile. Death surrounded her at his insistence, since he'd pressed her to continue helping, even after she tried to pull away. Because of him, she'd confronted raw brutality upstairs. It had been caged behind bars and chained to desks, but it was there.

Gabriel stared at her, watching as full lashes swept down over tired brown eyes in an effort to fend off fatigue. She would fight exhaustion, he acknowledged wryly, and she would probably win.

Frustrated by what he read in those simple gestures, he moved to stand in front of her and grunted, "I'm hungry. Time for dinner." On cue, loud rumblings from his belly echoed his pronouncement.

Erin ignored the sound effects and the edict and turned a fresh page in the legal pad. At the top, she noted the case number, the victim's name, and the officer in charge. Detective Iberville had forbidden the removal of any items or even a photocopy. Erin saw no reason to explain her eidetic memory, or that she would only use the notes as filler.

"I said, 'Time for dinner,' Erin." Taking matters into his own hands, Gabriel nipped the file from beneath her nose.

As expected, she snapped her head up and glared. "I was reading that." She stretched to reclaim the file, but he held it high above his head, beyond her reach. A cursory glance at the table height showed Erin that if she scrambled atop its surface, she had a shot. But she refused to lower herself to chase after information she had already memorized. Instead, she did the dignified thing and pouted. "I wasn't finished."

Gabriel shrugged as he strolled to the black cabinet. He opened the drawer labeled MARCH and located the proper date. Sliding the file into place, he shoved the drawer closed with a metallic click. "Now you are." Crossing over to the table, he sat on the edge. "We got what we came for. Time to go."

"You might be through, but I was looking for something," she fumed. The spectacles she'd perched on the tip of her nose slid askew.

"You're not a detective, darling." Leaning in, he used a finger to push them firmly into place. "But you're damned cute in glasses. Makes me want to have you teach me something. A one-on-one tutorial."

The blaze of infuriated heat she shot at him should have melted the glass. "Give me back the file. I'm not done yet."

Gabriel rolled his shoulders in disagreement. "We promised Sylvie we'd be out by now. She only let us stay because I swore we'd leave by midnight."

"It's not midnight yet," Erin argued.

As a gentleman, he declined to point out that it was ten past or that she didn't wear a watch. Instead, he gripped her fisted hands in his and tugged. "Close enough."

Erin strained against his efforts, not willing to be alone yet. As long as they remained inside the dank basement of archived files, she had company, as macabre as it was.

Here a killer couldn't creep into her apartment and leave threats in her mailbox. Here she couldn't be helped by a stranger and lie awake fearing the stranger would be the next to die.

She wanted to explain this to Gabriel but didn't dare. Instead, she did what had become habit around him. She resisted.

"Stand up."

"I'm not ready to go." Erin tugged at her hands,

a now-familiar fight. She tried to ignore the equally familiar sparks. Both efforts met with failure.

Gabriel stopped trying to bring her to her feet, and he allowed their joined hands to drop low. "Do you enjoy fighting me, Erin?"

"Not really." Abruptly tired, she closed her eyes. Her head fell back, as though her neck could no longer support the weight. "I'm tired, Gabriel. I came to New Orleans for a fresh start. To find peace. Not quiet, really. Just peace. And now I'm sitting in the basement of a police station with an investigative journalist trying to find a serial killer who wants me dead." She chuckled, the sound defeated, her eyes still closed. "I don't like fighting, but I don't know what else to do."

CHAPTER 16

"Look at me, Erin." Gabriel made the request quietly, his soothing baritone a balm. Unable to refuse, she blinked heavily and met his expectant gaze.

"Will you trust me? Just for tonight?"

With a tremulous sigh, she nodded.

He helped her stand and draped his arm across her shoulders. They walked to the door, where Gabriel flicked off the light, and then he led them out to the stairwell. Only Gabriel spoke as he told the new shift of cops good-bye.

Erin remained silent, her mind blissfully empty. When he led her out of the building, she barely noticed the strident rock that had replaced the earlier velvety notes of jazz. Strings of colored lights kept the deep of night at bay. Raucous laughter punctuated the swirl of light and sound, but the hazy feeling of relaxation didn't lift. They walked away from the parking lot and along Royal, not quite inside the Quarter. She didn't ask where he was taking her, content for the moment simply to walk.

Giving in to need, she tucked her head into the nook at his shoulder.

Staggered by the trust, Gabriel held her closer. "How do you feel about Italian?"

"Impartial."

The arm draped around her squeezed in punishment. "You can't be impartial about Italian food. That's like not having a favorite football team."

Shrugging, Erin confessed, "I don't."

"I think you've just broken my heart." Lifting his hand, he clutched vainly at his chest. "She doesn't like Italian food or football."

"Before you expire, let me explain," she said, smiling. "I said I was impartial about Italian food. I lived in Rome as a child, and I've never found anything Americans can make nearly as good."

"But football?"

"Could never choose between the Raiders and the Steelers. Franco Harris. Marcus Allen. Who can decide?"

Stopping them dead, he spun her out and bent into a deep bow, doffing an imaginary hat. "Darling, I think I'm in love. Say you'll be a Saints fan, and I'm yours forever."

"Win a Super Bowl and we'll talk," Erin teased.

When he suddenly lunged, she tried to dart out of his way, to no avail. Gabriel swung her up into his arms as though she weighed nothing. One arm balanced her, and she clutched his neck as vertigo struck. He took quick advantage, digging mercilessly into her ribs, tickling.

Erin started and gasped, struggling for breath shortened by laughter. "Stop it, you maniac!"

Gabriel shifted her into a more secure hold and continued punishing her. "Say the Saints are supreme!" he demanded. "All hail the Saints!"

"Never," she retorted. Wriggling in his arms, shaking with mirth, Erin realized how strong Gabriel was when she attempted to retaliate by poking him in his ribs. Her futile attempts met with solid flesh that scarcely moved beneath her touch.

"Sing the song, heretic. *'When the Saints Go Marching In'!'* To inspire, he began to hum the opening bars, then broke into the full song. Soon, passersby stopped and pointed at the madman and his captive as Gabriel high-stepped in time with his off-key singing. *"Oh, when the Saints, go marching in,"* he belted out.

"You fool," Erin giggled, and buried her head in his chest. "Cut it out. People are watching."

Gabriel continued, undaunted by the attention. More captivating was the pleasure gleaming in her eyes. To keep her smiling, he'd do a chorus line, he realized. He'd do anything. For the moment, it meant making a fool of himself as he marched down Royal singing, *"Yes, I want to be in that number."* He grinned down at the lovely woman in his arms and couldn't imagine a more perfect moment. "Sing with me, Erin darling," he crooned, and he carried her off the main thoroughfare onto a dimmer street. The sounds from the Quarter still reached them, but the tones were muted. Here a warehouse had been gutted in preparation for condominiums.

"When the Saints go marching in," she joined in, her creamy contralto meeting his over the last line.

Satisfied, he nuzzled her forehead with his own. Close enough to hear her mutter, "Go marching into last place."

"Heretic," Gabriel denounced. He drew back, watching the satisfied smirk spread across her mouth. "I could fall in love with you," he whispered dazedly.

Abruptly her smile faded. In his arms she struggled once, and reluctantly he allowed her legs to drop. At the same time, her arms stayed around his neck. Gabriel braced himself for the acid retort, knowing he deserved it. He'd ruined a perfect moment by making an insane declaration even he didn't want to examine too closely. He bent low to set her feet on the ground and moved to stand. But the arms around his neck didn't let go. Bewildered, Gabriel met her eyes.

"What?"

"Kiss me, Gabriel. Now."

"Why?"

"Because right now, standing here, I could fall in love with you, too."

"Erin." The name emerged on a wisp of longing.

"Don't let me think about it. Not too long," she begged. Then, unwilling to wait, she pulled him to her. In desperate passion, she pressed her mouth to his. For an instant he resisted, and she started to draw away. A ragged sigh rose between them, and her lips curved into a knowing smile. Oblivious to their audience, her past, his career, she fused them together in a kiss that swept through her like lightning.

He tasted both foreign and achingly familiar, and completely right. Leading, she searched his mouth for answers to questions she didn't dare to ask. Who was he, this man who could make her laugh? What did he want, this man who could steal her secrets and tell them to the world? Who was she, the woman who'd gone to such pains to reemerge, only to risk it all on this—this wonderful fusion of flesh and want and need? She angled her head and swept beyond the cool silk of his teeth to the delightful danger of his tongue.

In silent duel, he battled for supremacy, yearning to give her more. Gabriel dragged her flush against him, reveling in the arc of spine, the instinctive undulation of hips. Needing to see her, he watched as she gave herself to the kiss. In reaction, heat poured out of him, and he could have sworn the air shimmered in the seconds before passion forced his eyes to close.

When his name was murmured between them, he exalted.

In the vestibule on Sunday afternoon, where the congregants waited to speak with the pastor, noise milled through in waves of whispered sound. The sermon had been particularly affecting, cautioning attentive parishioners against the evils of sloth and greed. Given the mission trip to Panama scheduled for next weekend, no one failed to understand the message. Cash or coins were due.

Tom Farnen stood near the dehydrated ficus that welcomed visitors to St. Timothy. He curled callused fingers around the damp green check he'd been holding for nearly three hours. The sum on the crinkled paper represented what would have been the whole of his wages for the past month, assuming he still had a job.

He wasn't surprised when Ms. Rosalind fired him from Newell Bike and Go. For months his work had been shoddy, ever since he had discovered his true vocation.

Blessed be, he received his miracles these days in the merciful arms of Harrah's casino. By the time the slots played out last night, at three in the morning, his two hundred dollars in quarters had been multiplied by the Lord into eighteen thousand dollars.

"Hi, Ms. Abbott." Tom smiled shyly at the pretty teacher trying to slip out of the side door. She'd been the one customer he hadn't neglected. Every two weeks, like clockwork, she brought in her bicycle for service. He rushed to the door and grabbed her arm. "Ms. Abbott!"

"Mr. Farnen." After a brief hesitation, she came inside. Coming to church had been a risk; but under the circumstances, she had decided to chance it. She'd arrived late and slunk into the last pew. No speaking to anyone beyond a cursory nod. No chats with the minister. She slipped her collection money into the plate and planned to sneak out before anyone noticed. Her first thought was to be rude, to pretend she hadn't heard him.

"Haven't seen you around the shop lately, Ms. Abbott. Your bike is due for a tire check."

Glancing around her, Erin said quickly, "I haven't ridden much this week. I think it will be safe for a few days." She tried to free her arm discreetly. "I'll stop by in a few weeks."

Tom wiped his damp brow, the bushy red eyebrows glistening with sweat. She always made him sweat. "Can't be too careful in this heat. Tires could blow out on you."

Desperate to escape, not sure if anyone watched them, Erin bobbed her head in agreement. "I'll be careful, Mr. Farnen." She pried her arm loose and shot out the door.

Tom didn't take offense at her running away. A teacher had to watch who she associated with. Personally, he had a reputation for gathering sin unto himself like a brothel. Just last year, he'd confessed his fondness for Jim Beam and his cousin Jose Cuervo, a fondness that knew no bounds. The pastor had counseled him to helpful sobriety. Of course, when Tom tested himself in the bar of Harrah's last October, he'd resisted drink in favor of the swirling lights and siren sound of the slots.

If he told the pastor his theory, of God's bounty found not in the drudgery of fixing bikes but instead in the soothing darkness of Harrah's, would the pastor chastise him for the sin of gambling? Perhaps. So, to allay his conscience, he'd written out a check for 10 percent of his winnings.

The crowd around the pastor thinned, and Tom inched forward, clutching his donation. The lies to explain his windfall arranged themselves in his head. Unexpected commission? *Wouldn't work,* Tom thought ruefully. He'd never earned a commission in his life, and his laziness was legendary.

Could he claim it was a gift from a dead relative maybe? Good idea, except everyone in the parish knew the Farnen family. No Farnen had left Orleans Parish in seventy years, except his papa for parts unknown.

A satisfied grin spread across Tom's mouth, and he nodded his head. Why wouldn't his papa send him some money? No one needed to know about the casino or the slots or the eighteen thousand. As long as he paid his tithes, surely God would be satisfied.

Minutes later, Tom emerged into the sunshine, a lighter man. It was nearly one o'clock, which gave him time to shower and shave before returning to the leather stool of his new job. As he'd hocked his car last month, he decided to walk the seven blocks to his home. Tomorrow he'd take six thousand to the car dealer and buy a nice little vehicle to get him about town. No reason to buy a flashy auto, one that would draw attention. He needed the approval of no one, except his God, his church, and his slots. A good trio, he figured.

"Help!" cried a voice from a side street near Canal, two blocks from home. "Help, please!"

Filled with a generosity of spirit, Tom turned down the side street. He balled his fists, prepared to come to the aid of the downtrodden. An attack in broad daylight, on the Sabbath no less, could not be tolerated. Disregarding his pencil-stick arms and spindly legs and the fact that a light wind could knock him sideways, Tom charged into the breach, an avenging angel.

"I'm coming!" he called out to the victim, whose cries had stilled. "Where are you?" Tom halted a quarter of the way inside the dim corridor, where buildings blocked even fervent light.

"Here," came the voice, its tone muffled.

Tom turned, and his eyes widened in shock. The gleam of metal blinded him for an instant, and his body shut down. In his mind, he shoved past, ran out onto the street, ran home. In his mind, his balled fist felled his assailant. Legs of iron kicked while fists of steel pummeled. In his mind, he was a hero.

Before the blade cut into flesh, severing artery, freeing blood, Tom imagined himself invincible. The first strike released his bowels and he whimpered in disgrace. A second hit stopped even the sniveling. Bone cracked. It took a third strike, swung heavily toward the fallen body, to break through sinew and skin and bone.

The hacksaw vibrated for an instant. Pulling it free, gloved hands turned it toward the light, fascinated by the patterns of humanity on its blade. *How easily life ended. How precarious.*

The remains of Tom Farnen lay on the ground, head staring up at an awkward angle. Eyes frozen in fear asked the question he had not.

"Why?" as the killer checked the body for remnants of Tom's winnings, the question was asked for him. "Because you helped the bitch. Men, women. We're all the same. We help her, but she doesn't see it. She's too good for us. Men are the most gullible for her type." The hacksaw was placed near his neck. "She is a parasite. A fraud. And what she doesn't understand she destroys. But I will finish her first."

The paper thudded against her door at dawn on Monday, but Erin was already up. The muggy morning had stolen through the bedroom windows she left ajar, waking her from dreams of tall, handsome men chasing secrets. Chasing her. When the face in the dream shifted from Nathan to a shadowy figure, then to Gabriel, she hadn't known whether to keep running or to stop and be caught by one of them and face judgment.

Stumbling out of bed, she went into the living room, where she sat curled into the great chair, sipping tea and trying not to think. Since January, life had been blessedly dull. No stories on the missing Nathan Rhodes. Analise Glover had disappeared, after years of slowly evaporating. If nothing else, she could thank Nathan for giving her the courage to leave. Years as a curiosity to be devoured by scientists and press and passersby had stolen the daring she'd had as a child. . . .

"Let me come, Sebastian," a ten-year-old Analise had whined in the bathroom.

"I've already told you no a hundred times." Sebastian checked the collar on his shirt. Perfect. He looked like a nice young man out for a walk in the park. Then he patted the cards stashed in his back pocket. In a couple of hours, he'd have enough cash for a beer and cigarettes. Barely fifteen, he'd have to ask one of the older boys to buy for him. But since he'd be treating, they wouldn't mind.

Analise read his mind and the telltale pat of his pocket. She folded her arms and tapped her foot. "Take me, or I'll tell your mom that you're gambling in Gramercy Park."

Sebastian blanched and hauled Analise into the bathroom, slamming the door. If his mother heard her, he'd be grounded until Judgment Day, assuming Saint Peter showed some pity. "What the hell are you talking about?"

Tilting her chin up to give him a smirk, she taunted, "I'm talking about three-card monte and blackjack. I've seen you fleecing those stupid people. I saw you in Milan and in London. But I didn't tell. Now, I want to come, too."

"I can't bring a child with me," he argued in a low, furious voice. Part of his anger was at himself. He thought he'd been so careful. How was he going to be a professional snoop if a kid could catch him? Still, he consoled himself, Analise wasn't your average kid. He told her as much. "Plus, you're too famous. All the adults recognize you from that dumb-ass show you did. Queen of the geeks."

Analise flushed. "That was last year. I look older now."

He rolled his eyes. "Look like the same snot-nosed know-it-all to me. The freak-geek." As soon as he'd said it, he wished he could take the words back. Huge tears filled the brown eyes too wide for the narrow face.

She dipped her head and turned around. The slippery knob refused to twist, and she jerked at the door. When it mercifully opened, she whispered, "I won't tell Mrs. Cain."

Sebastian pushed the door closed. "Go put on some clothes, kid clothes," he warned, "and meet me at the fire escape in ten minutes." Gruffly he wiped at the tear that had trickled down her face. "And you're not a freak-geek, okay? Just a pain in my ass."

Nathan's betrayal had reminded her of who she'd once been. Not an experiment, but a woman of flesh and feelings.

Now someone was determined to force her to hide again, to flee emotions and feelings she'd thought weren't possible for her.

But Gabriel also called to her, demanding she come from the shadows. Become the whole woman, filled with desires and longings and wants. To emerge.

She made her way to the front door. The sun had risen fully, and a glance at the clock showed that morning had begun in earnest. She opened the door to the hallway and retrieved the paper from the landing.

Inside, she bolted the door and flipped past the headlines to the *Chronicle*'s obituaries. Tired eyes skimmed over natural deaths, hoping to see only those who had met a timely end. No one jumped out at her.

Grimly satisfied, she returned to the first pages of the news and read quickly through the stale recitations the *Chronicle* pretended were headlines. On the last page, in a narrow column of ink, a local story had made it past the banal national news.

A mechanic had been found murdered on Locust Street, an offshoot of Canal. Her breath hitched. The body had been left to fester, attracting the police only when someone noticed the smell. They suspected a crime of passion, given that the head had been nearly severed from the body.

Erin's hands began to shake. The weapon, the story noted, was a hacksaw. No fingerprints. No motive. Only a wallet identifying the victim as Thomas Farnen.

Quietly Erin wept as she read further. According to a neighbor, Mr. Farnen had recently lost his job as a salesman and had become a frequent visitor to the casinos. "He acted like slots were his job now," the neighbor explained. "He even dressed up, like he was going to work." The police had no other leads. Hoping for more news, maybe information that proved her theory wrong, Erin checked the *Ledger*'s online edition. They, too, carried the blotter item and a quote from a neighbor. Impulse had Erin shifting the mouse to a link for the ABC Murders article that had run earlier. Again she read her words, analyzing the victims, speculating about what had driven someone to murder them.

Through the sorrow, her mind supplied the words that would link his death to the others. That would make his murder the eighth in the series.

Tom Farnen was *H*. Another life had been added to the tally, as the killer had promised. Another letter closer to retribution.

Guilt gnawed at her as she burrowed into the sofa,

staring at the brief recitation of Tom Farnen's final minutes. Eyes closed, she recalled the moment in the vestibule, how he'd been sweetly concerned about her. She'd smiled at him, touched. Had that been the instant when Tom lost his life?

Tom Farnen. Rose Young. Harriet Knowles. *Three new names to add to the roster of death,* she thought. One name she may have been able to spare, if she'd avoided him yesterday.

Even as the distressing thought occurred, she knew better. Farnen had been the plan all along. The killer had known of his new avocation, had known of the trips to the bike shop. He knew her life inside out.

CHAPTER 17

Erin's first thought was to call Gabriel. When she couldn't find him at home or at the *Ledger,* she made a desperate call to Genevieve that proved equally fruitless.

Thinking he may have gone to the police station, she phoned Detective Iberville. A bored receptionist informed her that she hadn't seen Gabriel. Out of options, Erin asked when Sylvie would return. The detective was off-duty until two, and no, she couldn't give Erin her number. If Gabriel showed up, she'd give him the message.

Bemused by her urgency, Erin hung up the phone. She needed to hear his voice, to feel the touch of his hand taking hers. When had he become her talisman? Erin wondered. Before, always, she'd been better alone. Once, in crisis, she'd turned to Sebastian, but only because she was too injured to take care of herself.

It galled her to admit the need tying them together, binding her to Gabriel. More than attraction, he spoke to the woman she wished desperately to become. He saw in her, in a glance, what it had taken her years to see. What she still only half-believed.

He made her want in ways she never thought she could. When the phone rang, she rushed to answer.

"Hello?"

"Dr. Abbott? It's Jessica Dawson." On the other end, Jessica tugged the sheet higher. Behind her, attentive hands tried to distract her from the call. She slapped at him. "I wanted to know if we were still on for today."

Erin took a quick look at the clock. It was already nine in the morning. In the midst of everything else, she'd forgotten to cancel her meeting with Dr. Bernard and Jessica. It was too late to cancel, she decided, annoyed with herself. "We said nine-thirty?"

"I booked the media room for this morning. See you soon."

Too soon. Her mind was whirling with thoughts of murder and unfamiliar feelings. She was scared and confused, in no shape to advise a grad student on a project when she could barely help herself.

With sluggish motions, she turned the taps on in the shower, bundled her hair atop her head. As steam billowed, a glimpse in the mirror revealed what she expected. Bleary-eyed, she looked exhausted and anxious. How was she supposed to function when every person she touched could be in danger?

It hit her then and she gasped with the comprehension. The fear that crept into her dreams at night, the answer to the puzzling dream with Nathan and Gabriel and the killer.

"Why didn't I see it sooner?" She braced herself in the stall, the tiles slick against her clammy skin.

Nathan was the life she'd fled. Gabriel was the promise of what she could have. But turning to Gabriel meant the killer would follow. Her only choice was to run again.

No doubt, it was what he wanted from her. To chase her so deep inside herself, she would be easy prey.

"He won't win, Analise," she murmured. "We won't let him."

"By crossing disciplines, psychologists can better evaluate the data and advance new theories of criminal behavior." Jessica dimmed the slide on the screen and signaled for the lights to come up.

"Good work," Erin commended as she forced her thoughts back to the presentation. "I like your interdisciplinary approach. You have a great command of the intersections of social theory and criminology. I thought I heard threads of cognitive science in there."

"I have a number of friends in the field, Jessica. I mean, Ms. Dawson," Kenneth said. "Please stop by my office and I will give you contact information."

Jessica nodded. "Do you have any other suggestions, Dr. Bernard?"

"I . . ." He cleared his throat and loosened his tie. "I do think you are glossing over too many fields of study to reach your conclusions."

To Erin, he appeared to be flushed. Throughout the presentation, he'd been restless, squirming in his seat. More than once, he'd relaxed, only to start suddenly. Concerned, Erin watched him closely. "Are you feeling well, Kenneth?"

"Fine. I'm fine," he snapped. He readjusted his position and yelped in pain. When both Erin and Jessica stared at him, he demanded, "What are you looking at?"

"You were speaking, Dr. Bernard," Jessica prompted.

Clearing his throat again, he said, "I was saying, you need to narrow your focus. You'd do well to pay more attention to sociolinguistic studies, if you intend to focus on criminal communications with society."

"Sociolinguistics? Excuse my ignorance, Dr. Bernard, but what is that?" Though Jessica posed the question, Erin could feel her heart race.

Kenneth answered hastily. "It studies the interaction between language and the social life of a community. Criminals and words." He coughed lightly. "It could be useful."

"Absolutely, Dr. Bernard." She jotted down the suggestion. Catching Erin's eye, she asked, "Dr. Abbott, do you know anything about linguistics? Since Dr. Bernard is leaving town, I'd like to learn more before I make calls. Could you help?"

"I don't know much about the field," Erin lied evenly. "But I'm sure we'll find someone." Eager to be away where she could think, she stood, shook Jessica's hand. "I'll be in town all summer. Please be sure to check in with me twice a month, to alert me to your progress."

Jessica thanked them both and left the room. Before Erin could stop him, Kenneth hurried out, muttering about a plane to catch.

"Kenneth, we need to talk about Jessica," she called out after his retreating back.

He waved a dismissive hand, refusing to turn around. "I'm sure you'll take care of it."

Undeterred, Erin chased after him and caught him in the

lobby. She scooted in front of him, blocking his path. "This is important, Kenneth, and we should have discussed it earlier. Jessica is a second-year Ph.D. candidate. I'm worried about her moving ahead on her dissertation topic before she's completed her course work. Don't you think sociolinguistics is a tough subject to tackle so early?"

"She's quite ready." Kenneth shifted impatiently. Then he frowned. "I thought you weren't familiar with the subject."

Erin dipped her eyes. "I've done some reading, but not enough to guide her." In the light of the lobby, she noticed something she hadn't earlier. Kenneth's normally crisp pants were creased and crumpled, as though he'd slept in them. Running her gaze over him, she noted that the shirt he wore had the same look of dishabille. "Kenneth, what's going on?"

He flushed again. "Nothing. I'm in a hurry, Erin. If you can save the third degree until I return, I would appreciate it." With a brusque nod, he brushed past her. "Ah," he muttered, and continued out of the building. To her, it appeared that he favored his right leg.

Erin stood in the lobby, flabbergasted. The unflappable, impeccable Kenneth Bernard looked as if he'd slept in his clothes, and the chair of the department wasn't concerned about a student's progress.

Was it coincidence, Erin wondered, that Kenneth had recommended a field that studied the ties of language and crime? She hadn't thought to mention it, hadn't seen the place where it fit. Admittedly, she'd been less than alert through the presentation, but the topic seemed too convenient.

A signal, perhaps? One so subtle, he thought she wouldn't hear it?

She wandered to her office, replaying their exchange. There was something she was missing, something important. But she couldn't be rash. Not if the suspicion percolating in her mind had any grounding in the truth. Erin needed to go to her apartment and review her notes.

Jessica sat at her computer, printing. "Résumés," Jessica explained. "I got a lead on a couple of summer positions in Atlanta. I'm applying late, but I think I've got a shot."

Trying for normalcy, Erin lifted one of the résumés on fancy paper. "Let me know if you need a recommendation," Erin said as she signed off on her grade sheets. Jessica had already sent the grades to the registrar electronically, but this provided a paper trail. As calmly as possible, Erin asked, "Jessica, did you notice anything unusual about Dr. Bernard today?"

"Not really. He always seems kinda spacey, you know? Too good for this world. He should really loosen up." Jessica paused. "Is there something wrong?"

Erin smiled reassuringly. "Not at all. I was just wondering."

"Dr. Abbott!" The breathy, histrionic voice barely preceded Harmony's arrival. "How could you?"

Not now, she thought. Aloud, she asked, "How could I what, Harmony?"

"Give me a D? If I don't pass, I can't go to Greece." She whined, "All the sisters will be there but me."

"You should have thought of that before you turned in your final paper, Ms. Turner. When I added the grades for your paper and your last test, I was hard pressed not to give you an F."

Harmony's eyes welled with tears. "I tried so hard, Dr. Abbott. I really did."

"I'm not changing your grade, Harmony." Erin had no time to argue with her. The theory playing out in her thoughts was fast becoming a conviction. Once again, Harmony would benefit from a murderer's madness. To shoo her away, Erin said quickly, "I want an essay in my e-mail by tonight on the proper technique for profiling serial killers. One minute past midnight, and you keep the D."

Erin wasn't prepared for the bony arms to wrap around her or to be crushed into a sea of perfume. She awkwardly patted Harmony's shoulder. "You should get to work."

Harmony spun on a teetering heel and rushed out of the office, already on her cell phone to her friends. Erin wanted to rush out as well, but was stopped by Jessica.

"That was nice of you, Dr. Abbott." Jessica gestured to the door. "Hopefully, she won't take advantage of you."

Before Erin could respond, Kenneth Bernard appeared in her doorway. Sweat beaded his brow. "Dr. Abbott?"

Erin shifted away and her pulse jumped. Had she done something to reveal her thoughts? "Yes?"

Kenneth swiped at his wet forehead, his eyes darting around the office. "I ran into Ms. Turner. I hope you agreed to change her grade. We can't afford to alienate Harmon Turner. He's the most powerful real estate developer in Louisiana, and a generous benefactor to the university."

"I gave her an opportunity, Kenneth, but not because of her father." Erin's tone was cool. "I thought you had a plane to catch."

"My flight's not until tomorrow, but I have errands to run," he muttered. "It seems I forgot to bring my wallet. I don't know quite where I may have left it." He stared into the office. "Maybe I left it in the classroom." Turning, he limped away.

Erin watched him go. Erratic behavior, she knew, was often a sign of stress at a breaking point. Odd that he had been so eager to avoid her, as though afraid she would see something he wanted to hide, only to return so quickly. Alone, it meant nothing, but she could see a pattern emerging.

"Finished with the computer," Jessica announced. She shoveled her stuff into a knapsack. "I'll see you in a few weeks, Dr. Abbott."

"Have a good vacation," Erin murmured, distracted by the swirling possibilities. *Hide*. The word repeated itself, echoing, and Erin was chilled by its implications. Tamping down the panic that seemed a part of her, she forced herself to draw the connections. *Find the pattern*.

The killer had followed her from the shadows. The notes, their cryptic contents, revealed little. Even the calligraphy was an attempt at obfuscation. Too ornate to tie to any one person. Before now, when she and Nathan had presumably been in Callenwolde together, she'd had no hint of another person knowing her. In the cellar, on the mountain, he'd concealed himself, watching the world play before him.

He needed the anonymity not simply to protect himself from prosecution, she thought. It was part of his makeup. It helped define him, the obscurity. In New Orleans, he would seek anonymity, yes, but he would also want to be witness to her struggles to find him. For her to be the perfect audience, he would want to be close enough to gauge her reactions. He'd have to know when to ratchet up the tension, when to make the adjustments in timing and delivery.

Where better to hide than an unknown college, protected by status and with access to Erin's every move? He would know that she used the gym membership offered by the university. Most of the faculty banked where Burleigh Singleton was killed. From the shadows, he could have easily followed her to the menagerie or to the museum, seen her standing at the bus stop with Harriet Knowles. Even poor Tom Farnen had been easy prey, a routine part of her life. Rose and Margaret had their own ties to Burkeen and to Kenneth.

From the safety of his position as dean, Kenneth would be seen but hidden, able to act and observe.

Able to kill and not be suspected.

Terror pulsed through her as she thought of Harmony and Jessica. If Kenneth Bernard was indeed the killer, she would need Gabriel's help to reveal him before he got too far away.

Erin's first visit to the *Bayou Ledger* was a revelation. On the main level, reporters bustled in frenzied motion. Fingers typed hurried copy, the soft clattering of computer keys no less hectic than the murmur of voices.

"Can you tell me where I can find Gabriel Moss?" she asked the middle-aged woman who greeted visitors. "My name is Erin Abbott."

"One moment please." She dialed the phone, lifting the

receiver when the line connected. "Gabriel? Dr. Abbott is here to see you." She listened, then replaced the phone. "He'll be here in a moment."

"Erin," Gabriel greeted her quietly.

Dressed in black jeans and a plain white shirt, he should have looked plain. Instead he looked devastating. The quick flare of heat that came unbidden, followed by a disquieting sense that she was safe here, with him.

He closed the distance between them, and she saw that there were shadows in his eyes. Shadows, she realized, only those who cared for him would see. The thought caught her off-guard, and she stumbled away a step. "I left you a message this morning."

"I received it." He took her hand. "Will you come to my office? We need to talk."

Mutely, Erin followed him through the maze of cubicles and wires. When she asked, he explained the computer system that connected the newsroom to international wires and national reporters. The small pool of reporters faced a job expanded to daily online coverage of major stories and never-ending deadlines.

In the background, presses whirred. Gabriel pointed out the Plexiglas that boxed in the upper floors but allowed a view to the lower tiers of the warehouse. The conversion of the warehouse to contain printing facilities had been a gamble for him, but it paid off.

In a few nights, at close to midnight, broadsheets would slide onto conveyor belts and newspeople would mill about, checking for errors and shifting stacks for distribution. And the *Ledger* would publish its first daily edition.

Gabriel tapped Erin's shoulder and she turned fascinated

eyes to meet his. Wordlessly he pointed to the rear of the warehouse, where a bank of offices was arrayed along the far wall. She followed him, and, much as he had at the station, he stopped repeatedly to greet staff.

He cooed over a reporter's newest batch of baby pictures and celebrated with an advertising assistant who had scooped the competition. He remembered every name, had a personal word for each employee. Regardless of status and the obvious fatigue of the staff, one quality marked them all. Loyalty.

Erin marveled at his ability to conjure such a rare emotion in so many, but then she smiled wryly. Hadn't she thrown in her lot with him, too?

Her quiet existence of intentional detachment had become the life of an amateur detective, one on the trail of a serial killer. As dangerous was her transition from an isolated woman to one on the brink of wanting something more. Something heady and forbidden and untried. She wanted to trust him when the only men she had trusted were her father and Sebastian, who was more brother than friend.

And she wanted. With Gabriel, her senses were unbearably keen, her body unfamiliar.

And her heart, she discovered, had expanded to fill with her senses. She was out of her mind and out of her league with Gabriel. Yet she wanted him to know her, to understand her. To remove any trace of the shell of a woman she'd been. If Kenneth really was the killer, together, they might be able to stop him and she could begin living her life. A real life.

He ushered her into the office, unaware of her thoughts. When the door clicked shut, he shaded the glass for privacy. He pulled out a chair for her, dropped into the one next to it. "Tom Farnen was number eight?"

"I believe so. The word is *habitué*. It means one who may be regularly found in or at a particular place or kind of place. His friends told police that he'd been living at the casino lately. He'd lost his job at the bike shop a few weeks ago."

"Killed with a hacksaw. All right." Gabriel reached for his pad. "How was he connected to you?"

Erin glanced up at him, surprised by the clinical questions. In stark contrast to his friendliness with the staff, with her he was all business. Her throat tightened, but she responded calmly, "My bicycle. He did regular maintenance for me every few weeks."

"You saw him recently?"

"No," she answered. "I didn't ride much. I spent most of the time with you. But we attended the same church."

"Oh." The scratching of his pen was the only sound. Finished, he said, "I think we should turn this over to the police today."

"Agreed."

Gabriel rose and crossed to his desk. The tourmaline rock from his father felt smooth against his palm. He could remember his dad fiddling with it when he faced a tough decision.

His decision had been made when he'd heard about Tom Farnen dying in an alleyway. When he realized he wasn't falling in love with Erin, because he'd already gone under. There was no way he'd risk her life again.

The safest course of action was for her to get out of town, a decision she wouldn't like. He sat on the edge of his desk, his legs stretched out before him. "Gen tells me classes are over."

"I turned the rest of my grades in today." The shadows that she saw deepened. "Gabriel, tell me what's wrong."

"Well, for starters, there's a psychopath who wants you dead. He knows where you live, where you work, where you wait for the bus." He dropped the rock, and it clunked onto the desk. "He's been to your church. He's been to your bank. Hell, he's watched you ride horses."

Erin could hear the frustration. "We've been over this already. He's watching me. And I think—"

Gabriel cut her off, jumping down from the desk. Fear for her twisted inside him, rose like bile in his throat. He'd read about Farnen's death a thousand times that day, imagining what worse lay in store for Erin. Unable to hold it in, he raged, "What if he gets you?"

He could see the terror, no matter how she tried to conceal it, because it mirrored his own. Yet, it was the bravery that terrified him. "You need to leave New Orleans, Erin. Tonight."

"No." Erin laid a hand on his cheek to calm him. "I don't run anymore. I don't think I'll have to. I have a theory—"

"I don't give a damn about your theories, Erin. He's killed eight people. Eight. I don't think he'll wait until twenty-six," Gabriel argued, his fingers tightening on her hand. "He's after you. You probably saw him yesterday, and you didn't know it. What if he doesn't fit your profile? What if he gets tired of waiting, of playing games? He'll come after you. Other than locking you in a cell, I'm not certain the police can protect you. And what about the people around you? Will you continue to put their lives in danger while you play Nancy Drew?"

The words sliced her heart neatly in two. "I'm trying to help," she whispered. "I think I've found the killer, Gabriel." She inhaled sharply. "I think the killer may be Kenneth Bernard."

CHAPTER 18

"Kenneth Bernard?" repeated Gabriel. "The pompous ass who heads up the psychology department?"

"Possibly." Quickly she described his behavior. "The pressure is building in him. He's given himself a mission, but it requires too much. He can't maintain a place in both worlds for much longer."

"He doesn't fit the typical serial killer profile. I thought they were generally white men. Loners."

"They are, but there are deviations. Other than skin color, Kenneth shares many of the characteristics." Erin ticked them off. "He's smarter than average. Because of his position, and his naturally fussy tendencies, he's isolated himself from the rest of the faculty."

"You said before, because the victims were both male and female, the crimes could be asexual. Gen's told me about him, about how he interacts with the women at the university."

"He thinks of himself as a sophisticate, and he wants

to be seen as someone who is attractive and appealing to women he sees as his equals."

"Is he?"

"Not really. The limited social contact I've had with him has been uncomfortable. I dismissed it because academics often are ill at ease in those settings." Erin toyed with the silver ring on her hand. "The socially awkward will try to show an interest in a woman but fumble it. As though he's following a playbook, he'll try to compliment a woman to get closer. However, she will sense the insecurity and respond to it instead. She reacts by being nice to him because she doesn't want to hurt his feelings."

"And he thinks it's more," Gabriel summed up. Cursing, he asked, "Has he flirted with you?"

"Since I arrived. I've never been more than polite, maybe a bit friendly." She thought about last week, when he'd cornered her. And their first meeting. At her interview, he'd spent little time on her curriculum vitae. Then she had welcomed the lack of scrutiny, since Sebastian's handiwork went untested. Despite the fact that she had finished her doctorate at Callenwolde, the fake diplomas bore the seal of Gorham University in England.

But the worldly Kenneth had been so impressed by her knowledge of Europe, he'd glossed over the paucity of publications and teaching credentials.

At the time, she'd chalked it up to necessity. The semester had started and they needed a professor.

Now his casual decision seemed like more. "He asked me for a date a few weeks after I started. I declined."

"How did he take it?"

"He was cold for a while." Again his reaction matched the profile. "The man fitting this profile wouldn't handle rejection well," she explained. "Especially from women."

"What is the typical reaction?" Gabriel posed the question, but he knew the answer. "They become angry and sullen. Determined to retaliate."

"Julian. He asked me out just before Julian was killed."

"We need to get in touch with Sylvie." Gabriel punched in her number, fury tangling with alarm. Kenneth worked with his sister. A person he'd pressed into friendship with Erin. He didn't regret it, but he couldn't take chances with her life. He disconnected the line.

"You're afraid for Genevieve."

"Of course. Tell her to meet us here. I'll use another phone to call the police." She gripped his hand. "We won't let him hurt her, Gabriel. Or anyone else."

Half an hour later, Erin sat in Gabriel's office, drinking coffee and listening to Gabriel spar with Detective Iberville.

"That's not enough, Gabe, and you know it," she argued. "Doesn't come close to probable cause."

"You want to wait for another body?" Gabriel roared, slapping his hands on the table. He leaned forward, nose to nose with Sylvie. "He matches the damned profile. He's had motive and opportunity."

"What motive?" She shot a dubious look at Erin. "Dr. Abbott's pretty enough, but the first time I saw her, she looked like a maiden aunt." When Erin flinched, Sylvie muttered, "No offense."

Erin merely shrugged. "None taken. I realize I wouldn't seem to be the type to inspire obsession."

Sylvie heard something beneath the quiet agreement, but she didn't probe. Instead, she turned back to Gabriel. The boy was ready to breathe fire, she thought, just to protect his women. At his instructions, she'd swung by the university to pick up Genevieve on her way to his offices. She was pestering Peter Cameron next door, shut out by Gabriel. "I need more than an amateur profiler and alphabet soup."

"How about eight dead bodies? Eight men and women that Kenneth Bernard has killed? Or do you want to make it nine?"

Sylvie reclined in her seat. A thoughtful hand tapped the album that Erin had shown her earlier. She'd read the profiles they'd added, the composites. "I believe you, Gabriel. I didn't at first, but I do now."

"Then do something!"

"Can't." Sylvie focused on the silent Erin. "No judge in the world will give me a warrant based on this. I can run the notes, but the paper isn't high-quality. You can find it in every office supply store in the city. The handwriting wouldn't tell us much, either. Every crime scene was wiped clean, except for the weapons left there. We've got no fingerprints. No fibers. Not even a stray hair for DNA." At Erin's raised brow, she confessed, "After you left the station the other night, I did some checking. I owed you."

"What would it take to get enough for a warrant?"

"He's gotta make a mistake." Sylvie drummed her fingers on the table. "And fast. If we could lure him out, make him act carelessly."

Thoughtful, Erin rotated the album to read her updated profile. "He would need to feel humiliated, beyond bearing. And provoked. Jealousy and revenge are his triggers. Kenneth must feel that he's been exposed and found wanting. Worse, he needs to feel that his goal is slipping out of reach."

"Goal?" Gabriel repeated. "His goal is to kill you. Which means you should leave New Orleans."

"He'll follow." Sylvie rubbed at eyes that had seen too much. "If she leaves, he'll find her. He's already followed you once, hasn't he?"

Erin weighed her words carefully. When she agreed to let Gabriel show Sylvie the notes, she knew she'd have to explain their references. She could give them enough, she thought, to convince Sylvie. Enough to stop Kenneth without throwing her life away. The connection to Nathan still eluded her, but the rest of the profile fit. It had to be him. "From California. I was in a bad relationship there, and I got out."

"Like Lindy. Did you know him there?"

"No. I'd never seen Kenneth before in my life."

Sylvie read the note aloud. "What does he mean when he talks about the mountains and the cellar?"

Erin met Gabriel's eyes, nausea rising. Still, she kept her voice level. "I saw a man commit murder. In a cellar. I ran away, to the mountains. Kenneth obviously holds me responsible."

"Who died?"

Dropping her eyes, Erin confessed, "I don't know. I saw her body and I ran. I didn't even report it." Red, hot lights. Gleaming flesh. Piercing screams. Nathan standing over the still form, triumphant. Bitter shame coursed through her and she struggled not to tremble. "I left her there. With him."

"Do you know who killed her?" asked Sylvie.

"It wasn't Kenneth." Erin lifted her head. "And I know the murderer is dead."

Sylvie added a background check on Erin Abbott

to her to-do list. For now, though, she could offer some unorthodox advice. "If I have a reason to take Kenneth Bernard in custody, I can work out a way to keep him there."

Gabriel glanced at Erin. He noticed how her knuckles tightened in her lap. She was teetering on the brink, and he realized a puff of air could blow her over. "I'll do a story about him. About how it's come to the attention of the *Ledger* that his name has been mentioned in connection with the ABC Murders."

"That's not true," Sylvie objected. "He could sue the paper for libel and win. You could lose everything."

"I could lose my sister. I could lose Erin. That's enough reason."

Moved, frightened, she turned to Sylvie for help. "He could have known all of the victims. Why isn't that enough?"

"It's just a theory, Dr. Abbott. We need proof." Sylvie simply gathered her bag and stood. "But I'm not here to hear what Gabriel's planning, I don't know a law's been broken. But," she said to Gabriel, "you hurt him and I'll have to arrest you, too."

"I understand." Over Erin's continuing protests, he summoned Peter and Kelly to his office. Gen would come, too, and she wouldn't like what she heard. But his family was at risk. He would do as he must.

Peter fixed Erin with a glare. She hesitated to approach him, unwilling to engage the direct hostility. His dark eyes seemed to measure and dismiss her in a fleeting glance, and he towered over everything in the building, including Gabriel. But where Gabriel was lean and sleekly muscled, the giant was broad of shoulder, a solid mass of cynicism and distrust.

To prove her sense of his hostility wasn't a product of her imagination, he grumbled, "What the devil is she doing here?"

Blindly seeking an ally, or at least a warmer reception, Erin turned to the other person who had come in behind Genevieve. Kelly watched her with curiosity rather than the dark-eyed suspicion emanating from Peter. She bounded up to Erin, who shifted a few steps away.

Kelly paid little attention to Erin's retreat and grabbed her into a friendly hug. "Ignore the office curmudgeon," she warned sotto voce. "He blames you because he actually has to do some work around here."

"Impudent brat," he said in a low, rumbling growl. "You wouldn't know a hard day's work if it walked up and bit you on the—"

"Peter. Kelly. To your corners, please," Gabriel ordered. "Erin, meet my crack management staff. Peter is the managing editor here at the *Ledger*. Kelly runs the business department." He settled into the deep leather chair and clasped his hands behind his head. "I want to run a story on the Web site as a lead for the daily."

"More on the serial killer. You'd better have something about him," Peter said. He kicked the office door closed and propped his shoulder against the frame. "We've carried all the victim profiles. I doubled up with the two you brought in yesterday."

Kelly said, "We've been getting thousands of hits and phone calls from advertisers." Hearing her glee, she covered her mouth in shame. "God, Erin. I'm sorry. I didn't mean—"

"I understand," Erin said, trying to soothe Kelly's conscience. "If the newspaper is going to help find their killer, you need the financial support."

Peter wasn't as shy about the bottom line. "Which will run out if we don't get something new in soon, Gabe. I'm pacing this out, but we're running out of teasers."

"That's why I'm here." Gabriel cocked his head. "We're going to run a big story tomorrow. Make the serial killer angry enough to make a mistake."

"How?" The one-word question came from a suddenly pensive Genevieve.

"We're going to make ourselves bait," Erin answered. "Gabriel will use my profile to write a story that will break his control."

"Desperate times lead to stupid actions," Peter said angrily. He shook his head before Gabriel could respond. "I won't print it."

"That's not your decision," Gabriel said mildly. "The *Ledger* is my paper."

Gabriel rotated his chair toward Gen. She reclined against the sidewall, staring at him as though he'd lost his mind. Perhaps he had, but it might save her life. "The police can't help us, Gennie. Not without proof."

"Your dead body?" She glared at Erin, who squirmed under the accusation. "And hers?"

"I don't like this, either. But he won't listen."

"He wouldn't need to if you hadn't brought him into this!" The accusation burst out of her. Gabriel couldn't walk away from a fight, especially when there was an underdog. Usually the stakes were low, but this could mean his life. And all because Erin had brought a killer into their lives. "The killer is after you. Not Gabriel."

Before Erin could respond, Gabriel moved to Gennie's side. He clasped her hands. "Erin did her best to keep me away from her and this story. But I've never listened worth a damn."

"The killer is after her," Gennie protested. "And you're taking stupid chances because you feel responsible for her. I know the pattern, Gabriel. I've lived it."

When his eyes darkened, she plowed on. "When Mom got sick, you came home to help Dad with the paper. After she died, you nearly drove yourself crazy trying to hold on, even when Dad wouldn't."

"He needed me to."

"No, he didn't. That was your mission. Like protecting me by staying at the *Chronicle*. Afraid I couldn't handle losing Mom and Dad." She leaned toward him, resting her forehead on his. "You make yourself everyone's savior, Gabriel. Me, our parents. Even Peter." She ignored Gabriel's warning look as he pulled back. "Mirren didn't do right by Peter, so you start a new paper and give it to him to run."

Gabriel studiously avoided Peter's narrowed gaze. "I got fired."

"You got yourself fired. Because you think you let Mirren take the paper."

"Dammit," Peter cursed. "I told you I was fine at the *Chronicle*. And, by God, you didn't let them take it. Mirren Enterprises is a media beast and it eats papers for lunch. The *Chronicle* in New Orleans, the *Gazette* in Atlanta. The *Richmond Star*. It didn't matter. Unless you were Rupert Murdoch, Mirren was going to take the paper. He'd already started with your dad, before your mom got sick. You just happened to be at the wheel when we ran out of gas."

"Enough. I've made my decision." To Gennie, he said, "I survived wars and famine and your adolescence. I can do this." When she still refused to relent, he decided he'd give her time. "Erin? You want to tell them what you found?"

"We need to humiliate him," she began, and sketched out her theory.

CHAPTER 19

The showdown occurred at the *Ledger*'s office at high noon.

"I demand to see Gabriel Moss!" Kenneth's shrill order could be heard throughout the converted warehouse. Faces peeked over cubicle walls to watch the drama unfold.

The receptionist pressed the intercom. "Gabriel? A Mr. Kenneth Bernard is here to see you."

"*Doctor* Bernard!" Kenneth shouted. "My name is *Doctor* Bernard!"

Rolling her eyes, she dutifully repeated to the dead air, "*Doctor* Bernard."

Gabriel ambled up to Kenneth, shoulders deceptively relaxed. He thanked Patrice for her help, then took his first good look at a sociopath. They'd met before at university functions that Gennie had dragged him to. Kenneth Bernard wasn't the remarkable type.

But he was the murdering kind.

"How can I help you, *Mr.* Bernard?" Gabriel stressed the title. "Having a problem with your subscription?"

Nearly apoplectic, Kenneth waved crumpled sheets of paper in Gabriel's face. "This is libel, sir. I plan to sue."

"I'm not sure I understand why you're angry. Care to explain?" *Keep him talking,* Gabriel reminded himself. *Kelly should have phoned Sylvie by now. Wait for the signal.*

Kenneth noticed the interested folks watching him, and he tried to calm down. It wouldn't do to disgrace himself in public. No, what he planned to do would be done in private. "If we can go into your office?"

Gabriel smiled pleasantly. "I don't think so."

"I'd rather not discuss this out in the open," Kenneth hissed.

Relenting, Gabriel walked up to him and clapped him on the back. "We can use the alcove." Kenneth's shriek of pain careened through the building. Gabriel quickly drew his hand away. "What's wrong?"

Kenneth had fallen to his knees. There, he bent over, whimpering.

Patrice circled her desk and rushed to his aid. She tried to help him stand, bracing him.

He recoiled at the touch of her hand. "Don't touch me!" Kenneth reared up, shoving Patrice away. She slipped and fell against the desk.

The act of violence was all Gabriel needed. With a single swing, he smashed his fist into Kenneth's jaw. Down he went for a second time. Gabriel stood over him, waiting for another shot. Kenneth surged to his feet and rammed his head into Gabriel's gut. Both men went down. Fists flew, each man landing hard punches. Gabriel stayed down, letting Kenneth pummel him.

To keep him going, Gabriel taunted, "You get off on hurting women, Kenny?" He kneed him in the gut. "Like pushing them around, do you? Makes you feel like a real man?"

Enraged, Kenneth elbowed Gabriel, glancing a blow off his chin. "Shut up!"

Gabriel flipped the smaller man into the alcove wall. The sickening thud had onlookers wincing. He got to his feet and dragged Kenneth up. "You don't have the balls to pick on someone your own size!"

"You son of a bitch!" Kenneth yelled as he charged at Gabriel and both of them crashed through the plate-glass window beside the alcove.

Having arrived just in time to see them fly through the window, Sylvie and her partner pulled the brawling men apart. She wrestled Gabriel to his feet and thumped at his arm. "For pity's sake, Gabriel. Now I've got to take you in, too."

Erin bailed him out a few hours later. Gennie, Kelly, and Peter tagged along, all wanting to see their hero and his mug shot. Disappointed that they'd missed the booking, Sylvie had provided each one with an autographed copy. In the late afternoon, the air was damp with the promise of rain. Tourists packed every square inch of the Quarter, spilling out onto the streets beyond. Music and voices filled the air and dueled with the weather. For now, the weather was losing.

Genevieve broke away from the trio and fell in step

beside Erin, who had faded to the rear of the group. Leaning down, Gennie whispered conspiratorially, "The Moss family has a genetic disorder."

Erin didn't look over. "What's wrong?"

"It's called foot-in-the-mouth-itis. At least, I think that's the Latin name for it."

Refusing to chuckle, Erin kept walking. "Is there a cure?"

With a dramatic sigh, Gen admitted, "Copious amounts of groveling with a smidge of forgiveness."

Erin gave in then and laughed. "You're forgiven."

"Wait, I have to grovel first." Suddenly serious, she placed a hand on Erin's arm to stop her. Gen faced her. "Gabriel is my family. All that I've got left. It's hard, going from a group of people you just know will always love you and be there, to waking up one morning to nothing."

"I understand," Erin said softly.

Genevieve believed she did. Sighing, she continued. "I've seen Gabriel do this before. Take on a problem and make it his. Like he really is supposed to be a guardian angel."

"I didn't ask for his help, Genevieve," Erin said, protesting. "You saw me run."

"Yeah, I did. And I know that once Gabriel decides that he's going to fix something, no one can stop him. Not even those who love him," she added meaningfully.

"I don't—"

Genevieve held up a hand. "Whether you admit it or not, it doesn't matter. But you need to know, Gabriel's in love with you." She dropped her hand, tucked it into the pocket of her jeans. "It terrifies me, because my brother would die for the people he loves."

Erin shook her head fiercely. "I won't let him be hurt because of me. I swear it. Kenneth Bernard is behind bars. They found lashes on his back and thighs, fresh wounds. Sadomasochism is a warning sign in killers. Sylvie thinks she can get a warrant to search his place tomorrow. It could be over by morning."

"So I heard." Linking their arms, Genevieve towed Erin toward the trio that had gone ahead. As they joined them, Gen whispered, "I like you, Erin. I'm glad my brother likes you. But you break his heart and you answer to me."

"What did she say to you?" Gabriel asked, taking in the shell-shocked look. "Damn it, she swore to me she'd apologize."

"She did," Erin replied. Taking a chance, she reached for his hand. When his fingers twined with hers, she smiled. "Don't worry. We understand each other." She looked back at the station. Kenneth continued to deny the allegations, but Erin hadn't expected anything else. She had hoped, though, for some measure of relief. "I don't want to go back," she blurted out.

"Back where?"

"To my apartment. Not yet. I just—I just want to forget for a while, you know? Just for a night."

Gabriel brought her hand to his mouth. "Why don't we ditch the others and you let me show you New Orleans?"

With a slow smile that reminded Gabriel of sunrise, Erin agreed. "Yes, but you have to buy me a beignet."

For the next few hours, Gabriel showed Erin a New Orleans she'd never seen. It seemed to her he knew every priestess, bookie, and charlatan in the town. And they all adored him.

Erin had her palm read, her leaves read, and even her epitaph. Oddly, all of them seemed to involve a gray-eyed man in her future.

"You're bribing the fortune-tellers," Erin accused as they sat down to dinner. Gabriel had dragged her to the dingy little hole-in-the-wall with a crooked sign that promised the best jambalaya in the bayou.

"I can't be responsible for the whims of fate. If they say we're meant to be, who can argue?" He plucked a menu from between the napkin stand and the ketchup bottle. Flipping it open and spinning it toward her, he said, "Prepare yourself for culinary delight. Especially if you have the house special."

"I'll have the house special." As though he'd been waiting to hear those words, a chubby little man bounded over to take her order.

Two glasses of iced tea materialized in front of them. The man spoke to Gabriel in a stream of Creole that sounded like singing. When he grinned at Erin and bent low over her hand, she arched a brow at Gabriel. Shrugging, Gabriel gave the man their orders. As suddenly as he'd come, he disappeared.

Gabriel shifted his legs beneath the table, where they bumped into Erin's. She angled away, but like magnets, his followed.

"Should we ask for a bigger booth?"

"I'm comfortable," he said. "I like seeing you smile."

"I haven't had a lot of practice since we met." Not since she realized a killer hunted her.

"No." He covered her hand on the red-checked tablecloth and turned their hands to rest them palm to palm.

"Stop thinking about it, Erin. You're not to blame for Kenneth Bernard. He's sick."

"I know. At least, I know in my head." Nine deaths. Eight linked to her. She lifted her tea but didn't drink. Determined to keep tomorrow at bay she asked, "Did you always want to be a journalist?"

Gabriel heard a hesitation, and wanted to push. But he saw the fatigue in her eyes and relented. Tomorrow, he thought, he would have all of it. "I'm very nosey. It fit."

"And if you couldn't write? What would you do?"

"Middle linebacker for the Saints," he said without hesitation. "Their defense sucked this year." He reached for his tea, drained it. "What about you? All the kids have all the knowledge they need. What do you do next?"

Before she could answer, their dinner arrived. They ate in silence, knees nestled beneath the table. Later, when bread pudding sat in a dish between them, he asked again.

"I'd travel the world and study languages," she answered softly. "In East Africa, there are dialects that fewer than five hundred people still speak and remember. I'd love to learn them all."

He finished off his tea. "All the languages. To save them."

Not many would have understood. Absently, she slid her glass to him, taking the one he'd just emptied. "Words are vital, yet we treat them so cavalierly."

"Language is malleable. Fluid."

Erin disagreed. "There's a precision to language that we've forgotten. Words have precise meanings. They're not interchangeable."

"Semantics," Gabriel countered, enjoying the fight.

"Absolutely," she agreed. "I'd think a writer would appreciate that it's all about semantics. Words have particular meanings; otherwise, we wouldn't have quite so many of them, would we?"

"Like *passion*? What is its precise meaning?"

Her voice, when she answered, reminded him of smoke. "Passion. Emotions as distinguished from reason. An intense, driving, or overmastering feeling or conviction."

"And *desire*?" Gabriel stroked a long finger down the center of her palm, in imitation of the palm-reader. "Can you see its heart?"

"To have a longing for."

"Come home with me, Erin." Eyes dark and intense, he stood and drew her from the booth. "Say yes."

She met his eyes. Thought of her fate. "Yes."

Gabriel tossed some bills onto the table, dragged her outside to hail a cab. Soon they were at the station where Genevieve had left his Jeep. Tension stretched taut between them, but neither wanted it to end. Not until they could begin.

They hurried to the lot.

Suddenly a scream rent the air.

"The street." Gabriel took off, dragging Erin behind him. A second scream joined the first, and he veered. The next street, he realized. The third scream pierced the air and abruptly faded, as though cut off.

They reached the entrance to the alleyway at a dead run, too late. The crumpled body lay sprawled along the asphalt, a parody of sleep. In the distance, an engine roared to life and headlights flashed briefly when the vehicle turned the corner. Beyond them, the night blared welcome to the all-hours party, the muffled lyrics of James Brown proclaiming that he felt good. Not so for the broken body of the woman at Gabriel's feet.

He spun around and shoved Erin into the alley. By God, he thought, she would not end her night with an image of death. The angle of the young girl's head told the story, but he would check for a pulse.

"Wait here," he commanded.

The minute Gabriel returned to the body, Erin darted around him. "Oh, Lord," she prayed as she sank to weakened knees. "It's Harmony." Quickly, faster than Gabriel, Erin lifted the stiff wrist. The skin was cold, too cold for the vibrant girl she'd seen just yesterday. Though she understood the meaning of the cold, she refused to accept what logic told her. "I can't find a pulse. Gabriel, I can't find a pulse." She bent over the girl's body and pressed her head to the unmoving chest covered in a baby blue tee. The shirt revealed a strip of midriff that did not rise and fall with life. Still, there was nothing.

Harmony couldn't be dead, Erin thought, too sick of Death to give him another victim. Grimly she gently angled Harmony's head and pinched her nostrils. Timing the breaths, she puffed air into the unresponsive mouth, did compressions on the fragile ribs. Nothing. Over and over, she exhaled and pushed, but nothing. *Save her, Erin. Press on the rib cage, then count out the breaths. One. Two. Fifteen compressions, she remembered, then two more breaths. Find the pulse. One. Two. Again. Again. Again. Again. Again. Again.*

Meanwhile, Gabriel whipped out his phone. He hurriedly punched in the emergency number, adrenaline surging. The eternal ringing drew a smothered curse. When the line finally connected, he impatiently barked out information. "Possible homicide. Corner of Royal and St. Inverness. Two blocks from the Eighth District Police Station. Female, approximately twenty years of age. No pulse. We're doing CPR. Send help immediately." The last bit was purely for Erin's sake. He cut the line without waiting for affirmation and dropped to his knees beside Erin.

A closer look confirmed what his earlier guess had told him. The motionless body Erin called Harmony was an empty shell, brain and heart done with their duties. As much to have something to do as to check, he reached past Erin's futile ministrations for the girl's throat. Pale ivory skin gleamed in the garish lights. All the warmth had seeped away, perhaps into the concrete, perhaps earlier.

It was then that Gabriel really noticed the full pallor. He'd spent years in countries littered with corpses. He could identify the complexion of death. Right after death, the human body pretended to hold life near, with the illusion of rosy cheeks and warm skin. Before the onset of livor and rigor mortis, the body looked as if it enjoyed full health. Hours passed before the flesh chilled and the frame stiffened into final repose.

Still, they'd been taught in combat zones to check for proof of death. Gabriel made a tight fist with one hand and then squeezed Harmony's arm with his other hand. The taut muscles resisted his contractions. To be sure, he released his fist and squeezed the unbendable arm again. He'd need to ask the paramedics and the coroner to be sure, but the short fingers tipped with blush pink had lost their grip on life at least six hours ago.

Gabriel grasped Erin's shoulders. "Come on, baby.

Stop it. She's gone." He tried to pull her from the body, but Erin jerked away furiously.

"Move!" she shouted. She leaned protectively over Harmony, prepared to begin her count again. He wouldn't make her go. Wouldn't make her responsible for another death. "I've got to do CPR. I have to save her." It was her fault. The accusation screamed through her, pounded at her brain. Though she hadn't any reason to think the body had been left for her to find, the coincidence was harder to trust.

Fear misted around her and mixed memory with now. The body, cold and still. The ache splitting through her head like shrapnel. His body and the gun. The gun in her hand. She tossed it aside and scrambled to him. Nathan was so pale. Was he breathing? She had to save him. She had killed him.

She searched his cold, familiar body, but there was no pulse. No breathing. No life. Only a bloom of red to match the blood dried on her hand. Red flashed and the screams in her head grew deafening. Louder than the thunder. Brighter than the lightning.

"Oh, God, Gabriel! She's not breathing! Why won't she breathe? What did I do?" She broke into racking sobs, but no tears fell. Gabriel watched in horror as she seemed to turn inward, to a shadowy place where another body waited for her. Over and over, she asked the question: "What did I do?"

Uncertain about how to reach her, or even if he could, he tentatively clasped her shoulder, and behind him, sirens blared. Gabriel's head shot up at the sound. They'd be here any second, and the police wouldn't be far behind. His journalist's eye surveyed the scene. A dead girl, dumped on a street corner at midnight. A broken woman, sobbing out incoherent guilt.

If the police saw Erin in her current state, the odds were good that they'd assume the worst. The scared, wild look, the muttered imprecations, these were the stuff of suspicions and good copy. He had to get her away from here. Holding her firmly, he whispered to Erin, "Baby, the paramedics are here. We need to go."

The ambulance screeched to a halt, and the EMTs descended, hastily gathering equipment. The first person, a solidly built woman with sandy blond hair and a determined look, reached them first. Her badge identified her as Laurette.

She knelt beside the body and began checking for vitals. "Did you call it in?"

"Yeah. We found her here." Gabriel pressed Erin's face into his chest, both to comfort and to hide. "Tried CPR, but it was too late."

"CPR." Laurette repeated Gabriel's squeezing of the dead girl's arm. Looking over her shoulder, she shouted to the second EMT, "Bring the gurney, Jason. She's already in rigor." The look she shot at Gabriel changed from determined to suspicious. "You said you found her?"

"Yes. We were down the street, and we heard a scream. Came running. Found the body. Called it in and started doing CPR." He shrugged. "Then you arrived."

Laurette's partner joined her. The gurney had been unpacked and waited beside him. "What about your friend? What did she see?"

"Same thing." He held Erin tighter. "I need to take her home."

Laurette glanced over her shoulder at her partner. "She could be in shock. Maybe we should take a look at her."

"No, thanks." Gabriel stepped away from the body and the twin set of eyes watching him carefully. "I just need to get her home."

The partner shifted to block his exit. "You gotta name, sir?"

"Gabriel Moss." They stood toe-to-toe, with a quivering Erin between them. The massive paramedic topped Gabriel by at least two or three inches, and only one of them had a terrified woman in his arms.

"You planning on leaving?"

"Yes."

Laurette, smelling the rise of testosterone, edged between them. "The police may need to question you, Mr. Moss."

"Give them my name. They know how to find me." Finished, Gabriel scooped Erin into his arms. One glimpse at the glazed eyes sent a shiver of fear along his spine. He had to get her away from here. Damn it, he thought as he strode past the paramedics, what the hell could he have been thinking, letting her anywhere near the body? She was a freaking academic, someone who knew nothing about the nastiness of death, despite her protests to the contrary. He'd let himself forget that she inhabited an ivory tower littered with theory, not experience. And he'd let her try to save a dead woman.

The lights from the ambulance shirred the sky in white and crimson, its sirens muted. A crowd had gathered, drawn by the excitement. They watched in morbid curiosity as the paramedics confirmed the girl's death. They lifted her to the gurney and shrouded her in white.

Onlookers craned for a glimpse of the deceased, eager to
see the dead body.

.   Gabriel only had eyes for Erin as he crossed Royal.
Her slender body vibrated in his arms like a wire plucked
too harshly. He thought only to shield. Mewling sounds
issued from her throat. He couldn't decipher much, simply a name. *"Nathan."* Shaded with sorrow, the word
tripped over itself in a curse or a prayer.

He pressed her head into his shoulder. Her breathing
was warm on his throat. Emotion moved through him, a
tenderness he could not turn away.

"Gabe? What's wrong with her? Does she need help?"
Calvin, the desk officer, had just come off his shift. He'd
been with the NOPD for nearly six months. He still hadn't
logged any field time, but his detective intuition prickled
at the sight of Gabriel cradling the beautiful woman who'd
followed him into the station a few nights before. No
doubt, her shivering form had something to do with the
flashing lights down the street. "Wanna come inside,
Gabe?" he asked, trailing behind as Gabriel wound between the police vehicles to his car.

"I just need to get her home, Calvin." Gabriel fished in
his pocket for his key and shifted Erin to fit it into the
lock. Eager to help, Calvin grabbed the key, unlocked the
passenger door, and held it wide. Gabriel softly set Erin
inside, his heart twisting at her hushed whimper.

Calvin stared over his shoulder. "Man, she looks like
she's seen a ghost," he offered helpfully. "Hope she
doesn't get sick."

Wanting him gone, Gabriel shut the door and moved to
the driver's side. He climbed into the cab. "Look, Calvin,
there's a corpse on St. Inverness. I don't think any cops are

on the scene." When the rookie scampered down the street, ready to play hero, Gabriel gunned the engine. He peeled out of the parking lot. Aiming his car south, he headed for a place where he and Erin could be alone. Soon enough, he realized, Calvin would piece together his presence at the scene, and the police would come looking for them.

Before that happened, he would know what demons tormented the nearly catatonic woman trembling in his car. And what in the devil a dead man named Nathan had to do with it.

CHAPTER 20

Weeping willows lined the winding dirt road, their delicate green leaves brushing close to the earth. Trunks grew heavy with Spanish moss, and crickets serenaded with the lazy undulation of Lake Pontchartrain in concerto. Stars dappled the inky sky in glorious bursts of light. Gabriel usually enjoyed the dazzling scenery rushing past his windows. He relished the way the sounds of the city dropped away, as though nature had drawn a shade over the festivities. Out here, the scent of magnolia and musk defeated the smoke and oil of civilization.

In the earlier hours of what had become morning, Gabriel drove out of the city proper and onto one of the narrow, meandering roads that led into the swamps of Orleans Parish, unmindful of the natural panoply spread out along the path of scattered gravel and packed mud.

His singular thought was to get his too-silent passenger to safety. To get her home. That it was his home, rather than hers, didn't matter. All that concerned him was erasing the frozen look of horror from her eyes. The Moss family, like many of the natives, kept what the old folks called hidey-holes near the edge of the swamp. He would take her there and, he hoped, pry from her the secrets she held so close they seared straight through.

Unbidden, the image of a nearly catatonic Erin curled into the dead girl's body swam before him. Impotent rage, redoubled in strength, welled inside and demanded release. Unable to do more than swear ripely beneath his breath, he stomped at the gas pedal, and the Jeep shot forward. Headlights bounced over ruts, bent as they traveled the sinuous road at a clip.

Oblivious to his mood or his plans, Erin huddled against the metal door frame, staring aimlessly at the clear, beautiful night that seemed interminable. Intermittent shivers coursed through her, and she was powerless to halt their passage. The thin blanket Gabriel had tossed over her was gathered beneath her chin. Still caught between waking and nightmare, she breathed deep. It smelled of Gabriel, of strength and sandalwood and comfort.

Nathan had a different scent, she remembered. Expensive cologne, the fragrance of the season, had always been his choice. It had given her headaches, but she rarely complained, learning that complaints would lead to a different kind of pain.

The pain had pounded in her head. She'd been at his computer for hours, finishing the paper for him. Her own dissertation collected dust on the writing table he'd allowed her in the tiny pink bedroom upstairs. But his conference in Italy was in less than a month, and he needed her to finish this paper. She would make any changes silently. She'd learned years ago not to correct him aloud.

He read over her shoulder, his teeth clicking together impatiently when she made a mistake. She tried to type faster. But it was difficult to think clearly when her skull felt as though it had been driven through with spikes.

"Nathan." She kept her voice low, penitent. "I'm sorry, but I can't concentrate. Your cologne. I have a headache."

"Fine." Nathan jerked the chair and tipped it over. She tumbled to the floor, cowered there. He kicked the chair aside. "Get out! Get the hell out of my house!"

At his feet, Analise waited for the blow. Most of the time, it never came. But she couldn't tell. It was better to fear it, to brace for it, than to be surprised. It never occurred to her to run. Even when he told her to.

Knowing she waited for the blow, he held off. She made him look like a fool, altering his theories and changing his words. It didn't matter that he forced her to write for him, that he hadn't written a paper on his own in nearly a decade. All that mattered was that she laughed at him when he wasn't around. She thought him beneath her, that she was smarter than he. After tonight, he'd show her the painful truth. Looming above her, he lifted his foot as though to crush her beneath its tread.

"Leave! Go find someone else who will take care of you. Who'll let you play scholar, let you live off of his reputation."

She didn't protest that it was he who lived off of her. She'd forgotten. Instead, she felt the slippery mix of guilt and gratitude. He'd given her a home. A life. He was her only friend. All he asked in return was a little help now and then. How dare she complain?

He could see the contrition, the confusion. He would use it.

"I'm the only one who gives a damn about you, Analise." He smiled at her gently, lovingly. He helped her to her feet, cradled her against him. Forcing her face against his throat, where he knew the cologne was the strongest.

The sneeze caught her unawares. Angrily, he thrust her away from him, and she tripped over the fallen chair. Her elbow cracked against the steel base, shards of pain radiating up from the bone. Why was she so clumsy? From the ground, she whimpered, "I'm sorry. It's my fault. I shouldn't be so sensitive." Rubbing at her nose, at her arm, she begged for forgiveness. "I won't do it again."

"You're clumsy and thoughtless, Analise. That's why no one else loves you." Once more, he drew her to her feet. He shook her and tossed her onto the leather sofa. Grabbing at her, he dug cruel fingers into her arms. The slender bones shifted beneath the silken skin she wouldn't allow him to touch. "Who else would love you but me?"

"No one," she whimpered, trying not to upset him. "You're the only one who loves me."

"But you won't let me love you, will you, Analise?" Suddenly, he ripped at her blouse. The silk tore, revealing the plain black bra beneath. Desire twisted inside him and he clamped his hand onto one covered breast. "You're a tease, aren't you? You make me want you, but you won't let me love you." He bent down to the creamy flesh. Clumsy fingers fumbled with her pants. "Let me love you," he moaned, grinding his mouth to hers.

"No!" She surged beneath him, desperate to escape. "You promised you wouldn't do this!" After the last time, when he'd tried to take her and failed, he'd broken her arm. "Please, Nathan, don't."

The fist into her stomach stopped her screams. "Don't tell me no! Don't ever tell me no!" He could smell her terror and it excited him. She was his, and tonight, he would have all of her. If he had to beat her to take her, so much the better.

She scratched at the hands that tugged at her jeans, jerked at the head that bit her breasts. The cologne filled the air around her and she couldn't breathe. Couldn't see. Blindly, wildly, she kicked out and connected. Nathan's wail of pain echoed through the room and he collapsed to the floor. She scrambled off the couch and hurried to her bedroom. Barricading the door, she sat against it, bruised and aching. His punishment would be brutal, unless she stayed hidden until he left for Milan. She sat motionless against the door, unable to muster a single tear. His question wrapped itself inside her head. Who loved her?

No one, she thought hopelessly. *They sent me here because they didn't love me. They left me with him.* How could anyone have loved her and left her with him?

The Jeep climbed a steep rise, unexpected in an area known for sinking below sea level. Her face pressed against the window, her eyes fluttered open and she saw that they'd driven up a plank of wood. Curiosity died before she could see that the plank led into a garage. They'd stopped, she noted listlessly. She didn't move, unable to decide what to do next or to care.

Had Nathan told her to stay or go?

Gabriel made the decision for her. He opened the door and bundled her unresisting form into his arms. He bumped the door closed, not bothering with the locks. The aged ramp creaked gingerly beneath his feet, but the concrete stays beneath the treated wood guaranteed their stability.

Crossing to the tall, wide doorway, Gabriel fitted the key to the bolt. A slender beam of fluorescent light greeted him, the result of the hurricane lamp resting above the door. With practiced motions, he flicked on the kitchen lights and carried her through to the main room. He paused at the doorway to switch on the overhead light, but when it didn't respond, he walked into the room, knowing its contents.

His grandmother's wide green sofa dominated the space, its lines worn and comfortably shabby. Colorful quilts made by his Great-aunt Jeanette were stacked in a cherry bin on the left and draped over the antique rocking chair in front. On the opposite side was a gateleg table that had been carved from a felled oak by his father, and its surface held a shallow crystal bowl filled with hardened peppermint candy.

Along three walls, massive oval windows reinforced with treated glass peered out into the depths of the bayou. The central window was fitted to a door and opened onto a wraparound porch. Beneath an ivory-framed window, a varnished table with four sturdy chairs waited. Fishing gear rested in the far corner, rods leaning drunkenly against tackle boxes dusty from disuse. A hallway laid with a hand-woven rug in a deeper green than the couch led to two bedrooms and a single shared bath.

Unerringly Gabriel knelt on the cushions, tucking Erin into their soft embrace. He rummaged in the bin for a quilt, desperate to stop the shivers that continued to course through her.

"Erin, honey, I'm going into the kitchen. To make some tea. I'll be right back." Gabriel rose from his crouch beside her. Suddenly her fingers curled around his wrist, the nails biting in deep.

"No," she moaned brokenly. "Please. Stay."

"Always." Gabriel's hand twisted beneath her grip to hold her tight. He settled onto the sofa and lifted her across his lap. Stretching his long legs out, he tucked her along his side and stroked a tender hand along the silken mass of hair that flowed over her shoulders. "Go to sleep. I'll be here."

In the dimly lit room, he could see Erin's graceful profile, the face slack with exhaustion. And fear. Endlessly he held her, stilling her restive movements, soothing her brow with soft kisses. Beneath his touch she calmed, and nightmare receded into sleep. Only once did she stir. Then she whispered a new name. *"Analise."*

Gabriel continued to watch her, puzzled by the woman in his arms. More than the sight of a dead woman had wrought this devastation. She was shattered. And, though it may have bruised his ego, he recognized that her clinging wasn't to him. Hell, she wasn't really aware of him, not as a man. To her, he was simply protection against a darker, deadlier specter.

Before they left this isolated cabin on the edge of the bayou, he'd uncover her secrets. She'd fight him, but he was stronger and determined. Nathan, he figured, was somehow connected to California. The story he'd been unraveling with her had jumbled once more. The killer in New Orleans. A killer in California. A man named Nathan. A woman named Analise.

A wide yawn cracked his jaw, and he wrapped her still body closer, savoring the quiet. They wouldn't leave until he'd learned everything, he decided drowsily. Until she trusted him.

As dawn crested and topaz cascaded through the uncovered windows, he slid into sleep.

"Gabriel?"

Erin's voice was a pleasant susurration along his jaw. He turned, seeking the supple source of warmth that bowed along him in wonderful places. Slowly his mouth skimmed over creamy skin. His hands closed over firm, warm skin, and he allowed them to wander. Rounded curves filled his eager palms. When the slender body arched into him, he slid keen hands up, to knead the pliant flesh. "Hmm."

"Gabriel." The whisper became a muffled, urgent demand. "Gabriel, stop." Erin followed the command with an ungentle nip at his ear, the only flesh she could reach.

He emerged into full wakefulness when he conked his head against the wooden frame of the sofa's arm. "Ouch!"

Unfocused gray eyes shot open, and closed immediately on another groan of complaint. Bright, unfiltered light streamed into the living room and directly into his line of sight. Beneath him, a supine and deceptively lush Erin wiggled for escape. The triple assaults on his senses were too much.

"For God's sake, woman, stop moving," he growled, and threw an arm across her writhing body, trapping her where she lay against sensitive, rigid flesh. Erin bucked in protest, and Gabriel tightened his leg warningly. "If you have any compassion in you at all, you'll just be still."

The coarse tone carried a deeper edge of frustrated longing. Erin smartly lay still. She'd resisted waking, resisted abandoning the sensual oblivion that had become hers in sleep. During the night, they'd come together, so that she awoke to find her face snuggled into his chest.

Her traitorous hands had sought the sleek heat of his naked back, sliding beneath his shirt to hold him close. Hard hips cradled her between steeled thighs, and she could feel him growing impossibly harder. Awake, as in her dreams, she wanted nothing more than to pull him to her, into her, their union at once a safe haven and a dangerous prison.

"Good girl." Oblivious to her thoughts, Gabriel unwound bare arms that circled his waist and eased her into the dip between his tumescent body and the back of the couch. Without a word, he surged to his feet and strode off in what she assumed was the direction of the bathroom. Erin drew herself into a seated position and drew her knees up, beneath her chin.

Abruptly she recalled the events of the night before. How they'd stumbled over Harmony's body and how she'd tried to revive her. Gabriel had plowed over the paramedics to get her to the Jeep and away from the scene.

She replayed her panicked reaction. Gabriel would have new questions. More questions. He would want to know about Nathan and California. About Analise and her crimes.

Erin could hear Gabriel returning, and she cast desperately for the explanation she knew he'd demand. Why had she become so distraught over Harmony's death? And more damning, who was Nathan? Answering the first would be simple. A student's death was guaranteed to shock. Nathan would be harder to explain.

"I can see the lies forming," Gabriel remarked casually from the hallway, where he'd been watching her prepare. Pushing away from the doorjamb, he entered the room and sank into the rocking chair. "It's fascinating, really. Your eyes narrow in concentration, like you have to plan out the full story. Account for every detail. Then your mouth purses with determination. But I never see any remorse."

Beneath the even tone, Erin heard the disappointment, and tried to banish the shame. She would lie if she had to, be honest if she must. He would know the difference, but she thought about lying anyway.

He had no claim to her story. But she remembered his arms holding her close, his gentle murmurs of comfort, and they defeated her. "Ask your questions."

"Who is Nathan Rhodes?" The question had snaked around his heart, sinking venomous fangs deep. The name had followed him into agitated sleep and dragged him awake several times, when she'd called out the cursed name and scrabbled to hold Gabriel, or probably Nathan, closer. "Is he another lover? Like the phantom Sebastian?"

Slowly Erin shook her head in mute denial. "Sebastian is my best friend. And Nathan and I were never lovers." She shuddered at the recent memory. She paused then, searching for the most apt description that cloaked the reality. "He was my mentor."

Gabriel marveled at the rush of relief, followed quickly

by exasperation. He cared too much about a single answer. Yet he was determined to have all of them. "Where is he now?"

"California." She met his look steadily, and she wondered if she would eventually give him even that final satisfaction. "But you won't find him."

"Of course not," he agreed straightforwardly. "He's dead." Gabriel smiled at her, a thin, humorless smile. "Did you kill him?"

Her stunned expression, guilt layered with apprehension, should have answered his question. But the eyes, the huge, expressive brown eyes that telegraphed her thoughts so clearly, were filled with confusion. That was why, when she finally responded, he wasn't sure if he should believe.

"Yes."

"Why?" He leaned forward, his arms near her bent legs. Absently he lifted her cold hand, a habit he couldn't seem to break. "What did he do to you?"

The kind touch, the unexpected compassion, scorched her skin. She jumped up from the sofa, black tresses streaming behind her. Emotions, tangled and muddied, struggled to find their core.

She walked over to the window, the sunlight breaking through the glass. Resting her hands against the panes, she could feel the heat on her skin. She wondered if she could ever be warm again. "He took everything from me."

"Why?"

"Because I allowed him to." A sneer curled her lip. "I was weak. Pathetic."

Gabriel joined her at the window, not near enough to crowd. "You're not that same person, Erin. I've never known a braver woman than you."

He didn't understand her sad smile. "You don't know me."

Patience, an endless well, seemed to fill him. He didn't touch her, knowing it would make her run. He merely shrugged, the truth plain. "Yes, I do."

"Stop saying that!" she seethed, and the sun played through the clear glass, a beacon to highlight the anger that overflowed. "You don't know who I was!"

"Tell me."

"I was nothing! A wraith with no feelings except the ones he gave me. With no thoughts except the ones he let me think. I was nobody except who he made me!"

Gabriel caught her hand then, brought it to his cheek. Molten rage churned inside him, but he corralled the fury, knowing she didn't need his anger. Whether she could admit it or not, she needed him. "Tell me what happened to you, Erin."

As quickly as resentment had taken her, it fled, leaving her drained. "I can't," she said tiredly. She raised her free hand in a gesture of defeat, then pressed it to her stomach, as though to hold the pain inside. "Not yet. I can't."

"What else do you want from me, Erin? What will it take to make you trust me?" Anger flashed, and he let it spill over. "I've worked beside you. I've taken everything you've told me on faith. All I have ever asked of you is the truth. But you don't think enough of me to give me that."

Erin shook her head, stunned. "It's not you. God, Gabriel, I do trust you."

"Then why the lies? Why won't you let me all the way inside?"

"Because I can't go back yet!" she railed. "I can still see Harmony's body, Gabriel. I knew she was dead, but

I still tried to save her. I knew why she was dead. Because of me. Because of what I've done." She raised her eyes to his, begging for understanding. "I see him everywhere, and damn him, I can't escape."

"Let me help you. Tell me."

On a nearly inaudible whisper, she said, "Tomorrow, I'll be stronger. I promise." She shook her head. "Today, I just can't."

He stepped closer, and she sidled away. Relentless, he pursued her, and when her spine met the window he cupped her chin, his thumb resting lightly on the faint cleft. "Okay."

Startled, she met his look. "Why?"

"Because I have time. And, though I didn't know it before now, I can be terribly patient."

"Why?" she repeated, in a voice so small it broke his heart.

"Because you need me to be." He chuckled ruefully. "It seems I can also be sensitive. Who knew?"

Compelled, she moved into him. His hand slid to her throat and she tilted her head to hold his gaze. "Where've you been, Gabriel Moss?"

His mouth covered hers, as lightly as a dream. In restrained forays, he slipped inside, drawing out the moment, extending the pleasure beyond bearing. Warm breath sighed into him, and he cautiously explored the satiny recesses. Over, under, together, he claimed her mouth for his own.

Not to be conquered, she returned the kiss, wooed by the textures of tongue and teeth, by the caress of strong hands as they angled her for deeper access. A moan rose as softly as a wish, and she tried to draw him closer.

He relinquished her mouth to skim kisses across her face. Pulling away, he brushed a last kiss across her lips and whispered, almost too soft for her to hear, "I've been waiting for you."

CHAPTER 21

"Insulin overdose."

Gabriel read the coroner's summary aloud to two women in the poorly lit, cramped detective's office. He took a sip from a can of Coke he'd filched out of Sylvie's private stash. Erin's bottled water sat unopened. They were seated on the visitor side of Sylvie's desk, jammed between the beige floor-mounted air conditioner and overstuffed black filing cabinets. The unit rumbled to life, humming and spitting frigid air into the room.

The sound grated at Gabriel's nerves. As he scratched notes on the steno pad open on his lap, the sound of the pencil added to the dissonance. When the lead broke, he restrained a sigh and stole a fresh stylus from the cluttered desk.

Par for the course, he thought. Since the morning, he'd been unable to make anything work. The Jeep had barely sputtered to life and Erin had retreated into her shell once again. The hell of it was, he couldn't blame her.

Today she'd discover if she'd mistakenly accused her

boss of murder and left another man free to kill Harmony Turner. Their truce from the day before had ended at breakfast, when she'd been icy and distant. He hadn't helped matters, he thought, but maybe the distance was good for her. It might blunt the edges of what lay before them now.

Brutal photographs were spread across the desk. Though he'd learned long ago to cleave his emotions and divide feeling from fact, he could see again the pallid figure tossed onto the street like trash. When the second pencil cracked into jagged pieces, he muttered beneath his breath and snatched a pen out of the cup on Sylvie's desk.

Sylvie watched as he jerkily pushed the report closer to Erin, though both were careful not to touch. *Quite a feat to manage,* Sylvie thought admiringly, *given the tight space.*

Gabriel was as hot as gumbo, silver eyes flashing. He'd stormed into Sylvie's office a few minutes after noon. The prim professor had come in next, with an edge of ice that could have sliced and instantly frozen a lesser cop.

He'd dragged in a chair from the bullpen, and Erin had discreetly shifted closer to the filing cabinets. They hadn't spoken directly to each other. Not to be spared, though, Sylvie thought they'd gotten downright prickly over questions about what they were doing back at the station after Gabriel had been released. Her deceptively dull cop's eyes detected twin flags of embarrassment when they blandly described the moments before discovering the body.

She'd drawn out the preliminaries, issuing unnecessary warnings about privacy and secrecy and penalties for lying. The lady had stiffened at the naked threats, and Gabriel's usual even temper seemed to have abandoned him completely.

Which fascinated Sylvie even more. Like the finest exotic dancer, she'd drawn out the final reveal, waiting until Gabriel was perilously close to lunging at the folder lying in plain view on her desk. When she finally relented, he snatched at the thin file, quickly flipping through its pages. Erin reviewed it now, and Sylvie felt sorry for the girl. Her trash can sat nearby for nausea duty.

"It says she died between nine and eleven a.m." Erin traced the grisly lines of the report. "I didn't realize she was a diabetic."

"She wasn't."

Gabriel shifted toward her and tapped a sentence near the bottom of the page. Erin flinched slightly at his nearness. The instinctive movement away lashed through him like a whip.

Putting distance between them before he did something he'd regret, he explained in a taut voice, "That's why she died so quickly. In non-diabetics, an overdose of insulin is a poison."

The connection was too simple, Erin thought sadly. "Initiate."

"Come again?" Sylvie asked.

"She was an initiate into her sorority," Erin explained. "That's the connection. Insulin. Initiate. They were going to Greece to celebrate."

Gabriel heard the anguish, but he knew better than to offer comfort. "It fits. She's the ninth victim."

"Hold on. The captain isn't going to buy that so easily." Sylvie straightened and grabbed the report. "Was she a drug addict? This could have been a college prank. She thinks the injection is dope and ends up in a coffin."

Shaking her head, Erin refused to accept Sylvie's

explanation. "Harmony was too self-conscious and too much of an exhibitionist to be an intravenous drug user. The marks would show."

"Plus," Gabriel added, "the report says there was nothing else in her system."

Sylvie nodded. "Okay. Say I bite. The killer had to have access to insulin. It's not a street drug. You have to get it through a pharmacy or a hospital."

"Or be a diabetic yourself," Erin suggested quietly. She told herself she welcomed the space Gabriel had put between them. Any absence of warmth was a trick of her imagination and the result of a fitful air conditioner.

Gabriel closed his eyes to try to picture the assault. *A coed free from college on her way to vacation. Strolling through the Quarter. He comes up behind her and grabs. Harmony fights her attacker. She thrashes about to evade the shot, but it's no use. The heart attack does its work, and she dies. Her body is bundled inside a car or van and dumped on the street to be discovered by the crowds.*

But the autopsy showed no signs of a struggle. The only bruises came from her contact with the asphalt and Erin's attempt at revival. The rest of the tanned, smooth skin had been unblemished.

"She knew the killer," he murmured as he turned to face them again. "The autopsy shows no ligature marks, no scrapes or cuts. Nothing to say she didn't sit still, waiting for the injection."

"So why her?" The detective in Sylvie needed more than language tricks. "Why select the prominent daughter of a despised man, shoot her up with insulin, and dump her in the French Quarter?"

"It doesn't quite make sense. The others were kind to

me, but with Harmony, *I* showed *her* mercy." Erin finally locked eyes with Gabriel. She twisted the cap off her water and drank deep. The cool liquid eased her suddenly parched throat. "I changed her grade to let her join the sorority."

"Who else knew?"

"The registrar. My teaching assistant. Kenneth."

"So Bernard could have done it," Gabriel said as he got to his feet. He thought more clearly when he was moving. When he wasn't so near the rigid, terrified woman who was being tracked by a killer. He prowled the carpet between the window and the door, carefully avoiding Erin, despite the truncated area. "Sylvie didn't arrest him until one, but she died hours before. That was enough time to kill her and dump the body."

"Hold on a second," Sylvie interjected. "Erin, you told me your guy has a procedure. He kills his victims and leaves the weapon. All the other victims were killed near their homes or offices." She thumped the autopsy. "This one doesn't fit. The other bodies weren't moved. This one was. And there was no murder weapon. The paramedics didn't find a syringe."

Gabriel thought back to the evening they'd found the body and his tip to Calvin. "Uh, Sylvie, they may not have done a thorough search. There were a lot of people out there that night. I don't know that the cops would have known to search the area."

"We know how to do our job, Gabe." Impatiently, Sylvie scanned the police report again. Not a word about a sweep of the area. What kind of imbecile cop forgot to do a perfunctory sweep? Then she stared angrily at Gabriel. "Goddamn it, Gabriel! You sent the boy out there to keep him off your scent. If we missed the evidence, it's your fault. Holy shit!"

She thundered out of the office, yelling for Officer Rochon. Through the din of the squad room, Sylvie's righteous indignation and fury cut through the noise like a scalpel. Feeling sympathetic, Gabriel winced at the invective Sylvie used to describe the chagrined young man's mental acumen.

No good deed goes unpunished, he thought, blithely ignoring his role in Rochon's mistake.

Gabriel crossed the room and pushed the office door shut. Satisfied they had some time alone, he rubbed his hand along a spear of tension in his neck. He stood near the door and watched Erin pretend not to watch him.

Erin stifled an apology for her behavior. The strain between them had everything to do with her. She'd awoken that morning knowing today would be the end of it.

No more running. No more hiding. Nine lives had been taken, and she was the reason. Intellectually, she understood that the sickness in the killer hadn't begun with her. Julian Harris hadn't been his first victim. But the killer performed for her now, counting on her to remain silent. Knowing she couldn't stop him without revealing herself.

So she'd do the unexpected.

"Nathan was a diabetic." Twisting in her seat to squarely face Gabriel, she explained, "Nathan Rhodes. The man I killed." She sifted through the greasy layers of panic and guilt and degradation. This was familiar territory. Being the catalyst for a man's transgressions. She'd escaped, and with Sebastian's help, she'd made a new life. "He's repaying me for killing Nathan. Over and over again."

"How do you know?"

"There have been signs. Little things linking the victims to Nathan."

Bleak lines fanned out from Gabriel's thinned mouth. "And you didn't tell me?"

"No." She said the word without apology. "At first, I wasn't sure."

"You were sure enough to think you had to hide it." The accusation was quietly damning.

Erin accepted the judgment. "I can't do this here, Gabriel. I promised you the truth, but not here. Can we go somewhere private to talk?"

"Sure." Gabriel led her out of the police station and to his Jeep, knowing she wouldn't run now. They rode in wired silence to his apartment. The unit had a separate entrance from the newspaper offices.

She paid scant attention as he keyed in his access code to the elevator. The doors slid open with hushed efficiency. He drew her out of the car and into his home. Erin halted on the threshold and stared.

Lofts, particularly those owned by men, paid stark homage to metal and chrome. At best, they reflected the latest trend in mass-marketed furniture and accessories. Rarely did they look like home. Gabriel's did.

Sofas and a lush chair upholstered in deep green faced one another across a rug woven in muted colors. The warmth spread from the center of the room, along the rich woods that composed tables and chairs and frames. She moved a chair near the windows. He followed.

"It's time, Erin." The words were hushed, too low to reach beyond their bodies. "Time to tell me everything."

Her edgy frame shuddered once. She couldn't pretend

not to understand. After two years of hiding, of running, the past had found her.

Gabriel murmured, "Let me help you, Erin. Help us stop him." He touched her then, tipped dry, anguished eyes up to his own. With precious care, he stroked the furrowed brow, swept his thumbs along the proud cheekbones. Soothing, calming, he waited for her to relax. He waited for her to believe in him. That he would not abandon her to her past. Shifting his hold, he captured her cold hands. "Talk to me, Erin. Trust me."

It wasn't trust, she thought, that would make her tell him. It was fate. And like the condemned, she accepted her fate, that it had become entwined with his, with the innocent residents of New Orleans. There was no escaping what she'd done, no building a future with it hanging over her, a bloodied Sword of Damocles. "His name was Dr. Nathan Rhodes," she began faintly. "I met him when I was fifteen."

Unable to stand still, to feel the contempt that would surely seep into her skin, she pulled away. She would tell him the whole story and accept her punishment. Otherwise, she was no better than the man they chased.

"My father was a writer and my mother was a scientist. A neuropsychologist. As they describe it, I was an unexpected addition. I was born when they were already in their forties. When I was two, I demonstrated an unusual aptitude for language. By the time I was five, I could read in several different ones. My parents taught me themselves and brought in the top minds in every field to train me. Most of my childhood was spent in hotel rooms or in university laboratories, being tested."

Gabriel could imagine the child she'd been. Isolated, shy. "What about friends?"

"I had one. Sebastian. His mother, Mrs. Cain, traveled with us, took care of me."

"Did you ever attend school?"

"There was no reason to." She stared wistfully out of narrow windows. How many hotel windows had she stood at and pined for other children to play with, for her best and only friend, Sebastian? Shaking off the self-pity, she continued. "I had tutors, and we were always traveling." She turned and lifted her hands in entreaty. "Don't misunderstand. Mom and Dad weren't ogres. They did their best with me. But I was too . . . different. They'd never expected children, and definitely not me."

"It was their choice. Not yours," snapped Gabriel. "They had a responsibility."

"They tried. But I didn't make it easy. I'd become a minor celebrity, so my teenage years included a full complement of defiant acts. Shoplifting. Tantrums. In London, I tried to run away and live in a hostel. Dad found me, promised to let me have some freedom if I behaved. I demanded they let me try out for a game show on the BBC. Mom took me to the audition and I made it onto the show. I had to answer questions about etymology. I won. They kept me on for nearly six months. The teenage language freak."

Startled, Gabriel shook his head, the pieces falling into place. He'd been in London then, a twenty-year-old reporter interning with the *Times*. "You're Analise."

"That's who I was." She turned to face him, guarded and calm. "My full name is Analise Erin Abbott Glover. Abbott is my mother's maiden name."

He picked up the story, remembering. "You did an

interview once. They asked you about your hobbies. I remember, you said you liked to read obituaries. Said the people in them had much more interesting lives than yours." He smiled gently. "I remember thinking you sounded incredibly tired."

"My parents had a different idea. They got scared. Decided I needed structure and to be around kids my own age."

"They sent you away."

"To Callenwolde." Chilled by the coming memory, Erin moved past Gabriel to the chair to sit. "Dr. Nathan Rhodes was an exceptional linguist and appropriately older than I. He agreed to an arrangement. I'd work with him and he'd help hone my talent."

"You have a second degree?"

"No. I didn't finish my studies in linguistics. After my junior year, he refused to allow me to major in it. Told me my talents weren't up to it."

"What did your parents say?" Gabriel bent down next to her, refusing to allow her the distance to hide.

"My parents and Mrs. Cain died in a plane crash during my sophomore year. I only had Nathan. I was so lost," she said in a tiny voice he could barely hear. "So grateful for his attention. Because I was a minor, he petitioned the courts for custody. Later, I moved out of the dorm and into his house." She remembered the days in a blur. How she'd left the house for classes, driven there and back by Nathan. The few friends she'd made began to stop inviting her out, knowing she'd decline. "I didn't have to think about anything. He told me to cut my hair. I did. He told me to change my studies. I did. Everything he demanded, I did. I was a coward, a nebbish."

"You were a child." Gabriel gained his feet and towered over her. He heaved her up to stand, and she hung limply in his grasp. She watched him, defeated, broken. "You were a child, damn him. He used you!"

The shame burst out of her, a bitter torrent. "I let him use me! I gave him everything, and I didn't have the sense to try and walk away. After I left linguistics, he convinced me to let him use my ideas. We'd have weekly sessions where I'd tell him about my concepts and he'd tear them apart. Then he'd refine them and publish them under his name. I didn't fight him because he said he needed me. I needed him to need me."

"He stole from you."

"I let him. I let him take everything." She couldn't look at him as she spoke. "A few years after the plane crash, Sebastian hitchhiked from New York to California to see me. We hadn't talked for a while." Again humiliation suffused her skin, and she dropped her head down lower. "He knocked on the door to Nathan's house. Nathan told me to send him away. That Sebastian would only remind me of my parents. He told me that Sebastian would try to take me away, to exploit me for my parents' money. Seventeen years of friendship versus two years of subjugation. I told Sebastian to go away. That he and his mother had ridden on my coattails. I told him to never contact me again."

"Erin—"

"I hadn't known I could be cruel. Not until Nathan." Her shoulders quivered, like her voice, but her eyes remained tearless. She wanted the tears to come, but they remained hidden, unwilling to give her relief.

Gabriel sat in the chair and cradled her taut form. The grief, the self-loathing, tore at him, but he understood the need to purge the wound that festered. Tenderly he skimmed his hands over her. "You're not cruel. You're not a coward. You're a strong, determined, brilliant woman who saved herself."

When she tried to shake loose, he tightened his hold. "Finish it, Erin."

She didn't speak for several moments. "After Sebastian, there was no one else. Just the two of us. Nathan said I could finish my degree. I started grad school, but he didn't like it if I talked to the other graduate students. To my professors. He always knew. But since I'd always been peculiar, they thought nothing of it. I finished my dissertation, but Nathan wouldn't allow me to teach. I took care of his house and played hostess to his friends. Gave him theories to test and prove right."

"He never tried to—" Gabriel searched her face for an answer to the question he couldn't ask. Had no right to ask.

She read his expression and shook her head. She thought she'd known how deep the humiliation ran. She was wrong. Speaking just above a whisper, she said, "He tried once. When I was twenty-three. He was fifty." The words stumbled over one another, and she recalled his hands seeking. *A touch. A push. A clench. A rejection. He'd thrown her into the bedroom wall, breaking her arm.* "I didn't do it right. It didn't work. After that, he barely touched me, unless I made a mistake."

Understanding much more, Gabriel froze at her last statement. His eyes darkened. "He beat you."

"Sometimes." She had promised herself the truth. Hadn't she demanded the same of Lindy? "Usually, he was more careful than that. Words. Sarcasm. Accidental bruises. Shallow cuts." In her lap, she twisted the silver ring with its solitary stone and squeezed her eyes tight. "When I made him really angry, it was worse. Fists or his feet. Once, I tried to move out of the house. He caught me."

Her throat closed over a sob, and he gathered her deeper into his embrace, sickness as strong as the wrath churning inside. "Oh, God, Erin."

"I learned to see the signs. I never tried to run again. Not until the day I went into the cellar."

She'd thought about that decision every day since, wondering what would be if she'd ignored the tug of inquisitiveness. Would she be Analise or Erin? Would she be whole? Would Nathan be alive? She'd never know, she accepted fatalistically. Because she'd defied him, had crept down to the cellar and opened the door, never realizing she was changing everything.

CHAPTER 22

"Nathan had gone to Milan for a conference. He was due home that night. We'd had a fight. I made him angry." Erin twisted her fingers together, her voice a dull whisper. "I was selfish. Always whining about something."

"Erin, don't."

"No. I wasn't selfish. But that day, I had to make things right with him. Before he left, he threatened to send me away. I had nowhere else to go. There was just Nathan. He liked wine. The house had a cellar, and he kept his own stock. I wasn't allowed downstairs."

"Why not?"

A short, brittle laugh was her answer. "I was exploring the house one day, when he was out. I fell and broke a 1952 Château Latour. That was the first time he gave me a concussion."

Gabriel's mouth tightened, wanting to curse, knowing he couldn't. Quietly he asked, "How old were you?"

Erin splayed her fingers wide, palms up, as though perplexed. "Seventeen. I'd just graduated from Callenwolde.

Nathan invited me to live with him. I thought—I was afraid that he would— But he didn't. I had my own room. On the top floor."

"What happened when you went to the cellar?"

"I never really cared about wine. But I wanted his favorite. Pétrus. The cellar was so dark, so cold. All the labels looked the same and it took me a while to find the bottles. They were on the far wall." She remembered the smell of oak and grapes, the pungent aroma of reds. The crisp scent of whites. Closing her eyes, she brought her clasped hand to her throat. "It was warmer by the wall. I was afraid the climate control had failed. If his wine was ruined, he'd blame me."

She'd searched the walls for a switch or a box, not sure of what she was seeking. "Tucked away, behind the row of bottles, I saw a door. There was a faint red light. I went to it and I heard a strange noise. I thought it was the unit, understand?"

"Yes." Gabriel captured her cold hands, warming them. Her voice had grown thinner, fainter. He had to lean close to hear. "I understand."

"I turned the knob. There was a sound." Her shoulders began to shake. "A swish through the air. And a slap. Then I heard the noise again. It was a scream."

The door had been heavy when she pushed at it. Then it opened, swinging silently on its hinges. Her eyes tried to adjust to the light, the deep red that seemed to pulse through the room. The noises were louder, more discernible. Like a woman's screams.

From the doorway, she could make out a figure standing and a second one that appeared to be suspended from the ceiling. Chains rattled on walls; moans undulated in waves of torment and delight. Lights danced over leather and steel. In the room she'd never seen, bodies writhed in pantomimes of delight. Nathan stood before them, the whip dripping with crimson. She blinked, unable to accept what she saw.

"Nathan stood there. There were others on the floor. They were all naked. The swishing sound was a whip. The leather kept striking the woman and she'd scream. But not in pain. It sounded like—"

"Ecstasy." Gabriel felt the shudder course through her. "Did he see you?"

"No. The area was too dark. He was too engrossed. I don't know how long I stood there watching him beat her. Everywhere. But then I noticed she wasn't moaning. Not crying. Not screaming. Her head was limp. There was blood on her mouth. Oh."

"Finish it, Erin."

She lifted her hands to cover her own mouth. Jagged pain scraped nerves already throbbing from the dark recollections. "He was hitting her so hard, so brutally. They were all enjoying it. They didn't notice that she was gone, I thought." She swallowed, the motion painful. "Then he cut her down, Gabriel. Laid her on the floor. And they did things to her. Terrible things."

"What did you do?"

"Nothing." She stared at him fiercely. "I did nothing. I watched them, frozen. Then one of them saw me. I don't know if it was a man or woman. But I saw those eyes focus on me and it broke the spell. I ran."

"To where?"

"I had nowhere left to go except the cabin."

"Cabin?"

"Once a year, Nathan would take me to the mountains in Northern California. He had a house there. I didn't know where else to go. I ran until I found a taxi." Voice brittle, she curled against the solid strength that was Gabriel. "I was so pathetic."

She had watched Nathan kill a woman and done nothing. All the way to the cabin, she'd thought about calling the police, but she did nothing once more.

She'd tumbled out of the cab and wandered to the edge of the plateau. The welcoming distance to the deep thickets below. Hesitant steps and the tumble of stones into nothing. "I stood there, and I don't know what I planned to do. I just wanted it to be over."

His embrace trembled then, and she breathed deeply, determined to forge to the end. "I was there for two days. I walked in the forest, sat on the cliffs, and thought about everything my life had become. I was alone truly for the first time in decades. That second night, a storm moved in."

Erin fell silent again, and Gabriel brushed the top of her head with an encouraging kiss.

"I was out in the forest, running for the cabin. Nathan called my name." Remembering the scene, she frowned. "He'd always been beautiful. Not the way you are. You're sculpture. He was more illusory, an artist's rendering. The wind whipped the leaves into a frenzy behind him.

"He grabbed my wrist. I tried to pull free and he threw me into a tree. I could hear the bone splinter." She rubbed at the old wound. "I got to my feet and ran for the cabin. He chased me inside." Erin stared at the ring she'd taken from him after he died. "We fought. He had a gun in his pocket. I made him angry and he dropped it. I grabbed it and we struggled for the gun. It went off. I'd shot him, just before I passed out."

In a cool voice, banked with helpless fury, he questioned. He had no option but to question. To make her see her truth. "Why didn't you call the police?"

"The phones were out." She raised earnest eyes to meet his gaze. "When I came to, he was dead." Honesty prompted the last fragment of admission. About how she'd sacrificed humanity for survival. She braced herself for loss. The way Gabriel held her, the solid warmth of his hands on hers, the respect she'd seen in the deep gray eyes she adored.

She'd come too far to spare either of them with a final lie. So the horrible explanation streamed out unchecked, and she let it flow. "I didn't want to go to jail. Suddenly, I felt selfish. My tormentor was gone and a new life was possible for me and I didn't know if I could lose it. So I hid the body. Then I ran."

His reaction rippled through her. Unable to bear his disgust, she stood.

"Where did you go?" The question was flat. Deliberately so. Gabriel knew himself well enough to conceal the murderous rage thumping at his heart. To release it would terrify her, and he vowed he would never make her fear him.

Which meant he couldn't touch her, because if he did, the tenuous control he was fighting for would snap.

He would rail against the parents who had abandoned her, against Sebastian, who had left her in an evil man's clutches.

Instead, he circled around her and walked carefully over to the bar. Whiskey splashed into the bottom of a crystal snifter. He tossed the liquor down, grateful for the heat. His hands weren't quite steady as he poured a second shot. "Erin. Where did you go after that night?"

"I went to Sebastian." With her back to him, she didn't see his knuckles tighten on the crystal, didn't hear the glass stem break. Oblivious, Erin fought the urge to ask him what he thought of her. Didn't his reaction clearly spell it out? Tenderness was for victims. Not for women who committed murder.

"Sebastian." Repeating the name, Gabriel swept the glass into a paper towel and dumped the ruined snifter into the trash. "I thought he hated you."

"I thought so, too, but he was the only one I could call. After the storm ended, he came to California. He—" She stopped, unwilling to betray. "He helped me."

Swiftly, wanting the interrogation finished, she described the months afterward. Ashamed, she didn't tell him about the nightmares and the new fear of storms. "Eventually, I was able to get new papers. Identification. Passport. Doctorate."

His voice was gruff as he asked, "Why did you come to New Orleans?"

She wouldn't humiliate herself by begging for reassurance. Briskly she finished her explanation. "Mrs. Cain used to tell me about magnolias."

"And the position at Burkeen?"

"Maggie told me."

"Either the killer followed you here or your showing up was a lucky break."

Erin shrugged and wished for a glass of whatever Gabriel was drinking. "Yes."

Gabriel stepped from behind the bar. "We should get back to the police station. Sylvie will wonder what happened to us."

"Sure." Erin gave him wide berth as she made her way to the door. He pulled it open for her, brushing against her. Feeling her shy away, Gabriel shoved it wide.

"I'm not him," he snarled, unable to stem the frustration. Instantly, though, he turned from her, trying to find control. What did she see in him, he wondered, disgust eating a hole in him. Did she see Nathan when he snapped at her? When they fought, did she truly believe he would strike her? The fury crested again. Why couldn't she see he was nothing like the monster who'd terrorized her? Spinning back to her, he said softly, "I wouldn't hurt you, Erin."

Her head came up, the eyes dry and tearless. She shook her head ruefully. "I know. But I can't say the same. I am a liar, Gabriel. Like you said."

"Erin—"

She twisted the ring that seemed to burn into her skin. "And I have left bodies behind me. I was so desperate to save myself, I let him have them."

"You were scared," Gabriel reminded her. "Bernard isn't killing because of you. Didn't you tell Sylvie that he'd already likely killed before? You showed up in New Orleans, and he suddenly had an audience. That's all."

"That's not all. He knows about Nathan and me. About my murdering him."

"It was self-defense," he countered flatly.

"I took a human life. It doesn't matter why. What matters is that I'm guilty, just like Nathan. Just like Kenneth, if he's the one."

CHAPTER 23

They returned to the police station in an icy silence. Sylvie brought them to her office and summoned Captain Sanchez. Without speaking, they took up their positions in the straight-backed chairs.

Seconds later, a golden bear of a man, with massive hands and a shining bald pate, filled the doorway and glowered at them. A thin black mustache ran below a bulbous nose reddened by nature. The sober navy suit strained across shoulders layered with muscle and fat. At his belt, flesh strained against the leather, creeping over the top. Shoes, polished as high as his head, reflected the dim light. "This is the young lady with the neat little theory?"

"This is Dr. Abbott. And you know Gabriel Moss."

"Yes, I do. Which is why I'm not hard-pressed to imagine this tale is a concoction to make her famous and his paper successful. I've got half a mind to make up a reason to arrest them."

Gabriel leaped to his feet and shoved Erin behind him

in a single defensive move. He balanced on the balls of his feet, prepared to attack. Mixed with fear and loathing for a dead man and the living one who dared to threaten her, his voice was guttural. "Try it."

"Mr. Moss," Captain Sanchez said, "I can't let her run around terrifying the city. At best, she's a liar. At worst, she's crazy."

"No. What's scaring you is that you know she's right and that your department almost missed this one, Sanchez."

The captain advanced into the office. The confined space became claustrophobic. "Watch what you say, Moss. Your paper couldn't stand up to a sigh, much less a libel suit."

"Gabriel's got an excellent reputation. You're just mad he did that exposé last year." Too weary to stomach machismo in a battle with vain chivalry, Sylvie folded her arms over her ample chest. Neither man noticed that Erin remained upright by sheer force of will. Sylvie could, and because of what she understood to be true, she'd defend. For now. "We do have nine unexplained deaths that Dr. Abbott and Mr. Moss may help us solve," she challenged Sanchez. "You insult her, Captain, and we may lose our only chance to solve the ones we can."

Sanchez whisked around to confront Sylvie, not an easy feat for a man who nearly scraped the low ceiling. "Are you bargaining for her, Detective?"

"Absolutely. She's the only link we have to the murders." Sylvie wandered to her desk and lowered her impressive bulk into the creaking leather. "I'd wager that if you tried to make her a scapegoat, Gabe would skewer you on the front page of the *Ledger* so badly, the mayor would have your badge by his second cup of coffee."

The thought of a visit from the mayor stilled the angry retort trembling on Sanchez's tongue. He understood the value of a good bargain. His political aspirations demanded them. And the meddlesome Detective Iberville had a point. This case could introduce him to a national audience. With his sights on a nice white house in the East, it wouldn't hurt to find friends everywhere.

"I won't have you hauled in right now. However, I do expect your cooperation with this investigation of Dr. Bernard. It had better be good." The hearty bass that won over voters brooked no argument. He pierced Gabriel with flat obsidian eyes. "I don't want to read another word about this in your paper."

"Then don't pick up the morning edition," Gabriel retorted. "The daily edition comes out tomorrow. Headline on the ABC Serial Killer."

"I'll slap you with an injunction."

Gabriel snorted. "I'll meet you in court."

Sanchez knew it was an empty threat. He'd been filled in on the particulars of the ABC Murders by Sylvie late yesterday when Harmon Turner's daughter turned up in the morgue. The *Ledger* had been feeding the story for a while, and his detective swore the man they had in custody was the likely culprit. Though he hated being last on the bus, he was along for the ride.

He couldn't lose, he thought. If the serial killer turned out to be a hoax, he'd fire the detective with mixed loyalties and a poor sense of humor. If they found it to be true, he'd be spotlighted on news magazines from around the country.

But he couldn't make the upstart newsman's job too

simple. "I don't like a word I read and I go straight to the *Chronicle*. Give them exclusive access to autopsy reports and case files. Maybe take them on a tour of the murder sites with the detectives on the case."

"You sonofabitch." Gabriel had to admire the cold-blooded threat. "You know I don't write trash. Can you say the same about the *Chronicle*?"

"No comment." Because Sanchez remembered similar fights with Lincoln Moss, his dark eyes softened, though his tone remained cool. "I'm not as convinced as Detective Iberville." He cut his gaze to Erin, who shot out a dented chin, which wobbled despite her efforts. Grudging respect tugged at the corner of his unsmiling mouth. He didn't give in. "I don't trust you, lady. But you did come to us with this first. That counts for something."

"It counts for everything. She risked a lot coming here." Tucking his arm around her stiffened body, Gabriel brought her flush along his side. "We want this man as badly as you do. Worse. We'll work with Detective Iberville to stop him."

Sanchez looked around the dim, cramped office and at the motley gang crowded inside. He harrumphed loudly. "You'll work with me, too. Let's go to my office and see what we can coordinate." Without a backward glance, he stalked out of the office.

Sylvie circled from behind her desk to follow.

Gabriel stopped Erin and tilted her face up to his. "You up for this? If not, say the word and I'll take you home. I can handle it from here." He searched the shadowed eyes, trying to read what lay deep inside.

Erin straightened. His protective arm fell away. One more loss, but she would hold. "I can do this. I have to."

"You have a choice." He carefully kept his voice devoid of inflection. He wanted her to understand that it was her decision. To know he'd always give her one. She smiled at him, if the tremulous curve could be called a smile.

She stepped away. If he touched her now, she wouldn't have the courage to do what came next. "I'm going to confess, Gabriel."

"What?" He stared at her as though she'd lost her mind, fairly certain it was true. "Confess what?"

"To the murder of Nathan Rhodes." Before he could speak, she rushed through her explanation. "If Kenneth is the killer, then he might tell them to cut a deal."

"Who gives a damn? No one will believe him."

"Sanchez might. Someone might. But it doesn't matter." She took a long breath and placed her hand on his chest. His heartbeat thumped beneath her palm. "Kenneth might be innocent. If he is, there's a psychopath out there who won't stop. How do you think he'd react when his prey turns herself in?"

Pushing past outrage, Gabriel forced himself to consider the angles. "His hold over you is broken."

"And he'll want to punish me. He'll come for me. That's his endgame. Twenty-six deaths and then me."

"No."

"Yes." Her response was simple, absolute. Not only had she decided to stop running; she also planned to fight. "Help me, Gabriel. It's the only way."

An hour later, Peter answered the phone. Quickly Gabriel issued terse instructions to Peter, explaining the situation. The editor grunted in agreement. In the *Ledger* offices, Peter began to shout out orders as quickly as Gabriel fed them to him. When they finished,

Peter transferred him to Kelly. She cheerfully accepted his directives about drivers and distributors. It was past 7:00 p.m., and the inaugural daily edition of the *Ledger* would roll off the presses in six hours.

Erin turned the key in the brass lock and stumbled into the apartment. She braced herself against the door, unable to move farther. Every instinct, every fiber, shrilled at her to run. But, she accepted resignedly, this time they'd know to look for her. Sylvie had taken her confession. Sanchez wanted to book her that night, but Sylvie's logic had prevailed. Booking Erin would mean an open record and might undermine her plan. Grudgingly Sanchez gave in to letting Erin go, on condition that she surrender tomorrow after it was over.

Assuming she lived through it.

It was then she registered the muted hum of the television. The television that had been off when she left the apartment. Raw nerves trembled through her, and she thought of the killer whose sick mind held her in focus. Her hand scrabbled behind her for the knob. It wasn't running if she was evading a thief. Or worse.

Beyond the hallway, a laugh track sent its muffled hilarity through the apartment. Clutching her bag, she forced herself to be rational. What type of criminal would lie in wait, watching cable?

Breath seeped out of her and she managed his name through the receding iron grip of fear. "Damn it, Sebastian."

"Hey, kiddo." He strolled into the foyer, arms open, wry smile at the ready. Tall, angular, with gaunt cheeks and heavy-lidded ebony eyes that saw too much, Sebastian Cain possessed a mysterious unearthly beauty that reminded Erin of wizards and warlocks and fallen heroes. Without hesitation, she ran to him, her bag falling to the floor. Unerringly his arms closed around her, lifted her for inspection. "I guess you missed me."

She hugged him fiercely. "Oh, Sebastian."

He led her into the living room and settled her on the sofa. Brushing a kiss across her forehead, he cuddled her next to him. "You didn't sound good on the phone."

"You broke into my house." She pulled free to give him a warning look. "I thought we agreed you'd try to reform."

"Killed anyone lately?" was his droll response.

He wasn't prepared for her to dissolve into tears. They poured out of her, and Sebastian drew her to him. "What have they done to you?" he murmured into her tangled hair.

She didn't answer. Clinging to him, she wept for what seemed like hours. Finally empty, she sat back and scrubbed at her drenched face. "I've gotten you all wet," she muttered.

"You've done worse." Matter-of-factly, he reached for a tissue from the side table and mopped up the tears she rarely shed. Too rarely. "Remember the day before you moved to Callenwolde? At least, this time, you didn't draw blood."

Calmer, Erin chuckled. "That was an accident. If you hadn't gotten in my way, I wouldn't have broken your nose."

Sebastian shifted on the wide cushions, turning so he could face her. "We can leave the minute you say the word."

He made the suggestion simply, without asking questions, and Erin loved him for it. She didn't have to tell him about Gabriel or the serial killer or why she'd collapsed into tears. He didn't care.

For her entire life, he'd been the truest friend she'd ever known. Loyalty had stretched three thousand miles. Loyalty had met her in the mountains of California and helped her hide the man she'd killed.

"They know about Nathan." Erin sprang up from the couch, needing to move.

"How?"

"I confessed." She spun toward him. "Not about you. I'd never do that."

"Of course you wouldn't." Sebastian stretched his long legs in front of him. He was a man who never regretted his decisions. Life sifted through time at such a rate, regret had no place. Death had none, so why should he? But he'd broken his rule twice. Once when he let pride send him away from Erin's door, friendship shattered by nasty insults he should have known were forced.

But he had no regrets about his decision two years ago. The night a shattered Erin had called him, terrified, he caught the red-eye to San Francisco and drove to San Cabes without hesitation. It was his conclusion that the bastard Rhodes deserved no better than to be pushed over the jagged rocks into the ravine below. Then he'd bundled her into his car and taken her home.

It had taken him months to bring her around. To convince her of her worth. He'd come up with altering her identity, using the name he'd always preferred. With his less savory contacts, he'd forged her degrees from Gorham.

When Erin decided she was strong enough, needing him to let her try out her new wings, she left for New Orleans. Sebastian promised to watch over her.

He'd failed. Again.

"Give me the whole story."

He patted the seat beside him, but Erin preferred to stand. She started from the beginning. Had it only been a few weeks ago that she'd read about Maggie's murder? "The police believe me now. Gabriel is planning to run the story in tomorrow's paper."

"This Gabriel. You trust him?" Sebastian had his doubts. He didn't like reporters or cops, and the combination couldn't be any good. Plus, he saw the way her eyes shifted when she said Gabriel's name.

Images from the television screen flittered in the room. Erin watched them, trying to frame her response. "Gabriel is— He's a friend. He wouldn't hurt me."

Blunt as always, Sebastian disagreed. "Sounds to me like he's trading on your pain for his story."

Erin bristled. "I'm not an imbecile." Hearing what Sebastian didn't say, she relaxed. "He's not Nathan, either."

"How do you know?" Sebastian quizzed, apprehension coiled inside him but not in his voice. "You don't know men."

"I've learned." Erin walked over to the television and clicked it off. She sat on the low bench she'd placed near the armoire. Twisting the silver ring, she tried to explain. "The first time I met Gabriel, I was wearing this awful, frumpy suit. I ran into him, literally, in the hall. Most men ignore me now, and I want it that way." She lifted her eyes to meet his. "He saw me, Sebastian. Saw through the clothes and the hair and the makeup. He liked me."

"You're a beautiful woman," Sebastian argued grumpily. "No matter what you try to hide in. The fact that he can see it makes him a man, not a friend."

"Is it impossible that he could care about me?" she asked in a small voice.

Sebastian immediately crossed the room to kneel beside her. "Of course not. But I couldn't stand to have him hurt you. This Gabriel or anyone. You've always deserved more from life than you've gotten." Years of aggravation had him clutching her shoulders. "First your parents, then Rhodes. I couldn't stand watching you fall apart again. You've worked too hard."

Erin clasped the strong, wiry wrists and leaned close to kiss him lightly. "I'm stronger than I was then. I've gotten used to being content. Occasionally, I'm even happy. Gabriel, when I let him, makes me happy."

"Then why were you crying all over me like a baby?" The question was teasing. Sebastian was not. "I'm the closest thing you've got to a brother, Erin. If I have to break his legs, I'll do it." *And enjoy it,* he thought grimly.

Erin's smile fell. "I don't know if he despises me now. I told him I killed a man. I abandoned the body and didn't call the police. I must repulse him."

"Did you ask?"

"Well, no." Sometimes she hated the way he cut to the heart of things. "There really wasn't time."

"It's only nine o'clock. Seems like there's plenty of time to me." Sebastian nimbly gained his feet and he hauled her up beside him. It occurred to him that Gabriel Moss needed to understand Erin wasn't alone. She had friends already, ones who wouldn't put up with another tear from her wide eyes. Besides, Sebastian hadn't been in a good fight in a while. The prospect cheered him, and he draped an arm around Erin. "Let's go and meet your friend, shall we?"

Slightly dubious, Erin allowed herself to be led out of the apartment and down the stairs. Outside, a gleaming chrome and black motorcycle was parked near the corner. Sebastian strode toward it, but she hung back. He felt her hesitation and tugged at her hands.

"Come on, Erin," he cajoled. "Live a little."

"Why don't we wait for a nice, safe, enclosed taxicab?" If her voice whined, she didn't care.

"I forgot you were such a wimp." The childhood dare had its desired effect. Erin stomped over to the monstrosity and swung her leg over the seat. Sebastian sat in front and passed her a helmet. He strapped his in place and kick-started the beast. "Hang on!" he yelled. In seconds, they peeled away from the curb.

Erin shouted directions to him and held on for dear life. Sultry wind whipped past her cheeks. Honeysuckle and heat filled her senses. She reveled in the freedom and cautiously opened her eyes to watch their progress.

Too soon, Sebastian screeched to a halt beside the warehouse. A white neon sign declared the space the home of the *Bayou Ledger*. He locked his bike and helped Erin to alight. Lights burned in every window, oblivious to the late hour.

Erin pressed the intercom for admission, and Kelly's chipper voice asked for her identity.

"It's Erin Abbott."

"Hey, Erin! Gabe didn't tell me to expect you. I guess things are too crazy for him to remember all the details. I swear, if we get this issue out, it'll be a miracle."

Erin grinned. "Kelly, can you let me in?"

"Sure thing!" The locks clicked open and Sebastian hauled the metal door aside.

Together, they entered chaos.

CHAPTER 24

News made itself in an instant, in a second's thought or in-decision. Lives altered course, spun in wild, untried direc-tions. Information slithered in through whispered betrayals or bounded onto consciousness as shouted exaltations to the masses. Febrile and frozen by turns, the daily acts of randomly connected existences conspired to create hu-man drama destined to unfold on oversize sheets creased with ink.

Newsworthy events made themselves over hours and days and years.

The *Ledger* had one night.

From the confines of his office on the main floor of the converted warehouse, Gabriel surveyed the commotion. He'd expected to be anxious or excited, probably both. He hadn't expected to feel like a traitor. Even when the one he was about to betray asked him to do it.

The lead story on the twisted triangle of Analise Glover, Nathan Rhodes, and a serial killer was written. Right now, Peter was slashing through it with his green pen, punching up Gabriel's prose. By morning, readers would know about a murder in California that had come to haunt New Orleans.

By tomorrow night, a killer would be behind bars. As would Erin.

Fascinated, Erin absorbed the flurry of activity. She and Sebastian halted just inside the main floor as a runner sped past, a page fisted in his hand. From her perch overhead, Kelly waved down to them. The friendly greeting motioned them inside and signaled that she'd join them soon. Erin intentionally refrained from glancing down the length of the floor to Gabriel's office. But despite her best efforts, her gaze was drawn in that direction.

Sebastian impatiently observed the surreptitious glances. It didn't take a genius to guess what she was trying so hard not to look at. Or who. Gabriel Moss had a great deal to answer for, beginning with the smudged shadows beneath Erin's eyes. And the wounded catch in her voice when she said the man's name. And agreeing to sign her death warrant by running her struggle for survival in his paper.

Loose morals were Sebastian's specialty, but he drew the line at harming the defenseless. A line Moss didn't seem to recognize. Once more, Sebastian congratulated himself on listening to his instincts. His delayed task in New York could wait until he convinced Erin to come home with him before she was taken into custody.

In marked contrast to his restive thoughts, he drawled, "Have they done this before?"

"I explained that. They're moving to a daily issue. This is the inaugural edition." Erin twisted around, eager to

take it all in, and pain melted into pride. Gabriel had created a superb monument to the family he held so dear. For
better or worse, she would be a part of this creation and,
come what may, a part of him. "Gabriel should be proud
of himself."

"Hmm." Lithely Sebastian sidled out of the path of
two warring reporters, who seemed to be disputing the
closing bell on Wall Street. The duo stormed by and he
had to arch to avoid another collision. He lightly
clasped Erin's arm and tugged her into what appeared to
be a safe corner of the bedlam. Guiding them to an alcove, he mocked, "This is the crack team that's trying to
stop a killer?"

"Yes. And who the hell are you?"

Sebastian turned lazily and encountered a pair of glacier gray eyes that perfectly matched the icy voice. It
amused Sebastian that the cold stare was directed at
where his hand wrapped familiarly around Erin's wrist.
Deliberately he ran his thumb along the soft skin there.
When the ice melted into dangerous heat, Sebastian lifted
a brow in challenge. It had definitely been too long since
he'd been in a fight. "You must be the inestimable Gabriel
Moss. Nice shop."

"Thanks." The gratitude did not extend beyond that
single word. Gabriel could barely see past the red haze to
the face of the man who stroked Erin with such familiarity. Where Gabriel touched her. Where only Gabriel
should touch her. Infuriated, he started to snatch the hand
away, to demand she explain herself.

Nearly as tall as him, the newcomer looked rawboned
and lean and self-indulgent. For affectation, Gabriel
silently derided, he wore all black. The gaunt face had the

look of culture, but Gabriel could see it was a facade carefully slicked over rougher, less cultivated edges. The primal glint in the black eyes proved his point. "I guess your name is Sebastian."

A wily grin quirked lips women swooned over. The newsman definitely didn't like him, which suited Sebastian fine. Lucky for both of them, he felt the same instant antipathy.

Gabriel Moss wasn't a small man, but neither was Sebastian. Still, it was unusual for him to have to look up at anyone, even an inch. He didn't like the sensation. Irritated, he relied on his preferred weapon. Arrogance. "Way to use your powers of deduction. You'll be a success yet, young Clark Kent."

"Sebastian." Erin shot him an exasperated look. Waves of hostility poured off of both men. She had no energy left to referee a bout *mano a mano* tonight. "Gabriel Moss, meet my oldest friend, Sebastian Cain." She nudged Sebastian. "Shake hands like good boys," she instructed.

Gabriel quickly accepted the gesture, knowing it meant nothing. His eyes remained focused on where long fingers toyed with Erin's satiny skin. Misery throbbed hard and fast, because what he'd also noticed was that she didn't seem to mind the caresses. In fact, he could have sworn he saw pleasure flicker briefly in her wary eyes.

It appeared he'd been a poor substitute for her errant knight, he fumed. When Sebastian abandoned her again, as he had in California, she'd have no one but herself to blame. But he sure as hell wasn't going to wait around to watch her fall apart.

Love had bloomed hastily, and surely, Gabriel promised himself, it would wither as fast. When he finally met her quizzical look, his expression was deliberately blank. "I didn't expect to see you tonight."

"I wanted to see the story." Erin tried to read the impassive face, to no avail. He had a right to be annoyed, but surely she deserved more than this chilly reception. She'd done everything he asked. Told him everything.

But if honesty earned her his contempt, then so be it, she thought, hardening her heart. Tightening her hold on Sebastian, Erin explained briskly, "I told Sebastian our plan and he wanted to come along."

"Our plan? No, this is your idea, Erin. I'm just the fool too stupid to say no."

"Try harder next time," Sebastian suggested dryly.

Gabriel's urge to smash his fist into Sebastian's smirking face nearly overwhelmed him. Instead of succumbing to the violent impulse, he snapped, "I don't make a habit of leaving my friends to the wolves, no matter how badly they hurt my feelings."

The harsh accusation drew a stunned gasp from Erin. "I told you that in confidence."

"I'm a reporter. I don't keep secrets." He held her shocked look, refusing to apologize. She'd rejected what he had to offer, except for his newspaper. Well, she could have the front page, he thought tiredly, but that was it. "There's no room for you here, Erin." With a final, withering look, he turned to walk away.

The blow nearly buckled her knees. Hurt, she thought only to leave, and the rest happened in slow motion. A reporter rushing through with copy careened into her. They teetered on the brink of falling. Both men leaped to save her and succeeded in entangling all four of them in the process. As they swayed, trying to recapture their balance,

Erin thought she detected a hint of shoving between Gabriel and Sebastian.

In the end, Erin found one arm captured by Sebastian. Gabriel had a death grip on her hand. Enduring the silent tug-of-war for the time it took to secure her footing, she abruptly jerked free of both men.

"Listen here, you—" Sebastian's solid grip on his shoulder forced him around again. Gabriel cocked his fist, grateful for the provocation. Before he could land the ready blow, Peter grabbed his arm.

"Kelly needs to see you." The older man squeezed his captive elbow warningly. Bone ground against bone, though Gabriel refused to wince at the deliberate pain.

"This is none of your—"

Peter cut off the epithet in mid-sentence. "Upstairs. Now."

Prepared to remind Peter who was actually in charge, Gabriel glowered at the older man until he noticed work had ceased and forty faces gawked at him. Reining in his temper, he exhaled sharply. Brawls in the middle of the newsroom were not permitted, particularly those started by the owner. With a curt nod to Peter, Gabriel headed for the central staircase that linked the three floors. He muttered an obscenity beneath his breath.

Peter herded him into Kelly's office. "I'm not playing referee all night. This blasted daily edition was your confounded idea. Either send the girl home or put them to work. I don't give a fig which one you choose, but do it soon."

"I didn't ask her to come here." If his voice was sulky, Gabriel paid no attention. He pointed an accusatory finger at Kelly. "You let them in."

Stressed and exhausted, Kelly retorted, "She's your girlfriend. What was I supposed to do?"

"Tell her no." Gabriel folded his arms defiantly. "And she's not my girlfriend."

Peter rolled his eyes and Kelly released a disbelieving giggle. Looking at Peter, she pantomimed air kisses. "Oh, Gabriel. I love you. Be mine." She spread her arms wide, and Peter caught her around her waist, lowering her into a romantic dip.

"Erin, my darling. I will sacrifice everything for you!" Peter's bass, with its sonorous texture, rumbled over words infused with biting sarcasm. He planted a smacking kiss on Kelly's grinning mouth. "The *Ledger* be damned."

"Cut it out, you idiots." Gabriel scowled at the duo, refusing to be amused.

Setting Kelly on her feet, Peter stopped smiling. "We've got three hours to finish this thing, Gabriel. I need your focus. You need her help." Gabriel opened his mouth to protest. Peter spoke over him. "It's her story and she has the best insight into the murderer. Plus, she's here already. You've been holed up in your office since five o'clock and I still don't have a good draft. Time's wasting, Gabe."

Kelly decided it was safe to chime in. "The rest of the articles are nearly set, Gabriel. If the ABC Serial Killer is going to be our lead, we need it soon. I have it on good authority that Harmony Turner's murder is the *Chronicle*'s headline tomorrow."

Gabriel looked down at the lobby. Erin was talking to a young gofer who'd volunteered for the late shift. The proximity between the two was disturbingly intimate. Sebastian leaned negligently against the wall, covertly watching them. Gabriel recognized the protective stance and filed the information away.

Whether he liked it or not, he did need Erin. If only for tonight. Tomorrow, he decided, would take care of itself. He turned to his staff, his best friends. "You'll have your copy in time."

"Never doubted it for a minute," Peter lied with ease. "Kelly, see if you can't entertain Erin's friend for us, will you?"

The instant the words left his mouth, Peter found himself, for once, nonplussed. In the blink of an eye, Kelly's girl-next-door grin transformed into a sultry smile. And he didn't recognize the provocative voice that answered, "Anything for the paper." She skipped out of her office and bounded down the stairs. Soon Sebastian's appreciative chuckle wafted up the stairwell.

"Close your mouth, old man. You're starting to drool." Gabriel draped a comforting arm around Peter's frozen shoulders. "Back to work."

They returned to the lobby. Peter shot Sebastian a narrow look that the younger man blithely ignored. Kelly offered him a tour of the facilities, and he hesitated, looking askance at Erin.

"Go on," she encouraged with a wan smile. "I've seen it already. I'll wait here."

Prodded by Peter, Gabriel stepped forward. "I'd like for you to look at the article, if you don't mind."

"Of course."

Erin trailed Gabriel to his office. In silence, they sat at the conference table, and he showed her the rough draft. After a quick read, she fished a pen from his desk and started making notes. She returned the article, and Gabriel reviewed her suggestions, grunting occasionally.

"You disagree?" she queried after the fifth grunt.

"Hmm?" Gabriel tore his eyes away from the page and focused on her, as though he'd forgotten her presence. "What?"

She gnawed at her bottom lip. Testily she sputtered, "You've been grunting for a while now. Do you think I said something wrong?"

Gabriel examined the notes he'd made thoughtfully. When he finally answered, he gave her a level look. "I think you'd make an excellent reporter. Your writing is sharp. Clear. Concise." He turned the pages toward her, pointing at the phrases she'd added. "The analysis is clinical without being distant. That takes talent. The reader will understand what happened to you, why you made the choices you did, but he won't pity you. That's great journalism."

"You mean that?" The question escaped before she could stop herself.

His pencil tapped the article; then he used it to tilt her chin, and her befuddled eyes met his steady ones. "I always say what I mean, Erin. Don't ever doubt that."

"It's difficult not to." She shrugged feebly. "I don't have the best barometer for liars."

"You know me."

Erin nodded once, owing him that at least. "Yes. I do." Other words crowded in her arid throat. Pleas for reassurance tussled with passionate longings she'd never before given voice to, and the battle left her silent.

A skirmish played out in her eyes, and Gabriel waited

for her to say more. But he wasn't shocked when she remained quiet. *At least,* he thought morosely, *she didn't lie this time.* Drained, Gabriel pushed away from the table.

It was amazing, he mused, how mercurial relationships could be. He'd stick with the news, which rarely changed. Just the seven deadly sins repeated in creative patterns and never as treacherous as love. "Why don't you find the rest of them? Tell Peter I'll have the final copy for him soon."

Bemused, Erin left Gabriel to complete the article. Over the next two hours, she learned about the machinations to putting a paper to bed and having it ready for readers in the morning. Her admiration for Peter grew exponentially as he hustled stories into layout and caught last-minute errors.

In Kelly, she found a drill sergeant cloaked in sheep's clothing. Burly press operators, muscle-bound loading crews, and tough-talking drivers obeyed her slightest command. Gabriel guided the process with a firm, patient hand, appeasing fretful reporters and harried workers with banter and calm reassurances.

By 2:00 a.m., the inaugural daily *Ledger* rolled out of the loading dock and onto deserted streets and boulevards, thousands of copies. In a few hours, the city would meet a killer and the woman he performed for and no one would sleep easier at night. "Alphabet Killer Seeks Twisted Vengeance Against Local Professor."

The tension palpable, Kelly flopped onto a low divan near the break room. She peered at Gabriel with one eye at half mast. "You want to do this every day?"

"If your predictions net us enough revenue, absolutely." Gabriel playfully tousled her hair. "I hope you really can count."

"I don't plan to hold a column open for you tomorrow. Have your copy on my desk by seven, or I'm running another lead," Peter said, scrubbing at the streaks of green ink that striped his hands.

"My story. My copy."

"Territorial, aren't you?" Sebastian lounged on the opposite end of the divan, next to Erin, who'd squeezed into the center. Holding Gabriel's glare, he plucked Erin's limp hand from her lap, expertly stilling her small jerk of protest. He had a point to make, and he'd make it. "Mine, mine, mine. Sometimes, Moss, you have to learn to share."

"Sebastian," hissed Erin, snatching her hand free, "cut it out or you'll be sleeping on your motorcycle."

An image of where else the man might lay his head tonight hazed Gabriel's vision. Blindly he strode across the floor. Before he could reach Sebastian, Peter stepped between them.

Fed up, Erin turned the tables and grabbed Gabriel's hand. She plowed through the knots of celebrating staff that occupied the main lobby, their mouths agape at the sight of their boss being tugged along in the angry woman's wake.

As soon as they reached his office, she slapped the door shut on their audience. "How do we get upstairs?"

"The elevator." Gabriel jabbed the hidden button, and a panel opened to reveal the lift. The car doors slid wide and they entered. They rode to the fourth floor in silence.

Leading her out, he keyed open the loft door. He kicked at a package laid at the entryway, caring nothing for its spilled contents. He crossed to the window to stare down at the night.

When silence lingered, she asked neutrally, "What are you doing?"

"You dragged me in here. You tell me." He ground the explanation out without looking at her.

"All right. What the devil is wrong with you?"

Angst stiffened his shoulders and unfamiliar jealousy writhed inside. Declarations whirled inside his head, each demanding to be the first. *I love you. I won't hurt you. I hate Sebastian Cain for touching you. For leaving you to that monster. Let me love you.* Unable to choose, he said nothing.

When the quiet lengthened, Erin said evenly, "Words tend to help with the talking."

"Shut up."

The terse command cracked her serene veneer. She stormed over to the window. A few feet separated them, a healthy distance given her mood. He may not want her, but she'd be damned if he'd treat her like this. If anyone would ever again make her feel useless or unimportant or unworthy. She wasn't a piece of chattel. She was a flesh-and-blood, living, breathing woman who deserved an explanation for his attitude. "I asked you a question. What's wrong with you?"

"Nothing. I just don't appreciate you bringing lover boy into my office."

"I told you Sebastian was my friend," she grated out. Struggling for reason, she explained, "We're not interested in each other that way."

Gabriel sneered. "Tell that to him. He has every intention of winding up in your bed. If you can't see that, you're a fool."

The insult loosed her temper. "If you don't want me,

that's your prerogative. But you have no say in who else I choose to sleep with."

In three steps, he cornered her against the mahogany bookcase built into the wall. Cool silver now burned with molten heat. "Touch him and I'll break his arms."

"Why? You don't want me." She spat out the accusation, trying to take no notice of the intent blazing behind the silver.

His laugh was hard and furious. "Don't want you? I can't think of anything else!" He slapped his hands on a half-empty shelf, trapping her hips. "I imagine you in my bed every night, wrapped around me. Taking me inside you." In blatant torment, he pressed closer. "I imagine you here on the desk. In my car. In your bed. Everywhere. Anywhere."

Desire and apprehension battled for supremacy, and her throat tightened. "You're lying. I know I disgust you."

"You what?" Gabriel roared, stunned. "Are you insane?"

"No." She pushed at his chest. He didn't budge. Refusing to take the coward's way and give in to the tears threatening to flood, she glared at him. "I told you what I did, and you turned away. You haven't been able to look at me since."

When he saw how her brown eyes glistened, Gabriel started to embrace her. But he would clear the air first. "I haven't looked at you because I can't stand it."

"You mean, you can't stand me. I took a life and lied about it. I know what you think of liars." Her voice broke, but her eyes remained dry. "What you think of me."

"Do you?"

"Yes."

"Idiot." Fresh, raw, the helplessness consumed him. Forgetting his vow, he cupped her chin, his thumb drifting over the beloved dimple. "I ache for you. I hate knowing how you had to live. How alone you were. It slices at me, thinking about what you had to endure. What you had to do."

Forcing the whisper past a throat ravaged by unshed tears, she managed, "You walked away."

"It infuriated me, how useless I felt. How helpless I feel. You fought for your life and no one helped. Now I'm helping you put your life in jeopardy for a headline." Gabriel stared at her. "I'm no better than Rhodes."

Shocked, Erin laid her hand on his where it rested on the shelf. How could she have been so blind? How could he be so stupid? "You're nothing like him. He was a bully. A selfish, insecure man who had no compassion in him."

Gabriel retorted, "And I'm a desperate reporter willing to put your life at risk to save my paper."

She heard the remorse and wondered how she'd missed the misery in his eyes. He had no idea what he'd given her in their time together. More than passion, more than affection, with him she'd discovered a measure of peace that had eluded her for a lifetime. Sitting on the dock, dangling bare feet in the water, she'd felt something suspiciously like joy wending its way through her. Binding her to him. She hadn't told him, not trusting the vibrancy of feeling. She hadn't admitted it to herself, not believing it could be so easy. "You're doing what I asked you to do. What I need you to do."

"I should have said no. I shouldn't have pushed you so hard."

"Gabriel, you didn't force me into this. I volunteered."

"I didn't give you an option."

Bluntly Erin overrode his confession. "Get over yourself. A madman is focused on me. He knows my past and wants me to solve his ghoulish puzzles. If he wins, I'm the prize. Not you." Her voice shook over the last, but she resisted the fear. She'd spent too much of her life avoiding reality, hidden away. Gabriel helped her emerge from the shadows, and for that alone she could have loved him. It amazed her that he couldn't see it. Copying his earlier gesture, she caressed his chin where stubble shaded the copper tones. "This has to end, whether you write the story or not. But I'm glad you're a part of it."

"Then why do you cringe when I come too close?" Gabriel tore away from her. "My God, even now, I can't stop crowding you." He put more distance between them, certain in a moment he would beg. When the width of the room separated them, he sighed. "Please, Erin. Take Sebastian and go."

"You don't get it, do you?" Determined, she followed him, forced his back to the door. "I'm not afraid anymore. Not of Nathan or a killer or myself."

Gabriel grabbed her shoulders, reckless enough to believe. "You should be. You should run away from here, Erin. Away from all of this."

"I'm not going anywhere, Gabriel." She traced the hollow at his cheek, the proud line of his nose. This face belonged to her. He belonged to her. "Not without you."

CHAPTER 25

"Erin." Gabriel captured her hand where it singed his cheek. He thought to pull it away, but somehow the fragile skin grazed lips hungry for the taste of her. There, where her pulse beat madly, strongly, the scent of jasmine wafted up to him, and he breathed deep. Control remained by the sheer will. Want had never been so immediate. Visions of them together, satiated, clouded before him, and desire raked him with erotic claws.

But the part of him that remembered a frightened young woman finding herself refused to take in heat what no other had. With a ragged plea, he entreated, "Go. You don't know what you're asking."

In silent response, Erin moved impossibly closer. Power, feminine and timeless, filled her. For the first time in her life, she knew exactly what she was doing. What she wanted. Gabriel was hers. And, whether he knew it or not, she belonged to him. With him.

For nearly thirty years, decisions had been made for

her. Well-meaning, ill-intentioned, they wove together in a pattern of supplication that shamed her. But not any longer. Tonight she would seek and take for herself. Tonight she would offer and give of herself. Not from fear or obligation or timidity. From strength.

"Make love with me."

Tightening his hold on the slender wrist, Gabriel forced himself to force her hand away. "We can't do this. I can't."

Boldly she twisted the captive fingers free and sought tumid evidence to the contrary. When he gasped and shuddered, she reveled. "Apparently, you can."

His mind clouded, his heart raced. Unsteady palms lifted to push her away, but a surge of sensation ravaged him and he whispered, "Stop it."

Heady with power, Erin complied. As she angled closer, teasing fingers stroked his throat, scraped lightly at his jaw. Because her head barely brushed his shoulder, she couldn't reach the mouth that tempted. Instead, she focused on the regions within range. "I want you," she breathed into his bared skin.

"Don't." Rearing away, smacking his head into the door, Gabriel scrabbled for restraint. Downstairs, the *Ledger* was shutting down until tomorrow morning, which left him no reason to run. Inside the suddenly airless loft, his destiny stalked him. Wayward hands streaked over buttons, teased willing flesh. His voice trembled as her searching tongue found and lathed skin, as though with naked flame. Where she touched, he burned. Where she kissed, he ached.

To hell with it, he thought rashly, ready to jerk her mouth to his, to plunge deep and taste forever, until neither could walk away.

As though she felt the change, she raised herself toward him. His fingers dived into the silken black strands tumbling around her face, and seeking, he caught her eyes. In their endless depths he saw an echo of trepidation. In that moment, Gabriel found the last threadbare remnants of gallantry. He refused to take advantage, despite the erotic promise. Love, if it was true, demanded sacrifice. Denial. Gripping her arms, he gave her a none too gentle shove. Above her head, he explained gruffly, "Obviously, my body wants you. That doesn't mean I'll have you."

Hesitation faltered her hand, and she dropped it from his muscled chest. She wrapped chilled arms around her body. Staggering away, she refused to look at him. He'd tried to warn her, but she didn't listen. Kisses weren't the same as sex. What she'd imagined as restraint had actually been disinterest. She gathered tattered pride and lifted her head, determined to apologize before disappearing. It was then her distressed gaze met eyes that burned like the stars. Burned with unnamed yearnings and reflected cravings.

Doubts vanished, and gentle, unyielding affection made her want him more. And annoyed her beyond reason. Gabriel thought chivalry lay in protecting her from him. Didn't he understand salvation could only be found in his arms? She spun to him then, triumphant. "You want me. You can't think of anything else."

"This isn't right. You don't know what you want. What you need. I can't take advantage of that. I won't—"

She cut off his denial. "No, I've never been with anyone before. Because I've never wanted anyone before."

"Which is why this is a mistake. You need time. More

time." His appeal was desperate. "Stay, and I may never let you go."

"I'm yours." The words were erotic threat, voluptuous promise. Erin watched him with glittering eyes, waiting for his reaction.

Dragging her up, he fused his mouth to hers. Inside, his tongue streaked over and under, drew out ragged moans of pleasure. Their lips mated, parted, sampled. He bound her to him, and he plunged and devoured. Undaunted, she slid her arms around the hardened body and consumed. He tasted and grew impossibly hungry. He feasted and demanded more. His hands, too long denied, ripped at fabric, in quest of sleek skin. Torn clothing pooled at his feet, but it wasn't enough.

"Come," he insisted, lifting her into his greedy arms. Night pierced the dimly lit bedroom, the full moon a silent witness. In the moonlight, he stripped off the lace concoction binding her breasts, the triangle swathing her hips. When his reverent hand traced humid flesh, her knees buckled and he rejoiced.

"Come," he demanded, tumbling her to the cool sheets. Wanting to show her, needing to give, he stroked and cajoled and gloried when she convulsed beneath him, unprepared. Her keening cry filled his ears and he laughed with exultation.

Slick, sated, strangely empty, Erin rolled over him. "Your turn."

Spurred by imagination, she undressed him. Clothing slowly unraveled and fell unheeded to the floor. Then, in lascivious revenge, she strung hot, steamy kisses over dampened skin. She tasted him. Tormented him. Her eager

tongue traced the shape of quivering muscles of his chest.
She learned of the piquant flavors at his throat, the different
spice of his quivering stomach. Studious, she explored
long, corded thighs, lean hips, strong arms. When he
arched beneath her, she tested more exotic flavors, tortured
with flicks of untutored tongue and devilry.

Too near the edge, Gabriel pulled her away and up.
Blood pooled and surged, and he'd barely begun. Loving
her should take forever. "Let me see you," he murmured.
He turned them, determined to adore. Tracing the line of
her body, he savored the elegant beauty of her form.
Creamy skin and lovely, rounded curves. High, full breasts
tipped with chocolate rose above the slight mound of her
belly. Generous hips tapered into smooth, graceful thighs,
impossibly long legs.

He dipped his head, drawing a rounded, full globe into
his mouth. The pull and scrape and tug at her sensitive skin
made Erin writhe against him. She slid eager fingers into
his hair, held her to him. Gently he nipped at the captive
peaks and her body arched in fevered response. Skimming
his hands over her, he watched as sensations flooded her.
He caressed and plucked and nibbled. Over and under. Inside. When her body was a quivering length of damp skin
and tattered sighs, he whispered, "Let me have you."

"Not yet." Slithering against him, she returned his sensuous torment in full measure. Heated caresses redoubled, and she paid him back, stroke for stroke.

Soon they wrestled in rapturous battle, each determined to give. Gabriel felt himself falling and he flipped
her beneath him. He fumbled for protection, groaned as
she sheathed him. Then he yanked her up to face him, to
see him. To know it would only ever be him.

She circled him, enticed him. "Now."

He tried to ease into the wet heat, wanting to spare her pain. She closed around him, a damp fist of delirium and control stretched thinner, finer. Her body bucked once, and he surged forward. "Wait," he gasped. "Be still."

"I can't." Reaching for the unknown, her hips tilted and he slid deeper. "Please."

"I don't want to hurt you." Forcing their hands above her thrashing head, Gabriel clutched her wrists, joined their fingers. He pressed their lips together in a kiss that seized her heart. "I couldn't bear to hurt you."

"I know." Erin stirred restlessly against the corded body of sinew and skin, the body that promised her ecstasy just beyond her reach. Her slim back bowed like a reed, trying to take all of him. "You won't."

Slowly, inexorably, he moved within the satiny pulse of heat, surrounded and captivated. At the barrier, he captured her mouth in a frenzied kiss. When her body trembled and his vibrated in counterpoint, he knew.

"Now," they moaned in aroused unison.

He flowed inside her. She surrounded him. Control, tenuous and thready, snapped. Frantic, urgent, their bodies joined together, hips dancing in sinuous motion, building heady enchantment.

They sank into each other, unwilling to be apart.

They chased their pleasure, unable to be still.

They came together, knowing no other way.

Erin, Gabriel discovered to his amusement, slept with mindless abandon. Pale moonlight filtered through sheer curtains and highlighted the naked figure sprawled across the bed. Mussed hair tickled his chin, and even, peaceful breaths warmed his chest. One slender leg draped over his thigh shifted slightly, awakening his loins in a rush. Elegant fingers curled around his shoulder, and turning his head a little, he saw the other hanging off the bed. During the night, he'd roused himself enough to cover them with a tangled sheet, but it now bunched at her narrow feet.

Rather long, narrow feet for someone who beat five-two by an eyelash. The incongruity pleased him, as did the sight of fuchsia polish on her toes. Intrigued, he gingerly slipped from beneath her. The wide bed allowed room for him to reverse his position, so he could take a closer look. Never before, Gabriel realized, had he been aroused by the sight of a woman's feet. But the graceful construction, smooth skin, and irrepressible polish necessitated attention. And salutation.

She shifted and lay back, sighing in unconscious pleasure. Gabriel grinned and set himself to his task in earnest. Soft, open kisses traced dainty ankles, anointed tapered legs. He lingered over the tender skin behind supple knees, the faultless sweep of thigh. As he cupped her lush bottom, his mouth lazily explored the hollow of her navel, suckled at the luxurious apex of perfect breasts. Languidly, masterfully, he sketched shallow creases with licks of wet fire, tantalized mounds with restrained greed. Complicated flavors burst on his tongue. Piquant, sharp, sweet, resilient. "Erin," he sighed into her humid skin.

She emerged from sleep, damp and ready, into a morning shot through with sumptuous flames. Enthralled, she watched as he feasted, feeling the punch of release in shattering tremors. Her cry of satisfaction alerted him to her waking, but he paid her no heed. Before morning fully broke, he would memorize every valley, every peak. He would imprint himself on her, defying her to forget.

When she begged for completion, he denied her. Kisses singed her questing arms, rough licks of tongue sampled the hands he adored. Once he finished his journey of discovery where his mouth committed to heart lips and cheek and eyelids, he ranged over Erin's twisting form and began a sensual voyage down the smooth skin of shoulders, the faint ridges of her spine, the shadowed cleft beneath her hips.

Finally, having mapped what no other man had, he covered himself and slid inside. In concert, he took her mouth and her body, parried and thrust with a recklessness that he couldn't control. Discipline, restraint, control had no dominion. Only now. Only the glide of dewy skin, the violent tenderness of passionate kisses, and the race for more.

But Erin refused pliancy. With quick motions, she straddled him, taking them deeper. She rose above him, triumphant and wanton. He guided her, then gave himself to her devastating lead. Lightning flashed through her hips. Thunder rolled in his veins. The climax, when it came, pitched them together into the dark, into the dawn.

"I love you." Gabriel stroked her trembling form, his lungs strained for air. His mind cautioned silence, but his heart had other plans. Before she could respond, he hurried into muffled explanation. "All that matters is you. I love you." He heard her inhale, prepared to speak. The possibilities sprinted through him and he realized he could only bear one answer. But she said nothing. Fighting lassitude and the dull ache of disappointment, he shut his eyes and drifted off.

Devastated by her frozen silence, Erin curled into him.

She wanted to tell him what she felt, but she couldn't trust the words. Or the riot of feelings that reeled inside her. In mute response, she pressed a fervent kiss to the chest rising and falling with signs of sleep. Above his heart. There, the steady beat was strong and true. Like Gabriel. She hadn't known her capacity for joy until him. Hadn't realized her ability to feel until he held her.

She'd thought of herself as emotionally numbed, too different to love or be loved. Nathan had told her so, too many times. Irritated that he would intrude upon this moment, Erin angrily thrust the image aside. Nathan was the past. Gabriel was her present, possibly her future. If she could find the words.

CHAPTER 26

Erin awoke to the scent of coffee and pancakes filling the apartment. Slipping on one of Gabriel's shirts, she wandered into the kitchen. Gabriel stood at the breakfast bar.

"Good morning," he said, sliding a cup of coffee to the edge of the bar. After a couple of hours' sleep, he'd bounded out of bed with renewed determination to woo Erin. Starting with breakfast.

"Morning." She rubbed at her eyes, remembering the last moments before she'd succumbed to exhaustion. Of his mumbled confession that he loved her. Of her glaring silence. Faltering, she paused at the entryway, uncertain of her next move. She had absolutely no experience to draw upon.

Gabriel saw her hesitate and he suddenly realized he had no idea what he should say to her. Running his fingers through hair that definitely needed a cut, he exhaled sharply. He'd have to wing it. "Breakfast will be ready in five minutes." With deft motions, he flipped omelets onto a serving plate. Soon they sat down to breakfast.

"Erin," Gabriel began after taking a bracing gulp of juice, "we need to talk." *Great,* he thought disgustedly. *You sound like the morning after in a bad movie.* "I mean, we need to think about what happened last night."

"And this morning," Erin corrected lightly. "Several times, I seem to remember."

"Uh, yeah." Gabriel stared at her, unable to read her expression.

Seconds ticked by in absolute silence. Finally, Erin giggled. "Oh, Gabriel." She laughed uncontrollably. "You should see your face."

"What's so damned funny about my face?"

"The fact that you're terrified the poor deflowered virgin is expecting a proposal of marriage."

Red skated along his cheeks. "I'm not scared of you."

"You're scared witless." Erin got up and came around to his side of the table. She kissed him sweetly. "It's adorable."

"You think my attempt at chivalry is laughable?" Gabriel caught her around the waist and pulled her, protesting, into his lap. Impossibly, he was as rigid as steel. Did she realize he was only this way with her? "Erin—"

"I have you, Gabriel. That's all I want." She let him draw her to him, felt the sweet slide into oblivion when he kissed her and carried her back into the bedroom. Felt the liquid pull of paradise when he moved inside her as dawn broke.

He made love with her, felt himself explode within her warm, satin embrace. Felt his heart break when his confession was met by a scorching kiss, rather than words. Felt the painful tug of unrequited love when he cradled her into him.

Breakfast forgotten, they spent the early-morning hours

in bed, learning each other. How Gabriel writhed in agony when she tickled his sides. The wide streak of adventure in the wary Erin. And they learned about themselves. Erin hadn't known the dimensions of lovemaking, the art of bringing your partner laughter as well as ecstasy. Gabriel hadn't realized his capacity for generosity, driven to see pleasure overtake her before he followed her over the edge.

Too soon, the phone shrilled for attention. Gabriel fumbled for the receiver. "Moss."

"Get your ass down here." Peter pounded the desktop, and his lunch of coffee and a stale croissant bounced under the reverberations. "It's nearly nine o'clock. We've got another paper to put together. Advertisers have been ringing Kelly's phone off the hook. Stroke of brilliance, Gabe. Sheer brilliance. So get down here and steer the ship."

"You're the managing editor," Gabriel protested, exhausted and unwilling to leave the sleepy body wrapped so close to his. He stroked the long, slender limbs, marveling at their perfection. "Manage."

"You're the damned fool who decided we should become a daily." In a rare show of discretion, Peter lowered his voice to a muted roar. "Let Erin get some rest and come downstairs. Better yet, bring her with you. That young wolf she brought with her yesterday has been prowling around since morning."

Gabriel stiffened. "He's downstairs?"

"Yep. I've gotten Gennie to entertain him, but he keeps coming in here, demanding I produce the professor."

Gabriel had stopped on a single phrase. "You left my sister with Sebastian Cain?"

Gleefully Peter corrected him. "No. You left Sebastian Cain alone down here and he discovered your sister."

"Son of a—" The reasons for pummeling Cain redoubled in legitimacy. "I'll be down in fifteen minutes."

"Ten. I told Kelly to get us orders for a Saturday edition." Satisfied, Peter rang off. He sipped at his mug of coffee. Articles sat stacked high in front of him, and he merrily set about trimming the fat. By God, he loved his job. At the *Chronicle,* he'd been an important cog in a well-oiled machine. With the *Ledger,* he was the engine. Gabriel's story had caught fire and hopefully, Peter thought, a criminal. The *Ledger* would outpace the *Chronicle* in a year's time. In three years, the *Chronicle* would be birdcage fodder.

Relishing the image, he winnowed through pages of copy. In the middle of the stack, he found an unread piece on gentrification. The writer had crisp prose and clever wordplay. Peter made several notes in the margin, punched up a line or two, and inserted queries. When he finished, he scrolled through the copy until he was satisfied. He searched for a byline but saw nothing. A flip of the page revealed nothing. No byline. No submission date. No nothing.

Before he could attack the staff for shoddy workmanship, Gabriel swung into his office. "Where's Cain?"

Hoping Erin was on her way, Peter stalled and handed him the gentrification piece. "Read this."

Gabriel dropped into the chair on the other side of Peter's desk and fished in the cup holder for a pen that wasn't green. After a second pass, he looked up. "This is good. Damned good. Who's the writer?"

"Dunno." Peter jabbed the intercom. "Whoever wrote the article on gentrification, get in my office now!"

Peter muted but didn't kill the speaker. It amused him

to hear the anxious reporters out in the newsroom scramble. *Good for their development,* he thought. An eagle eye kept the pressure on. The fact that he kept his shades drawn so he couldn't see out was for his privacy alone. It had nothing to do with giving them breathing room.

A timid knock elicited a booming, "Come!"

"Peter?" Genevieve paused on the threshold. Her eyes widened when she spotted her brother. "Gabe."

"Gennie. What can I do for you?" Peter glanced at the clock. A few more hours before the dummy had to be set. "Looking for Gabriel?"

She fiddled with the handle in a nervous gesture Gabriel recognized. Hiding a smile, Gabriel beckoned her in. "She's not here for me, Peter."

"No. I came to see you about the gentrification article."

"You know who wrote it?"

"Yes." She screwed up her courage. "I did."

Saying nothing, Peter picked up the article. "It's wordy. And you announce your personal sentiments very clearly."

"Oh. Well. It was just—"

"What? A lark? You think we have time to play here?"

"Of course not." Genevieve stood proudly. "I may not be a reporter, but I understand the business. I wouldn't waste your time."

"Then why slip it into the pile without a byline?"

"Because I wanted your honest reaction. And I got it." *Dreams die hard,* she thought. But at least she'd finally tried. "I'll get out of your way."

"Sit down, Gennie." Peter waved her to a chair beside Gabriel and slid the copy across the surface. "Go on, take it. Read what I wrote."

She read the green script. "A column?" Her hazel eyes widened in astonishment. "You think I could write a column?"

Peter's obsidian eyes twinkled. "Since your accursed brother is determined to make this a daily, I need the copy. You academics get the summer off, so I thought I'd start you out on a probationary period. Three columns per week. We still like you in the fall, we'll talk."

"What's the pay?"

"Non-negotiable." He named a sum and she nodded briskly.

"I can live with that."

"Good. Ask Payton to find you a desk. I want the revised version on my desk by three."

"Yes, sir." Gennie bussed Gabriel's cheek with a grateful salute. "I won't let you down."

After she danced out of Peter's office, she halted and ran back inside. Euphoric, she planted a smacking kiss on Peter's cheek. "Thanks!"

"I didn't know she wanted to write," Gabriel grumbled when she shut the door. Why hadn't she told him? Did she think he'd disapprove?

"I doubt she could have told you without you trying to give her a job."

"Of course!" he returned. "I'm her brother and I happen to own a newspaper."

"She has her pride, Gabe," Peter grunted. "Runs in the family. Her wanting to be a crusading columnist was probably hard to admit when she lived in a house with Lincoln and Gabriel Moss. After Linc's death, the paper was all you talked about. All you cared about."

"No, it wasn't. I love my sister!"

"Yes, you do. But you've spent a lifetime living vicariously through your stories. Then you switched gears and made the *Ledger* your life." Before Gabriel could retort, Peter held up a silencing hand. "Lincoln Moss was a legend before you wrote your first piece. Between the two of us, you were hooked. The adrenaline, the power. You became a foreign correspondent to carve your own mark on the profession."

"I was good."

"You were the best," agreed Peter. "When you gave it up to come home, I thought you were ready for balance."

"Is this a lecture from the pot to the kettle?"

Peter snorted. "I've been alone longer than I've been a part of anything, except the *Chronicle*."

"That's your excuse?"

"I don't need an excuse. This isn't about me. It's about Gennie and you. You've always dived headfirst into the world, Gabe. 'Cause you have the devil's own luck, you wind up plucking pearls instead of drowning."

"Interesting metaphor."

"Shut up." Peter pounded the desk. "You don't have anything to prove. Not to me. Not to your sister. Not to your father." He saw Gabriel frown but plowed ahead. "The *Ledger* is a lifeline, son. Take it and wrap it around you and yours. Make the *Ledger* your own. Don't let it make you." He ceased abruptly. Advice-giving made him cranky.

Aware and grateful, Gabriel winked at Peter. "Am I crazy, or is she exceptional?"

"She'll be a phenom." Peter clicked off the intercom.

The buzz of the newsroom faded, leaving them in quiet. Friendship ran deep between them, and it was friendship that gnawed at Peter now. "What's the plan today?"

"The police will meet us at Erin's apartment at ten. Bernard's being released this morning, with a car on him. Assuming things go as expected, either he or someone with a grudge will be at her apartment. He won't be able to resist."

"I still don't think this is a good idea. They don't call 'em lunatics for nothing. What if he doesn't flip out like you expect?"

Gabriel had worried over the same question all night. But this was their last hope. "He'll show. I'll have the article ready by closing. Plan on using the same column inches on the dummy." He lifted an article from the stack on Peter's desk and scanned the pages. "You should think about whether the *Ledger* could use a food and wine section."

"We need to talk about something else, Gabe." Erin had yet to show up, but Peter thought he'd rather do this without her anyway. He pushed away from the desk and came around to sit beside Gabriel. "It's about Erin and her past. About your relationship with her."

At his solemn tone, Gabriel shot him a wary look. "My relationship with Erin is my business."

Peter shook his head. "Once you asked me to investigate, she became my business, too. Who she is impacts everyone at the *Ledger*. Everyone who sacrificed their jobs and paychecks to follow you from the *Chronicle*."

A vise tightened around Gabriel's heart, a war of loyalties. Forty men and women had placed their faith in him. In his dream. And he'd promised them triumph. One woman had shared her secrets with him. Her freedom. And he'd promised her sanctuary. "I can't betray her. I won't."

"I'm not asking you to. Not yet anyway." Peter leaned forward and propped his elbows on denim-clad knees. He wished there were another way to handle the situation, but he'd wrestled with possibilities since he got the report. They had no choice. "I've pulled up everything I could find on Analise Glover, Nathan Rhodes, and Callenwolde University."

"I don't need to hear it. She told me everything yesterday."

Peter frowned. "Everything? You sure?"

Experimentally Gabriel's fingers creased the article into folds. He parried Peter's question with one of his own. "What did you find out about him?"

"Rhodes was a jerk. Misogynist and egomaniac. Colleagues hated him. Girls loved him. Especially the barely postpubescent. Erin must have been fresh meat to him when her parents sent her to him."

"She was fifteen." The folded page crumpled into a fisted ball.

"I know. They'd whisked her away from London after she managed to wig out even the avant-garde of the BBC." He flipped through several pages. "I couldn't find any record of reports mentioning him. Except two, from a few years ago. A student's father filed charges against Rhodes. She refused to testify at trial. In the end, she transferred to another school with a perfect transcript. A Terry Watson."

"And the other?"

"A graduate student in linguistics. She vanished. Less than a week later, so did Analise Glover and Nathan Rhodes."

CHAPTER 27

"It's time to go." Erin spared Gabriel a glance as she buttoned up the shirt she'd borrowed from his closet. "Sylvie called. They just released Kenneth."

"Are you sure you're ready?" he asked as she calmly passed him to go into the bathroom. Too calmly, he thought, for his taste. As she combed her hair, he watched her in the mirror. What he saw clutched at him, squeezing his throat. In the next hours, she would confront a madman and her past. Where was the fear? The apprehension? He couldn't find either in her eyes. "The police could still send in a decoy. Erin, you don't have to do this."

"Ten people are dead," she replied evenly as she bundled her hair into a band. "I have to account for taking one of them myself. And the others won't have justice without me." In the mirror she could see the gray eyes grow stormy, and she braced for it.

He didn't disappoint. "You've given the police all the information you have. They can do their job without you."

His voice rose, ringing with the impotence he felt. "This is not your responsibility! Damn it, Erin, don't go!"

"He'll be watching the apartment. If it isn't Kenneth, he'll know I'm not there. That I didn't go home last night." *That I spent it here with you. And he'll come after you next.*

Gabriel saw something shift in her eyes. "What are you thinking?" She ducked her head and moved past him, but he blocked her at the door. "Oh, God, you're trying to protect me, aren't you?"

Her head shot up, expression fierce. "Ten bodies, Gabriel. I can't let it become eleven. I can't let it be you."

"The police can protect both of us, Erin." He cupped her cheek. "You don't have to pay penance by sacrificing yourself. I'll call Sylvie. They'll send a detective into your apartment and—"

"And what?" The horrible visions she'd wrestled with all morning flashed before her, filled her words. "He's vicious and cruel. And smart. Smarter than Sylvie or Sanchez or any of them." She flung her hands out, imploring Gabriel to understand. "He's patient. Patient enough to wait two years to come after me. Nine lives that we know of. I won't risk another death on my conscience, Gabriel." Now she shuddered. "I couldn't bear it."

Gabriel wrapped her close. "Okay. Okay. But we go together."

Erin pulled away. "You can't come inside. He'll know."

"I'm not waiting in a car while you risk your life. Either I come with you, or you don't go," he announced.

She cocked her head, fascinated. "How do you plan to stop me?"

The crooked grin warmed and infuriated her. "I'll leak the story to the *Chronicle*. And WBCC and WNOG and—"

"Fine. I get it." With a defeated sigh, she shoved him out of her way. "I need to grab my bag. Is Sebastian still downstairs?"

"I'm driving you," Gabriel growled. "Not him."

Amused by the spark of jealousy, Erin returned to where he stood. She reached up and pulled him down to her mouth. The kiss was hard and fast and exciting, and both struggled to catch their breath when she released him. Erin traced his lips with her fingertips. "I've never done that or several other things with Sebastian. But he drove me here and he's taking me back. Otherwise, he'll just show up and ruin everything, trying to play Lancelot. See you at the apartment."

Her bravery survived the ride to her apartment and the endless ride up the elevator. Along the way, she identified several faces that had never been inside 216 St. Bennett before. Sylvie hadn't been kidding about providing protection. With Sebastian on her heels, she unlocked the apartment and froze.

It lay on the floor. The cream envelope taunted her, dared her to lift it and read its contents. Behind her, Sebastian waited, knowing that she had to make the decision.

She inhaled deeply and scooped up the paper. Willing her hands to be firm, she broke the seal and reached inside. This time, the envelope contained a torn strip of paper with letters scrawled in blue ink.

SANSKARIDAUORTHIPHASCABESTHAI

Sebastian read over her shoulder, then looked at Erin for a sign of comprehension or a flicker of recognition. He saw nothing. "What do we do, Erin?"

Erin studied the line, but she'd already decoded the message. "Call Gabriel. Tell him the killer has already come and gone."

With meticulous care, Erin packed a small leather suitcase, remembering the vagaries of Northern California weather. Particularly in the mountains, the wind could whip through layers of cloth like a lash. She swept the case and her bag off the comforter. The jeans she hadn't worn in years fit snugly, and the fitted long-sleeved shirt would be layered by a sweatshirt when the temperature changed.

"I'm not going to fight with you about this." Turning, she saw Gabriel and Sebastian arrayed in front of her door, blocking her only exit. "I have to finish it," she said, echoing Gabriel's instructions from the day before.

Gabriel advanced into the room, having been briefed by Sebastian. Erin had talked to Sylvie alone. Whatever she'd told her, the detective refused to remove the guards from the perimeter of the building, but Kenneth Bernard was almost in the clear. He'd deal with writing the retraction after the current crisis passed. Erin and Sylvie were planning a trip to California, straight into a trap. "How do you know he's there?"

In answer, Erin handed him the slip of paper. Gabriel stared at the line of gibberish. He shot a look at Sebastian, who shook his head. He couldn't read the damned thing, either.

Gabriel turned it upside down. "Is this in a foreign language?"

"A few of them." Erin sat on the edge of her bed and beckoned them to come inside. They sat on either side, like schoolboys waiting for a lesson. Erin pointed to the script. "Give me a pen."

Gabriel handed her one from his pocket.

"I have to go to California. These are his instructions."

Sebastian looked dubious. "This nonsense makes sense to you?"

"Of course." Taking the pen, she drew lines along the page.

SAN | SKARI | DAU | OR | THI | PHAS | CABES | THAI

"I don't see it." Sebastian stared at the page. "Wait. I see 'San Cabes.' That's where the cabin is."

Erin nodded. "Once I saw those words, the rest was simple. He didn't spend much time on the threat."

"Threat?" Gabriel read the paper again, annoyed that Sebastian had seen the words before he did. "What's the threat?"

Erin drew links across three of the segments. "*Skar-iphasthai* is the Greek root for 'scribe.'"

"Writer." Gabriel paused. "Reporter."

"And *dauthi* means 'death' in Norse."

"What about the letters *o* and *r*?" Sebastian asked, eager to show Gabriel up again.

"You're thinking too hard," chided Erin. "'Or' is just the word *or*."

At her side, Gabriel froze. His voice, when he spoke,

was hard as iron. "The message says: 'San Cabes or the reporter dies.' You're going to him."

"I have to. I won't let him hurt you, Gabriel." She stood, facing them both. "First Maggie, then Harmony. I won't let him have you."

Sebastian leaped to his feet. "San Cabes is a trap, Erin. You go and he'll kill you."

Her face was impassive. "I don't and more will die." She shook her head. "This ends tonight."

Finally, Gabriel accepted what he'd seen in her eyes this morning. What she'd been unable to say to him last night. Because he loved, he would do the same. "I'm going with you."

"Erin's my responsibility," Sebastian argued, but without any real heat. He realized Gabriel would be going with her, but he needed to make it look good. Whether Erin accepted it or not, the reporter planned to stick close to her for the rest of her life.

Gabriel heard the concession. "I need you to go over to the *Ledger*. Tell them what's going on." *And that I might not be back.* He wasn't sure he would let Erin come back and face a possible prison term. But he'd argue with her about that later.

"Don't do anything foolish," Sebastian warned Erin. "You've got nothing to atone for."

She met his look steadily. "I want a life, Sebastian. My life."

"Be careful."

Erin dozed fitfully as they crossed the continent. The plane angled for descent, cutting through summer storms that battered the mass of metal and glass. In concert with the storm, the night of Nathan's death churned in her restless mind. The crash of wood against stone as he barreled inside. Wind whipping trees into a frenzy of sound. Rain exploding like bullets against the cabin. Her pleas, his demands. A struggle for the gun. The crash of wood against stone. Then darkness and a slow awakening to find the gun in her hand.

Ripping herself from the nightmare, she turned to Gabriel. "He was at the cabin that night."

"Are you sure?"

"Yes." Erin clasped her hands to her mouth. As though a veil had lifted, she remembered. "The door opened when the gun went off. I'd always thought of it as an echo. But it opened."

"Do you know who it is, Erin?"

She clenched the armrest. "I can't figure it out. The clues keep spinning in my head, but I can't find the pattern."

"I can't, either." Gabriel took a deep breath. "We'll do this together. Tell me what you see."

Erin scrubbed at her weary eyes and tried to marshal her thoughts. "He knew me in California. Or knew Nathan."

"He lured you into the position at Burkeen. May have convinced Bernard to hire you. Could follow you around and learn everything about your life. Do you have any idea?"

A fleeting thought occurred; she dismissed it. Crimes had three elements: motive, means, and opportunity. The only person she could imagine lacked the means to open a space for Erin at a university. *No,* she thought, *it couldn't be.*

At that moment, the plane skidded to a stop and rolled

to the terminal. Gabriel got their bags. In step, they hurried through the airport. Sylvie took charge. After Gabriel stored Erin's bags, she hurried them into the car. He climbed into the backseat, stretching his long legs across the divider. "Where are we going, Erin?"

"Highway 1. To the mountains."

Sylvie would have no jurisdiction here, so she wouldn't be able to cross lines like this to apprehend a criminal. Sylvie called into the county sheriff's office, having already alerted them to their plan. They'd reluctantly agreed to joint jurisdiction because the captain went to college with the sheriff. Together they drove along the winding California highway, the sedan climbing higher along the steep cliffs and edging close to the sheer drops into the Pacific. Thick, hearty redwoods decorated the route, ancient sentinels to the passage of time. The entire highway stretched almost 650 miles, cutting through forest and farm, from above San Francisco to below Los Angeles. Their journey was little more than a tenth of the length, but the difference was startling. San Francisco's famed arched bridges and glittering spires of light gave way to quaint villages and isolated towns.

The car was quiet except for the occasional directions issued by Erin. They'd explained their theory to Sylvie, and she concurred. It explained why he needed Calvin to feed him information on the murders.

Finally, they left the highway and followed a twisted road cut into the side of the mountains. At a plateau, the route had been graded with a better-quality asphalt, acknowledging the perseverance of its users. Abruptly, out of the deep night, a structure emerged from the darkness.

"This is it," Erin whispered, and Sylvie put the car in park. More than anything she'd ever desired, Erin wanted to beg Sylvie to turn the vehicle around. To take her back to the airport and let her go. Let her run away.

But Gabriel's life depended on her. She owed him for so much, for so many things. It was debt that propelled her out of the car and up the stone walkway. Sylvie and Gabriel hurried after her.

Gabriel caught her midway. "Don't be a fool, Erin." Casting a pensive glance at the door, he hissed, "There could be a killer in there. Let Sylvie do her job."

Following protocol, Sylvie pounded on the door, announcing herself as an officer of the law. The cabin was dark, and she hadn't noticed any tire tracks leading up the road. She motioned them to stay back and did a quick sweep inside. The cabin was two stories, one wide room with a loft above. After she checked the rear door, she returned to the front. "Place seems deserted."

"I want to go inside."

"Can't." Crossing over to Erin, Sylvie patted her arm. "I think it's best if you wait in the car."

Erin stared at the site of her greatest sin. Before she could forgive herself, she had to face what she'd done. In a sudden burst, she shoved Sylvie aside, knocking her into Gabriel. They tumbled to the ground, both yelling for her to stop. She darted inside the cabin, drawn by conscience and destiny.

The thick door slammed closed, locking Erin inside and Gabriel out. He hurtled his body at the door, but the solid wood did not budge. "Sylvie! Sylvie, he's got her!" he bellowed.

Inside the cabin, Erin whirled around to face the killer. But she felt no shock to see Jessica standing at the threshold, covered in dust, gun in hand.

"Jessica? What are you doing here?" She asked the question because the scene demanded it. Jessica's twisted ego demanded it.

"Defending my dissertation, I suppose." Dropping the wooden plank into the grooved slot, she grinned at Erin as she bolted the locks. "Are you impressed?"

"Yes," Erin answered honestly. "I didn't see it. You gave me all the clues, and I didn't see it."

"Of course not." Jessica waved the gun toward the bed. The naked mattress sagged from disuse. "Sit down, Dr. Abbott."

Erin did as she instructed, realizing Jessica had hidden beneath the bed. Her heart pounded in her throat, and she could hear Gabriel hammering at the door. Jessica had dragged the rocker to the other side, and the teaching assistant sat down regally. With the gun trained on her forehead, Erin thought only of buying time. "You saw me with Nathan that night."

The butt of the gun smashed into her lip. Pain arced through her and her vision blurred. Jessica stood over her. "Don't you dare use his name. You destroyed him."

"I tried to leave him." Erin managed to speak through the pain and she levered herself up. "The night you found us here, I was trying to leave him."

"You were going to turn on him. I could see it in your eyes." At Erin's confused look, Jessica explained patiently. "I was the one who told him that you saw him with Kendra. I saw you lurking in the shadows, judging us."

Erin remembered the eyes that stared at her through

the pulsating red. The eyes that made her run. "You were a student of his. At Callenwolde."

"No, not a student of Nathan's. More like a protégé. Of his darker passions. My major really is psychology. Always has been." She smiled, a slow, deliberate baring of teeth. "I've always been fascinated by pain and death. Nathan was a master."

"I didn't recognize you."

"How could you? Princess Analise. Darling of the school. Perfect manners, perfect grades, perfect dissertation. You never had time for the rest of us peons."

"I'd already graduated by the time you arrived, Jessica."

"But you still had him. No one else measured up." The crazed, bright smile Jessica shot Erin curdled her stomach. "But you could never be to him what I was. He said I was a natural. I did for him what you wouldn't. Couldn't. And then you took him away from me."

"The shooting was an accident. Jessica, you saw it."

"If you hadn't forced him to punish you, he never would have died." Her voice broke and the gun dipped. "I had to do it for him. Avenge him."

"You could have killed me a thousand times, Jessica. Why did you kill the others first?"

Jessica frowned. "I thought you'd have realized that by now. I killed them for research, naturally. My dissertation is on the interplay of disciplines in criminal behavior."

"The connection of linguistics and psychology."

In a reasonable tone, Jessica explained her theory. "How language can subvert generally accepted theories of criminal behavior. Sociolinguistics, as Dr. Bernard so elegantly put it."

"As you commanded." The connection snapped into

place. "The lashes on his back. Your work?"

Jessica nodded in approval. "Excellent, Professor. Kenneth likes being told what to do. I'm very good at telling him." She smiled knowingly. "We had an understanding."

"He hired me because of you." That explained the lack of scrutiny to her application. "How long have you been in New Orleans?"

"Two years. Two very long years, waiting for my chance. Then, like a Christmas present, there you were." Jessica crossed her legs demurely. "I saw you in the Quarter one day, buying trinkets. I wanted to kill you then. Shoot you in the heart. But then I saw Dr. Fordham with you, and I knew. I knew what had to be done."

The banging on the door had stopped, but Jessica didn't seem to notice. Erin leaned forward, scooting away when the gun waved her back. Her mouth still throbbing, she asked, "Why Julian? Why did you kill him first?"

"I watched you. For weeks. Every morning, you would go to the gym and tease him." Disgust edged her words. "He would watch you like a dog in heat. Salivating over you. Lusting after you. And you just ate it up." The gun wavered slightly.

"He was nothing to me."

"You didn't see him. You never saw anyone. But I did. I paid attention." Her eyes shone with resentment. "I went to his office. Invited him home with me. He said no. I asked him about you and he smiled."

"So you killed him." Erin blanched, her stomach turning. "Because he wouldn't sleep with you?"

"No!" Jessica's eyes grew hard. "I had a theory. About you. Want to hear it?" Not waiting for Erin's response, she said, "The subject would be oblivious to the pain and suffering around her unless it became an intellectual exercise. How much more interesting if the victims were the ones to show her mercy?" Her voice trembled with sullen pique. "How badly would she suffer if she had to actually feel?"

"Why? Why hurt those who were kind to me?"

"Because then you'd feel like Nathan felt every time you turned him away. Rejected his love."

Erin used the tail of her shirt to dab at the blood that trickled to her chin. "Nathan was incapable of love, Jessica. He was a narcissistic tyrant who abused women for his own ends."

"He was a great man under too much pressure. Everyone wanted him to be perfect! You wanted him to be more than any mortal could."

Enraged, Erin surged up from the bed. "Kill me if you have to, but understand this. Nathan was a bully and a thief. He preyed on the weak and the innocent and he used them. You and me and the woman in the cellar."

"There was only one," Jessica countered shrilly, gesturing with the pistol. "You. Always his precious Analise. Because of you, he pushed me away. Said I was inferior. That you were the most brilliant at everything you tried. Linguistics. Psychology. But I was better with the games. I knew how to please him."

Over Jessica's shoulder, she saw a swirl of light through the cabin's front window. Out of the corner of her eye, she saw movement near the side window. She had to stall, give them a chance to rescue her. Erin returned to the bed, penitent. To pacify her, Erin said, "I couldn't have done what you did, Jessica. The combination of weapon and occupation was inspired."

"I researched every word."

"Where did you find your weapons?"

"You'd be amazed at what the university has lying around."

"Not insulin." Erin needed to keep her talking. "How did you get it?"

Fondling the gun, she explained, "I'm diabetic, like Nathan. That's how we first met. At the university pharmacy, getting our prescriptions filled."

"I didn't realize you took insulin."

"How could you? You never asked about me or my life."

"I'm sorry, Jessica. I owed you better."

"You owe me respect. I beat you." Jessica preened as she talked. "That day Harmony begged for another chance, all to join that sorority, it came to me."

"An initiate." Erin held back the grief. There would be time, she had to believe. "I admired the intricacy of your clues about Nathan. It must have taken you a great deal of research to find all of those links."

Jessica preened. "I got the idea after I killed Julian Harris. He had all of those books. I added Nathan's to his collection."

Glad she had calmed, Erin kept her talking, one eye on the weapon resting against the young woman's thigh. "I couldn't figure out Harriet Knowles. What was the clue?"

"They were both from Philadelphia." Jessica cocked her head quizzically. A student eager for praise, she asked, "Did you figure out the other ones?"

"Phoebe went to Juilliard, like Nathan. The Chinese artifact for Rose Young. The photo in Mr. Johnson's cabin. And you took Maggie's ring." Erin realized instantly she'd gone too far.

"I saw you wearing his ring at school. He loved that ring." Jessica aimed the gun at Erin's finger. "I defiled her body, just like you did to Nathan's. When you made me kill him."

The confession froze Erin. "You? You killed him?"

Madness brightened her eyes and she nodded. "I had to. He went after you, left me there with Kendra's body. He chose you over me. I knew about the cabin. I followed him to you. But you were too weak to save him from himself. I struck you with a branch." Jessica smiled wanly. "The bullet had hit him in the stomach, but it wasn't fatal. He begged for me to save him. Whining, mewling. A whimpering dog. He was supposed to be the master, but he was no better than a supplicant. I took the gun from you and stood over his body. He cried. The bastard cried. It wasn't Nathan. Not my Nathan. I had to kill the impostor."

"I didn't kill him." The knowledge ripped through her.

"But you took his ring." Jessica stared at her hand. "Give it to me."

Dazed, Erin looked past Jessica and saw her signal. She tucked her hand behind her back. "Come and get it."

CHAPTER 28

Jessica lunged for Erin, who jumped out of her path. She ran for the door, stopped by a vicious tug on her hair. Erin lost her footing and fell. Kicking out, she knocked Jessica off-balance, and they both hit the ground.

Erin straddled Jessica's writhing form. Jessica bucked and they tumbled over the rough wood and braided rugs. They wrestled for the gun, a haunting echo of two years before.

But this time, Erin was wide awake and furious. "You're not going to win, Jessica!" She levered her body to aim a knee at the younger woman's kidneys. The blow elicited a screech of pain, and Erin felt Jessica's hands loosen on the gun. She heaved the weapon away.

This time, when glass shattered as Gabriel dived inside, Erin stood over a live body. Behind him, police officers swarmed into the cabin. Kind hands pried the gun from her rigid fingers. "We've got it now, ma'am."

Erin could hear Jessica's shrieking cries but only had eyes for Gabriel. Stumbling, Erin made her way to him, meeting him near where Nathan had died. Gabriel cradled her bruised cheek in a cautious hand. "Oh, honey. I'm so sorry."

"I didn't kill him." The immensity of her vindication crumpled her into an exhausted heap. "She did it," Erin sobbed in a broken litany. "Gabriel, I didn't kill him. I didn't kill him." Crouched beside her, Gabriel could do nothing but hold her as she wept.

When she subsided, Gabriel gained his feet and scooped her body into his hold. Purple colored her cheekbones, swelled the ripe mouth he adored. He'd let her walk in alone. She'd never be alone again. Giving voice to his oath, he pledged, "I'm taking you home."

Erin awoke to find herself swathed in crisp cotton sheets. And nothing else. Her jaw ached from Jessica's gun, and her stomach growled in hungry protest. Next to her, Gabriel sat on an upholstered chair, feet propped on the bed. She realized, with a start, that he'd been there for hours. Dawn hadn't broken, but the sky was lightening.

She watched Gabriel, flooded by emotions too huge to comprehend. Shadows bruised the skin beneath his eyes. Stubble darkened his chin. One hand held hers in an unyielding grip. Touched, Erin pressed a kiss to the warm skin. Gabriel blinked once.

"You're awake," he murmured in a voice scratchy from sleep.

"Why are you over there?" Erin patted the empty space beside her. "You didn't have to sleep in a chair, Gabriel."

"I didn't want to crowd you."

The wide expanse of the king-size bed belied his explanation. "Are you trying to tell me something?" she teased.

Gabriel didn't smile. Instead, he loosened his hold on her and stood up. "I'm sorry, Erin." He stalked over to the balcony, where the drapes framed the Golden Gate Bridge. Fog hung low over the night city, a gauzy blanket over the pastel and stucco houses below.

Pushing her tangled hair away from her face, Erin struggled to sit up without dislodging the sheet. When she finally managed to lean against the headboard, she remarked evenly, "You have nothing to apologize for. You saved my life."

"I put your life in jeopardy." He shoved his hands into his pockets, afraid to touch her now that she was awake. Through the long night, he'd grappled with his guilt. He'd get this out before he asked her the question that would complete his life. "Before I bullied you into helping, you were safe."

"I started investigating on my own. I found the clues."

"You wanted to quit."

"My teaching assistant was a serial killer who blamed me for stealing her lover." The absurdity of the situation demanded that she either laugh or weep. She chose to laugh. "Jessica planned to kill me, Gabriel. If I'd given up, more would have died and then she'd have come after me. You're the reason I was able to fight back."

Stubbornly clinging to his remorse, he challenged, "You'd have run if I hadn't taunted you into staying."

"Because I was a coward."

Gabriel erupted. "You're not a coward! You're the bravest woman I've ever known."

"So brave, I let someone cut me off from everyone I loved. I changed my career for him. My life. I was a coward." The summary brooked no argument.

Before Gabriel could contradict her again, a rap sounded at their door. Gabriel checked the Judas hole. "It's Sylvie."

Erin tucked the sheet around her more firmly, grateful for the interruption. "She can come in."

Because he wanted to hear Sylvie's report, he stepped away to admit her. "Come in."

"Erin, you doing okay?" Full of motherly concern, Sylvie trundled over to the bed, which dipped beneath her. She patted Erin's undamaged cheek. "I was proud of you back there. You kept her occupied long enough for help to come."

"I had to know the truth."

Sylvie sat up. "Truth is, the kid's as crazy as a loon. SFPD is gonna charge her in Rhodes' murder and extradite her to New Orleans, but she'll be in an asylum. Turns out she's been in and out of mental facilities since she was nine. She was abused as a child but showed promise in school. They sent her to Callenwolde, where her med list would fill a novel."

"Nathan used her. He gave her a focus for her rage."

"One that she turned on you," Gabriel reminded them both harshly. "She brutally murdered nine innocent people."

"She's not responsible, Gabriel. She's sick." Erin could see the struggle in his eyes. Compassion warred with anger over how Jessica had hurt her. Erin felt the same, but training demanded that compassion win. "When she goes to trial, I plan on testifying in her defense. She needs help."

"We'll discuss that later." Gabriel turned back to Sylvie. "What about the other matter?"

A satisfied smile wreathed her broad face. "All charges

against Analise Glover have been dropped. Erin is free to leave the jurisdiction."

She gave Gabriel a startled look. "I was under arrest?"

"No. Just forbidden to board a plane. Sanchez thought I might try to make you run."

A week later, Erin curled on the sofa to read the morning edition of the *Ledger*. The lead story, written by Gabriel Moss, reported on the DA's agreement to accept a plea of not guilty by reason of insanity from Jessica Dawson, aka Terry Watson. Captain Lynn Sanchez railed against the prosecutor's decision, but it didn't help that the next victim and his investigating officer had lobbied on Jessica's behalf.

Erin reached for the phone, wanting to call and congratulate him. The *Chronicle* had been hounding her for an interview, but all exclusives went to the wildly popular *Bayou Ledger*. But her hand faltered above the phone. It had been a week since they'd talked about anything other than Jessica's case. A week since he'd made love to her. Told her he loved her.

The urge to go to him thrummed through her every day. How could she, though, when she had no idea what she felt? Love was more than the flutters in her belly and the tightness in her throat or the tingling of her skin when they touched. It was more than sacrificing herself for his safety or wishing for his happiness.

Love was a daily endeavor of compromise and forgiveness and trust. Trust most of all. She wasn't sure she could do it. With a sigh, she got up from the couch to head to the library, prepared to spend another day buried in her latest project. Over Sebastian's rather crude objections, she planned to write a book to explain why Jessica Dawson deserved to be hospitalized rather than executed. Luckily, Sebastian had returned to New York, so his threats were in word only.

Erin rode her bike through the streets, unaware that she traveled downtown. When she stopped, it was outside the *Bayou Ledger*. She parked her bicycle and buzzed for entry.

Gabriel stood in the lobby. He didn't smile when he saw her. "Erin."

"I read the *Ledger* this morning," she offered as she moved toward him. His expression remained impassive, slightly annoyed by her interruption. She tucked her hands into her pockets. "I've canceled my subscription to the *Chronicle*."

"That's good." She looked beautiful, as though she'd finally been able to put Nathan's specter to rest. He was happy for her. At least, he would be when he could bear to feel again. "What's wrong?"

"Nothing. I came to talk to you."

"Let's go to my office." Gabriel decided he'd prefer to beg in the sanctity of his own space. Once inside, he engaged the lock and levered the electric blinds to block out the rest of the newsroom. He gestured to a chair, taking a seat on the edge of his desk. "How can I help you?"

"You haven't returned my calls, Gabriel."

"Returned your calls?" He said the phrase slowly. "The ones where you thank me?"

She shifted on the cool leather, unable to sit still. "Yes. I wanted you to know how I felt." *I wanted to hear your voice.*

"Did you call to tell me you love me?" The question was bland, almost perfunctory.

"I can't do that, Gabriel."

"Then we don't have anything else to discuss." He stood and marched to the door. "I love you, Erin. I don't want your gratitude or your friendship. I want you."

Erin shook her head. "Jessica may be insane, but she was right about one thing. I couldn't love Nathan." She met Gabriel's hooded gray eyes, the color of San Francisco fog. She wanted him to understand. Restless, she crossed the room to stand beside him. When she cut out her heart, she would do it with her head held high. "If I was ever going to be in love with someone, it would have been you and it would have been that night."

Gabriel nodded in agreement. "But?"

Hollow, beaten, she hung her head. "But I can't be in love."

"With me?" His voice was mildly interested.

"With anyone." She waved off the next question. "Because it's impossible. I'm impossible. I'm secretive and afraid and never sure I'm good enough. I'm neurotic and controlling."

"True." Gabriel quirked an inquiring brow. "But you're also brilliant and kind and willing to risk your life for others."

"I'm a freak, Gabriel. An oddly wired brain with an eidètic memory for strange words. Only now I can use my carnival skills to solve murders."

His teeth snapped together. "Don't you dare belittle yourself in front of me. You used your empathy, your smarts, and your bravery. You used years of training and teaching. You used your powers of observation to find her. You used your powers of communication to stop her. So don't give me any bullshit about eidetic memory. You solved this case, Erin. Not Analise. You."

"But—"

"No. And I'll tell you something else. You are in love with someone. Me. And it isn't just that night, when I saved your life."

"When you saved my life?" she sputtered. "I stopped Jessica—"

"Shut up and listen." Patience vanished, Gabriel stalked her, forcing her back to the door. "You fell in love with me in a school hallway weeks ago, when I saw through tweed and bravado and saw you. When I fell in love with you. California was one more night, one more hour, of loving you. And tomorrow will be another. Until we have forever."

"Aren't you listening to me?" She poked his chest with a warning finger, wanting to believe. "I've never been in love before. I can be mean and petty and clumsy."

"I've never been in love before, either. And we both know I'm domineering, driven, and occasionally rash. And I love you, Analise Erin Abbott Glover."

He swept her into his arms and fastened his mouth to hers.

The torrid kiss drew her in, and she sank into the embrace. His mouth danced over her eyelids, caressed her throat. Hard, reverent hands kneaded and held until she couldn't breathe. In sensual retaliation, she licked at his bottom lip, enjoying how his breath stuttered.

Fear crumbled, washed away on a tide of possibility. She'd given him an out, and he'd ignored it. Now, she'd made her choice. To stand. To love. Reaching up, she circled her arms around his neck. "I could love you for the rest of my life and never come close to being finished."

"Say it, Erin." His mouth floated above hers, refusing to give them both what they'd waited a lifetime to feel. "No more teasers. Give me the headline."

"I love you, Gabriel Moss. End of story."

THE
Midnight Hour

A Madaris Novel

Essence Bestselling Author

BRENDA JACKSON

"A super-hot hero, a kick-butt heroine, and non-stop action! Brenda Jackson writes romance that sizzles and characters you fall in love with."

— Lori Foster, *New York Times* bestselling author

"*The Midnight Hour* is a roller-coaster read of passion, intrigue, and deceit."

— Sharon Sala, *New York Times* bestselling author

ISBN: 0-312-98997-0

AVAILABLE WHEREVER BOOKS ARE SOLD
FROM ST. MARTIN'S PAPERBACKS

Sometimes you have to forget what you want

to find what you need...

All
the Man
I Need

TAMARA SNEED

"Sneed really knows how to deliver."
—*Romantic Times*

ISBN: 0-312-98730-7

Coming in August 2004

AVAILABLE WHEREVER BOOKS ARE SOLD
FROM ST. MARTIN'S PAPERBACKS

She knows exactly what she wants—and how to get it.

Whatever Lola Wants

Niqui Stanhope

Author of *Changing the Rules*

"Romance with a hip attitude."

—*Publishers Weekly* on *Changing the Rules*

ISBN: 0-312-98624-6

Coming in September 2004

AVAILABLE WHEREVER BOOKS ARE SOLD
FROM ST. MARTIN'S PAPERBACKS